MORGANA
TRILOGY

ALESSA ELLEFSON

ISBN: 1482065444
ISBN 13: 9781482065442

Library of Congress Control Number: 2013905248
CreateSpace Independent Publishing Platform
North Charleston, South Carolina

Jacket art © 2013 by Sammy Yuen
Author photo by Dhel Reed of deeReed Photography

To my dear friends, Kate, Thomas and Cici

who suffered to help me shape this story,

To all the friends who supported me,

and to my most beloved family

without which this book and I would not be.

Legends say that, in the beginning, angels were free to roam through all planes of existence. Some chose the physical world and became so enamored with it that they could frequently be found roaming about in nature and interacting with its inhabitants. But when the War broke out, and the Fallen Ones were cast for ever out of Heaven, these angels found that they'd been locked out of Paradise as well.

Not evil enough to be sent to Hell, they were forced to spend their nearly eternal lives on Earth, where they became known as the Fey People. But living with near-unlimited powers amongst mortals brought about inevitable abuse and subsequent retribution from those they had oppressed.

The Fey saw their fortunes reversed, and their dominion gradually diminished until only one place was left for them to escape to—Avalon.

For the Fey, only a completely selfless and noble act could change their fate...

Chapter 1

The truth of the matter is, when you're in deep shit, there is no Prince Charming who'll come to your rescue, let alone one who'll do the dirty work for you. A precept that's been pounded into my head with a twenty-ton mallet since I first saw the light of day. Still, as I stare at the detritus[1] floating around my calves, I wish this wasn't the case.

Gritting my teeth, I wade deeper into the frigid waters of Lake Geneva. I stifle a sneeze. Despite the ungodly hour, I don't want to draw anyone's attention, especially when I'm supposed to be safely tucked in bed back at school. Last time I got caught on a little outing, Sister Marie-Clémence had me do penitence at four every morning for a month. Not that I dislike my dates with the Lord—I sign myself in case He's listening—but at the ripe old age of seventeen, I need all the beauty sleep I can get.

The reeds sway with every one of my movements in a sleepy waltz, oblivious to the small knife in my hand.

---

1 Loose accumulation of silt.

"I'm so very sorry," I murmur to them as I go about my reaping, "but it's for your own good."

Or at least the good of the school's greenhouse. For two weeks now, I've seen our plants—those precious beings I've tenderly watched grow—inexplicably wilt and darken, and nothing either I or Sister Marie-Bénédicte have done has helped.

"And so you must understand," I tell the alga as I snip off one of its tendrils.

As I reach into my pocket, the glass container slips out and falls into the water.

"Saint George's balls!" I mutter through clenched teeth. "That's all I needed."

Thankfully, I find the vial floating amongst the rushes and fish it out without any other incident. My sample safely stored away, I plow through the weeds in search of my next victim. I sigh. Doesn't look like anything here has been infected, which brings me back to square one.

I stare up at the Alps, wondering whether I should check uphill instead for the source of the disease. The sun peeks over the Rochers de Naye, firing its blood-orange rays at me, like a prison guard on an escapee; a definite sign I've been gone too long.

I put away my tools and make for the shore, when something catches my eye. Amongst the rushes' thin stems is a dark patch of algae I've never seen before. Intrigued, I make my way over and pick a few strands. Odd...The algae have the same consistency as moss...

As I reach for my knife once again, something big and round pops out of the water a foot away, gelatinous eyes staring straight at me.

I gasp, let go of the hair, and stumble back. I slip on the muddy floor of the lake and fall into the reeds, gulping down some of the foul water.

"Help," I squeak. I lurch for the lake's bank and manage to make it to solid ground. "Help!"

My weak cries must have gotten someone's attention, for the next thing I know, a gendarme's[2] standing next to me while another's fishing out the body.

"Your name?" the potbellied officer asks me through his thick mustache.

"M-M-Morgan," I manage to say.

"Last name?"

"P-P-Pen…" I sneeze, and some of the water that has filled up my hip boots squishes out.

"You want to write it down?" the gendarme asks, handing me his notepad.

Teeth chattering, I shake my head. "D-D-Drag-g-gon," I manage to say.

The man's eyebrows lower dangerously, blotting out his beady eyes. "Listen, missy, if you think you're being funny…"

"Pendrag-g-gon," I say again, tearing my eyes away from the scene below, where an ambulance has arrived. But I can't get the sight of the bloated body out of my mind, the girl's porcelain skin striated with black veins as if she's shot herself up with ink. I shiver.

"Do you need another cover?" the officer asks me.

"N-No, th-thank you." I don't think anything can dispel the cold I'm feeling, and, never having gotten ill, I'm not afraid of sickness.

"What were you doing here?" the officer continues, licking his pen.

"S-Sampling."

"The water?"

2 Police officer.

4

I shake my head. "Macrophytes. For p-pollution."

"And that's when you found it," the man says, taking copious notes.

"Agnès," I say, my voice catching.

"Excuse me?" The gendarme's pen has stopped over his notebook.

"Agnès Deschamps," I say, watching the people pack her body up. "She was my classmate."

I don't have to see the gendarme to know what he's thinking. I've never been very good at making friends, concentrating instead on not getting bullied all the time. A little investigating and he'll find out how, just last week, I broke down and punched a molar out of Agnès in gym class after she'd slammed the volleyball in my face, twice. An act I came to regret immediately with the relentless retaliation that followed. An act I regret even more now.

For there's no doubt I'm going to be their suspect number one.

The room is small, gray, with a camera stuck in one of the ceiling's corners like some fat spider. The desk is cold under my fingers as I wait, wait for the detective to come question me again, to accuse me of doing the worst of things, things I've never even imagined, as he waits for me to break down. But what he doesn't know is that I'm used to this type of treatment. All I need to do is keep my mouth shut and wait for the nightmare to stop.

Except this time, it's not ending, and the hours creep by while images of Agnès's corpse float about in my mind.

You could always plead guilty. I'm sure they'd move you then.

"And be in jail for the rest of my life?" I retort. "For something I didn't do? No thanks. I just need to survive through this, like I have with everything else, and then I'll be free. I won't let you jeopardize this, so shut up."

For once in my life, my alter ego—the one I like to pretend is my guardian angel—complies.

The door slams open, and the inspector strides in. He slaps his file down, and a few pictures jump out onto the table.

Without meaning to, I find myself staring once again at Agnès's ballooned body as it lay on the shore like a stranded blowfish. I swallow the bile that rises up my throat and force myself to look up into the little man's steely eyes.

"Consider yourself lucky," he says, his fetid stale-tobacco breath wafting over to me.

Lucky? I stare at him, wide-eyed. What happened? Did Agnès miraculously resurrect?

"I don't know who your parents know," the inspector continues, "but you can tell them that when I find definite proof of your involvement, I will come for you."

My parents are here? I straighten up in my seat. My parents actually came to see me? For the first time since I found Agnès's body, I feel my heart pound against my rib cage like a boxer on a sandbag.

"A mute lawyer," the cop growls, glaring past my shoulders. "I've seen it all."

A tall shadow makes its way through the still-open door. I look around in time to see Dean, my family's lawyer, walk up to me. My heart leaps at the sight, and I want to rush to him, throw myself into his arms where I know I'll be safe, but I hold myself back.

Despite the circumstances, he seems collected. But then, in all my years knowing him, I've never seen a single hair of his stand out of line. He motions for me to get up, and, like a good soldier, I obey at once.

Without even acknowledging the seething detective, he shuffles me down the hallways under the other officers' disapproving stares. I hunch over, hating all those judging looks, but Dean sets his arm around my shoulders protectively, and I know I'm going to be all right.

It's not until we step outside and the late summer breeze tickles my face that I open up.

"Are they here?" I ask Dean, following him down the steps toward a black car.

He pauses and looks down at me, his dark eyes inscrutable, then shakes his head. My shoulders slump. No. Of course not. My parents have never bothered to come see me in all my years at the boarding school. Why would a little incident like the murder of a classmate make them change their modus operandi?

I try not to show how much this hurts, however expected it may be, and smile at Dean as I pass him to get into the open car. The leather soughs as I slump into the seat, and I slide over to let Dean sit next to me. God knows what's going on inside that elegant head of his. Something brilliant and devious, I'm sure, or he'd never have been hired by my family. Yet somehow I feel like he understands me, that he knows me like no other person does, and for that I'm grateful.

"Back to school?" I ask.

Dean shakes his head, and I let myself unclench my hands. I don't think I'm up to facing Sister Marie-Clémence's wrath or the accusatory looks of the rest of the school. The momentary relief vanishes, however, when I realize what this actually means.

I swallow hard. "H-Home?"

Dean gives a curt nod. As I feared.

Lake Michigan at our back, the limousine that's taking us from the airport to my parents' house is eating the miles at a solid clip. I stare outside the windows without paying attention to anything. I can't keep my thoughts from returning to the daunting prospect of meeting my parents for the first time since being sent away, despite spending a whole day flying over the Atlantic to get used to the idea.

Once upon a time, I would have been brimming with anticipation, but something tells me that, after having been accused of murder, hugs and kisses are not what's on the *menu du jour*.[3]

"You don't think they've prepared a surprise party for me?" I ask with a tense smile.

Without looking at me, Dean pats my hand while remaining focused on whatever business my parents have for him. I look over at the foldable table before him, strewn with papers and maps, and lose interest. There are more important things at hand, such as preserving my own life, however others might disagree.

I clear my throat. "Does Wisconsin have the death penalty?"

I redden at the squeakiness of my voice. But when faced with the possibility of the electric chair, I'm afraid it's hard to keep up my composure.

My question, however mousy it might have sounded, draws Dean away from his work. His eyes look me over carefully. Then a tiny smile lifts a corner of his lips, and he shakes his head.

The Gordian knot that my stomach's become loosens somewhat. I return Dean's smile, then look back out the tinted windows at the rolling hills of yellow grass, the sharp angles of the city of Fond du Lac rising behind them like uneven teeth. I wipe my hands on my jeans as the car speeds past the first rows of Monopoly houses that ring the outside perimeter of the town.

---

3 Menu of the day.

A large, dark monolith of a residence rises before us. The gates open before the car can even stop, and a few moments later, I find myself standing before the empty porch steps.

Heart thumping, I follow Dean inside the quiet hallway, where a minuscule, ghostlike servant awaits. Eyes downcast, she presses her tiny body against the wall as Dean walks by, as if afraid to be seen.

"Nice meeting you," I whisper before Dean and I make a turn into another, wider hallway.

My words echo in the still air, and I repress a shiver. What is this place? Are people not allowed to talk here? Do my parents only hire mutes? I grimace. All I know about them is what everyone else knows, which is to say not much. They're very rich, and travel lots, and from the limousine and private jet we used, I would assume in style.

Looking around the mazelike house, I think "eccentric" is a better term. Displayed along every wall are hundreds of artifacts from all over the world. If it weren't so quiet, I'd think we were in a museum. As it is, the whole place is more of a mausoleum—an apt setting for my demise.

We make another turn and find ourselves before a large, dark wooden staircase. The plush carpet muffles our footfalls as we go up to the second floor. As I step onto the landing, I get dizzy and waver. I fling out my hand to catch myself on the wall, but knock down the bust of some long-dead bearded man instead.

In a blur of movement, Dean catches both the old man's head and my arm before either of us can crash to the floor.

"Thank you," I breathe.

I didn't think the idea of finally seeing my parents after all these years was going to affect me this much. I thought—I hoped—I would be immune to all feeling for them by now. But no matter what I may tell myself, my body can't lie.

After a pause, Dean lets me go, though he keeps close to me. I force air back into my lungs as we arrive before a set of imposing doors. With a final look in my direction, Dean knocks on the wooden panel and opens it.

My mouth runs dry. After a moment's hesitation, I follow the lawyer into a library, the parquet floor reflecting the multitude of lights from the chandeliers above. Lining the red-papered walls are ceiling-high shelves filled with books.

Two dark shapes in the back of the room draw my eyes away from the threatening volumes. I wish I were brave enough to run over to them and finally hug them, as I always do in my dreams, but I'm too scared of their reaction and remain frozen.

"I do believe your daughter's here," says the man, leaning against a high-backed chair in which a small woman sits reading.

"You married me. Hence, she's yours as well," the woman replies.

They're both wearing matching black clothes that look straight out of one of those Victorian romance novels some of the girls at school sometimes snuck in. Frilly blouses cinched in tight jackets, tight pants for him, and a billowing skirt for her with so many ruffles one might mistake her for a doll—except for the leather army boots.

The man's upper lip twitches. For a split second, I see disgust etched in my stepfather's features, and I try not to flinch.

"Well, what have you got to say?" says my mother, her black-lined eyes never leaving the pages of her newspaper.

I feel the sting of tears despite myself. I take a deep, shaky breath, pull my shoulders back, and raise my chin. "I didn't do it."

Mother looks up then, her unblinking stare boring into me. After having the time to do two Paternosters and an Ave Maria in my head to calm myself down, she finally speaks again. "Just go to your room."

Not exactly the warm welcome I'd imagined, but at least they haven't executed me on sight. Which, relatively speaking, is a rather good turn of events.

Chapter 2

I watch the distant waters of Lake Winnebago turn from glittering blue to brilliant orange, then dull down to gray before turning a blue black indistinguishable from the fields before it. My stomach grumbles, in total agreement with my thoughts—despite this being the first time in nearly two decades my mother's seen me, she's already forgotten about my existence and left me to die of famine in this godforsaken place.

Hands in fists, I face my prison. The bedroom's spacious at least, I'll give them that. There's hardly any furniture though, just a bed, a desk with accompanying chair, and some cumbersome wardrobe. All look solid, if not comfortable, and clearly state I should refrain from punching them.

Instead, I grab the first thing my hand falls on—a large book—and hurl it across the room. The volume bounces off the door and lands with a dull thud on the floor. My blood drains from my face—Saint George's balls, I've just thrown the Bible!

I rush over, pick the sacred volume up, dust it off, then carefully set it back down on the desk.

"I'm really, *really* sorry," I say, darting glances about to make sure nothing's going to strike me down. "It's all her fault."

My mother's features spring back before my eyes—all compact coldness, like an ice cube. Any thought I've ever entertained that she didn't raise me because of my stepfather has vaporized, and, for the first time in my life, I let myself get angry at her.

There is no way I'm the fruit of her loins. For one, I'm probably twice her height. Then, I don't have any of her angular features, and where her hair's a darker shade of blonde, mine's jet-black. Quod erat demonstrandum.[4]

I sink to the floor next to my luggage that's been placed at the foot of the bed. If only I were adopted, then I'd have no qualm about leaving this horrid place. But if she believes sharing her genes makes me indentured to her, then she's barking up the wrong tree. In fact, I might as well leave right now instead of waiting for my eighteenth birthday, for all the difference my presence makes.

Filled with newfound purpose, I grab my small suitcase, march to the door, and carefully crack it open. I peek through into the hallway, then, the coast clear, ease my way out of the bedroom, and stop.

What exactly am I doing? I don't know this town, this country…this continent! I don't have a dollar in my pocket. I don't know anyone, except perhaps for Dean. For a moment I consider asking him for help, but quickly give up on the idea. He is, for better or worse, my parents' bona fide lackey, and though he's always helped me in hairy situations before, there's no doubt this is not one of those times.

---

4 What had to be proven.

I rub my aching head. This is way-too-intense thinking for me to be doing when I'm jet-lagged and starving. Ah yes, that *is* how this whole mission started: food first, then escape.

I don't know who designed this house, but whoever it was ought to be hanged, and quartered, for good measure. I make another turn and find myself in the living room. Again.

I retrace my steps around the perimeter of the mansion, careful to check every door and passage for a sign of the kitchen. This has got to be a trick, a ploy to keep me sequestered here so I can never tarnish my parents' good name again! As I find myself once more in the living room, I give up, and face the embers glowing in the fireplace.

Hanging above the mantelpiece is an intricate metal-and-wood carving of two dragons standing back-to-back on their hind legs, each holding in its talons a large, glittering jewel. The Pendragon family sign! I draw nearer the sigil until I walk into the chimneypiece.

"You called, mistress?"

I jump nearly twenty feet in the air at the voice. Standing behind me is the small maid I'd seen upon my arrival.

"I didn't hear you come in!" I say shrilly.

"Apologies, young mistress," says the little woman. She readjusts her bonnet over her perfectly round head.

"Wait," I say before the maid can disappear in whatever hole she's come from. "I, uh…" I fidget, unsure whether she'll report my unapproved activity to my mother or not.

The maid's eyes look as big as apples in her pale face.

"Uh, the kitchen?" I ask.

"Is the mistress ready for her dinner?" she asks.

"Yes," I answer, then add as an afterthought, "and as many snacks as you can come up with."

The little woman nods. "As you wish, mistress. It shall be delivered in the dining room in—"

"No!" I look quickly around to see if my outburst has caught anyone's attention, then resume, more quietly. "In my bedroom. Please."

The servant curtsies, and, as quickly and quietly as she appeared, she leaves me alone once again. I take one last look at the foreboding dragons, having no difficulty pretending their faces are those of Irene and Luther. No, it definitely won't be hard for me to leave.

I carefully make my way back upstairs, wishing for the maid to be quick. I don't know whether the house is ordinarily so quiet and empty, and I don't want to jeopardize what may be my one and only chance to flee.

"The Lamoraks have sent us notice that, apart from Notre-Dame du Chablais, they haven't seen another instance."

I freeze at the mention of my school. I slowly turn around toward the sound of my mother's voice, for there is no mistaking her clipped tone.

"But Clarence says that he's gone to investigate a murder that's taken place in Annecy," Luther says.

Step by cautious step, I make my way toward the library door, which has been left ajar, letting a wedge of flickering light fall on the red carpet. Another murder, in Annecy? That town's only a few miles away from my school…They couldn't possibly think I'm a serial killer now, could they?

"And if that's the case," my stepfather continues, "that means there's a clear path between the first case and Morgan's."

My feet reach the edge of the light beam streaming past the door. I can hear the crackle of the fire now and smell the faint scent of burning wood. I tilt forward until I can see my parents. They're both standing by a long table, poring over what looks like a map.

"Luther, could they know?" my mother asks. It's the first time I've heard her sound nervous. "I mean, that's exactly how her father died."

I feel like I've just been hit by a train. I lean against the wall to prevent myself from collapsing. My father, dead before I was born, was killed by the same strange poison that got Agnès? How is that even possible? I cross my arms to stop myself from shaking.

Luther bends further over a second map. "More importantly," he says, "our team's extrapolated three different sources for the nefarious activity we've detected."

Irene has to rise on the tips of her toes to see what Luther's pointing at.

"No!" she gasps. "There's got to be a mistake."

"I'm afraid not," Luther says.

He starts pacing the room, hands behind his back. I pull away, afraid they might see me. If only they could say something that made sense to me. Like the fact the inspector has given up his search for evidence against me, or that Agnès turned out to have died of some severe case of diarrhea.

"All we can do," Luther says, "is wait to find out whether the murders will pop up again, and where. Maybe then we'll be able to narrow the epicenters down to one or two."

Goose bumps rise along my spine. They talk about those murders like they're nothing more than items on a grocery list.

I hear a furtive sound behind me and spin around just as a hand clasps around my mouth and someone drags me backward.

"Who is it?" I hear my mother call out.

I try to fight back, but my opponent is taller and more powerful than me. He lifts me off my feet and drags me away into a dark room. The door closes just as I see Luther's face poke out of the library.

Panic makes me lash out. It's the murderer! He's somehow tracked me down to this house and is now going to kill me! I kick furiously and feel my heel connect.

The man lets out a muffled curse and releases me. I trip against something hard and fall down. A green light flashes out of the corner of my eye, and I somehow find myself lying comfortably on a thick rug. I hear the killer move, and then the lights turn on.

Blinking, I sit up, noticing the coffee table laden with articles next to where I've landed; its sharp corners look angry to have missed my head. I then look up to find a tall boy staring down at me from behind dark blond strands of hair, his muscled frame reflected in a mirror that takes up a whole wall. He doesn't look quite as ogreish as I'd imagined, but then again, the spark in his hazel eyes tells me he isn't that innocent either.

"Who are you?" I ask. Then, deciding I don't quite like the lack of vantage I have while sitting on the floor, I get up.

The boy smirks. He doesn't look quite that young anymore, about my age. "I should be the one asking you that," he says. "You're the one who was caught spying."

"I wasn't spying," I say, offended. "I was just…on my way out."

"Leaving?" He looks at me for a long second, and I feel myself blush. It can't be that bad of an idea, can it? "You do realize," he finally continues, "that should you disappear after having been accused of killing off your classmate, there's bound to be a price on your head?"

I feel myself turn a couple shades darker. To hide my embarrassment, I pick up a newspaper cutting that's fallen on the rug, and its title jumps at me.

Are Alien Abductions Behind The Disappearance Of Will And Ava Krueger?

For a moment, the strangeness of it makes me forget where I am entirely, until the guy takes the article from my hands and replaces it on the table.

"Look, I'm saying this for your own good. You better not get caught snooping around here."

"I wasn't snoop—" I start, but he takes a few steps toward me until I'm backed up against the wall. His eyes are so close to mine I can see the specks of gold spattered over the light brown of his irises. I swallow hard. Apart from Dean and the inspector, who are both much older than me, I've never been this close to a guy before.

"Fortunately for you," he whispers, his breath brushing my burning cheeks, "I won't say anything... *Sister*."

He pulls away suddenly, strides back to the door, and opens it with a flourish. "By the way," he adds, "you probably shouldn't be found lurking around our parents' office either." And with that warning, he's gone.

My knees go weak, and I slide to the ground. Brother? I take deep breaths to clear my foggy mind. Now that I think about it, I vaguely remember Dean mention to me once, ages ago, that my mother had given birth shortly after I was sent away.

Somehow, I'd conveniently forgotten that detail. Now, however, I remember seeing him mentioned from time to time in the few articles dedicated to my parents' work around the world. A quiet, polite little boy named Arthur.

Except he's not that little, and far from polite. I glare at the door as if he were still standing there. "Jerk!"

ChAPTER 3

Not for the first time since this whole ordeal began, I can't bring myself to fall asleep. Who would've thought that the wish of meeting my family, held for so many years inside me like a rare and fragile orchid, would turn into a nightmare?

Whenever I close my eyes, I see Agnès's corpse taunting me, her cracked lips black against the white of her skeletal smile. A smile once shared by my father, whose face I've never seen, not even in pictures.

I toss around in bed and kick at the covers. Then, with a worn-out sigh, I resign myself to dealing with the next worst thing that's happened to me since the murder: meeting my family. Perhaps, if my father had still been alive, all those letters I sent for years on end would have gotten responses. Instead, my mother's shriveling looks are inked to the back of my eyelids like some insipid tattoo I can't get rid of. Anger broils in me as I relive the moment of my dismissal, like I was some booger she'd flicked off her dainty little finger. But before I can garner the strength to punch my fat pillow, another face flashes before me, all crooked smile and mocking eyes.

"You!" I mutter, shaking my fist in the air. "If I weren't so tired, and you so big and strong, I'd teach you to be dutifully respectful to your older sister."

The words feel strange in my mouth as I utter them, like tasting a chili-covered candy for the first time. I let my hand drop back down on the covers. I don't think I'd like that kind of candy.

Seeing Arthur, my brother, live the life I've always wanted, surrounded by parents who have never kicked him out or would even dare think he could commit a murder…My eyes prick with the onset of tears, and I sniffle them back down.

"Life is just not fair," I whisper. "I've tried everything I can think of to conform and be accepted, but nothing's worked. Then again, when my own mother doesn't want me, there's no reason for the rest of the world to want me either." I feel like toxic waste.

Stop whining. You're not five anymore.

I glare at the ceiling. "Who asked for your advice?"

That was more of a recommendation, actually, because I know you'll be kicking yourself come morning.

"Can't you, for once, just allow me a minute, make that five, of self-pity? It's not like I ever asked you for anything."

Except to listen to you every time you have a problem.

I growl. "That's your role. You're my guardian angel."

You'll feel better once the light of day comes, he says. *Things always seem worse when it's dark.*

"But I feel like the night's never going to end."

No answer comes, of course. I'm not quite sure what's worse right now: the fact I was expecting one, or that I'm talking to myself again.

A loud bang startles me awake.

"Get ready, or you're going to be late for school."

Blinking, I stare at Arthur's tall frame obstructing my bedroom door. He's dressed in a burgundy-and-black suit, a sparkling metallic belt at his waist, and what I can only assume are steel-toed cowboy boots on his feet. A strand of hair falls in his eyes, and he brushes it away with a hand heavy with rings. I blink some more. This is way too sparkly a way for me to wake up.

"School?" I manage to mutter.

"Uniform's in the closet," he replies.

"For what?" I say. "Rodeo clown school?"

Arthur's not paying attention to me. Or rather, he's paying too much attention to me and not at all to what I'm saying.

I realize that I'm only wearing my pajamas, a decidedly improper attire in front of a boy. Sister Marie-Clémence would not approve. He takes a step closer, and I shrink away.

"You, uh," he starts, then pauses.

"I what?"

He clears his throat. "You may want to wash your face first. You've got drool on your chin and goop in your eyes."

With a quick grin, he storms out of my bedroom. I stare after him. Then, unable to come up with anything better, I yell, "Jerk!"

I'm really going to have to work on better swear words. Then it hits me—am I really going to school, not juvenile hall?

It's not until I finally get downstairs that I realize it's still pitch-black outside. The house is dead quiet, as I've come to expect it, with no trace of either my parents or the house servant. Apart from Arthur, only Dean's there, dressed impeccably as usual, his dark hair slicked back over his blank face.

"What time is it?" I ask, stifling a yawn.

"Four thirty," Arthur says, "now get a move on."

Before I can protest, he ushers me outside and into the already running car, and seconds later, we're on our way. The streets are completely deserted as we make our way north, every sane person still sound asleep. Arthur's not saying a word, seated up front next to Dean, who's driving for once.

"What happened to our parents?" I ask to fill up the uncomfortable silence—it's obvious those two don't like each other, not that I can blame Dean.

"Irene and Luther had to go to the airport," Arthur answers without looking up from his lap.

"Oh, another charity event?"

No one answers me this time, and I resume picking at my pleated skirt. Despite its airy look, it's actually quite heavy, a fact I've realized is due to tiny metal threads weaved into the fabric. Why anyone would want to dress kids like ambulant lightning rods, I have no idea. Upon closer inspection, it seems that Arthur and I may be going to different schools. Whereas his school's logo is a bunch of crowns—no doubt to represent kids born with a golden spoon in their mouths—mine is a simple cross.

Dean accelerates, and I look out the window. Under a bright single light is a sign:

Winnebago Mental Health Institute
5 miles

Despite the heat blasting in the car, I turn cold. Surely that can't be our final destination. I've never told anyone that I sometimes talk to myself, except once, to Father Wilhelm at confession, when I was six! And wouldn't my mother have sent me to a shrink sooner if that was what she was worried about? Unless...

I glare at Arthur. Maybe they've placed a spy on me.

"No need to stare so hard," Arthur says. "You might wear your eyes out."

"Where are we going?" I ask. We take the hospital's exit, and I see another sign, for the State Hospital Cemetery this time.

I lean forward so I can look Arthur in the eyes, but a gleam draws my gaze downward to his lap instead. I gasp as I realize that the thing Arthur's been playing with all along is nothing but a long, nasty-looking knife.

"Where are we going?" I ask again, unable to hide the rising panic in my voice.

This is what they were planning all along, isn't it? To bring me to a secluded place in the middle of the night, kill me, and dispose of my body before I can taint the family name any further.

Startled, Arthur's eyes finally meet mine. "School, of course," he says as Dean parks and turns off the car.

"With a knife?"

Dean opens the door for me, but I refuse to get out. If they think I'm going to make it easy for them, well they better grow a brain.

Except nobody's forcing me out of the car, and this *is* Dean, isn't it? When a second, then a third, vehicle arrive and park next to us, I'm forced to admit that Arthur told the truth. Unless this is going to be a public execution instead of a private one.

To my surprise, I hear the sound of waves gently rolling in the dark, reminding me of Lake Geneva and my occasional unsanctioned excursions there. Tucking my hands deep in my pockets, I follow the ever-increasing crowd to the shores of Lake Winnebago, where Dean is already waiting for me.

"Where's Arthur?" I ask, looking around at the gathered sleepyheads around us. Everyone seems to be waiting for something or someone.

Dean points toward the lake with his chin, and I turn around. Though there aren't that many lights about, I manage to see a dark figure wading into the water. The wind picks up, and I shiver.

"Arthur!" I yell out. "Arthur, what are you doing?"

But that little twerp doesn't even bother to answer. I pull on Dean's coat sleeve. "We've got to help him!"

I remember the knife, the stupid-looking belt, his boots. I feel the weight of my own uniform as it settles around me like some armor. With all that metal...

"He's going to drown!" I exclaim.

I hear a few splashes as other people get into the water, but whoever they are, they're too far from Arthur. I spare one last look at Dean, but the tall man is just shaking his head.

"Fine!" I spout. I should've known my brother was mental. All the signs were there: the kooky look, the knife, the mental institute. But being wacko is not a good enough reason to let him die. If that was the case, people would have lynched me ages ago.

I make to go after Arthur, but Dean grabs my arm.

"Let go of me," I say, trying to pull away. "We can't let him die!"

But he shakes his head and points to a long, slim wooden boat that's appeared and into which other kids are now climbing. I stare back at Dean, round-eyed.

"Seriously? What is a rowboat full of crazy kids gonna do?"

I manage to free myself from Dean's death grip. I run before he can stop me again, then jump into the lake.

"Saint George's balls!" I yelp. "It's freezing cold!"

After the first shock, I hurry after Arthur, who's now an indistinguishable dot in the distance.

"Arthur, don't do this," I yell.

I try to go faster, but my uniform is dragging me down. All I can do is watch helplessly as Arthur dives and disappears beneath the lake's dark surface.

"Arthur!"

I dive after him, forcing my numb limbs to move, kicking my feet in what's possibly the worst swimming style the world has ever seen. I pause where I think I last saw him and try to feel for his body. Nothing, nothing but water.

"Arthur," I gasp as I emerge to the surface again.

I take another look toward the shore. Nobody seems to care about what's happening, just Dean waving frantically at me. But I can't go back, not until I find that brother of mine. A lump as fat as two years' worth of cat hair balls forms in my throat.

Before I can let myself truly panic, I take a deep breath and plunge down into the cold water again. I concentrate on my strokes, keeping my movements regular. Down here, where I can't hear or see anything, I lose track of time and distance. The only thing present in my mind is that I have to save Arthur.

I try not to think about Agnès as I continue swimming down, deeper and deeper. I don't know how much longer I can hold my breath. My lungs are burning. Something grazes my arm, going from my wrist to my elbow, then back. I jerk away and open my eyes out of reflex.

It's all I can do not to gasp and breathe in water. I see two white-blue orbs head in my direction, followed by an elongated jaw the size of my hand and filled with sharp teeth. I make to swim away, but something grabs my ankle and yanks me farther down into the lake's aphotic depths. I try to kick at whatever's holding me, but my head feels heavy, and my limbs are barely responding to my fuzzy brain's commands. If only I could get some air...

More of those strange glowing orbs appear, like the antennae of anglerfish I've seen in biology class. And there's a lot of them. Fancy meeting so many down here…

I giggle, and water rushes into me. I want to cough, but only manage to swallow more water. I make one last attempt to free myself. I reach for my feet, feel around my ankle…Something slick and bony is wrapped around it. If this is one of Arthur's jokes, he's so going to pay…for…it…

Something then grabs me around the middle, and I give up. I let go and let it take me away. I'm weightless, free. Soon, all my worries will melt away as well. No more deaths, no more accusations…no more rejection…just…peace.

A punch to the sternum wakes me up, and I cough out water. The coughing doesn't stop as I gasp in air. I roll onto my stomach, a loud roaring sound in my ears, or is that heavy purring? More water spews out of me, and I shudder. I feel like I've just been pulled out of a washing machine and wrung out to dry. I hear someone laugh.

"Morgan!"

I groan as someone pushes me over and I roll onto my back, my drenched clothes squishing beneath me.

"Morgan!"

Someone slaps my cheeks.

"Ssstooooooop," I croak.

I blink through thick strands of hair stuck to my face and find myself staring into a pair of ever more familiar hazel eyes. I slap the face away. Definitely not the first thing I wanted to see upon dying.

That laugh comes back. "Well, she's alive an' kickin' at least."

Alive? My hand falls back onto my chest, and, despite my labored breathing, I can feel the quick thump-thumping of my heart. By all that's holy on this earth, I *am* alive!

For a moment, all I can do is look up at the inky sky above, where a few stars manage to wink at me before disappearing again.

"Probably should get her to the infirmary," Arthur says.

I shift my gaze to the four people around me, their profiles lit up by a lantern hanging somewhere behind them—Arthur, a couple of other boys, and a girl, are all staring down at me. I really, really hate always finding myself being looked down upon. I push myself up into a sitting position and immediately regret that decision, as my head feels like it's about to split in two.

"Whoa there," says the laughing boy, reaching for me before I can crumple to the ground again. "Take it easy now. You just had one hell of a swim!"

Swim. Right. I glare up at Arthur. "I almost drowned because of you!"

"Who is this, Arthur?" asks the girl. Her voice would've sounded divine if it hadn't been filled with disgust.

"Morgan," Arthur finally says after a long pause. "My sister."

"You had a sister, and you never told me?" the girl exclaims, outraged.

Arthur pulls her off his arm. "She was away all the time. What was there to say?"

The girl sniffs. "Well, you've checked up on her, and she's fine. Let's get out of here then."

Without another word, the three of them turn around and head down the hill, leaving me alone with the last boy who's still propping me up. I sigh. So much for family ties.

CHAPTER 4

"So why didn't ya come on one of 'em freshman boats?" the guy asks in a low drawl. "Woulda been a lot dryer."

"Thought Arthur...was gonna...drown," I say, still trying to catch my breath before I manage to process everything he's said. "Boats?"

"Yeah, they've just landed, see?"

A few hundred paces away, two wooden boats are discharging a slew of students onto the grass to the flickering light of torches. Waiting before the gleaming keels is a woman, her short red hair whipping about her face with the wind. But what draws my attention aren't her strange clothes that seem an amalgamation of dark leather and silver plating, nor the very long scabbard at her waist from which a dark hilt is clearly protruding, but the fact that she's directing a longboat down from the air, onto the ground, next to the other two. I shake my head; the lack of oxygen must've affected me more than I thought.

"Boats, of course," I say. Falling from the sky, how quaint. "And, where exactly are we? The hospital? Did I suffer a concussion by any chance?"

The boy smacks my back, and I nearly swallow my tongue. "Looks like ya had a lil too much to drink is all! This is the International School of Lake High, o' course." He gets up then, with a wide grin, holds out a callused hand to help me up.

"You mean that our"—I pause, picking my words carefully—"school is on a lake?"

"Under would be more precise, miss."

"It's Morgan," I mumble automatically, taking his hand. "Did you say under?"

With much reluctance, I let go of him, the only thing that tells me this may not be a dream after all. Looks like America truly does have some impressive technology.

The boy, a head shorter than me, brings his hand to his forehead as if he's used to wearing a hat. "Pleasure to meet you, Morgan," he says, drawing out my name so it sounds like More-Gun. "My name's Percy, at your service. Now ya better get back there, or Lady Ysolt'll skin ya alive."

I look back toward the group of students that's now filing in two perfect rows down the hill, toward what looks like one gigantic five-sided stone honeycomb cell and some kind of shrub at the top that makes the building look like it's wearing a toupee.

"With the freshmen?" I ask, confused. "Shouldn't I wait for the seniors?" There's no way I'm going to be sent back three years—I was never *that* bad a student!

Smile glittering in the waning darkness, Percy points to the embroidered cross on my drenched uniform. "Not accordin' to yer blazon."

"What, this doesn't mean I'm going to another Catholic school?" I ask.

But Percy just gives me a small bow before rushing down the grassy hill.

I watch him disappear in the ever-growing throng of people herding toward the strange-looking school, their way lighted up by so many torchlights it looks like some of the constellations have sunk beneath Lake Winnebago as well. Maybe it is a mad-house, after all.

Behind me are empty fields with the dark outline of a forest cut out against the lightening sky-lake. If I want to escape, now's the time to do it. I take a few rigid steps toward the unwelcoming expanse, then stop, eyes blinking rapidly. Did I really just see a fish poke its head out of a cloud? I breathe in deeply, letting the chill air fill my lungs and hopefully clear out my obviously delirious mind.

"Miss Pendragon!"

I whip around, sheepish. Poking from over the hill is the face of the red-haired woman.

"If you don't hurry," she says, her tone sharp, "you'll miss Mass, which means you won't get breakfast."

I hesitate only a moment longer before following her orders. Better the devil you know, I suppose. Besides, with food in the equation, how can I refuse?

I join the last rank of freshmen, behind a boy with a severe limp and next to one with dark hair.

"You ask her," another boy with short black hair says, nudging the one next to me with his elbow.

My neighbor pokes him back in the ribs, and he yelps. I roll my eyes—not only have I somehow been held back three years, but on top of that, I'm a full head and a half taller than everyone else, which makes me stand out like an ogre amongst children. How utterly humiliating.

The tall torches fizzle and crackle on both sides of us as we march down the gravelly path toward the school.

"My name's Bri," the boy next to me whispers to my shoulder in a high-pitched voice—a girl then. "What's yours?"

"Morgan," I whisper back, keeping my eyes trained on the teacher's back. She strikes me as the type of person one does not want to cross, and in this crowd, I make a very obvious target.

The black-haired boy in front turns around, and it's clear now that he and Bri are twins. "So how come we've never seen you here before?" he asks. "I can't believe you swam all the way down here, by the way. That's so rad! Didn't think people could do that without the use of oghams."

I blink at the boy's dialect, completely unsure what an "owe-em" is.

"Don't be rude," Bri says, kicking him in the calf before adding for my benefit, "That's Owen, and the other's Jack."

Very violent siblings, it appears, which reminds me of Arthur. For a very brief moment, I wonder where he is and whether he can help me clear things up so I can avoid the torture of going through high school all over again. But seeing how he's already abandoned me to my own devices twice now, I seriously doubt it. All thoughts of my brother, and any subsequent murderous intent, disintegrate the moment I take in the full massiveness of our school.

The granite building rises five stories high, straight out of the ground, and stretches the span of a stadium. Dotting the ramparts like gaping wounds are arches and windows, soft light glowing through them. As we pass through the titanic wooden doors, I can't help but gawk first at the hunting scene carved into them, then at the rows of colorful standards hanging along the high walls of the entrance hall.

"There's over seven hundred of them," Bri says. "But the most prestigious ones are hung in the KORT room."

She pulls on my sleeve to force me to accelerate. We turn left into a narrow hallway, then engulf ourselves in a dark staircase where the din of voices is amplified tenfold. On the third landing, we encounter a young woman, dressed in an old-fashioned full-length black skirt and apron, who bows to us as we pass by before we head up another set of stairs.

"Just a servant," Bri explains when I ask her, but she's too engrossed in her brother's conversation with his neighbor Jack to pay much attention to me and I have to quell the thousands of questions warring in my already overtaxed brain.

"Didn't you see the news?" Jack asks, limping ahead. "They had to close all the schools in the Bayou Bartholomew area of Louisiana"—he lowers his voice even further—"for frog invasion!"

"I'm sorry, did you say frogs?" I ask.

"I would love for that to happen to us," Jack continues as if I'm not there.

"You're crazy," Owen says. "This is the week we finally get to practice EM!"

"That's exactly why," Jack says.

I have absolutely no idea what these people are saying, and the farther up we go, the more lost I feel.

"We're in the mental hospital, aren't we?" I finally ask Bri.

She looks askance at me. "Does it look like we're in an asylum? Am I wearing a straitjacket?"

"The asylum's next to the church," Owen says as we arrive at the final landing, which does nothing to reassure me. "So I know that they usually start off with sprites," he says, switching topics, "but I want to try a salamander first!"

Bri chortles. "Right, like they'd let you. You nearly turned our yard into a swamp when Hadrian let you play with his ogham this summer." She turns to me and adds conspiratorially, "Mother had a fit. You should've seen how he tried to hide behind the chicken coop."

"Do you eat salamanders here?" I ask.

All three turn to me, shocked into silence, then burst out laughing.

"Not unless you want your intestines to burn," Owen says.

I nod and try not to let the smile melt from my face—the fewer questions I ask from now on, the less I'll stand out. I'll just figure things out as I go along.

"Right then," Lady Ysolt says, her voice ringing out around the rafters, "time to leave your school material here. And perhaps get a little cleaned up." Her eyes linger on me for a moment. "Miss Pendragon, I believe you are not yet acquainted with the layout of the grounds or school proper. Your room's the third door to the right, which Miss Kulkarni will be glad to show you." She raises her voice over the din. "Miss Kulkarni? Come over here, please, and show your new roommate around."

A dark-skinned girl with plaited hair makes a short curtsy, then heads straight down the left hallway. The room we are to share is small, with bunk beds set over their respective desks, and two large trunks lying at their feet. One side of the room has already been claimed, as I can tell from the slew of pictures hung over the bed and around the desk.

Most of them are of a set of three boys, and it doesn't take me long to recognize them. Percy I can very well understand why; his easygoing manners have already won me over. The second boy is the tall, devilishly handsome but moody boy who'd been with him when they rescued me from drowning. But the third…

"Looks like someone's got a crush on Arthur, eh Kulkarni?" I say, braying out a laugh.

The girl draws near me, her perfume hanging in the air behind her. She doesn't look too pleased with my reaction. "My name's Keva," she says, "and he's the head of KORT. Who *wouldn't* like him?"

"Is that right?" I mumble.

The girl darts me a malevolent glare; she clearly can sense sarcasm, and does not appreciate mine.

"Great," I hear her mutter, "now they give me a Sudra[5] to live with. Next thing you know, they'll pick a frigging untouchable!"

Before she can gouge my eyes out, I promptly head for my side of the room, where I rummage through what I assume is my trunk for a change of clothes. Thankfully, amongst a slew of very battered books that constitutes the majority of its contents, I find what I'm looking for. But before I manage to get more than my skirt on, the lights go out, and the door slams shut.

"What the——" Great. Just great. Not only does my roommate have poor taste, but on top of that, she's vindictive. Couldn't have hoped for more luck than that.

Not wanting to trip on anything, I feel my way over to the door and try to find the light switch. But my fingers only encounter the coolness of the stone wall.

"Are you done?" Bri asks, slamming the door open smack on my face. "Oops, sorry. What are you doing in the dark?"

"Looking for the light," I mutter, rubbing my sore nose.

"Oh, here you go." She taps on the wall, and the light fixture on the ceiling, a glass ball, turns red to display a creature stuck inside it.

Rooted to my spot, I point a shaky finger at the incandescent lizard still clearly visible. It stares at me for a second with one large eye, sticks its tongue out, then becomes too bright, and I'm forced to look away.

"I think we just killed a lizard," I say.

---

5 Caste of unskilled workers in India.

Bri stares up at the ceiling. "You mean the salamander?" She slaps her hands together. "Cool, huh? But don't worry, the elemental's well controlled. It won't set fire to this place. Come on, let's get to Mass, or we'll get detention. Besides, you definitely can't miss the oath taking," she adds, tapping the wall so the light shuts off.

"I knew you guys were high-tech, but to use radioactive animals like that..." I say, craning my neck up as we walk out, but the light fixture is now empty.

The sound of bells in the distance makes Bri jump. "Malediction! We're going to be late for Lauds! Hurry up and put on your jacket, unless you don't mind showing up to mass half naked!"

She flashes me a grin before dashing back into the now-deserted hallways. Struggling to put my shirt on the right way, I hurry after her.

"North," Bri tells me when we hit the ground floor.

We hurry after a couple of other stragglers. The bell rings once more, then remains silent.

"Oooh, not good," Bri says, bolting through the north door and into the open air.

At the other end of the long paved path stands a large white church with a single steeple and long, narrow stained-glass windows. We make it inside before the double doors close and, gasping, stop long enough to dip our fingers into the holy water bowl and make a hurried cross sign, then head down the aisle to find Owen and Jack.

"What took you so long?" Owen asks, scooting over to let his sister and I sit.

"Hey, we're on time. Give us a break," Bri says.

"Just in time," Jack says, pointing toward the front.

Dressed in a long black cassock, a priest is now making his way to the front of the altar. He bows, crosses himself, then turns to face us.

The heady smell of incense reaches me before I see two boys and two girls walk down the nave toward the front, then settle to each side of the altar.

"Greetings, brothers and sisters, daughters and sons," the priest intones in a steady voice. "Let us begin this day in prayer. In nomine Patris, et Filii, et Spiritus Sancti."

"Amen," I say in unison with the rest of the congregation.

Once the first notes of the Kyrie Eleison ring out, my brain clocks out. From where I sit, I have a direct view of the priest and, in front of him, a cordoned-off section of pews where, to my surprise, is Arthur, his back straight, dark blond head held high.

My gaze roams about my new surroundings, resting occasionally on some of the people assembled—more students, I guess from the uniforms. Even with the whole school present, only a third of the benches are filled, giving the place an impression of emptiness.

Large votive candles hang along the pillars above us, their flickering lights turning the capitals' carved figurines into grotesque demonic forms that seem to be laughing at me from their lofty heights.

Despite my best intent, my eyelids start to droop, and I nod off. I get brutally awakened when Bri jabs me in the ribs with her sharp elbow.

"Ow, what?" I snap, blinking.

My words echo under the now-quiet ribbed vaults. Bri gestures toward the front of the church, where the priest is focusing his whole attention…on me.

"What?" I mouth to Bri, shrinking lower on my bench.

"You're supposed to go up there," she replies in the same manner.

I force myself to my feet and nearly trip on the kneeler. I hear a couple of people laugh, but I remain stoically standing.

"We are welcoming today our newest member," the priest says, motioning me forward.

Legs shaking, I manage to make my way over to the chancel, where the priest has me kneel down. One of the altar boys brings him a thurible,[6] and the priest proceeds to incense me, which only makes me feel more drowsy.

"Dear God Almighty and Victorious," he says, "you sent your Son into this world to banish the power of Satan and his evil horde, to rescue mankind from darkness, and to bring your servants into your light.

"We pray for Morgan Pendragon, who has decided to join our ranks today. Set her free from sin. Make her a temple of your glory, a warrior of your kingdom, and a defender of our brethren against the demons who try to take us over. Send your Holy Spirit to dwell within her and help her in these troubled times to resist the lures of evil. We ask this of you through Christ the Lord."

I nearly jerk back when he steps away; what is this mumbo jumbo about warring and demons and whatnot? I squint at the man. Despite the severity of his features, he doesn't seem to be a cult leader, but then again, wasn't Lucifer the most beautiful of angels?

The priest makes a small cross on my forehead with his thumb, leaving a damp mark on it.

"We anoint you with the oil of salvation, that Christ our Savior may strengthen you. Do you, Morgan, accept your place amongst us?"

---

6 An incense holder used during certain Masses.

I look back down, noting in passing the spots of mud on the priest's black shoes. Does he expect me to be honest, or is this a rhetorical question? Because, to be quite frank, I have no inkling of staying here, at least not past my eighteenth birthday, which is in less than a year. Nor do I want to go to any war!

My silence stretches for a long minute until I hear people shifting uncomfortably in their seats. Sweat beads on my forehead as I try to decide what my best course of action is.

On the one hand, I'm going to be stuck here for a while still, so why not give them the answer they expect and do my best to remain as inconspicuous as possible? On the other, if I say yes, I may be doomed to remain with them or die. Which is not exactly my current life goal.

Just go with the flow, my guardian angel chimes in. *You can figure out how to deal with the consequences later.*

"Yes," I say out loud.

"Amen," the priest says, laying a hand on my head in benediction before stepping aside.

Before I can get back up, however, another pair of feet enters my line of vision—black steel-toed cowboy boots. I snap my head up and find myself staring straight up into Arthur's nostrils.

"Rise, and come make your pledge of allegiance," he says.

Great, *now* what did I get myself into? I follow him to the edge of the altar, a large, rectangular block of stone with strange design patterns carved into it, similar to those I've seen on the mantelpiece back home. The odd characters spiral around a large black jewel set into the center of the stone itself.

"Raise your hand before us all," Arthur commands.

Casting furtive glances at the sea of faces turned to me, I raise my hand in the air.

"Over the altar," Arthur adds quietly, raising a few chuckles from the crowd.

"Right," I say, shifting positions.

In a silvery flash, Arthur pulls out a knife and pricks my palm with it.

"Ouch!" I exclaim, pulling away in outrage. "What did you do that for?"

A burst of laughter erupts at my reaction, and Arthur grabs my hand before I can escape.

"Trust me," he whispers through clenched teeth.

"Why should I?" I reply in the same way.

Arthur doesn't bother to reply and instead forces my injured hand on the gem. Reflexively, I clutch the smooth stone as he keeps pressing my hand down.

"Do you swear," he says, "on pain of death, never to reveal what you will see and learn here to the laity, nor to disclose our location to anyone outside our order?"

I struggle against his hold, but his grip only gets stronger.

"Let me go, you maniac," I whisper harshly. "I take it back. I don't want to be a part of your swag crew."

"You can't take it back," Arthur says, keeping my hand firmly anchored to the large precious stone below. "Swear it if you have the slightest desire to survive this."

"Is that a threat?" I ask.

The temperature around us seems to drop below freezing level. Even the students have stopped fidgeting and are watching us with bated breath.

"It's a fact," Arthur says, sounding genuinely worried. "Now make the bloody oath."

Biting my lip, I take in a few short breaths, then say, "I swear."

Arthur removes his hand, and I try to pull away as well, but for some reason, I can't seem to move. The gem beneath my fingers takes on a glowing red tint, turning my hand translucent for a moment; then it dies down, and whatever pressure kept me locked on it releases me.

As if burned, I yank my hand away quickly. "What was that all about?" I ask Arthur, cradling my hand to my chest protectively.

"You just sealed your oath," he says. "Now bow."

We both bow before the altar, then join the rest of the assembly as it files out. Everyone's all smiles again.

Everyone but me.

CHAPTER 5

The moment we step into the nave, the beautiful girl who'd witnessed my near drowning grabs Arthur's arm, casting me a disdainful look as she pulls him away.

"There you go," Bri says to me with a big smile. "Now you're one of us!"

"Who is that?" I ask, pointing with my chin to the blonde girl's back.

"You don't know Jennifer?" Bri asks.

"Only the hottest girl in the whole wide school!" Owen says.

"You don't say," I mumble.

"And a member of KORT," he adds.

"By association," Bri says. "But I guess it's the prerogative of the president's fiancée."

"She's engaged to the president of the United States?" I exclaim.

"The president of KORT, of course," Owen says, holding the door open for us.

"Didn't they say your name was Pendragon?" Bri asks me.

"So?"

"So aren't you related to Arthur?"

"He's my brother," I admit, pulling a face.

"You're kidding!" Owen exclaims.

"Trust me," I say, "it's really nothing to be excited about."

"You're joking right?" Owen asks, his voice reaching unmanly octaves. "You're related to the head of KORT, who also happens to be the youngest president in three centuries, and you think it's nothing? Do you even know that he fought his first battle, and won it, at the age of seven? That he's set a record of elemental captures just over the summer, and that he has the ear of most of the Board?"

I back away under this verbal assault; not only is this way more information than I'd ever wanted on Arthur, but all that jargon is giving me a headache.

"Hold on," I say, then lower my voice so no one else can hear me. "What's this court you're talking about? Is there a king or something like that down here?"

"KORT stands for Knights of the Round Table," Bri says before either of the two boys can voice their obvious shock.

"You're his sister and you didn't even know he was the president?" Jack asks.

"She didn't even know he was engaged," Owen adds.

Bri punches him in the shoulder. "She's new here. Be nice."

I stumble to a halt as the coin finally drops. "You mean...you mean that my brother's engaged, and to her?" Not that I care who has the bad luck of being stuck with Arthur, but I don't want to end up being related to someone who, with a single word and a twist of the mouth, makes me feel like I'm no better than bat droppings.

"They had their handfasting this Lughnasadh," Bri says.

"It's a trial marriage," Jack says before I can ask. "If they choose to, they can annul it after a year and a day. Otherwise, they stay married."

I knew that my family was weird, but this proves it.

"Wait," Bri says, stopping Jack from entering the school.

"Now what?" Owen asks.

"You're telling us you really don't know *anything* about this place?" Bri asks me. "Your parents never talked to you about it?"

I swallow hard—my parents never talked to me, period. I shake my head, hating how conspicuous this makes me.

To my surprise, Bri's face lights up. "Then you need a tour!"

Jack and Owen groan, but Bri shushes them. "Come on, guys. At least we got to go through orientation."

"But there's hardly any time for breakfast—" Owen starts.

"It'll be quick, promise," Bri says, grabbing my arm and steering me around another gravelly path to the end of the building.

The two boys hurry to keep up with us.

"Shouldn't we go through the school?" Jack asks, the pace making his limp more obvious. "It'll be faster."

"Just to let her see the stadium," Bri says as we round the corner.

And there, on the other side of an empty patch of dirt, lies a perfectly circular arena, its solid stone walls reaching high up into the sky.

"Nice, ain't it?" Owen asks, sticking his hands deep in his pockets. "It's where all the tournaments take place and the knights practice."

I lick my lips, staring at the gray structure. "You mean...real knights fight there?" I ask. This whole KORT thing isn't just the name of a drama club?

"Of course!" Owen says, flinging his arm out as if holding an imaginary sword. "They get to fight with weapons and elementals in their noble quest to defend the world against the Fey. Whoosh, he creates a wall of fire for diversion"—he dodges and twists around an invisible foe—"dashes around the Fey's attack, uses an air shield to protect himself from the poison, and then"—he jumps toward Jack, bringing his arm down in a swinging motion—"defeats the enemy and captures his ogham."

"Stop," Bri says. "I think she's going to get sick."

And she's right. My vision's a fuzzy blur of grays, and my breath comes out in short gasps. I feel someone move me, and I find myself sitting down. The coolness of the stone bench seeps through my clothes, slowly helping my mind to clear up.

"Are you all right?" Bri asks, her small face concerned.

"She looks pale," Jack says, pushing his glasses up the ridge of his nose. "Maybe we should take her to the infirmary."

I shake my head. "I'm OK, thanks," I lie. Just a little panic attack, nothing I haven't dealt with before.

"Didn't think she'd faint at the mention of knights," Owen says. "Girls can be so delicate."

"I thought this was a Catholic school," I say.

"It is," Jack says. "Weren't you in Mass with us?"

"I thought I was going to go to a *normal* school," I retort, tears streaming down my cheeks, "with normal people, and learn normal things, not..."

"Not learning how to become a knight and fight?" Bri asks, sitting down next to me and patting my back. "There, there, it's not so bad, really."

"Not bad?" Owen exclaims. "Being a knight is an honor! Only those who pass the test are able to come down here and train, and even then, not everyone gets to be knighted! It's very difficult to even make it to that level."

"But I didn't ask for any of this!" I say, yelling despite myself. I wipe my runny nose on my coat sleeve. "I don't care about your knights and your Fey creature thingies!"

Owen's eyes widen, and he snaps his mouth shut.

"It's really not that bad," Bri says again, grabbing Jack's tissue and using it to dab my eyes. But that small act of kindness only makes me cry harder.

"Truly," Bri says, looking pleadingly at the two boys. "I mean, what Owen says is right; not everyone gets to become a knight. There's lots of people who end up having a pretty regular life after school."

I blow my nose hard. "Really?" I ask with a hiccup.

Bri nods emphatically. "Yeah, and even being a knight isn't so bad these days, compared to what it was like centuries ago, when they were constantly at war."

"Actually, it's been reported that Fey activity's increased in recent years," Jack says.

"You're not helping here," Bri says, throwing him a warning glance.

But I've cried so much, I'm left feeling strangely empty, and Jack's comment doesn't stir me.

"So you're supposed to take a test to get here?" I ask, trying not to think too hard beyond the present moment.

"It's usually pretty straightforward," Jack says. "They see if you have any affinity for controlling elementals, and then you're good to go."

"Elementals?" I repeat.

"Fey creatures that are linked to the elements," Jack says.

"You know, fire, water, and all that," Owen adds.

"They used to be the lowest angelic form," Jack explains, "which is why their powers are so basic. But there are all sorts of Fey, and some of them are quite powerful—those are the ones you really want to avoid."

"Wait, wait, wait," I say. My hands clench convulsively around the edge of the bench. "You mean…these Fey are angels?"

"Fallen angels," Bri says, "so more like demons."

"Well, technically, they weren't bad enough to end up in Hell," Jack corrects her. He clears his throat at a look from her. "But yes, in essence."

"And these demonic angels have…magic?" I ask, feeling lightheaded once again.

"Well duh!" Owen says, giggling. "They're ex-*angels*!"

Two pairs of arms grab my shoulders as I sway on my seat, preventing me from toppling to the ground. Just breathe, I tell myself. This will all be over soon. I'm going to wake up and I'll laugh at myself for being this ridiculous. And to prove my point, I let out a nervous chuckle.

"I think she's lost it," Owen whispers.

Someone slaps me, and I stop laughing, the sting making my cheek feel warm.

"What did you do that for?" Bri exclaims, holding me close.

"That's what they usually do in movies," Jack retorts. "Besides, it worked, didn't it?"

More tears spring to my eyes, for I realize what this means— it's real, it's all real!

Jack eyes me suspiciously, his hand still raised. "Do you think she's going to need another one?"

Holding my cheek, I recoil. "No, I'm fine. I'll be good now."

"Are you sure?" Bri asks.

I nod. "Let's just keep going."

The three of them look skeptical, but I jump to my feet and force a smile. "Where to now?"

"I suppose the dining hall," Bri says hesitantly. "We could do the rest of the tour some other time…"

"Perfect!" Owen exclaims, already heading back. "I'm starving."

"Let's take the shortcut," Jack says as we step inside.

We head down a narrow hallway and burst out through the opposite door into a vast courtyard. Despite the dim light, I can make out an enormous dark shape in the center, one so large it blots out the other side of the building completely.

"What's that?" I ask, stopping when I see movement in the hedge that seems to spring out of its trunk like a hairy leg.

"Just an apple tree," Bri says, pulling on my arm. "Come on, this side. The other's blocked off."

"Unless you wanna make out with someone," Owen snorts.

Bri slaps him across the head. "Don't be such a ninny!" she says, then adds quietly to me, "Though it *is* true what he says. That's a notorious kissing spot."

We veer left, hop over a low row of shrubs, and peel down the dirt path toward the opposite side. I can't take my eyes off the tree's massive shadow as we reach the other end of the inner courtyard. They open another door, and we find ourselves at the tail end of a thinning crowd of students that's heading past a wide, arched door, through which I can already detect the smell of fried eggs and sausages.

"Just a moment," Jack says as we're about to enter the dining room.

"Can't this wait?" Owen asks. "All the sausages are gonna be gone!"

"Forewarned is forearmed," Jack retorts.

We move to the side of the corridor where a large board filled with news clippings and regulations takes up a whole span of the wall.

"Anything you like in there?" Owen asks, growling with impatience.

"Nothing we didn't know before," Jack says with a sigh. "Nothing more on those kidnappings either."

"Why anyone would want to go on Island Park beats me," Bri says, and I remember the news clipping found in my parents' office.

"Are there aliens too?" I ask, scared of the answer.

"Of course not," Jack says.

"I'd think we have enough with the Fey," Bri adds.

Somehow, her answer makes me feel a little better, and I follow her inside.

"Don't worry," Owen repeats for the umpteenth time. "We've only covered theory, so you're not that far behind."

"You shouldn't dismiss what we've learned," Jack says.

Owen shrugs. "In my humble opinion, practice is the best way to learn."

"There's nothing humble about you," Bri retorts, and her twin answers with a grin.

I nearly collapse into my bowl of oatmeal when something heavy lands on my back.

"My, isn't this Arthur's sister?" a loud, deep voice says, nearly ripping my eardrum apart. "*Enchanté.*"[7]

The weight lifts from my back, and I find a pair of massive boys making deep curtsies before me. They straighten up gracefully, their smiles bright within their dark faces, and an insane amount of silvery studs adorning their ears. I'd almost think they were twins as well, except where one is broad and completely bald, the other is tall and has a full head of dreadlocks.

"Wonderful performance," the tall one says, "at church, you know."

"The best we've seen," the other one adds, "forever and ever."

7 Charmed.

48

"It's 'in a long time,' you sophomoric buffoon," the tall one says.

The other one frowns. "I don't like being called a monkey."

"I said buffoon, not baboon," the tall one says. He then extends a large hand toward me. "Gauvain, at your service."

"And Gareth," says the other, pushing the first one out of the way.

Tentatively, I shake their hands, getting my hands reduced to a pulp in the process.

"I had no idea Arthur was keeping such a pretty sister away from us," Gauvain says.

I blush and find myself completely tongue-tied, but considering I'm facing a man nearly twice my height and quite evidently all muscle, I feel I'm excused.

"Shut yer big bazoo," Percy says, playfully punching Gareth in the arm despite barely reaching his navel.

They could easily crush him if they wanted to, but the two boys don't seem to mind, and instead make more room for him around our table.

"Be sure to ask if you have any problem with lessons," Gareth says. "I'd be delighted to help you."

"She'd be better off getting help from a baboon," Gauvain retorts.

Gareth's brows lower. "Did you call me a monkey again?"

"No," Gauvain says. "I said you were worse than one, my—"

He doesn't get to finish, for Gareth punches him in the stomach, sending the taller boy flying over the table and into the solid wall.

I cringe at the sharp ringing Gauvain makes when he rebounds off the stones, but the moment he hits the ground, he's back up on his feet again.

"You're going to pay for that," he says, flexing his hands, a bluish glow throwing sparks around his knuckles.

"Enough," Percy says. "Mind the company."

Gareth and Gauvain weigh each other up for another full second before finally relaxing their stands. With a jerk of his head, Percy gets them to follow him out, stopping by just long enough to talk with two Asian girls at another table.

Moving very slowly, I set my fork back down on the table before I stab someone with it. Next to me, Owen, Jack, and Bri are staring with their mouths agape.

"You-You saw it too, right?" I squeak.

"Aren't they amazing?" Owen says. "Full KORT members!"

"And they came to you," Bri adds in awe. "And not just the cousins, but Sir Percy as well!"

"You didn't..." I sputter. "You seen it, you dididii..."

Giving up on trying to make sense, I gulp my tea down, then gasp as it burns my throat.

"You OK there?" Owen asks, patting my back.

"His hand!" I rasp.

"Yeah, he was about to use an elemental!"

"Which he shouldn't have," Jack says, frowning. "It's dangerous, especially with all these people around."

"Oh, come on," Owen retorts. "Percy stopped them. Besides, they know what they're doing. They're KORT members!"

"See?" Bri says. "It's a good thing to be related to the president. Then everyone likes you."

"Well, not everyone," Jack says, pointing to the other end of the dining hall.

Still fanning my tongue, I look over my shoulder and find myself locking gazes with the haughty Jennifer, who appears to have been ditched by my brother.

50

"Beautiful people don't like it when others become the center of attention," Jack whispers.

"Not Jennifer," Owen retorts. "She's a true angel!"

As I watch the blonde girl strut out of the room, I have a feeling that Owen may be delusional.

Classes starting at seven, we leave the dining hall the moment we hear the church bells ring the hour. I relegate the fight to the deepest recesses of my mind, willing the whole incident never to have occurred—if only to keep my sanity for a while longer.

As we make our way up another narrow staircase, the sunlight filters through the slitted windows, crisscrossing the steps like a bar code.

"I still can't believe you know so many people from KORT!" Owen says, jumping up a couple of steps. "I mean, even regular knights don't usually bother with us, unless it's for chores."

"Morgan!"

We all pause to find my roommate, Keva, descending the steps toward us. Panting, she stops a step above me and hands me a bag.

"Your books," she says. "You forgot to bring them with you."

Staring incredulously at her, I grab the heavy bag and hoist it onto my back. "Uh…thanks?"

"Maybe if you hadn't shut her up in the dark, she wouldn't have forgotten," Bri says.

The two girls stare at each other for a long moment, and I worry they're going to go for each other's throats, when Keva smiles.

"That was an accident," she says, and she pushes Bri away to stand next to me.

As we make our way down the third floor, I notice people stop in their tracks to stare at me and whisper behind their hands. I feel myself turn crimson, and I accelerate my pace.

We find the rest of the class already seated, though no teacher in sight.

"What happened to Boris?" Keva calls out, dumping her books on the first desk next to the windows.

"How should I know?" a portly boy with a big nose retorts. "Hey, who's the tall girl with you? Is she some half giant you've brought for a presentation?"

The boy and his two friends snort out in laughter.

"Daniel, if you can't come up with better insults, you may as well shut up. Besides," Keva adds as I find a seat near the back, "she's Arthur's sister, so you better keep your tongue extra civil."

"Oh yeah?" Daniel says, turning in his seat so he can see me. "How come I've never heard of her? Maybe she's so dumb her family was afraid to show her in public!"

I ignore the jab and pretend to be looking through my books.

"Of course that's not why," Keva says, complacent. "Otherwise she wouldn't have been allowed here. Right, Morgan?"

I sink lower into my seat, wishing she wouldn't involve me. What am I supposed to say? That they only brought me in after I was accused of killing one of my old classmates?

"I'm just his half sister," I say instead.

Smiling, Keva draws closer to me, a well-worn notepad open in her hands. "So tell me, what toothpaste does he use? And what's his soap brand? Does he wear slippers or go barefoot? And what about bedtime?"

"What about bedtime?" I ask.

"Well, what does he wear?" Keva asks, sitting on top of my desk. "Pajamas or the more common shorts and T-shirt? Or better yet"—she lowers her voice to a loud whisper—"does he sleep in the nude?"

"How should I know?" I say, pulling away. "It's not like I sleep with him."

"But you live with him," Keva says.

"As of yesterday," I retort. "Until then, I was away in Europe."

Keva's hand falls limp in her lap. "Yes, but there were summer vacations, and Christmas holidays," she continues with dogged determination. "I mean, surely you must know something! Did he ever wear braces? Did he get grounded often when he was little?"

"I think I need some fresh air," I say, rushing outside.

Thankfully, she doesn't follow me, and I manage to have a respite from the onslaught of questions. Closing my eyes, I lean against the wall and take a shuddering breath.

Surely you're not having another panic attack because of some crazy fangirl?

"Shut up," I say. "I don't need your sarcasm right now."

But I can't deny my guardian angel's right: her probing shows that my family only sent me away to forget all about my existence, and letting others know would be like accepting it, and that would hurt too much.

When I feel I've regained some composure, I open my eyes again and see, like a vision from Hell, a large shadow fast approaching, dead silent along the cobbled walls, stretching from floor to ceiling. The half-man, half-animal shape, the long, double-pointed beard, the sniffling and grunting…there's no doubt about it.

I shriek, and dash back inside the classroom.

"Demon!" I yell. "In the hallway!"

Keva and Owen rush over to poke their heads out the door. "Where?" they ask.

"It was this close to me," I say, bringing my thumb and forefinger together until they almost touch. "And it was making weird noises, and it had horns, and—"

A shiver courses through me as a light *clippity-clop* reverberates down the corridor. Every cell in my body's poised for flight, but I can't make myself leave my new friends behind, defenseless.

I try to pull Keva and Owen away from the door and the danger lurking outside. "We need to get out of here!"

Owen bursts out laughing. "You mean Puck?" He's so incapacitated by his chortling that he has to hold on to a desk not to fall.

I look back outside to find the owner of that terrifying shadow appear around the corner, its beady eyes staring me down beneath a pair of small horns. It lurches toward us on a set of hairy hooves, its fists swinging from side to side with every step.

My hands unclench as the strange creature reaches the level of our class. Belying his gargantuan silhouette, it barely manages to reach my knees, and I do feel somewhat foolish at my initial reaction.

"Puck?" I say.

The creature looks around at the mention of his name, but otherwise doesn't stop.

"Our resident hobgoblin," Bri says, wiping tears from her eyes.

"Hobgoblin?" I repeat feebly.

"Another Fey type," Owen says. "Kinda like elementals."

Keva tsks. "Daniel, I must apologize to you," she says. "You were right. She is just a backwater dimwit who's been held back. There's no other explanation for it."

Chapter 6

Breathe, just breathe, I remind myself.

"You really don't look too good," Bri says when I sit next to her.

Eyes closed, I rest my head on my books. "I'm OK," I say, more for my sake than hers.

"It's really not that bad," she says.

"So you keep saying." I straighten up. "But I thought angels had"—I flutter my hands about my sides—"wings, you know?"

Bri cocks her head. "Well, some do, of course. Just like some of them look like us, but there are some who look... different."

"And don't forget about those who can change shapes," Jack says, sitting before her.

"But then, how can you tell them apart from us?" I exclaim.

I hear Daniel snort on the other side of the room. "I would think it's rather obvious, wouldn't you?" he says, and his two friends snicker. "Puck doesn't exactly look human."

"Obviously!" I snap, then point at Bri accusingly. "But she said they could look like us!"

I bite on my lip to stop myself, but I know it's too late when I see the hurt look on Bri's face. Cheeks burning, I turn away. No matter my best intentions, I always end up ruining everything I touch, one of the reasons I never keep any friends.

A tall, burly man enters the room, the light from the chandeliers reflecting off his shining pate. He eyes us, his long mustache hanging severely low like the tusks of a walrus.

"All rise," says a surly girl at the front. "And bow."

At once, the class obeys and says, loud and clear, "Good morning, Sir Boris."

The teacher's gait is slow and uneven as he makes his way to the lectern, his clothes clanking and clinking with every step.

"I don't like how you talk to my sister," Owen whispers to me over his shoulder. I try to ignore him as he turns around. "And for your information, she *did* say Fey didn't all look like us."

Sir Boris clears his throat. "Mr. Vaughan," he says, setting a large book down on his desk.

Owen spins around.

"Considering class has started, you may share what you have to say with the rest of us."

"I was just telling her some Fey look like us," Owen says, sheepish. "Sir."

"So they can," the teacher says, nodding so his mustache comes to rest on his large stomach. "So how can you distinguish them from us?"

"Uh...pointy ears?" Owen ventures.

The class bursts out laughing. "Always ready to entertain, aren't you, Mr. Vaughan," Sir Boris says. "But perhaps your neighbor will once again enlighten you?"

"The Fey don't like iron, sir," Jack answers automatically, and I see Owen slap his hand to his forehead. "So anyone who wears it is human. It's also how we identify ourselves."

"Right," Sir Boris says. "Now everyone sit and put your books away. We're having a quiz."

A collective groan rises from the seats, but the teacher makes his slow way from desk to desk unfazed, distributing his sheets.

When he arrives besides me, he hands me a test as well, but adds, "No need to worry, Pendragon. This time I'll let you find the answers in your book."

"Thank you, Professor," I say.

"It's 'sir,'" the large man says, moving on to the next desk.

While everyone's writing away madly under the pressure of a ticking grandfather clock, I open the book in question: *A Field Guide to Elementals.*

With trembling fingers, I flip the pages to the introduction and start reading.

Many believe that, being the simplest form of elvins one can find, elementals are also the easiest to tame, but that is not so. This field guide was created with the intent to discuss the four major families and their sixteen genera, their strengths and weaknesses, and the best methods to subdue them. This edition also has an extra section on the maintenance of the creatures once captured.

I pause, take a deep breath, then turn the page. The first chapter talks about the classification of various elementals with four main branches linked to the four elements: gnomes for earth, undines or nymphs for water, sylphs for air, and salamanders for fire. I pause at the last illustration—a drawing of the incandescent lizard that lit up my dorm room! And now I wish my high-tech nuclear version was correct.

I hide my face in my book, on the verge of tears again. What have I done to deserve this? This, there's no doubt about it, is a book of witchcraft. And the Bible's clear on its stance on anything related to sorcery—it's the same as transacting with the Devil himself! I cross myself at the thought, but…

Surely having a quick look isn't going to be enough to send me to Hell, is it? And, unable to resist my curiosity, I resume my reading.

This is, by far, the strangest class I've ever taken, and the more I read, the more I realize the world is a lot more vast and unfathomable than I've ever realized. Which I find both terrifying and…a little exciting. Sister Marie-Clémence wouldn't have recognized me if she'd seen the avidity with which I peruse the book, or the keen interest I take in the lecture that follows the quiz.

"Gianakos," Sir Boris snaps, "where is the most likely place for a gnome to keep its ogham?"

I sigh. Again with the big words, and I'm too afraid to draw attention to myself again by asking questions.

The boy who was called on stammers, "Its f-feet, sir?"

"Are you asking me, Gianakos?"

"N-N-No, sir," the boy replies, his face as bright as his red hair. "The-The feet."

"A plausible answer," Sir Boris says, "considering many of them have rather large extremities, but wrong. As usual. Watkins?"

A girl sitting at the front answers eagerly, "Most have them hidden in the ground, sir. Usually a cache or under a rock."

"Because, as you ought to know," Sir Boris says with a particular look at the red-haired boy, "Fey can voluntarily separate themselves from their oghams and have their powers unaffected. As long as the ogham remains surrounded by their natural element, of course."

He goes to the blackboard and writes down a list of possible places that gnomes—or earth elementals, as I've just read—like to use as hiding places.

I'm not quite sure what these sources of power, or oghams, look like, and copy everything down in the hopes that I'll soon find out.

"The key to finding these hiding places," Sir Boris continues, "is to trick these creatures. Their powers are usually proportional to their smarts, and they're prone to using deception and arts to outdo you."

"But never lie," Keva says.

Sir Boris's stare makes my roommate cringe. "But they can't lie," he finally says. "Though there are ways of twisting the truth."

He unfurls a chart hanging from the board. On it are the same four elemental illustrations pictured in my book. He turns to the diagram of a lumpy, hirsute man with a bulbous nose and large, hairy feet.

"Fey people always hide their oghams where they're safest," the professor continues, "which makes sense. Look at us: all our vital organs are protected within our rib cage."

I nod in agreement—at least *that* I understand. Out of the corner of my eye, I see Daniel's friends push their chairs back, and something flashes. I snap my head around in time to see a glowing wave of green hurtle toward me. I try to duck, but the desk is in my way. Then, about an inch from me, the green current rebounds in the air as if it's hit an invisible wall, and hurtles back the way it came.

There's a loud crash, and the whole class turns to find Gianakos sprawled on the floor, the legs of his chair broken.

"Causing trouble in class today, Mr. Gianakos?" Sir Boris asks. "Guess I'll see you in detention later today then."

The boys at the back snigger, but I catch Daniel giving me a long, considering look.

The dull sound of the bell reaches our classroom, and everyone jumps up to leave.

"Everyone is to write a five-page essay on two gnome types, their behavior patterns, and the best ways of approaching them by next class," Sir Boris says. "And don't forget, what's the one thing you need to remember about EM?"

"Iron is the only true weapon against a Fey," the class intones.

As I hurry by, the teacher calls me over. "Pendragon, I believe this is your first time being exposed to the topic?" His blue eyes seem to be dissecting me from the inside out, analyzing every little defect of mine.

I nod. "Y-Yes, sir."

"You've got quite a lot to do if you want to catch up with your classmates then," he growls, his mighty mustache quivering. "I expect you to turn in all the homework you've missed in the next two weeks. You may ask Vaughan for the list, since she's evidently waiting for you."

A month's worth of homework to do in two weeks? Is the guy out of his mind? But the teacher's too intimidating, and my nerves deflate before I can utter a sound of reproach.

"You shouldn't have said that to her," I hear Bri say outside. "She's new. She's scared—"

"That's no excuse," Owen cuts her off. "You were helping her! No, she's annoying, and I don't like her."

I hang back to hear what more they have to say about me, shame burning my insides.

"You don't even know her," Bri retorts. "It'll get better once she's more used to this place." Owen chortles in derision, and she adds, "For once, try to put yourself in someone else's shoes!"

Before they can get into a full-blown fight, I walk out of the classroom.

"Sorry for making you wait," I whisper, avoiding their eyes.

"How was your first class?" Bri asks as if nothing was wrong.

We head up a narrow staircase tucked away in a corner, and Owen hurries ahead of us without waiting.

"Don't worry about him," Bri says. "Or about Boris. He's not so bad, as long as you do what he says."

Jack coughs lightly, as if afraid to disagree openly with her.

"Well, he *is* rather bad," Bri says, and before Jack can cough again, she adds, "and I really hate his class, but I'll still help you."

This time, Jack coughs so forcefully that Bri glares at him. "Actually, Jack here will help you out since he's so eager to help and has the top grades. Besides"—she turns to me with a bright smile—"you can always ask Arthur, since you're his sister."

However unlikely it is that's ever going to happen, I just smile back, concentrating instead on not destroying my budding friendship with Bri and proving Owen wrong.

We sprint together to the other side of the building and skid to a stop across the way from wrought-iron doors that guard a library.

"This place is huge," I say, admiring through the gaps the rows upon rows of bookshelves bursting with volumes and scrolls.

"Trust me, you'll get sick of it soon enough," Bri says. "Now come on, we've got to go in for our hour of doom lore. History," she adds, when she sees my questioning look. "You'll see when you hear Lincoln talk."

I follow her into a wide auditorium where a short, energetic man greets us. "Come in and have a seat," he says, making a sweeping gesture with his one and only arm.

I find a spot close to Keva this time, who doesn't seem too pleased at the sight of me.

"Now that everyone's here," Sir Lincoln says, "let us resume where we last left off." He jumps onto his podium, sending his full head of white hair quivering. "You all know how humans had to live under the heavy yoke of the Fey, those lost angels who got caught on Earth after the last battle between Heaven and Hell."

I spy Bri yawning profoundly in the back, but the professor doesn't seem to notice.

"We also covered the terrible wars that we were forced to undertake," Sir Lincoln continues, striding along his dais, "all because of their little games. As if we were nothing more than pawns.

"Look at Troy. A great, mighty city fallen because they refused to pay tribute to certain of the Fey. Roman times were not much better, and by then, Carman's influence was so great that even our own morals and standards of conduct started to degenerate."

Baffled, I pause over my blank page. My version of history wasn't quite the same—at least there was no Spanish lady involved with the downfall of the Roman Empire. I hesitate for a second longer, then decide to risk it all and raise my hand.

"Yes, Miss..."

"Pendragon," I say. "Who's Carman? I thought Rome had been sacked by Visigoths?"

Sir Lincoln blinks at me owlishly while the class lets out a collective gasp. Then the teacher clears his throat.

"Anyone wish to answer Miss Pendragon?" he asks.

Keva's hand shoots up, and she immediately begins reciting, "An angel whose soul was so tainted by evil she should have gone to Hell. But the Archangel Michael missed her in his cleanup, so she got to continue her business here on Earth, bringing chaos and destruction everywhere."

"Exactly," Sir Lincoln says. "And—"

"She also brought the ten plagues along with her," Keva interrupts him, on a roll. "But then she was defeated and sentenced to prison for life."

"Very good," the professor says. "And a piece of her lore can be found—"

"On the stele inside the library," Keva says with a proud flick of her hair. "I can't believe you didn't even know that much," she adds under her breath for my benefit.

"However we haven't reached that part of history yet," the teacher says, resuming his pacing. "Indeed, today we shall discuss the peak of her reign, before we humans rebelled: the Dark Ages.

"Now, everyone turn to page sixty-eight of your book. Mr. Smith, if you'd be so kind."

While Jack stutters his way through the chapter, I draw closer to Keva.

"I don't understand," I say. "How did this woman even cause all of this? And what are the plagues you mentioned?"

Keva rolls her eyes, but she enjoys showing off more, and answers, "Look, the woman's Fey, all right? That means she has insane powers. And I don't mean just the elemental kind, which is pretty basic, but a lot more."

"So…she could create fire and water and—"

"Not create, control," Keva whispers harshly. "And many other things too! Haven't you been paying attention? This world is crawling with demons that could reduce humans to ashes in the blink of an eye!"

"Then why haven't they already?" I ask. "If, by your logic, they're all evil and want nothing more than our death—"

"Well they're not all like that," Keva says with a slight grimace. "And besides, we're here, aren't we? To protect the innocent, yada yada yada…What's the matter?"

"I feel sick," I mumble, the blood draining from my face. I've reached my limit; I don't think I can stay in this crazy place any longer.

"You better not throw up on me!" Keva says, stumbling out of her seat. "Sir! Morgan needs to go to the infirmary!"

The short man adds another entry to the growing list of dates on his blackboard. "Go right ahead," he says without stopping.

With the help of Bri, who eagerly volunteers to help me, I get my books packed up and leave before I can lose the contents of my breakfast on anyone.

"Look," Bri tells me once we're in the empty hallway, "I know what you're going through." At my look of incredulity, she adds, "Well, I don't really, but I can imagine it. Since you grew up away from all this"—she motions around us—"it's only normal for you to be overwhelmed. And you're old...well, older anywho, and so probably less adaptable. So I'm concluding you're already half-way—make that three-quarters of the way—to the loony bin."

I miss a step, and Bri has to hold on to me so I don't plummet down the rest of the staircase; though getting a concussion right now sounds somewhat appealing.

"My point is," Bri says, "that you should just accept this new reality as is. Look on the bright side. If this world is real—and I assure you it is—then you're part of a few who know the truth. If it isn't..." She shrugs. "Then at least you're not the only one who's crazy around here, and you can join the club."

"In, two, three. Out, two, three," Owen says, no longer mad at me now that he and Jack have rejoined us outside where I'm taking some fresh air—doctor's orders. "You feeling better?"

"I think so," I say, releasing my breath.

In the light of day, I can clearly see the apple tree's massive trunk rising from the center of the courtyard, its heavy foliage expanding over the school like a wide umbrella. The grounds around it are separated into alternating flower beds and vegetable patches.

He sets his foot next to me on the bench. "I just don't get it," he says. "The moment we took our test, we were told about Lake High and how this place works. How come your parents never did it? I mean, they're Pendragons! Their families have been going here for generations!"

I shrug. "I don't remember a test. Does everyone take it?"

Jack nods. "Though the ability to manipulate elementals is usually passed down to the children, it does happen that someone's born without the talent. In which case, they're not allowed to know about this world."

Owen nods emphatically. "Which is why some think you—"

Bri kicks his foot from underneath him, and he falls down. "Just like some people are born with it in families that never had a knight for an ancestor," she says.

"So did your parents go here?" I ask.

The twins and Jack nod. And so did my parents—or at least my mother...A thought strikes me, and I jump to my feet.

"What's the matter?" Bri asks, suddenly concerned.

"If my mother went here," I say, "then my father must have too!"

"That's what I was saying," Owen says with a pout. "All the Pendragons—"

"No, I mean my *real* father."

Silence greets my words, and I start to fidget, uncomfortable with the sudden admission. Face as red as his hair, Gianakos approaches us. Close on his heels is the rest of the class.

"Was your father a layman too?" he asks, so quietly I have to lean forward to hear him.

"Elias's mom ran off with a layman," Owen whispers in my ear. "'S why he's a little, you know, slow."

"I don't know," I answer. I never knew him, I add silently with a pang.

"It's unlikely." Keva speaks up for the first time since Lore class. "Have you seen Lady Pendragon? She wouldn't dare get caught with anyone who wasn't of the Blood."

Elias's face falls. "I see. I thought, maybe…"

"But perhaps he's right," Daniel says, wrapping his arm around Elias's neck. "Maybe that's why she kept her own daughter locked away—because her shame was in her daughter's own lack of talent and would show the rest of the world how she'd hooked up with the wrong kind of people." He pats Elias's head. "And you should avoid those people too, if you want to make up for your own mother's errors."

I know he means it as an insult, and in other times, I'd have been stung, but right now I'm too busy thinking about my father, the one I know nothing of, and wondering whether he ever was a knight here too.

"Man, I don't think I have the patience to deal with stupid plants right now," Owen says, kicking a stone into a small water basin as we make our way to our next class.

"You shouldn't dismiss them because they're not as flashy as EM," Jack says.

"That's not why," Owen retorts. "They're just…useless."

"That's not true!" Jack and I exclaim at the same time.

Grinning, we both look at each other until I look away in embarrassment.

"Well, whaddaya know," Bri says, punching Jack's shoulder playfully. "You've finally got someone you can nerd out over herbs with."

For the first time that day, I'm actually excited—not only because I'm going to work on what I love best, but also because, nearly twenty years ago, my father may have been taking these exact same classes too. And maybe, just maybe, Bri is right, and things might not be so bad down here after all.

Botanics is held inside a long, simple greenhouse that opens onto the inner courtyard. Boxes of plants are set in rows along one side of the room, while a set of worktables adorn the other, over which potted plants hang. I can already smell the heady scent of lilacs, and the delicate fragrance of roses.

"Good morning, children," a soft voice says. A girl pops up from behind a shrub of thyme, waving a tiny sickle in one hand. "You should put on an apron and some gloves for today's lesson." She moves toward the far end of the greenhouse.

Grabbing a set work clothes for each of us, Bri and I follow the rest of the class to the back.

"At least we get to wear skirts," Bri mutters, pointing at her brother and Jack, who are desperately pulling on their pants to keep them from sticking to their legs in the intense humidity.

"Is she really our teacher?" I ask, eyeing the brown-haired girl with circumspection. She can't be more than a year or two older than me.

"What, Professor Pelletier?" Owen asks. A devious gleam appears in his eyes. "Guess who really liked her last year?"

Bri answers him with the same look. "Hadrian," they say together before bursting out laughing.

"Who's—" I start.

"Their older brother," Jack says.

"He never had a chance," Bri says. "I mean, he's so prissy, he hates getting even a speck of dust on his uniform."

"And she rolls around in dirt all day long," Owen adds with a knowing nod. "It was doomed—"

"From the start," Bri says. She lets out a heavy sigh and leans on Owen's shoulder. "Poor soul, condemned to forever watch his love from a distance."

"Maybe she could teach him," Owen says.

Bri shakes her head sadly. "He'd be running away every five minutes to change into a new set of clothes."

The twins roar in laughter, and Jack shakes his head at them. "Their humor is often somewhat...dubious."

"What's going on over there?" Professor Pelletier calls out.

Bri and Owen straighten up, their faces scarlet.

"Nothing, Professor," Owen says.

"Sorry, Professor," Bri says.

I watch the teacher collect some pink, bell-shaped flowers in a small basket.

"The foxglove, or digitalis," she says, "is easily recognizable because of its elongated bell shape. It comes in several colors, going over the whole spectrum of pinks, as well as gray and white. Who knows some of its uses?"

"They're usually used to help regulate the heartbeat," I say, after making sure no one else knows.

Professor Pelletier nods. "Correct. It's particularly used in instances of atrial fibrillation. However, and this is what we're going to focus on, they also happen to be a plant favored by the Fey."

My initial excitement peters out. Here I was, thinking that I'd finally be able to show everyone that I was actually good at something.

"You need to gently pluck—*gently*, Mr. von Blumenthal! No need to squeeze them to a pulp." The teacher walks down between the two rows, looking over at our work. "When you're done with your pickings, you may grab one of the glass vials by the windows, fill it up with water, then place the flowers in it."

"What are we going to do with them afterward?" a curly-haired girl asks.

"When you've placed the flowers inside, you'll replace the vials by the windows and let them simmer for three hours," Miss Pelletier answers. "Which will result in what, Miss Adams?"

The curly-haired girl looks about, uncomfortable. "Scented water?"

"Which we can then turn into essence of—"

The sound of breaking glass cuts the teacher short.

"Elias Gianakos!" Miss Pelletier yells, rushing over to him. "What do you think you're doing?"

Shaking, the boy holds out his bloody hand before him. "S-Sorry, miss," he says. "I didn't mean to..."

"No, you never do," the teacher says. "Go see the nurse. Miss Henderson, come help me clean this mess."

Without a word, a tall blonde girl grabs a broom and sets to sweeping up the broken shards.

"Happens all the time," Bri says. "It's a wonder they ever accepted him into Lake High."

Jack comes back with one of the few round glass vials left and hands me one.

"One thing's for sure," Owen says, nearly dropping his own container, "he's never going to make it as a knight if he keeps at it."

"You mean not everyone does?" I ask, carefully dropping the flowers into the water. "Not even after passing the test?"

"Nah," Owen says, flicking the remains of a flower off his fingers and gingerly picking up another one. "Only those who get through all the trials."

"Which means you've gotta demonstrate your abilities in fighting," Bri says. "Barehanded and with weapons."

"And with elementals," Owen adds.

"And those who don't want to fight?" I ask, stoppering my vial.

I look up when no one answers. All three of them are staring at me like I've just sprouted a pair of horns.

"What?" I ask.

"Why wouldn't you want to fight?" Owen says. "It's the greatest honor you can get! To defend our world against the Fey who would otherwise kill us all!"

"The Bible clearly says to put your sword back," I say. "I don't see why I should fight when I don't—"

Owen throws himself at me, and we both land among Miss Pelletier's foxgloves moments before one of the large hanging pots comes crashing down, shattering the table beneath.

I cough as clouds of dust swirl about us before settling back down on the remains of my workstation.

"What happened?" Miss Pelletier cries out. "Is anybody hurt?"

"I-I don't think so," I say as Owen helps me up.

"Just your plants, miss," Bri says. "They're completely squished."

"As long as nobody's hurt," the teacher says, sounding on the verge of tears.

"Trust the new girl to cause trouble on her first day here," I hear Keva say two tables over.

"It wasn't her," Owen says, angry. "It was Daniel. I saw him use EM!"

"Don't be silly, Mr. Vaughaun," Professor Pelletier says with a frown. "Elemental manipulation's not allowed outside of training until you've reached squire level. Go get a broom to clear this up."

"But that's not fair!" Owen exclaims. "I didn't do anything wrong!"

"Did I say you did?" the teacher snaps. "Now get a broom and start sweeping!"

Muttering under his breath, Owen complies, but I grab the broom from his hands.

"You saved me," I explain.

"Sweet, thanks," Owen says.

But Bri slaps him across the head. "Don't be a ninny. You can sweep too."

Their fight brings down the teacher's wrath upon us, and we all end up on cleaning duty. By the time the bell rings, the place looks as it had before, minus a few plants.

As we leave, I see Daniel high-five his two friends, and I remember that strange glow I'd seen coming from him in Sir Boris's class. Something tells me that Owen was right, and that spells trouble for me.

The next couple of classes are mercifully easy and mundane, which I thank my guardian angel for, not that he had anything to do with my schedule. By the time three o'clock hits, I've already managed to get two of Sir Boris's assignments completed, and the third one well under way. If this keeps up, I'll have all twenty-seven of them done within the week!

"Miss Pendragon, would you mind telling us what you're doing when you're supposed to be listening to me?"

I look down to find that I've turned Lady Ysolt's instructions to shreds.

"I suppose you feel you don't need this class," she states, circling me like a vulture. A gust of wind poufs up her hair so she looks like a rooster. "Very well then, what would you do if you saw a crack in your brace?"

I see Bri's hand shoot up, but Lady Ysolt ignores her.

"Have it repaired?" I venture.

"And how can you tell it needs to be repaired?"

"Because…there's a crack?"

A few people chuckle, and Lady Ysolt snaps her boots together, her sword clanking against her side.

"And if there are no cracks," she asks, her voice dangerously low, "does that mean the brace is uncompromised?"

"Yes," I manage to say around the lump that's growing in my throat.

A tight smile appears at the corners of her full mouth, not a good sign. "What happens if a rune's overused without being properly tended for, even if no cracks are apparent?"

Why is she asking me so many questions? This is my first day here. Can't she give me a break? I see Bri raise her hand again, and I stare at her, willing for her knowledge to pass into my brain, but it's no use.

"Well, Miss Pendragon," says Lady Ysolt, "we're all waiting for your wisdom."

"I'm not sure," I say.

"It's simple, Miss Pendragon. You die."

I shudder at the words, and can't help but think back to Agnès and her strange and unexplained death. Could it be that she'd stumbled upon a Fey? But that isn't possible. We were going to a regular boarding school! And what about my father?

I rub my clammy hands against my uniform in a vain attempt to dispel my unease.

"Which is why you need to pay a little more attention to my instructions," says Lady Ysolt, jolting me away from my unpleasant recollection. She jostles a basket before her. "Now, everybody grab a ring and fan out. Just don't forget to return them when lesson's over."

The class erupts in a general brouhaha. Even Bri can't control the excited glimmer in her eyes as she reaches for a ring. When it's my turn, however, Lady Ysolt pulls the basket out of my reach.

"Not you, Morgan," she says. "You'll be observing this week."

With a sneer, Daniel pushes me aside. "Guess Stupid will never become a knight now," he says to his two buddies.

They laugh as they head for the farthest end of the training field.

"Fine," I mutter to myself, walking over to the side. "I don't want to learn how to fight anyway."

Don't lie. Admit you're jealous.

"Don't be ridiculous," I say, slumping into the seat. "Look at them. They look ridiculous."

A few feet away from me, Elias is scrunching up his face in concentration, yelling some strange word over and over again. Not even Bri nor Owen seem to be making much progress with their manipulations either, while Jack, for once, looks completely lost.

They all look like they're suffering from constipation, my guardian angel notes.

I chuckle. Maybe it's not so bad to have been left out then.

"Remember your lessons," Lady Ysolt says, marching before them. "Breathe deeply, and call the elemental out."

There's a loud whoop. Over at his end, Daniel's managed to create a fountain of water, the jet spurting in the air and showering everyone within a five-foot radius.

My eyes widen at the sight. Saint George's balls, that's really impressive!

"Very good, Mr. von Blumenthal," Lady Ysolt says, the plates of her strange clothes reflecting the waning light of day. "I see talent hasn't skipped a generation in your family. You may want to control where the element goes now."

She catches the rest of the class staring and claps her hands. "Did I say you could stop?" she yells.

The rest of the students scramble to resume their practice and I, noting nothing more interesting is happening, decide to take a nap instead.

Their methods are so backward, my guardian angel chimes in.

"How would you know?" I retort, placing my arm over my eyes.

And why is there only one supervisor? My guardian angel tuts. *Elementals can be quite dangerous, and accidents happen so easily...*

"Stop always being such a downer," I say. "This school has taught this for centuries. You don't think they know what they're doing?"

Doing something dumb over a long time doesn't make it any less dumb, he continues in his usual mocking tone. *How long was it again that humans believed the earth was flat?*

"Seriously?" I ask back. "You can't even let me rest for five minutes?"

My guardian angel doesn't reply immediately, then says, *It seems awfully quiet all of a sudden, don't you think?*

Realizing he's right, I scramble into a sitting position and find Keva frowning down at me.

"Who were you talking to?" she asks.

"No one," I say with a flush.

Keva narrows her eyes at me. "You're schizophrenic, aren't you? That's why your family kept you away all these years." She grimaces. "Class is over. Ysolt wanted me to let you know." As she leaves, I hear her add, "Worse than I thought, she's completely mental!"

The rest of the week passes by in a blur. By the time Friday hits, I don't think I'm making any sense anymore, not to myself nor to anyone else willing to listen long enough to my babble.

"You're never going to catch up if you keep doing that."

"Doing what?" I ask.

Jack points down at my notebook, where a large ink stain has spread over my latest essay on the habits of bogeys and their lesser-known cousins, the domovois.

Jack snatches the notebook from under my hand. "Really, Morgan. Bogeys aren't afraid of books, not unless you think you can him bash their heads in with them, which is highly unlikely."

"Just hand that back to me," I say. I tear the sheet of paper out and apply myself to copying my first answer over.

"Can't you just finish it for me?" Owen whispers across the table.

"You're not going to learn anything if I do," Jack retorts without looking up from his book.

"I will," Owen says. "I'll just memorize what you wrote for the exams."

Jack wrinkles his nose in disgust, but picks up Owen's essay. Giving up, I let my pen drop and recline against my seat. Over the last five days, I think I've spent more time in the library than in any other room.

I stare up past the arcing bridges at the vaulted ceilings five floors up. Bri was right. Despite my initial awe of the place, I'm already getting sick of it.

"You can't call domovois Peeping Toms, Owen," Jack says, crossing out Owen's answers furiously.

"Why not? I distinctly recall one got caught trying to sneak into this woman's bed while her husband was gone."

"That's because she'd let the stove run cold and the domovois was freezing to death," Jack says. "You have such selective hearing."

"It's so creepy," Bri says, "to have a Fey live with you like that, don't you think? And those poor people were so afraid, they couldn't even do anything if the critters got pissed at them all of a sudden."

"You know, I've been thinking," Owen starts.

"Well that'd be a first," Jack retorts under his breath as he rewrites a whole section of Owen's essay.

"What if people can have stronger affinities for certain elements, and not others," Owen continues, unfazed. "Maybe Daniel's just better at linking up with nymphs and sylphs than the rest of us, and that's why he's gotten so good so quickly."

"Or maybe he's better at it because his blood's purer," Bri retorts. "He's from one of the original families, after all."

"The original families?" I ask, looking away from the unicorn weaved in the tapestry closest to us.

"Back in the Middle Ages," Jack says, tossing the notebook back to Owen, "the original knights who were first taught to use elementals were extremely powerful. Less blood dilution over the generations generally results in a greater ability to control the Fey."

"Unless you're you-know-who," Bri says, dropping her voice lower as Madame Jiang, the librarian, passes by with a cart of books.

"Who's you-know-who?" I ask.

"She means Jennifer," Jack says, who turns out to be uncommonly patient with all of my questions—maybe from having been friends with Owen for so long. "She never had the qualifications for being a knight, but because of her family background…they kind of let it slide."

"I still think that if I were to use a salamander," Owen says, "things would be different."

Bri flicks him on the head. "Don't be such a nincompoop. Salamanders are the most dangerous. You're going to burn your hair off."

"Says who?" Owen retorts, rubbing his forehead.

Madame Jiang stalks over, a frown creasing her otherwise smooth forehead. "This is a library," she whispers harshly. "Which means no speaking or you'll be sent out."

76

"It's time for our last EM class anyway," Owen says, hopping up onto his feet.

We pack up and hurry outside, laughing. As we round a corner, we cross the path of two older boys coming in the opposite direction. The moment they see us, they turn sideways until they're walking down the hallway like a pair of giant crabs, but not before I notice their blackened faces and their very obvious lack of eyebrows.

"Busted!" Owen yells after them.

The pair flinches, then hurries away, presumably to the infirmary to get treated. A large, beefy arm comes down around my shoulders, its weight forcing me to stoop over like an old granny.

"That was our work. Very pretty, don't you think?" Gareth asks.

"Playing with live fire," Gauvain says, shaking his head so his dreadlocks swing around it. "And so close to the face too!"

"Morgan, my *chère*,[8] how are you doing?" Gareth asks, flexing his biceps so I'm nearly choking.

"On your way to practice, hmmm?" Gauvain asks.

"Yeah," I reply, trying to move from under Gareth's crushing arm. "Last lesson of the week."

Gareth nods understandingly. "Today's a special day for us too."

"We're going to play a trick on that one," Gauvain says, his French accent thick from excitement. He points at a boy a few yards ahead of us.

"Percy?" Keva asks, suddenly next to us.

"Why?" I ask.

"He got us in a pigeon of trouble," Gareth says.

"It's 'smidgen,' you oaf," Gauvain says.

8 Dear.

"No thanks, I'm not hungry," Gareth says, finally lifting his arm off my shoulders. "But you watch, Morgan. Tonight, he's going to get spanked."

"And not by us," Gauvain adds with a dazzling smile.

"Make sure to stop over!" Gareth says as the two cousins dash away, the floor shaking under their steps.

"We will!" Keva shouts back, waving energetically. "See you later, suckers," she adds to us, leaving after them.

Bri jumps from foot to foot. "That means we better check out the arena tonight!"

"No way," Owen says. "I've a feeling I'm going to have a breakthrough today. I'm not wasting a single second of training until I get it this time."

"Whatevers," Bri says with an indifferent shrug. "I still say watching Percy in a fight's way more entertaining. What do you say, Jack-Jack? Morgan?"

"Sure," I say. "I've got nothing better to do anyway."

A loud cheer erupts from the stadium next to us, and everyone looks up, gaping.

"It's the fight!" Bri yells.

She pulls off her ring, tosses it back into the basket, and drags Jack limping after her.

"Owen, you coming?" she calls out as more students run by to get to the arena.

Owen waves her away. "Not now. I told you I'm gonna have my breakthrough today."

"Suit yourself. Morgan?"

"I'll be right there," I say, lingering behind.

The training field is now empty, except for Owen and myself, Lady Ysolt having been forced to take Elias to the infirmary after Daniel pretended to lose control over his nymph and shot the boy down instead.

"You sure you don't want to come?" I ask.

I may be behind when it comes to all this Fey stuff, but I'm still older than they are, and I don't like the idea of leaving Owen behind alone.

"Just go," Owen says, fixated on his ring. "I'll be fine. I've been doing the same thing for the last week."

And with very little progress, my guardian angel adds. *But no surprise there.*

The crowd lets out a roar of surprise, and I turn toward the sound. From where I stand, I can see people gathering at the entrance to the stadium, cheering on the fighters.

"Be careful," I say over my shoulder as I trot over to see what the fuss is all about.

"What's happening?" I ask the first person I reach, a bucktoothed girl with severe strabismus.

She ignores me, and so I push forward through the mass of bodies, getting my feet trampled in the process.

"Oh, that one's a fine young man," I hear a girl say, giggling.

"True, true," replies another, a woman with a slightly greenish tint to her. "But he's still a far cry from Lance. That one's made to charm the ladies."

The first girl laughs. "I won't disagree with you there. I'd give my ogham to spend a night with him!"

The other grins. "If only you still had it."

With a shock, I realize that they're both Fey, finally noticing the wide berth the students are giving them.

The first Fey girl catches me staring. "What do you want?" she snarls.

I jerk away and do my best to disappear in the crowd, my mind reeling—how could there be so many Fey here when the whole point of this school is to get rid of them?

The sound of metal hitting against metal gets suddenly louder, distracting me from my own thoughts. I elbow my way through the throng, feeling the crowd's excitement peak around me.

"Fifty on Arthur!" someone yells.

I duck beneath an angry fist.

"Seventy on Arthur!" says someone else.

A couple of heads down, I see Gauvain, writing frantically in a small notebook. "Won't anybody go for Percy?" he calls out.

"Seventy on Percy!" says Gareth next to him, and they both flash their dazzling smiles.

My heart beats faster as I make my way to the center of the crowd. I freeze. Arthur's standing over Percy, a long sword aimed at the shorter boy's head. Both are wearing the same type of leather-and-metal gear that the teachers wear, but I have no doubt that, should Percy get hit with that sword, he's going to be in trouble.

"Aren't they breathtaking?" someone whispers next to me.

I cast a sidelong glance and find Keva, her hand over her chest and her mouth slightly open as if on the verge of swooning.

In a shining blur, Arthur's sword swings down, and Percy intercepts it with his. The twang that results is so loud it makes my ears ring. The cry of outrage I'd been meaning to yell dies on my lips. Mesmerized, I watch their deadly practice.

Without warning, Arthur attacks. Percy parries the thrust, then pushes forward, feints, and makes another cutting motion.

This time, it's Arthur's turn to defend his position, and, slowly, Percy forces him back toward the crowd.

Before Percy can strike again, however, Arthur's mischievous grin flashes on his sweaty face, and he opens his left fist toward the ground. A green flash sizzles from his gauntlet to the ground, propelling Arthur into the air. I watch him spin, then land gracefully on the ground behind Percy.

"Surrender," he says, his sword aimed at the open part of Percy's neck.

I hold my breath as I wait for Percy's next move. For a second, it looks like he's going to give up. People boo as he extends his hand out and deliberately drops his sword. But the moment the weapon hits the ground, Percy rolls backward into Arthur, kicks up, and disarms him.

Before I can blink, Percy's sitting on Arthur's chest, perspiration running down his grimy face. "Do you surrender?" he asks, his breath short.

I snort, enjoying the bewildered look on Arthur's face. Then, with a smile, I make my way back out to the groans of people counting their losses.

As I reach the end of the crowd, a terrible cry rends the air. Every single hair on my body stands up, and I know at once its source: Owen.

I run, dodging confused onlookers. My skin prickles as I emerge from the slowly dispersing crowd in time to see a large blaze of fire reach up to the sky.

"Owen!" I yell.

The flames slowly dissipate to make room for a large red bull the size of a cottage. I gasp, slip on the ground, and nearly lose my balance. I can see the boy, lying between the gargantuan bull's front paws, seconds away from being trampled to death.

Before I know what I'm doing, I find myself sprinting toward the bull, yelling and waving my hands frantically like my arse is on fire.

Without breaking my run, I swoop down and grab the biggest rock I can find, then hurl the stone as hard as I can at the creature. "Over here, you measly piece of steak!" I yell, trying to draw it away from Owen, toward the empty fields.

The missile ricochets off the bull's hide with all the effect of a gnat. But the bull swings its massive head toward me, steam puffing out of its cavernous nostrils like a forge. The insult must've gotten to it after all.

My stomach lurches, but I can't stop now. Owen hasn't moved an inch, which means either he's fainted with fright or— and I don't like this idea at all—he's badly injured.

"Come over *here*!" I yell to the monster, pointing at my feet. I can't believe I'm talking to it like it's nothing more than a puppy.

To my surprise, the bull hesitates, then takes a step in my direction, then another. The ground shakes under its weight. I hear people scream in the background, the noise muffled by the beating of my heart.

"Good boy," I say as the bull moves farther from Owen. One of the knots tying my insides uncurls. "Keep it steady."

Another step and it will be trampling me. The heat emanating from its body hits me like I've walked into a sauna. Sweat drips into my eyes and soaks my uniform. The bull stops in its tracks and bellows, and my mouth runs dry—what am I doing?

The blaring sound of a distant horn cuts through my concentration, and I break my gaze away from the creature. The horn sounds again, its piercing cry overwhelming every other sense. The bull answers with a deep bugle of his own, then rushes at me.

My legs turn to mush, and I sink to the ground. The creature lowers its head, but all I can do is watch as a glinting black horn draws nearer and nearer to me.

A sword swings before me, diverting the horn down and spearing my skirt to the ground.

"Move!" Arthur yells.

We roll away just as one of the bull's hooves hits the ground where I was lying. I blink the dirt away as Arthur pushes himself up. I see something shimmery fly over the bull, then fall onto its wide back with a sizzling sound. Screaming in pain, it rears up on its hind legs in a desperate attempt to get the metallic net off him, but Percy and another boy use that moment to cut him up.

Flames spout from the unexposed parts of the bull's body, but it's too late. I can see it clearly: Percy, Arthur, and the hot guy from before are distracting the Fey while a team of four teachers, Gareth, and Gauvain attack it from behind. Another net is thrown, and the bull stumbles, its rear legs unable to support it anymore. It gives a pitiable cry, smoke billowing out of its mouth, before it collapses onto the ground.

A chill sets over me, but I can't look away. Slowly but methodically, the nine of them hack at the creature, reducing it in size until I can't see it anymore. Finally, Gauvain hands my brother a metal box. With precise movements, Arthur bends down, picks up what seems to be a stone, sets it inside the box, then snaps the lid shut.

CHAPTER 7

"Somebody help me, *please!*"

The plea comes as a high-pitch shriek. I barely register Bri, kneeling next to her unconscious brother, his head in her lap. I lick my parched lips. Somehow, I'd forgotten about him. I make to stand up, but can't feel my legs, and I collapse like an old rag doll.

"Owen," Bri cries, holding his bloodied hand to her tearstained face. "Owen, open your eyes!"

Lady Ysolt's suddenly next to her. Her face strains as she lifts Owen in her arms and carries him away.

"Tell Daphne to get the surgical room ready," she tells Percy, who sprints away.

As they hurry by, I call out Bri's name, but her paper-white face doesn't register any of her surroundings. A hand grabs me by the elbow and helps me up.

"How about you?" Arthur asks, his hazel eyes scanning my face.

"Owen—" I start to say.

"Do you need to go to the infirmary too?"

I shake myself free. "I'm fine. But what about my friend? Is he going to be all right?"

Arthur looks away, his brow furrowed. I notice that he's still holding the metallic box in which he's placed that stone; the stone that used to be a magical bull.

"I don't know," he says. "We'll have to wait until Dr. Cockleburr's done with him." He takes another quick look at me, seemingly satisfied. "You should still get a checkup."

I think instead about Bri waiting for news of her brother. No one should ever have to face that sort of ordeal alone, and I'm not going to let her. I take a shaky step after her and nearly pitch forward.

Keva appears at my side, a dreamy look on her face. "Amazing those three, aren't they?" she says, keeping me steady. "And right when Arthur and Percy had just had a grueling match to boot! But it's to be expected from the Triumvirate.[9] There's nothing they can't do."

"Can you just shut up?" I say. "There's more important things going on right now."

I take another step and wince as my ankle twists. I must have injured it when Arthur dragged me out from under the bull's hooves. Biting on my lower lip, I proceed through the now-quiet field as fast as my injury will allow.

"You, page!" says a sharp voice behind me.

A few paces back, her golden hair streaming in the breeze, is Jennifer. Her pale blue eyes are staring at me, emotionless but for a cold anger I don't understand.

I point at myself. "Me?"

"Where are you going?" she asks.

9 Group of three men.

"To the infirmary."

The remainder of the crowd stops its exodus to train hundreds of questioning looks on me.

"You should be cleaning the mess you've created," Jennifer says.

I lower my fists to my sides before I can punch her. She may be beautiful, but she's really starting to get on my nerves.

"I can't," I say, proud of myself for my unusual diplomacy. "My friend needs me."

Jennifer stalks up to me. "And I," she says, "need you to clean this area up, page."

"My name. Is. Morgan."

Before I can go berserk, Keva nudges me. "You've got to listen to her," she whispers, fear and awe in her voice. "She's higher ranked than we are."

"Why?" I ask. "Because we're only freshmen? For your information, I'm probably old—"

Keva shakes her head, then taps the cross on my jacket's front pocket. "No, we are pages. She's a knight. Pages have to follow orders from everyone above."

I stare at her, dumbfounded. "What is this nonsense?"

But Keva's moved away from me before Jennifer can unleash her anger on her as well.

"I will have you clean the entire practice field, on your own," Jennifer says, her full lips curling up scornfully. "And nobody's to help you. Got it?"

With a toss of the head, she strides away, drawing the remaining crowd along with her.

"You better get to it," Keva says. "You've got to take all the equipment down to the armory, and there's a lot of it."

I stare at the empty stadium, taking in the discarded weapons strewn about the dirt floor.

"But, isn't it dangerous?" I ask, darting glances about. The sun's low on the horizon now, and every shadow seems longer and deeper than before. What if there's another Fey monster lurking somewhere around here?

"Don't be stupid," Keva says with a smirk. "That Fey escaped because its iron restraints shattered, not because it appeared out of nowhere. Besides, they can't just come to Lake High without permission. Really, I can't believe I have to be your roommate." She shakes her head and starts to go after the others.

"But I'm going to miss the boat back home!" I tell her.

She stops. "You think they're going to let us go home after what just happened? This is a state of emergency. Nobody leaves until it's all been cleared up." She pauses to consider something, then adds, "And you better not make Jennifer go after me, or you'll really regret it."

I grab the last of the equipment and place it inside the now-thousand-ton basket. My back's aching, and my ankle's so sore I can't feel my foot anymore. The worst part is going up and down the stadium's seats for any additional gear I might have missed.

With a mighty huff, I sit down, leaving the basket aside. Of course, with a prat for a president, it's only normal the rest of the student body wouldn't learn to put their own things away.

The wind nips at me, mocking my plight, and I shake my fist in the air. "It's all your fault!"

A questioning meow startles me. I find a cat sitting a few levels up from me, its golden eyes almost glowing against its raven-black fur. I extend my hand toward it and make small, friendly noises.

To my utter annoyance, the cat royally ignores me. Fuming, I grab the first thing from the basket I can find and throw it at the feline. The cat easily dodges the projectile, a glove with iron meshing, spits at me once disdainfully, then, tail held high, trots away.

"Yeah, just leave me behind," I grumble. "Let me do all the work on my own, like everyone else!"

Joints stiff, I slowly make my way up to retrieve the gauntlet, regretting my burst of anger—as if a cat could actually understand me.

"What an odd thing to wear…" I say, turning the glove in my hands.

I slip it on. It's too big for me and jingles when I move. Lodged inside the metallic rings, I notice a small emerald-green jewel. As I angle it toward the remaining daylight, a strange symbol flashes just below its surface. I shake the gem around like it's a Magic 8 Ball, but nothing more appears, and I wonder if my vision's playing tricks on me.

I put the gauntlet back in the basket and pick up a dagger instead. It doesn't take me long to find what I'm looking for: set deep within the handle are three small round stones of a creamy white tint. I drop the knife back in and grab another weapon. Again, I find what looks like a ruby set into the blade itself.

I squint in the near darkness. What are these things? A picture of Arthur propelling himself into the air during his practice fight with Percy comes back to me. Are these the sources of power I've been hearing about, those things called oghams?

I grab the glove again and put it back on. "How, exactly, does this work?"

Tongue stuck out, I point my hand out, as far away from me as possible. The last thing I need now is to lose an eye or an ear because I don't know what I'm doing.

I squeeze my eyes shut, imagining the green flash coming out of my hand. Nothing. Tentatively, I open an eye, then the other. Maybe something happened, but I didn't see it because my eyes were closed. I concentrate again, pretending laser beams are shooting out of the gauntlet. Still nothing.

"Open sesame," I say, shaking my arm.

I tap on the stone, but no symbol appears, not even the tiniest bit of a glow.

"Stupid thing's broken."

I fling the glove back amongst the rest of the gear and lug the basket back into the armory. It takes me another half hour to put everything away, but, finally, the task is done, and I dust off my hands.

All I need now is a hot bath, a warm meal, and heaps of sleep. I limp to the door and freeze at the sound of something rattling.

"Is-Is someone here?" I call out.

Stillness greets my words, and I slowly let out my breath.

As I open the door, the sound comes back again, louder. I fling myself against the wall, wary of any attacker. I gasp as a large trunk in the opposite corner hops and shakes furiously, bouncing over the tiled floor. I feel the blood drain from my face. Is this another demon beast?

I inch outside the room, then waver. Keva was clear that what happened to Owen had been an accident and that no Fey could enter the school uninvited.

Unable to decide what to do, my thoughts grind to a painful stop, until, at last, I make up my mind. Slowly, I tiptoe up to the chest, unfasten the lock, then carefully ease the cover open.

Something small and black bounces out of it. It lands on my head, sharp claws digging into my face, then latches on to my hair. I shriek.

"Gerroff! Gerroff!"

I reach back to find scruffy fur, then try to pull the thing off of me. Finally, after much effort and many tufts of hair lost, I hold before me the hobgoblin from my first morning here.

"Puck!" I say, shocked. "What are you doing here?"

The little creature flinches, and I soften my tone.

"What were you doing in there?"

I glance down and notice the bottom of the box is strewn with small shards of glass and spilled...

"Milk," I say. "Did someone play a prank on you?"

The small creature's shaking so badly that I'm afraid to let it down. Despite my initial disgust, I cradle Puck in my arms like I would a small child.

"There, there, you're fine now." And if I ever get my hands on the one who did this to you, it's going to be someone else's turn to lose hair!

A few moments later, the hobgoblin falls asleep in my arms, snoring peacefully. I look around, but quickly realize I cannot leave him in here, not after what's been done to him, so I take him with me.

"Incoming!" someone yells.

I duck as a jet of water blasts into the wall next a foot from my face. An older boy laughs as he runs past me, his uniform soaked. He then turns around and punches the air. A blue glow surrounds his hand, then propels itself into another boy, farther down the corridor. Some girls squeal as water splashes onto them.

"Enough!"

The two boys disappear around a corner as a plump woman hurries behind, her hair undone from too much running.

"Ewww!" says one of the splashed girls as I head their way. "What's *that* thing?"

I instinctively hold Puck closer to myself. Avoiding any eye contact, I try to hurry past them but they block my way.

"It's Puck," the second girl says with a grimace. "How disgusting!"

The first girl chuckles. "What are you doing with it? Breast-feeding?"

All three girls laugh at that. I want to ignore them, prove that I'm above petty insults like these. But I've never been good at being the center of attention, mainly because it's never been for a good reason, like now.

"Just leave me alone," I say.

I try to push through them, but one of the girls grabs my arm and jerks me backward, hard. I wince and drop Puck. I try to catch him again, but the hobgoblin lands on the stone floor with a sickening crunch. For a moment, I feel like the whole world's stopped spinning, and I hold my breath. But Puck seems merely stunned and shakes his head as he sits up on his furry hind.

"Look at that filthy thing," says the girl who grabbed my arm. She kicks Puck in the ribs, sending him flying a few feet away.

"Stop!" I cry, horrified.

"Or what?" the girl asks with a smirk. "What are you worried about a demon for?"

She makes to go after Puck again, but I yank her by the hair. "I said stop!"

The girl shrieks like I've just stabbed her, and, quite frankly, that's exactly what I want to do. But I let her go. The girl starts crying, and her friends glare at me.

"How dare you go against your superiors?" says one of them.

I grit my teeth. "You? Superior to me? Please!"

But the girl points at me. "You're just a page, a gofer. You have no right to do this to those in higher stations than you. You ought to apologize, right now!"

Out of the corner of my eye, I see Puck get back up, then scramble away. I grin at her. Is she really hiding behind a stupid high school standard to tell me what I ought and ought not to do?

"Make me," I say.

When none of them make a movement, I spin around and march away, back to the dorms. Different country or different world, it doesn't matter. People can be as loathsome here as anywhere else.

The energetic ring of the church bells wakes me up. I roll out of bed feeling like I've been kicked all night long like a ball at a soccer game. Outside, the sky-lake is a gray pink, and I wonder idly if it ever rains in this world.

Keva's already awake, adding the final touches to her makeup. She admires her work in the mirror, then sighs. "I wish I had dimples. Then my cheeks wouldn't look so fat."

I drown my laughter in my pillow as she puts her mirror down.

"Well, toodles," she says before strutting out.

With a start, I hear the last peal of the bells echo through the arched windows—I'm oh-so-very late. I let out a slew of curses, struggle to get dressed, and sprint out of the dorms. I skid around a corner, nearly run a servant down, then beeline through the outside gardens to the church.

I try to make an inconspicuous entrance, but the door squeaks as I shut it, and the eyes of all the teachers standing at the back swivel around to stare me down. Hunching, I make my way to the freshmen pews—or the pages' section, as everyone keeps reminding me.

I find Jack in his usual spot, but no Bri here this time to greet me, and of course, Owen's absent too.

"I heard you got in trouble again," Jack whispers to me as I sit between him and Keva.

"That girl hates me," I whisper back, "and for no reason."

"You talked smack to her face."

"She was bossing me around!"

"She has every right to," Jack says. "She's a knight."

"Yeah, thanks, I've learned my lesson," I mumble, tracing the school crest embroidered on my jacket's front pocket. "Cross and shield for squire, add a sword, and you've got yourself a knight. I know now. Still, it doesn't make it right."

"I know it's not always easy to tell," Jack adds after the Credo is sung and we resume our seats, "but there's a trick."

"What is it? The size of their heads?"

"The more rings and earrings they wear, the higher ranked they are," Jack replies. "Usually."

"Well in that case, I'll just get some of these practice rings Ysolt hands out. If that's all it takes for Jennifer to be entitled to act like a bitch, there's no reason I can't do the same."

"Nice try," Jack says, "but you're only allowed to keep those oghams you capture, or family heirlooms."

I sigh. There goes my brilliant idea.

"So where's Bri?" I ask.

"Home."

A few of the squires in front of us turn around to shush us, and I return my attention to the homily.

"...sad event is to serve as a reminder that we're never safe until all demons have been cast back into Hell!"

The words send goose bumps down my arms. I know that Father Tristan's referring to Owen's attack yesterday.

"This comes as a reminder to never let our guard down," the priest continues, "even in times when peace seems to be presiding over our world. We were placed on this earth to serve as its keepers, and a good keeper does not fall asleep on his watch. These devils will stop at nothing to see our demise. They will find any way to tempt us, to lead us astray into the ever-damning flames of Hell.

"Satan's avidity will not be sated until every single one of us, every single one of our *souls*, is his to command. But we know the truth of his ways, we know how deviant and wily his emissaries on earth are, and we shall never give in! We shall never bend to these Fey, these great seducers of men, but we will send them back into Gehenna, where they belong, to expiate their sins for all eternity!"

An assenting murmur rises from the nave as the first rays of the sun creep through the rose window behind the altar, showering the congregation with motley hues.

"Now let us pray to God for Owen's recovery, that He may protect that innocent boy's soul from the devil's torments."

Keva leans into me. "Isn't Father Tristan inspiring?"

I nod, though I can't shake a certain unease the sermon brings me. His thoughts parallel what those three upper classmen said last night about Puck, and I just can't make myself think they were right. Shouldn't one always stand up for the weak and defenseless, no matter what their background is? Or, as Father Tristan seems to imply, are there creatures whose existence should automatically be abolished just for being who or what they are?

I stifle a groan; thinking in this roundabout way is bound to give me a migraine for the rest of the day.

The moment Keva, Jack, and I walk into the dining hall, we're assailed by the voices of hundreds of students debating what's going to happen next.

"I say we should march into that forest and flush all that vermin out," says the boy ahead of me in the food line.

"That's too dangerous," his friend says, slopping a plateful of gruel into his bowl. "We'd be attacking them in their own territory." He shudders. "Just thinking about all those trees surrounding us makes me cringe."

The first boy laughs. "You're such a sissy. You're never going to be knighted if you keep thinking that way."

"I'd at least live long enough to reach knighthood age," the other boy retorts as they head to find seats.

I fill my plate with buttered toast and yogurt. "What were they talking about?" I ask my roommate.

Keva tosses her long hair over her shoulder and shrugs. "The forest is where most of the Fey are now," she says with a pout. "It's the last place left that's truly wild enough for them to live in. Which incidentally makes it the most dangerous place for us." She leans in conspiratorially. "I hear that their headquarters is in a place called Avalon."

"But...aren't we located just next to it?" I ask.

As we make our way through the tables, people's conversations stop.

"It's her, isn't it?" I hear a boy ask in a loud whisper.

"Course it is. She's the only page that old."

"Over here," Keva says, setting her tray down on a table by the back wall.

Before I can follow suit, a boy jumps in front of me. "You're Morgan, right?"

"What do you want?" I ask, already imagining him taunting and mocking me. I take an involuntary step back, but the boy only smiles.

"That was really brave of you, what you did yesterday," he says, looking down. "And, uh, you're really cute." He blushes furiously, then quickly retreats to his laughing friends.

"Well, aren't you Miss Popular all of a sudden," Keva says.

Dazed, I sink into my seat. Never in my wildest dreams have I imagined this to happen to me, and I'm not quite sure how to handle it.

"What, you expect to give out autographs now?" Keva asks.

I clear my throat. "So, why do we live so close to the Fey then?" I ask to switch topics. "And in a magical place, when we want to...get rid of it all?"

"How does the expression go again?" Keva says. "Keep your enemies close and all that." She frowns at Jack stabbing his bacon with his fork like it might run away from him otherwise. "What's up with you?" she asks him.

"I don't know how you can be so carefree," he says. "Owen's still in the mending wing. He hasn't woken up, not even to go to the bathroom."

"How would you know?" Keva says. "I thought we weren't allowed near him."

"I've got my ways," Jack says, his ears turning pink.

"But the surgery went well, right?" I ask.

Jack exhales loudly. "We won't know until he wakes up."

The food turns to ash in my mouth, and I have difficulty swallowing. With a twinge of guilt, I look at the place where Bri and Owen should be, and am amazed to find how quickly their friendship has grown on me and how I now miss them.

"Does this kind of accident happen often?" I ask.

"Not really," Keva says. "Oh, it's happened before, but the last incident was, like, twenty years ago, and it was nothing compared to this. I mean, the records state nobody got seriously hurt."

I set my fork back down, unable to take another bite. On my first week here, one of the worst accidents in Lake High's history takes place. I force myself not to think about my last days in Switzerland, but it's as effective as carrying water in a sieve. There's no denying it; I'm bad juju.

"So you say there are records of the school?" I ask, an idea springing to mind.

"For the whole school's history," Keva says, pulling out her pocket mirror to check her teeth. "That's about a thousand years right there."

"And it lists all the students that have attended here?"

Keva flicks her gaze toward me. "Amongst other things. Why do you ask?"

I stuff my mouth with bread to avoid having to answer. How can I tell her I want to find out whether my father ever came to this school too, and if they state anything regarding his death?

"But that's not the important thing," we hear a boy say at the table next to us. "I want to know if our practices are going to stop now."

"Why would they?" a girl asks.

The boy pushes his plate away and leans forward. "That page didn't follow the rules," he says. "He didn't check his gear before using it. He wasn't even cleared for it. And now..." He splays his fingers out before him to describe the ensuing chaos.

"Didn't you hear Father Tristan?" the girl retorts. "We're probably going to go to war. Knights are too valuable, and we need to continue the training. Anyway, the news board said KORT will tell us their decision before practice tonight. Guess we'll find out then."

A chair falls to the floor with such force that we all jump in our seats.

"You done that on purpose!" Gareth shouts on the side of the dining hall reserved for KORT members. His bulky shoulders are smeared in what appears to be a full portion—or perhaps two—of oatmeal.

"Did you see me throw anything at you?" responds Gauvain's silky-smooth voice.

Gareth points a finger at his cousin, sitting a table away from him. "Give me your coat."

Gauvain's laugh bounces along the room's walls. "Why should I?"

A predatory smile spreads on Gareth's dark features. "It would only be fair."

I see the tall senior reach for a dish behind him, but Gauvain's still laughing and doesn't notice. Percy, however, moves his chair farther away from him, and that finally catches his attention.

Gauvain's halfway turned around in his seat when the dish hits him square in the face. Pieces of omelet and sauce drip down his head, onto his lap.

"No exchange, no clean coat for you too," says Gareth with a self-satisfied smirk.

Keva sighs next to me. "We should probably get out of here before it gets real messy."

How much trouble can they cause? I wonder, but I'm spared from having to ask, for Gauvain launches himself at his cousin's throat, and they both tumble to the floor in a cacophony of crashing cutlery and breaking glass.

"And the fight is on!" cries Percy, now crouching on his table like an umpire, calling out the shots.

Gareth kicks the taller boy in the stomach, and Gauvain, despite his bulk, is sent a few feet up in the air. And stays there.

Before his cousin can hurl himself at him, Gareth launches himself into the air as well, uses a column to push off, and both boys meet each other with blows just feet from the ceiling.

"They're flying," I say, craning my neck up to watch the pair fight.

"EM, stupid," Keva says next to me. "It's what we train for."

I nod, unable to tear my eyes away from the scene. I've seen Arthur's elemental manipulation during his fight with Percy, but it was nothing compared to this. People below the fighting cousins run, ducking for cover as lumps of oatmeal and eggs rain down around them.

Suddenly, the door slams open, and someone walks in, heavy boots ringing on the pavement. "That is enough!"

Everyone halts, even Gareth and Gauvain, who are still hanging in the air. The beautiful boy I've seen so often with Arthur glares up.

For a moment, I feel like he's going to swear at them, but instead he says, "Get back down, you two. KORT's meeting in five, and the Board's going to call."

Looking sheepish, the two cousins fly back down. "Uh... we'll clean this up after the meeting," Gauvain says.

Gareth pushes him toward the exit. "No time," he says as the KORT section empties out. "Let the staff care for it."

"That was amazing," I say once they have left.

Already two tiny men are going about the hall, picking up debris and wiping breakfast remains away, and I wonder for a moment if they, too, are Fey.

"Yeah," Keva breathes. "KORT's amazing, especially Lance. He's *so* dreamy...Hey, have you ever considered introducing me to your brother so I—"

"What's this Board?" I ask.

Both Jack and Keva laugh at me, and I feel the ever-familiar blush rise to my cheeks.

Jack pushes his glasses back up. "So you know how KORT's made up of the thirteen best knights at school—"

"Twelve, technically," Keva says.

"Well, the Board's made up of a hundred and fifty people who are in charge of affairs in the surface world," Jack says. "All graduates of this school, of course."

"Most of them are old geezers now," Keva says. "And not all of them got there because they deserved it. But that's the way of the world, isn't it, Morgan?"

"Right," I say, choosing to ignore the sarcasm behind her words.

Whatever the politics involved, it's clear things are a lot more serious than a training accident would warrant. And I'm going to find out why.

Chapter 8

By the time the weekend ends, I'm as knackered as I was when it started. Maybe it was to keep our minds busy, but the professors have given us mounds of additional work to do, and if it weren't for Jack, I don't think I'd ever get my brain right-side up again.

So when we get to Miss Laplace's math class, I let out a sigh of relief.

"Oh, look, the troll has arrived."

Daniel and his posse, Ross and Brockton, snigger in their usual corner.

"Did you know that the Fey hate to reveal their true names," Keva says loudly to Nadia, sitting next to her.

Nadia, a tall and spindly girl, doesn't respond, but then she never does, and I often catch myself wondering if she's mute like Dean.

"It's because it gives the one who knows their name power over them," Keva continues, "which is why we need to call their oghams in EM if we want to draw their power out."

The whole class sits a little straighter, wondering where she's going with all this. Even I know this much about EM by now. But one thing's for sure: my roommate's got a sharp mind on her, and an even sharper tongue.

"Now imagine if that worked on us! For instance, my last name means 'record keeper.'" Keva throws her hand up before her as if to stop Nadia's objection. "I know, not very exciting. Not like Pendragon, whose meaning is rather obvious. But far better than, say, Foreman." She throws a sly glance at the three boys. "How does it feel, Ross? Do you have the soul of a pig herder? Or maybe that of a pig?"

The greasy-haired boy jumps over his desk, toppling his chair over, and makes for Keva, who easily sidesteps him. He trips over his own feet and lands headfirst on the teacher's desk.

"What is going on here?"

Miss Laplace has arrived, her eyes bulging behind her glasses. Red-faced, Ross straightens up and sets her table back straight before shuffling back to his seat.

"Nothing, ma'am," Keva says. "He just won't accept that I'm refusing his advances."

Miss Laplace's features soften. "Ah, young love. I can understand your plight, Mr. Foreman."

The class giggles at her words, and she looks about her, confused.

"You shouldn't mock your classmate's feelings," she says severely, eliciting only more laughter. "Even at such a young age, one can feel the agonizing pangs of jilted love."

By now, even stuck-up Laura and Dina are laughing so hard that they're falling off their chairs.

"Enough," Miss Laplace says, slamming her book of sacred geometry on her desk. "Since you're all so wide-awake, we might as well start the lesson. Chapter seventeen. What's the ratio associated with circles? Miss Kulkarni?"

"Pi," Keva answers immediately.

"And its uses, Miss Kulkarni?"

"Depends," Keva says, "but it's usually associated with protection, especially with a pentagram inscribed in it."

"And the pentagram is associated with which sacred ratio? Miss Kulkarni?"

This time, Keva has to think a little longer before she answers, "The golden ratio?"

"And how," Miss Laplace continues, drawing on the board a circle with a five-pointed star inside it, "does a pentacle work? Let's not ask the same person every time." Her large eyes swivel over the ranks of students, then finally come to rest on Keva. "Miss Kulkarni?"

"By keeping things out," Keva says.

"Can you give me an example?"

"Well…" Keva stops fidgeting in her seat to concentrate, and I hear Ross snigger in the back. "It's not exactly a pentagram," she says, "but the school?"

Miss Laplace looks a little annoyed, but returns to the blackboard. "It may not look like one to the untrained eye," she says as she retraces the outside circle of her pentagram, "but the pentagon that is our very own school building is the center of the five-pointed star, as you see here." She colors in the inside section of the star, and I realize with a jolt that she's right. "And, of course, we have our stone markers at each vertex, which finish the pentacle that protects our school from any outside invasion.

"But that's not the only thing circles and pentagrams can do. Apart from keeping things out, what else can they do? Miss Kulkarni?"

"I don't know, ma'am," Keva finally admits.

"They can keep things in," the teacher says with a note of triumph from catching Keva off guard.

After that, the whole class ends up being a tennis match between the two, tiring everyone else out in the process. When the bell finally rings, we all let out a collective sigh.

"Now's the time," Jack says, drawing near me.

"Time for what?" I ask, hurrying to put my EM homework away before Miss Laplace can see it. I still have seventeen more to do, and I don't want to get this one confiscated.

"To see if EM practices are going to resume or if we're going to go back to jousting basics."

"Jousting?" I ask. "As in...a horse and lance and everything?"

"No," Jack says, "that's not till we become squires. I meant regular sword practice." He glances at the clock. "We better get going, though. KORT's very strict about time."

We join the rest of the student body gathered on the practice field by the arena. The buzzing of half whispers mixes with the low moaning of the wind as we wait, when there's a sharp cry, and we see a girl collapse onto her neighbor.

"What's going on?" I ask. I look about for any sign of Fey attack, adrenaline pumping.

Apparently, I'm not the only one worried, as people look about, but Keva points to a boy holding something over the unconscious girl.

"Just a fish that's fallen from the lake," she tells me. "Happens from time to time, when there's a storm up there."

Up there. I raise my eyes to the sky-lake. No clouds are ever present that I can see, just a gray expanse that can only be the bottom of Lake Winnebago.

"She got lucky," Jack says. "This one time, an old, rusted car fell down. Landed on the south side of the forge and caused a massive fire. Took hours to get the flames out!"

"Shut up," Keva says. "They're here."

A group of seniors is now standing on a makeshift platform at the edge of the field, Arthur at the forefront. I can't quite tell from this distance, but for a moment, he seems to look straight at me. Then he raises his hands for silence.

"In light of recent events," Arthur says, his voice clear, "we have long debated what the best direction would be for our school. And that is to keep up with training lessons as they were originally scheduled."

I hear Jack let his breath out, and everyone around me seems to be feeling less tense.

"The reason being," Arthur continues, "that we cannot let ourselves get weak. No one knows how many more Fey are out there, and the fact that we've encountered fewer of them in the last couple of decades does not necessarily mean their numbers are dwindling or that they've weakened.

"However, and I would like to insist on this point, we are now requiring every student to carefully tend to their respective weapons—including the ones used in training. One cannot be too vigilant, and Friday's tragedy ought not to be repeated. That means you are required to spend the time necessary before and after each practice to check your gear for any defect and perform the necessary cleaning duties instead of letting the staff handle it."

The crowd doesn't seem to like this new rule, but Arthur keeps on talking.

"As for the elemental that tried to escape," he says gravely, "we have the unpleasant task of informing you that its ogham was felled in two."

I feel a shiver run through me at those words. The Fey's ogham, its source of power, is gone, which can only mean one thing—we've killed it.

"A deplorable fact," Arthur proceeds, "since it could, and should, have been prevented. We are now one weapon down, and as you are aware, finding replacements is becoming more difficult, so this is a heavy blow."

Arthur lets his words sink in, and the students' initial annoyance turns to embarrassment.

"Today's lesson will therefore be spent going over our gear," he says. "I want you to make sure every ogham's iron casing is solid and uncompromised. Any defective piece is to be sent to the forge. And all other equipment is to be thoroughly cleaned and its power reserves restored.

"But before you set to your tasks, I want every page to be associated with an upperclassman to supervise. Ask Jennifer or K here to help you find a partner if need be. Dismissed."

"Great," Keva says, puffing her cheeks. "Now I'm definitely going to get a chipped nail."

Everyone scrambles at once to get to work—the faster we are done, the faster we can finish our day. I'm amazed at how orderly everything is as I watch the school file toward the armory and come back, arms full of weapons and armor.

When we reach the arsenal, Gauvain's the one who hands me a set of knives and a shield, though not without a doubtful look.

"Sure you can handle this?" he asks. "You're still a *bébé*[10] here."

"That's why I'm going to get paired up with someone who knows what to do," I reply with a smile.

Gauvain relents, and when I get back outside, people are already set into circles or pairs about the stadium's floor, checking the equipment, while others are tasked with taking the flawed gear to the forge.

A large fire blazes in the center of the arena, next to two large vats.

"What are they doing?" I wonder, but I discover that both Jack and Keva have left me to my own devices—no pity for the dummy, I guess.

10 Baby.

To the right of the entrance is Jennifer, giving Laura and Dina directions before she helps a squire out. I shudder—she's the last person I want to ask for help. But as I look about the blonde girl, I don't see this Kay Arthur mentioned, so, with a deep, heartfelt sigh, I approach the curvaceous girl.

"What do you want, page?" she asks me.

I can see tiny beads of sweat hanging around her temples, but even so, Jennifer seems to be glowing. Some people are just born lucky, no matter how undeserving.

"I don't know who to partner up with," I say.

"Well, that's a problem. I doubt anyone wants to pair up with you. It'd be too much work."

She looks about, and then a cruel glint enters her light-blue eyes.

"Marcos," she yells.

A large, greasy-looking boy looks up, surprised at being called out. As he nears us, I realize why she picked him for me. An indescribable stench seems to emanate from him, the smell of something sweet and of eggs gone bad.

"Well, there you are!" Percy shouts, striding toward us with purpose.

Jennifer's smooth brow puckers as Percy throws his arm around my shoulders, forcing me to bend my knees a little.

"I hope you don't mind," he says to Jennifer. "I've bin told to help this little dogie[11] out, considerin' she don't know much about the lay of the land."

This time, Jennifer looks decidedly unhappy. "Get back to work, Marcos," she snaps at him.

11 Motherless calf.

I throw her a bright smile and wave at her as much as my load permits, then follow Percy. We find an empty spot close to the large bonfire, and I settle next to him, a dagger in my lap.

"Is it Arthur who asked you to keep an eye on me?" I ask casually.

"Nah, it was Gauvain, got worried since you're new and all." He raises his eyebrow. "Why, ya wanted it to be Arthur?"

"Of course not!" I exclaim, hunching over my weapon to hide my embarrassment. "Just curious."

"Gimme that before ya cut yerself," he says.

I hand him the knife reluctantly.

"The way ya go 'bout it is simple," he says, holding the weapon up so the light of the fire reflects off the blade. He then points at the gleaming black stone wedged inside it near the handle. "See this ogham in the bolster? Ya wanna make sure it's secure. The last thing ya want is to find yerself with a captured Fey that's accidentally been set free."

"Is that what happened to Owen?"

"Uh-huh," Percy says, testing the gem's casing. "See, the Fey's source of magic ain't the stone itself."

I stare, wide-eyed, at the black stone. "So why do we call it that?"

Percy shrugs and sets the knife aside. "Shorthand, I guess." He picks up the first of a pair of vambraces and holds it to the light of the fire. The dull metal of the piece of armor glimmers, and I notice rows of pearls lining its edge.

"It's more of a...a link, I s'pose," he drawls, giving me a lopsided smile. "Sorry if my explainin' ain't too good. I ain't got a flannel mouth[12] like yer brother."

I shake my head. "So the oghams link to the real source?" I ask.

---

12 Smooth talker.

"Tha's right."

"Which is what?"

"Nature, I guess," he says after a moment of thought. "Some used to say it was to their queen, Danu, but that was ages ago and must've been wrong, 'cause I ain't heard of her no more, and she's thought to be long dead now." He frowns and brings the vambrace closer to his face.

"Come 'ere," he says.

I crawl over, and he points to a hairline fracture leading out from one of the pearls.

"It's cracked," I say.

"Precisely. Back to the forge it goes."

"So what does the iron do to them?" I ask, carefully placing the piece of armor to the side.

"It cuts off their link. Fetch me the other one, will ya?"

"Which means what, exactly?" I ask, handing him the second vambrace.

"That all it's got left are its own reserves, and it can't even use those without a catalyst."

"A catalyst?"

"That's us," Percy says, slapping his thorax. "Sweet, ain't it?"

The sudden hiss as the bonfire's flames are reduced down to embers startles me. I stare as, one by one, the gear is buried under the smoldering coal.

"What are they doing?" I ask. "I thought we were supposed to take the defective ones to the forge?"

"That'd be a recharge station," Percy says, screwing his eyes to look at a spiked mace without poking himself. "They're puttin' those with fire elementals in there, the water ones in one of the big vats there, the ice ones in the other, and—"

"And the earth elementals in a pit?" I finish.

He beams at me. "Bull's-eye! I told ya their source of power was cut off and they couldn't access 'em no more, right? Well, if we use them too much, they get depleted. So the only way to recharge them is to put them in contact with their primary element again."

"What about the air elementals?" I ask. "How do you recharge them?"

"There's no need to," Percy says. "Everythin' around us is air, so it naturally keeps its energy levels up. Which is why they're a favorite with defensive gear."

"How come you've modernized your armor, but you haven't done the same with your weapons?" I ask. "Wouldn't guns be more practical?"

"Nah," Percy says, "it's hard to beef[13] a Fey, let alone capture one. See, they control elements, right? So you can't just shoot 'em up an' expect 'em to just lay there an' wait to get hit without liftin' a finger. A sweep of the arm, or tentacle, or other thing-amajig, and it gets diverted. Or worse, returned to the sender, postage-free." He wipes the sweat from his forehead and grabs a dagger. "But if ya had to pick," he adds, "ya'd go for arrows. A lot more quiet an', if ya catch 'em off guard, just as deadly."

All in all, everything he's said seems logical, which speaks wonderfully to my mathematical mind. For the first time tonight, I'm grateful for Arthur's orders—I've learned more in an hour with Percy than I have in almost two weeks of school.

Yet there's still one thing that's been nagging at me since yesterday.

"Why…" I start, then stop.

"Shoot," Percy says, expectant.

I take a deep breath, wondering how to word my thoughts in a way that's diplomatic—a very difficult thing for me to do.

13 Kill.

"It's just, I've been wondering why we're going through all this training. I mean, we're still just kids. So why are we being recruited and brainw—that is, trained for war?" I can't make myself look him in the eye. "It just doesn't seem right," I add under my breath.

For a while, we both work in complete silence, with only the sounds of other students going about their business to distract us. As the light of day ebbs away, Percy mutters something under his breath, and a series of small flames spark to life over his head, then float above both our heads like gentle spirits.

"Thanks," I say, finally able to see what I'm doing and stop injuring myself.

"No problem," Percy says, wiping off sweat from his wide forehead. "Now, goin' back to what you were askin'. It ain't that easy. First off, there's the history."

"History?"

Percy nods, his eyes distant. "People have always been trained to fight at an early age. Back in the olden days, you were considered an adult at twelve, so there's that to consider. Then, there's the whole mind thing."

Bursting with impatience, I wait for him to continue with his explanation, but Percy seems to be content to just work on his shield. For a moment, I wonder if there's a button I need to push to make him talk, like a punch on the nose or a pull on an earlobe.

"*What* mind thing?" I finally ask.

A small smile plays at the corner of Percy's mouth as he notices me wringing the gauntlet I'm supposed to be checking.

"That's the hard part to explain," he says. "See, at our age, our minds ain't all formed up yet, so's easier to get round all the Fey's tricks and all."

It looks like he's going to add something, but he just shakes his head and resumes his silent inspection. Out of frustration,

I throw the gauntlet onto the recharge pile and pick up what appears to be part of a boot.

"No, no, no," Percy says, picking it right back up. "See how this plate is pratically covering the amethyst? Means it's almost completely cut off from its element, which ya don't want neither."

He pushes the metal part down to reveal the purple stone beneath.

"Remember what I just told ya. Now this is an air rune," he continues, "so it ain't so bad, but ya can't be too cautious, 'cause you sure as hell don't want to get caught with your pants down at the wrong moment."

CHAPTER 9

The week goes by in a blur of activity so that by the time the weekend arrives, I'm ready to crawl into a casket, never to rise again. I don't know why my mother decided to sign me up here—except perhaps for the fact that it's in a place where the police will never think to look for me—but I'm willing to trade my old, regular life for this one anytime. Except for one minor detail: I still don't know anything about my father.

This time around, I stay with my class as we board the long-boats that are to take us back to the surface.

"What are you going to do this weekend?" Keva asks me, a sudden glint in her dark eyes.

A glint I've learned to be wary of. "I don't know. Why?"

She tosses her long braid back over her shoulder. "Any plans for a soiree or an afternoon picnic, by any chance?"

"Not that I know of," I reply.

Keva's smile slides off her face like a dead slug. "Ah, well, there's always Bri's tea party then, if my parents will allow me to go."

"Bri's having a party?" I ask, surprised. "Even with her brother…"

"Her parents are," Jack says. "They usually organize some form of get-together once a quarter."

Keva snorts. "I don't think any of that's going to change the fact that they've never amounted to much more than squires and blacksmiths."

"Their great-uncle was part of KORT," Jack says indignantly.

Keva shrugs. "An oddity in their genealogy."

"Wait," I say, "so you mean not everyone becomes a knight here?"

"I thought I told you that already?" Jack says. "You have to prove your worth first, usually by getting your first big catch."

"Well, sorry for not remembering the billion things you've told me in the last two weeks," I say.

We step into the wooden boat headed for Oshkosh and sit down. When all three barks are filled with students, a teacher boards each one and stands at its prow.

"All right, everyone," Sir Boris says to our group, "hold on tight!"

I grip the side, somewhat nervous to entrust my safety to a flying object with no wings or motor. Sir Boris places his hand on the figurehead, the carving of a fierce dragon. A moment later, the green glow of a sylph spreads out from beneath his fingers then extends to the rest of the boat, enveloping us in an airtight bubble.

Then, in one nauseating lurch, the longboat rises into the air before flying away. I watch our school rapidly diminish in size, some of the servants waving at us from the fields.

My view of the Lake High and its environs suddenly changes to one of algae, fish, and the odd boot or car tire, before we break through the surface of the lake, in total silence and completely dry.

I let out a slow breath, happy to have made it back to the regular world in one piece. When the boat lands, I find Dean and Arthur are both waiting for me by the car, though they look like they've just had a fight again.

"Let's go," Arthur says, turning on his heels the moment I touch solid ground. "Irene and Luther are waiting."

"See you Monday," I say over my shoulder at a discomfited Keva.

The car ride back home is one of the most boring moments of my existence. I try a few times to start a conversation, but Arthur remains resolutely mute.

We arrive home at the crack of dawn, the neighborhood as quiet as the inside of the car except for a dog barking in the distance. I trip over the threshold in the darkness and curse. I understand that traveling between both worlds needs to be as discreet as possible, but I just can't get used to this awful schedule.

The moment the door closes, I hear Dean's car roar to life and drive away. As I take my shoes off, Arthur disappears upstairs without a word.

"Why good day to you too," I say to the coat stand by the entrance. "Yes, I had a very trying week. What about you? Oh, the usual, was it? Well, so long as you've got your health, old chap."

I choke on the last word as I catch Irene standing in the doorway, eyeing me like I've completely gone bonkers.

"Hello, Mother," I say, the word sounding strange to my ears.

She frowns at me, her corset barely rising with every breath she takes. "Get cleaned up and let Ella know if you want any breakfast," she says, turning away again.

I start to climb, then pause on the steps. "I have a question," I say.

Irene's small frame stops in the doorway.

I lick my lips. "Who was my father?"

"I said to get cleaned up," she says, her voice clipped. She retreats to the back of the house.

"Please, I just want his name," I cry out, holding on to the banister.

A door slams shut, and, with a heavy heart, I make my way to my room. My movements sluggish, I change out of my uniform into more comfortable clothes and crash onto the bed.

"Morgan! Come down this instant!"

With a grunt, I push myself off the bed and drag myself downstairs. The door to Irene's office is wide open, and the rustling sound of paper and drawers closing forcefully rushes out of it.

"What is it?" I ask, standing a safe distance away.

Reflected in the wall mirror, I see a large map of the United States marked with a myriad of crosses and connecting lines. Superimposed on it is another, smaller map of Wisconsin, on which three large red dots have been marked. One of them, I realize with a jolt, is dead in the middle of Lake Winnebago. What are they looking for that could be located close to my school?

Irene flings a bunch of newspapers aside, and a few loose sheets float over to land at my feet, displaying a number of politicians covered in pustules.

"Where's my cartogram?" Irene asks, her small face red from ransacking her own workroom.

"How should I know?"

"Don't play games with me, missy! It was right on this desk this morning when you came in."

I clench my hands into fists. "And as you may recall," I say, "you sent me straight to my room."

"Don't be impertinent!" Her tight curls bounce up and down around her flushed cheeks. "I did not raise you to be rude."

"You did not raise me at all," I retort. "If you had, perhaps you wouldn't be accusing me of theft right now instead of accepting that you're getting old and losing your mind."

A resounding smack echoes in the room, followed by a stinging pain. My vision blurs with tears. Openmouthed, I stare at the short woman before me. Not once have I been hit like this before, not even by Sister Marie-Clémence. I clench my teeth to keep myself from crying.

"Out!" Irene yells, striding back inside her office and pressing on the runes traced above the fireplace. "Ella!"

The air in the opposite corner of the room shimmers, and the maid's small form materializes. I stifle a gasp—Ella's a Fey?

"Did you not hear me, Morgan?" Irene says, distant and cold again. "Get out of my sight."

I don't need to be told a third time. My first impulse is to go back up to my room, but I don't want to be cooped up inside. This whole house is making me claustrophobic.

I storm outside through the kitchen door. The backyard opens up into a wide vista of green grass, flowering shrubs, and trees, cutting us off from the rest of the world. My cheek still burning, I hurry down the small dirt path, ruminating thoughts of vengeance and rebellion.

Without knowing how I get there, I reach a wooden cabin so decrepit it seems abandoned. I circle the shed, looking for an entrance, but find only a small window so dusty I can't see anything through it.

"What is this?" I kick at the boards. A cloud of dirt swirls up in the air and makes me sneeze. "Fine!" I shout. "Be that way!"

I start to walk away, then stop. Why would they build a cabin with no entrance if not to hide something, a secret the family doesn't want to spread? A plan forming in my head, I look over my shoulder at the solitary building. Vengeance may be mine at last!

Making sure no one's around, I smash the window with my elbow. I bite my lip hard not to cry out at the pain spreading down to my wrist and concentrate instead on removing the remaining glass shards from the sill without cutting myself.

It takes me longer than anticipated to climb through the opening, but I finally come crashing down into a pile of old boxes. Not my finest moment, but at least there's no one here to bear witness.

The thin sunrays penetrate through the broken window, displaying disappointingly banal contents. Gardening tools, some discarded toys, a broken birdhouse…and definitely no human remains or stolen goods.

I spot a couple of wooden swords in one corner, next to a rusty shovel. I would smile if it didn't strain my already swollen face.

"Practice it shall be," I say. "What do you think?"

I think you're going to get in trouble, my guardian angel answers.

"Puh-lease. We're far from the house, and you saw the state of this place. It's been abandoned for ages!"

I don't know, the inside looks pretty clean to me. Not a single speck of dust.

He's got a point. But before I can dwell on it long enough to make me lose my nerve, I grab the longer of the two staves and hitch back outside.

Don't say I didn't warn you, the voice inside my head continues.

"Who asked for your opinion?" I mutter as I pull myself through the window.

I let out a shout of victory. I've made it back outside, safe and sound, and not a soul around to reprimand me. Grabbing the wooden sword with both hands like Sir Ywain has taught me, I point it at the hut.

"Thought you'd get the best of me, huh?" I strike the wall with a satisfying *thwack*. "Thought you were better than me, didn't you?" *Thwack*. "You think I…" *Thwack*. "Like it…" *Thwack*. "Here?" *Thwack*. "Thought you could intimidate me into submission? Well guess what, I'm too old now for that crap to work on me." *Thwack*. *Thwack*. *Thwack!*

"Uh, Miss Morgan?"

I pivot so fast I nearly lose my balance, and find myself facing a scared Ella.

"Sorry, I didn't hear you," I say, panting. But now I know why, and I wonder who else knows she's not human. I drop my practice sword and go for an awkward smile. "You needed me?"

"This came for you, mistress," the tiny woman says, handing me a beige envelope with trembling hands.

"Thank you."

I take the letter and turn it over. Who would be writing me, and here of all places? Nothing shows on the creamy paper except for the sigil of an anvil inside a horseshoe, and my name.

"If this is another joke from Arthur," I grumble, "I'm going to strangle him."

But the envelope contains a pretty card with gold lettering from Bri.

Miss Morgan Pendragon and guest
are cordially invited to
the Vaughan family's tea party
at three o'clock this Saturday.

Directions verso.

The first thought that comes to me is that I'm finally going to be able to see Bri again. The second is that this is the perfect excuse for me to get out of here.

I kiss the card and mentally thank Bri. Before I can head over to freedom, however, I must put everything back in the shed. I groan at the prospect of climbing through the window twice more, but I think I'm getting the knack for it, because this time around, I only manage to bump my head on the windowsill once.

As I put the wooden sword back in its place, I step on something soft. I pick it up and find that it's an old glove, the leather falling to pieces. I'm about to toss it onto a shelf, when a flash catches my eyes.

On the biggest part of the glove, where the knuckles should be, is a set of three small, but very sharp-looking spikes, linked to a couple of metal plates around the middle finger. And there, to my utter dismay, is a small, and intact, gem.

"You've got to be kidding me!" I try the decomposing glove on and extend my hand before me, admiring. "My very own ogham!"

A gleeful sense washes over me, and I have the sudden desire to laugh maniacally. How brilliant! All Sir Boris's warnings against my use of oghams before I've been deemed suitable for actual EM training float away. With this, I'm going to be able to practice all I want on my own. Then, when I've gotten really good, I'm going to show everyone what I can do!

"So how does it work?" I wonder out loud.

I turn my hand left and right, make a fist, punch the air, but nothing happens. Just like before. And the lack of result is exasperating.

"You stupid thing!" I exclaim, hurling the glove to the ground.

When my blood pressure drops back down, I retrieve the glove from behind a musty basket, checking the ogham's casing like Percy's taught me. I feel relieved when I see that nothing's damaged.

"There must be a trick. Like, a magic word or something."

What if there isn't? Then what?

"Then I don't know," I say. "Ask for help?"

But my guardian angel's no longer talking to me, as if disapproving of my new pastime.

I end up spending the next few hours practicing all sorts of movements and random incantations, but only end up dizzy and with a pounding headache. Finally, giving up the battle but not the war, I put the glove in my pocket and head back to the house to get ready for Bri's tea party.

Freedom my ass. I try not to glare at the back of my parents' heads as they park the car in the Vaughans' wide driveway. The house, though smaller than ours, seems so much grander to me as we head over to the front porch.

"Mrs. Pendragon," a man says, rising to his feet to bow at my mother, who barely acknowledges him.

Luther holds the door open for her, and she sashays her way into the house. Ignored by everyone, I drag my feet after them.

"Have you even bothered to check up on your son?" a shrill voice asks, coming from the other side of a closed door.

"Don't start with that again," a man's burly voice says. "I will go see him when I have the time."

"All you do is keep entertaining people, day in, day out," the woman retorts. "Don't you realize that they're mocking you?"

Irene and Luther share a knowing look filled with condescension. "This is the last time you're dragging me to one of these, Luther," Irene says. "I don't have time to deal with rabble."

"He's vying for a position on the Board, darling," Luther retorts, setting his hat down on the coatrack. "We can't just dismiss him."

"For now," Irene says with a sniff.

I watch them greet another couple dressed in the same goth and leather trappings my parents always wear, and disappear together into a room.

"We can't even afford to have all these people here," I hear the woman behind the door say. "How are we going to pay for Owen's care now?"

"If we're part of the Board, all that will be covered," the man who can only be the twins' father says. "Owen will be able to get all the care he needs."

There's a rustling noise, and the door opens wide to show a dark-haired woman. She seems startled when she sees me, then puts on a smile belied by her red and puffy eyes.

"What is it, dear?" she asks, her voice soft.

"I, uh, was looking for Bri."

"She should be up in her bedroom," she says distractedly as we both hear the distinct sound of dishes breaking. "In fact, why don't you call her down?"

Bri's mother then dashes over to the living room before more plates can be broken, while I head upstairs.

The second floor is peaceful compared to the racket downstairs. I find Bri's room at the end of the house, facing the front door, and knock.

"I'm not ready," comes the grim reply.

"Bri, it's Morgan. Can I come in?"

A moment later, the door cracks open, and Bri peers out at me. I raise my hand in salute before she opens the door all the way.

"How've you been?" I ask. I want to bite my tongue, because it's obvious she hasn't been doing well at all; her plump cheeks have sunk in and are making her eyes look alien big.

"Have seen better days," she says, getting back to her sofa, where ten dresses are laid out waiting to be picked.

"How's Owen?" I ask and see her flinch.

"Same," she whispers.

Bri picks up a pretty blue gown with small flowers sewn around the bodice, then tosses it back down before holding up a red one.

"What are you doing?" I ask, sitting down on her bed.

"Picking a dress, can't you tell?" she snaps. She takes a deep breath. "Sorry, I'm a little on edge."

"I can tell. But it's OK. I understand."

"No, you don't," she says. She faces me, and I see angry tears pool in her eyes, accentuating the dark rings under them. "You haven't been around us people for long, so you wouldn't know. The pressure of society, of trying to fit in. You're lucky. At least your family's rich. You don't have to parade around as if you need to prove yourself to everyone all the time."

I bite back a snarky retort. I can only sympathize with Bri right now and the struggles she has to go through, except…

"But I thought you did fit in?" I ask.

She laughs mirthlessly. "That's all part of the show, isn't it? Pretend you're above it all when, in fact, you're striving to be the best, like everyone else. And now…" She looks out of her window to the cars that keep coming in. "Now with what's happened to Owen"—her voice cracks, and she has to clear her throat—"it's like a blow to our honor."

"A blow to your honor?" I exclaim. "But it was an accident!"

"Precisely." Bri chews out the word. "An accident. Not in the middle of a battle, where he could have gone down in style."

"Well, that's a dumb way to look at things." Though it fits perfectly with my square family.

"Are you kidding? Not since Duke Gorlois has a Fey been liberated, and he got exiled! There's no way my dad's going to make it on the Board now, which means he won't be able to afford the costs of me becoming a knight either. It's like a vicious circle."

Defeated, Bri sits down next to me. "And with Hadrian avoiding us like the plague, everyone's looking at me now, to see if I'm going to be the next one to shame the family."

I circle her frail shoulders with my arm. "Look, what happened to your brother was a horrible accident, nothing more. People shouldn't judge you or your family on that. Also, you are not your brother, no matter how creepy people find twins!"

"Creepy?" Bri asks. "That's silly."

"Exactly my point. So put on that dress, put some cold water on your eyes, and then go show all those stuck-up people downstairs who's the boss."

Bri nods and sets herself to the task. "You know," she says, "there's still hope for my brother. Father Tristan made it out fine in the end. I'm sure Owen can too."

"What's your brother got to do with the priest?"

Bri takes the first dress at hand and slips it over her head. "Well, when that Gorlois I just mentioned disappeared on one after he was exiled, Father Tristan went to find him." She zips up her dress and combs her fingers through her short hair. "They were best friends, he and Gorlois, and both part of KORT. But when even he didn't show up for years, everyone thought he'd gotten killed. But he did come back, alone, and completely unhinged."

"He seems fine now," I say. Except for the excess of fervor in his quest to exterminate all the Fey.

"Exactly," Bri says. She swirls around. "How do I look?"

I grin. "Like a girl."

Bri rolls her eyes. "Guess that'll have to do. Speaking of puffiness, though, what happened to you?"

I raise my hand to my face. Despite my best efforts, I haven't been able to completely hide my mother's latest gift to me.

"I broke into a storage cabin in our yard," I say offhandedly. "I wasn't too successful."

Bri's shoulders shake with her laughter. "How do you do it?" she asks. "How do you do it to not care about what other people think and do what you want?"

Try living your whole life alone in the middle of people who avoid you like the plague. "But I do care," I say aloud. "It just doesn't always show."

There's a knock at the door, and a gruff voice rings out, "Come down, now, Briana! You need to entertain our guests."

Bri's face clouds over. "I'll be right down, Father." She turns to me with a strained look. "Time to go to the hyenas."

Downstairs, we find most of the adults congregating in the dining room behind closed doors.

"It's an informal Board meeting," Bri explains, sounding sad. "Probably the last my dad will hold."

"What do they do?" I ask. I force myself to walk away before I succumb to the temptation of poking my head in.

"Talk about the state of affairs, mostly," Bri says. "Even though most of the Fey fled to the New World during the Renaissance, they're still all over the world. So the Board keeps tabs on things here in the upper world to make sure the Fey aren't up to something."

"What could the Fey possibly do that would be so terrifying?" I ask. "Change the world climate?"

"That's a possibility. But the Board's more worried about human enslavement."

"Excuse me?" I sputter.

"Yeah," Bri says dismissively. "Let's see what they ended up barbecuing. Hear there was some viral disease that wiped out the herds in Texas; all the ranchers were blaming it on illegal immigrants retaliating or something. If you ask me, sounds more like the type of pranks Fey like to pull instead."

We head to the back of the house. "It used to happen all the time back in the day," Bri continues. She pauses, a smile dimpling her hollowed cheeks. "Ah, they did come!"

Out on the veranda, shrouded in the last of the sun's rays, stand Arthur and Jennifer. My heart skips a beat at the sight of them smiling into each other's faces—they must've made up because I've never seen them look so close before—and it makes me want to gag. Can't I at least get a break from loathsome people on weekends?

"This is sure to be a good sign for my dad," Bri says, excited. "After they got engaged, they became so busy."

"Engaged at seventeen," I say, making it a point to look elsewhere. "It's so...medieval."

"I find it quite romantic," Bri says, hearts in her eyes. "I'm surprised they haven't set you up with anyone yet. It is a custom with the old families of the Blood, after all."

"Pass," I say. "They're all a bunch of inbreds anyway."

I look back when I get no answer and find Bri's been sucked away by the other guests. Left to my own devices, I grab a cup of tea from the waiter's tray as he passes by, then stuff my pockets with pastries.

Out of the corner of my eyes, I see Arthur detach himself from Jennifer and head in my direction. I gulp my tea down, burning my tongue, and nearly choke on it when our gazes lock.

I panic and run away in the opposite direction. If Arthur's found out about my morning exploration, I don't want to hear about it. Especially with Jennifer around.

I find a small bench outside, tucked behind wilting rosebushes. No matter that the spot is somewhat windy and humid, in the shade, and far from all the sweets, as long as it's away from everyone else, and by everyone else, I mean two people in particular.

"The whole family's gone."

My ears prick up at the unknown voice floating in from above. I look up and find that my bench is situated beneath what I take to be the living room's windows, which have been cracked open.

Holding my breath, I settle further into my bench and listen in.

"Now, now, Jorge," says Luther's voice. "They could very well have left on vacation without telling anyone."

"And leave the island without their boat?" Jorge asks back. "I don't think so."

"You don't think they've been murdered?" a woman asks.

"Let's not jump to conclusions here," says Irene, her voice grating on my ears. "Something more mundane may have happened to them, such as meeting up with friends. However...we can't rule out that possibility either."

"Especially considering the location," Luther says.

A tense silence settles on the assembly, and then somebody barks a laugh.

"You can't be serious!" says a man's deep voice. "You really believe that, after all these centuries—what am I saying?—after over a millennium, someone's going to be messing with Carman's cairn?"

"That is what we've been investigating," Irene says, her tone so sharp the man's ears are probably bleeding now.

"Anything we can do?" someone else asks.

"Just keep your eyes and ears open," Luther says, "and your head on your shoulders. A lot of strange events have been happening. It doesn't hurt to be extra cautious."

The remainder of the meeting is spent poring over numbers and lists of people and places, a cue for me to zone out.

"What are you doing here?"

I jump to my feet and yelp when I crash face-first into something solid. Looking through my tearing eyes, I find it's only Arthur.

"You broke by doze!" I accuse him, holding my hand to my appendage.

He raises an eyebrow. "Stuffing your face, I see." He pats my head. "What a cute little hamster you make!"

I slap his hand away, glowering. "No touchy!" I exclaim.

Arthur shrugs. "We're leaving in five," he says, then leaves me to fume on my own. How does he always have the knack to be so annoying? Must be in his genes.

CHAPTER 14

"I never thought I'd say this, but I missed you, and I'm so glad the weekend's over!" I exclaim when I join my friends by the dock.

Keva stares at me like I've turned into a gargoyle. "Don't go loco[14] on me now. I'm not feeling well. I think I got food poisoning."

"I can make you a special tea to help," I say, too chipper to be out from under my mother's yoke to care about her tone.

"Will it give her hives?" Bri asks hopefully.

"It's an infusion of tarragon, sage, and chamomile," I say, "basic plants against food poisoning."

"That would be splendid," Keva says with the fervor she usually reserves for members of KORT. Lower, she adds, "And if I do get hives, you're dead."

Standing closer to Jack, Bri gives me a tight smile.

"So how come you guys didn't show up at the tea party?" I ask Keva and Jack. "I mean, you're the ones who told me about it."

14 Crazy.

Jack blanches and wipes his glasses to avoid having to answer.

"With your tact, I guess you didn't have a lot of friends growing up, did you?" Keva asks me with a smirk.

"You can't expect Keva to show up at Bri's place," Jack murmurs in my ear, pulling me aside, "not after her family's been demoted."

"But I saw lots of people from the Board there," I say, incredulous. "Even Arthur and Jennifer showed up!"

Jack nods. "Just because the meeting had been set a while back and it was too late to change it. But did any of them stay long?"

My anger cools down. "I'm not sure…" But I clearly recall leaving as soon as the meeting was over. I sigh. This whole politics thing is so confusing and illogical, it's giving *me* hives.

"So what about you?" I ask him.

"I, uh, I knew that Owen wouldn't be there," Jack says, evasive, "so there was no point for me to show up."

"So he's still in the hospital?" I ask.

Jack looks distinctly uncomfortable at the question. "In the ward, back at school."

"Well at least he's in good hands, right?" I ask. "The doctors down there know what they're doing."

"Not the hospital wing," Jack whispers, looking fearfully at Bri who's doing a good job pretending not to hear us. "The asylum. Where they put the mental patients."

Mental? "But I thought he was just injured," I start. "All the blood…"

Jack shakes his head, and an indescribable sense of sadness overtakes me. I'm saved from expanding on this painful subject by the arrival of Lady Ysolt, the longboat floating silently to shore.

The moment I'm inside the boat, I wave Dean good-bye and see him raise his hand in return. One by one, the cars leave, and we find ourselves in complete obscurity except for the hospital and city lights in the distance.

"Everyone ready?" cries Lady Ysolt. "Righty then."

A now-familiar green glow surrounds our boats in an air bubble, and then we slowly sink into the lake.

"Can I ask you for a favor?" Bri asks me while we're making our descent.

I lean back toward her so I can hear her better. "Sure, what is it?"

"Could you come with me to see my brother at breakfast time?"

I look back at the quiver in her voice. A useless act, considering all I can see in the murky waters is her jawline, outlined by the sylph's faint green glow. "Of course," I say, quailing inside at the prospect. "Whatever you need."

The moment we leave the chapel, Bri and I slip away and head west toward a wide, squat building with red brick walls. A single torch sputters as we arrive before the entrance, throwing deep shadows at a plaque hung beside the doorway that reads:

BE SOBER-MINDED; BE WATCHFUL.
YOUR ADVERSARY THE DEVIL
PROWLS AROUND LIKE A ROARING
LION, SEEKING SOMEONE TO DEVOUR.
~1 PETER 5:8

"Lovely," I mumble with a shiver.

The inside of the asylum is as unwelcoming as its outside. The walls are smooth and barren, with sparse flambeaux in deep sconces the only source of light. How are people who are mentally ill supposed to get better in this oppressing environment?

"May I help you?" a man asks, dressed in white garb and very square looking—square shoulders, square jaw, square feet.

"Yes," Bri says. She has to clear her voice before she can start up again. "We've come to see my brother."

"Name?"

"Owen. Owen Vaughan."

The man looks through a ledger on a low table, then nods. "Only two visitors at a time," he says, "so one of you has to stay back."

We both look at him with round eyes, and the man looks back down. "A Sir Hadrian's already with the patient."

Bri's face lights up. "My brother's here?"

Guess my usefulness has expired. "Do you want me to wait for you?" I ask.

"Yes, please." Bri squeezes my hand, then hurries after the attendant, leaving me to roam the lugubrious mental institute on my own.

I end up in a small room with benches and tables set around the perimeter. At this time, I don't expect many people to be awake, but I'm surprised to find that a good two dozen patients are present. Most of them, I realize with a pang, are staring vacantly ahead of them. I walk by a disheveled woman mumbling to herself in a tongue I do not recognize, but she doesn't seem to notice me.

"Is this seat taken?" I ask an old man sitting straight as a rod in a high-backed chair.

As he doesn't utter a word of protest, I plunk down into the chair next to his, rest my head against the wall, and close my eyes.

At least the room is somewhat quiet, and I'm so tired I think I can manage a nap.

But my brain won't shut up, roiling with thoughts of my father, murders, and the Fey.

Funny how that works, eh? my guardian angel says, mocking me. *Then again, you are in a mental institute.*

"Which is precisely why I don't like being here," I whisper back. "What if, by some Fey magic, they find out about my split-personality disorder? I wouldn't want to get locked up in here."

It might fit you better. You'd be the queen!

"Thanks a lot," I say.

"It's nice here, isn't it?" the man next to me asks, startling me.

I find him staring at me with moss-green eyes. Despite his mile-long beard, I can tell he's smiling.

"It's got some comfortable chairs," I reply, sitting up.

"The best are the pies," he says conspiratorially. "They're too hot once they come out of the oven, but they get the perfect amount of time to cool down on the way over from the kitchens."

"Is that so?"

There's a short pause, during which I wonder whether I shouldn't just wait for Bri outside. But the man seems harmless enough.

"So how long have you been here?" I ask. I bite my lip—probably not the best question to ask anyone here. Keva was right—I am completely tactless. If only my tongue didn't always beat my mind.

"Oh, a few centuries, on and off." The old man chuckles, a deep rumbling that makes his gray beard shake. "You wouldn't be able to tell, though. This place does wonders on your aging process."

Oh-kay then. Moving on to the next topic. "How did you end up here?"

Saint George's balls, Morgan, I tell myself, can you please stop saying the first thing that comes to your mind?

"I'm sorry," I say. "I meant, what do you like to do here?"

But the man's attention has sharpened on the woman at the other end of the room, the one talking to herself.

"I said stop that!" he yells, spittle flying across the carpet. "You're going to call them over!"

I tense up. The woman's now moving back and forth in her seat, like a pendulum on a tight cord, faster and faster.

"You dumb hag!" the old man yells, getting up.

In the blink of an eye, the bearded man's standing next to her, shaking the woman by the shoulders so violently her eyes are rolling in her head.

"I. Said. Don't. Call. Them!"

"Stop!" I run over to the woman's aid, but the old man is surprisingly strong and pushes me away hard enough that I trip and tumble to the floor. "Somebody help!" I yell, my knees smarting from the fall.

Two burly men in bland white uniforms hurry in. They quickly seize the situation and rush over to the old man, whose face is now carmine.

"Calm down, now," one of the attendants says, grasping the old man by an arm.

"You can let her go," the second man says, grabbing his other arm.

Finally, like a balloon that's been popped, the old man becomes limp in their arms.

"There now, we'll just take you to your room," one of the nurses says as they drag him away. "You'll be able to get a nice rest."

It takes me a moment to recover from the shock. The woman's still lying halfway out of her chair, saliva foaming at her mouth.

I limp over and struggle to get her back in her seat, then finally slide down to the floor next to the wall.

A quarter of an hour later, Bri finds me still sitting in the same position, unmoving.

"What happened?" she asks, helping me up.

I shake my head to wipe the slate of my mind clean of the incident. "Just exhausted." I don't want to have her worry more about Owen than she already does. "I do wish they didn't have that 'maximum two visitors' policy, though," I say when we reach the exit.

As the morning bells ring the start of class, I breathe in deeply, letting the dawn air clean out the asylum's cloying smell of antiseptics and herbs out of my lungs.

"Come on," Bri says, picking up the pace. "We're already late for Sir Caradoc's class."

We wait for Sir Caradoc, our Runes teacher, to turn his back before we sneak in.

"Miss Vaughan," he says without turning around. "I see you've managed to join our class. Along with Miss Pendragon."

Dean sniggers while Ross and Brockton pelt us with just-made papier-mâché balls as, red-faced, we head for our respective seats.

"Now that everyone is here," Sir Caradoc says, facing the room again, "I want everyone to go to the comparison table between the Futhark runes and the Beth-Luis-Nion runes. Can someone explain the difference between them?"

To everyone's surprise, Bri's hand shoots up. "They're both different runic systems, used by different people," she says.

"The first one is the most common and has been most prevalent amongst the Fey as well."

"Precisely," says Sir Caradoc. "Though the Futhark runes are commonly found amongst the Fey, however, we cannot ignore the Beth-Luis-Nion runes. The reason is that, though much rarer, a number of earth elementals and other Fey linked to the woods respond better to the older runes. And as we all know, we cannot control the Fey without knowing and understanding their names."

Eyes flashing, Sir Caradoc pauses in the middle of the room. "Well, why isn't anyone taking note of this?" he asks.

There's a mad scrambling to get our pens and notebooks out. As I write the final word, a flash of inspiration strikes me. Was that what I was missing to make that old glove work?

Exhilaration washes through me. I wish I could retrieve the gauntlet, but unfortunately, it's tucked safely away under my mattress back in the surface world, so I won't be able to test out my theory until next weekend.

I'm so excited I don't even protest when Sir Caradoc tells us to spend the rest of the hour translating the ogham found on standing stones around the Isle of Man, off the coast of Great Britain, nor does it diminish when I realize I have no clue what I'm reading.

"Sir?" Laura asks, raising her hand before the hour is over.

"There's a small dictionary at the back," the teacher answers without looking up from his book.

"That's not what I wanted to ask, sir," the curly-haired girl says.

"What is it then?" Sir Caradoc asks, lifting his eyes to her face disdainfully.

"Is it true what that we're no longer allowed on Island Park?"

"That's in no way relevant to class, Miss Adams," the teacher retorts.

136

"But we thought maybe the message was wrong," Dina says.

"You can read, can't you, Miss Gonzales?" Sir Caradoc retorts, annoyed.

"Yes, sir. But——"

"But I believe the post was very clear," Sir Caradoc interrupts her. "There is no strolling to be done among the island's trees. Is that clear?"

"Yes, sir," Laura and Dina say, sounding disappointed.

Pretending to be deeply involved in the runic text before me, I lean toward Bri. "What was that all about?"

"There's a festival coming up," Bri whispers, scribbling in the margins of her book. "It's called the Triduum of All Hallows, and it takes place——"

"At the end of October," I say, remembering the extra hours of prayer Sister Marie-Clémence would make us do in remembrance of all the saints.

"Well, the first night, there's this big feast, and during the party, a lot of people like to skip out and frolic about."

I snort back a laugh, drawing Sir Caradoc's attention.

"Frolic?" I ask when the teacher's back to reading his book.

Bri blushes. "Yeah, well, one of the places the knights like to go to is that island, 'cause it's more...private."

"Not only do you dare come to class late," Sir Caradoc says, his eyes burning into me from across the room, "but on top of that, you spend the whole time talking. That will not do, Miss Pendragon."

Chastised, I scoot back to my side of the desk and spend the remainder of class trying to decipher the text.

"What are you so uptight about?" Keva asks as we finally get to leave Sir Caradoc's class, but not before he assigns Bri and me extra homework as punishment.

"I just got about twenty years' worth of extra homework," Bri retorts, waving the assignments in Keva's face.

"It'll take me twenty years just to do one of them," I say with a big sigh. "And I still have to do eight more essays for Sir Boris."

"I wasn't talking to you two," Keva says, "but to Jack Be Nimble here."

"Me, uptight?" Jack asks, walking into a post. "Not at all," he adds, rubbing his head distractedly.

As we approach the library, we see three KORT members disappear up the staircase, their faces somber, and talking in low voices. Jack slows down, and it's obvious he's trying to catch what they're saying.

"You'd make a very sad spy indeed," Keva sneers. "Man, I cannot believe I'm stuck with a tomboy, an outcast, and a gimp."

"Nobody asked you to hang out with us," Bri says. "And you," she adds to Jack, "why are you so twitchy?"

"I'm not—" Jack starts, his limp accentuated as he tries to catch up with us. "It's not—"

"There's no point trying to hide it," Keva says. "Either you spill the beans now or we wear you down till you do. And I can promise you that won't be pleasant for you."

Jack scowls, but considering who he's talking to, he doesn't stand a chance and gives up. "Don't you think it's strange that they've forbidden us to go on the island?" he asks.

Bri shrugs. "Could be heightened Fey activity."

"Or that they're the ones behind the kidnappings and are performing weird experiments on them there," Keva says. We all stare at her. "What? I'm only bringing up another possibility here."

"But you do know what else is on that island, right?" Jack says, his voice dropping lower.

"Hmmm, houses?" Bri says sarcastically. "Trees? Shrubs?"

"Oh, ha ha," Jack says, completely unamused.

"Isn't that the island where those people got kidnapped?" I ask, remembering the articles I'd seen back in my parents' office.

"They weren't supposed to be there," Keva says. "It's a private island. They got caught. Big deal."

"You're missing the point," Jack says. "On that island there's an ancient black standing stone."

He looks at us like it's supposed to mean something. All he receives in return are three blank stares.

"Oh, you girls are impossible," he says. "Black standing stone, Lore class, chapter twenty-three, fifth paragraph? The warning?"

"If you expect me to read ahead of what's scheduled," Keva says, "then you're completely off your rocker."

"Yeah, I think you're just being a little paranoid," Bri says, slapping his back so hard he staggers forward. "It's OK, though. You're still cool in my book."

I make to follow the two girls into the library—my homework won't, unfortunately, get done on its own—but something in Jack's face makes me stop. Though I've only spent a couple of weeks at Lake High, I've gotten to spend plenty of time with him, due mainly to the fact that he's always helping me, and I can't stand seeing him look so troubled.

"I have no idea what you're talking about," I tell him, "but if you say there's something wrong, then I believe you."

Jack gives me a wan smile. "It's OK. Maybe Bri's right, and I'm just seeing things where there aren't any."

I hold the door to the library open for him. "In that case, sir," I say with a mock curtsy.

We find Bri and Keva sitting at one of the tables farthest away from Madame Jiang's desk. Within minutes, I'm completely absorbed in my essay on the Fomori: monstrous amphibian creatures that grow to be twice the size of an adult man, with an elongated skull, no nose, lipless mouths that contain two rows of teeth and can open wide enough to swallow a human head whole, and luminous blue-white eyes.

"These are disgusting," I say, shuddering at the picture showing a Fomori's webbed hands that end in sharp claws. "And to think I once imagined most Fey people to be cute and cuddly."

"There's no such thing as a cute and cuddly Fey," Bri says, getting up once again to go check out the massive rune dictionary standing on its own table in the middle of the room.

"Dark Sidhe are the worst kind," Keva says with a grimace. She finishes filing her nails, blows on them, then admires her handiwork. "But at least they're easy to tell. They're all so ugly."

"That is a very moronic way to describe them," Jack mutters.

"What did you just say?" Keva asks, shooting him a dirty look.

"Says their skin is scaly and really hard to pierce," I say, "like the hide of a crocodile."

"Yeah, they were tough suckers, all right," Keva says, reapplying her lip gloss. "A good thing they were all killed in the last Great War."

"They were?" I ask. "Huh, I thought I'd seen them somewhere before…Glad I didn't, though, they look like the worst."

"Nope," Jack says. He rests his head in his hand, still holding his fountain pen. "There's been worse."

"Like dragons," Keva says, but with such a dreamy look on her face I doubt she thinks of them as monsters. "I don't know who caught the last sea dragon, but the last land one was killed—"

"By Saint George," I say, grinning. "Yeah, I've always liked him too. He was so ballsy."

"He was one of the last knights of the old order," Jack says, "before we were taught how to do EM. And, for your reference, Keva, the Leviathan was never captured or killed."

"Whatevs," Keva says, resuming her bored look. "Just so long as it stays away from me."

"In any case, most dragons disappeared after Carman was captured," Jack says. "Whether killed or not." He jerks his hand down, leaving a long trace of ink down his nose. "Want to see something cool?"

"What?" I ask.

"There's this really old stele—"

"Oh, not *that* old thing," Keva says with a yawn.

"I'll go," I say. Anything's good enough an excuse for me to procrastinate.

I follow Jack down to the opposite side of the library, through rows and rows of bookcases. Out the window, I can see the arena loom closer and closer until we finally arrive at a large tapestry of Saint Michael bringing down a seven-headed dragon—a very familiar scene.

"And the great dragon was cast out," I quote, "that old serpent, called the Devil, and Satan, which deceiveth the whole world. He was cast out into the earth, and his angels were cast out with him."

Jack nods. "And that's when things got bad for us. Look."

He points at a large stone embedded in the floor beneath the tapestry, on which hundreds of runes have been carved.

"Yeah, unless you want to see me grow old and die here," I say, "you're going to tell me what that says. 'Cause there's no way I can decipher all of that."

Without even reading, Jack starts to recite: "Four men to raise the stones their blood did shed, Four Fey their essence over the cairns did spread, Four of the Nephilim to Avalon's protection their lives vowed, And Danu, to seal the spell, her power over all bestowed. Finally, as a measure of precaution, a warning was cast. And a black sentinel over the prison now stands fast. To warn all of its ward's great and terrible threat And remind—"

"Humanity its evil deeds to never forget," Bri finishes, appearing behind us. "Yep, had to learn that by heart when I was ten." She grabs our arms in hers and starts to steer us away, but I stop her.

"A black sentinel?" I ask Jack. "Is that what you were talking about earlier?"

Jack nods. "My interpretation is that it's probably a warding stone. They used to be raised to keep people away from dangerous places. But, because they're very rare, people have forgotten about them." His voice drops. "There's a story about this man who went digging around the base of one of them once, back in Wales. The next day, they found his remains. It looked like he'd been chewed up, then spat back out again."

"OK," I say, trying to get the disgusting picture of a half-eaten, half-digested man out of my mind, "so you're saying there's one of these stones next to this Carman woman's tomb."

"Yes," Jack breathes. "And one of them's on that island."

Chapter 11

Having grown up in a Catholic boarding school, I've always struggled not to use violence, and I'm glad to find nothing's better than weapons practice to work out your pent-up frustrations.

Sweating profusely, I bring down my dagger in a cross slash followed by a thrust. One hundred! I drop the knife to the ground, my whole body shaking from the effort like a hairless monkey in the snow.

I plunk down onto the nearest bench, enjoying the early night's breeze on my face; I don't know how there can be wind down here when it never rains, nor why the temperature's always warmer in Lake High than on the surface, but I'm not complaining.

Watching the knights practice on the opposite side of the stadium, I find myself wishing once again for the ban from using elementals to be lifted from me so I can try my hand at all those fancy manipulations too.

"Miss Pendragon, what do you think you're doing?"

I barely manage to loll my head around to look at Lady Ysolt. She's standing by my classmates as they unsuccessfully try their first earth elementals.

"I've finished my practice, ma'am," I answer.

"No," the tall woman says, "you've finished a set. Now go run ten laps around the field."

"T-Ten?"

"Ten, Miss Pendragon!" Lady Ysolt shouts. "Hop to it!"

With a groan, I push myself up and start trotting along the edge of the field.

"Don't drag your feet!" the teacher yells after me.

I've barely managed to make it halfway around when a stitch doubles me over. Wheezing, I stop and look over to the freshmen's side of the field, but Lady Ysolt's too busy helping an injured Elias to notice me.

"Down!"

Hands on knees, I look up in time to see a glob of water hurl my way seconds before it hits me. My feet lift off the ground, and I land hard on my backside, my breath whooshing out of me.

From the corner of my eye, I see people sprinting over.

"Oh, it's Morgan." I recognize Percy's voice.

"Would it have made it better if it wasn't?" says the other boy.

Two faces appear above mine, the light of the nearest torches giving them angelic halos. Percy looks sheepish—I take it he's the one I have to thank for my current state. But it's the other boy who catches my attention, his deep blue eyes nearly black in the shadows.

"Ohtheprettyboy," I whisper in one breath.

Two pairs of eyes widen, then Percy guffaws. "Well, it sure seems her brain ain't too addled."

Lance helps me sit up, his hands surprisingly gentle. In my hazy mind, I wish I weren't so sweaty.

"Anything hurt?" he asks, the first words he's ever said to me.

"I don't think so," I say.

"You might have a broken nose," Percy says. "You should have it checked out."

I feel my face, and my hand comes back with blood on it. Lance helps me to my feet, catching me again as my legs give out. We both look up as a shadow crosses our vision. I feel Lance's warm hands instantly leave my shoulders.

"What happened?" Jennifer asks, her voice like poison to my ears.

"Got carried away," Percy says with a grin. "Ended up gettin' Morgan instead."

"She seems fine to me," the blonde girl says, still not moving.

I really don't know why she hates me. Is it because I'm Arthur's half sister? Maybe I should tell her I'd be delighted to switch spots with her if she weren't already engaged to him.

"Look," I say, tired of being the brunt of her anger, "if you want a bloody nose so you can have an excuse to go to the infirmary, I'll be happy to oblige."

The words escape me before I have time to think. Everyone around me freezes, even Percy. Jennifer's eyes are throwing daggers at me, but she ends up smiling at me instead. I'd rather take the daggers...

"Why thank you," she says in a honeyed voice. "Today has been a rather grueling practice session, for everyone around. I'm sure they'll be more than pleased to hear you've volunteered to help them by taking over the cleaning duties."

Cleaning, *again*? I bite on my cheek to avoid throwing a stinging retort that's bound to get me into worse trouble.

"But she needs to 'ave a look at," Percy says, without much conviction.

Jennifer tosses a handkerchief at my feet. "You can stick that up your nose. Now you can't say I'm not looking out for you."

"All that because you have an inferiority complex," I snap. "You shouldn't take it out on me, though. You and I are very similar, you see, both of us pretending at being knights."

Jennifer's nostrils flare. "At least *I* know how to use elementals," she remarks before stomping back to the dorms with Lance.

Shaking his head, Percy picks the tissue up and hands it to me. "Mighty foolish of ya," he says before trotting away.

I look around me, miserable, as I see people eye me before discarding their training gear. I have a feeling this is going to be a very, very long night.

On the other side of the arena, I see Bri and Jack hurry over to me, followed, to my surprise, by Keva.

"What the hell happened to your face?" Keva asks. She tuts. "Such a shame, your one lovely attribute."

"We heard you got disciplined by Jennifer again?" Jack says.

News sure travels fast around here. I nod. "Looks like she's making a habit of it."

"You want to be careful," he says. "She's not someone you want on your bad side."

"Do you need some help?" Bri asks.

My face lights up at the idea; that would sure make things go faster.

"You'll get in trouble if you do," Jack says.

Bri's about to retort when Keva interrupts her, "And you don't need any unwanted attention, especially not after what happened to your brother."

Jack elbows Keva in the ribs.

"Ouch! I'm only telling the truth. You don't have to give me a bruise for it."

I use the back of my sleeve to wipe the blood off my face. "It's OK, guys. I'll manage. But if you could save me some food, I'd appreciate that."

The three of them wave farewell, and I'm faced with a deserted field. "Twice in two weeks, Morgan," I say to myself. "Let's not make this a daily occurrence."

By bedtime, I feel like an old pair of distended, holey socks. I lie in bed, staring at the ceiling, too tired to even close my eyes.

"I'm turning the lights off," Keva says before climbing into her bed.

The imprint of the incandescent lightbulb still shines before my eyes despite the darkness. I hear Keva toss and turn in her bed.

"Can I ask you a question?"

Keva doesn't answer at first, then sighs. "What is it?"

"Did your parents come here too?"

"Just my dad," she answers. "My mom wasn't allowed to leave her family till she got married. They're very traditional. Why d'you ask?"

There's more rustling, and I have the distinct impression Keva's rolled onto her side to look at me.

"Is it 'cause you wanna know more about yours?" she asks, oozing with curiosity. "You really don't know anything about your father?"

"Does your dad ever talk about what it was like here?" I ask in return, skirting the uncomfortable topic.

"No," she says, sounding morose. "There was an incident here when he was a page. Then things changed for the worse. He doesn't like to talk about it."

I continue to stare at the ceiling, wondering whether my father ever met hers. If they'd perhaps been friends, or even roommates, like us.

"Didn't you mention something about school records?" I finally ask her.

"You're not gonna find anything about your dad in there," Keva says, bored.

Her words destroy my last hope like a house of cards. "Why not?"

"Got destroyed in a fire, the first and only in the school's history. It was set by the then president of KORT too. He went crazy."

A name springs to my mind. "Would that be...Duke Gorlois?" I ask.

"Well, well, well," Keva says sarcastically, "look who's getting her history lessons down? Yeah, it was him. Now go to sleep."

I try to fall asleep, I really do, but now that the subject's been opened, I'm wide-awake, and I need to get at least some of my questions answered.

"Can I ask you another question?"

I can feel Keva's murderous intent from across the room. "*What?*" she snarls.

"Who was this duke? What happened to him?"

"Nobody knows," Keva says. "Now leave me alone."

"Really?" I ask. "Not even an idea?"

"You're not going to stop unless I tell you, huh?" she asks, sounding defeated

I grin despite myself. "Nope."

"Duke Gorlois was the president of KORT about, oh, twenty years ago," she says. "He was great with his studies, especially in his tactical courses, and was renowned for capturing a lot of Fey. Kinda like Arthur, if you want.

"But then something happened. Nobody really knows what exactly, but it happened on one of his hunts. When he came back, he seemed fine at first, but he started acting all erratic. Unfortunately, we'd lost the Sangraal centuries before, so we couldn't heal him, and he was sent to the nuthouse. But then this one night, he set fire to the school and used the confusion to steal the most powerful weapon we owned. When the Board found out about it, they exiled him from this place for ever."

"What was it?" I ask.

"A sword," she replies wistfully, "that makes anyone who holds it practically undefeatable. Excalibur…"

Keva lingers on that name, as if able to taste its power.

"So where is it now?" I ask.

Keva sounds bored. "Who knows? He and the sword both disappeared, and they were never seen again. Father Tristan went to find him. And that turned out to be the biggest mistake of his life."

"Because he went crazy too?" I ask, recalling Bri's story.

"Not that." Keva chuckles. "He'd been engaged to Ysolt before leaving to find Gorlois, but he was gone for so long, everyone thought he was dead."

"And when he came back, she was married to Sir Boris," I say, struck by the sadness of the story. It's no wonder Father Tristan always sounds so cross.

"At least the forest didn't spit him back out a hundred years later like it sometimes does," Keva says. I can tell she's enjoying telling me this—maybe she's trying to scare me, a very plausible explanation. "You know, there's supposedly one of them in the asylum now. They say he's, like, three hundred years old and has turned into an albino from living inside all the time."

"I don't know," I say, thinking back on this morning's visit. "I didn't see anyone like that." Just some crazy Father Christmas trying to choke a poor lady to death.

"Well then," Keva says, annoyed, "since you know everything already, you can shut up now. I need my beauty sleep."

I leave Keva alone, and, soon enough, I hear her steady breathing. Could fighting Fey people really be that damaging to the mind? What is it exactly that they do to us? Hypnosis? I think back to Owen, then to the duke, who had been the best knight around. Just like Arthur, Keva said.

A knot forms at the pit of my stomach and I punch my pillow into a more comfortable shape, annoyed at my getting worried about him. And, in the middle of all that, I still don't know zip about my father.

The first pink tones of dawn are already bleeding into the sky when I manage to fall asleep, only to be immediately woken up by the morning bells. I hear Keva shriek, and roll over on my bed to see what's the matter.

"Mwhaddizit?" I ask, bleary-eyed.

"Why is that filthy thing touching my stuff?" Keva yells.

Holding on to her mirror, she wrestles something from a small, furry creature.

"Puck——" I say, yawning.

Puck snaps his little head around, lets go suddenly, and runs over to me, his tiny hooves ringing against the flagstones. He jumps into my arms, and I collapse onto my bed.

"What didja do?" I ask, grabbing his face spattered with red between both my hands until his lips pucker.

"He ate my makeup, that's what he did," Keva says, tossing her a small tube into the trash can. "And you owe me a new lipstick."

I hear her slam the door behind her, and then the world gets all fuzzy.

When I wake up again, there's a loud roaring sound above me, and my whole body's vibrating. I crack my eyes open to find a black cat purring on top of my chest, looking down at me with eyes of gold, and Puck curled up in a ball at my side.

"Hello." I cough. My mouth is parched, and every limb feels like it's been doused in acid. "What are you doing here?"

The cat jumps off me as soon as I try to pet him. Blinking, I try to get my bearings again. From what I can see of the sky, I take it it's almost lunchtime.

For a second, I feel a surge of panic—I've missed classes! And I haven't even caught up with all of my lessons yet. I hurry down the narrow steps, tripping over my bootlaces. But as I hobble toward the courtyard on my way to Runes, my steps falter. Why am I even bothering when I don't get to do any of the interesting stuff and I get punished all the time?

My emotions in turmoil, I let my feet take me out a side door, then head due north until I reach the church. After a moment's hesitation, I sneak inside in search of peace and quiet.

"What are you doing here, child?"

I startle at the quiet voice uncomfortably close to me. I hadn't even seen Father Tristan when I walked in. He resumes his sweeping.

"Shouldn't you be in class?" he asks. His black cassock seems to float about him as he moves away, giving him the air of a jellyfish.

"I, um, wasn't feeling well," I say. I sign myself before I can get struck to death for lying inside a holy place.

"Were you hoping for a confession?" he asks.

"Not exactly," I reply. "I just…needed a break."

Father Tristan stops his sweeping to look at me with eyes that are so pale they're almost white. He sets his broom against the wall and holds his hands at his sides, fingers splayed.

"If you seek some form of asylum, or counsel, you are more than welcome here," he says. "The house of God always welcomes His children."

As he picks up dusting with an old rag, I make my way to an alcove where a dozen votive candles are lined before a statue of Saint George defeating the dragon. A very appropriate place for me, I muse as I kneel on the prie-dieu to pray.

Despite my best intent, all I can think of is this new world, a world where, no matter how hard I try, I don't fit.

Did you expect anything else?

I ignore my guardian angel's voice. The initial excitement I'd felt at one day being able to control elements has abated. I wonder now if this isn't a ploy to keep me from running away so I won't cause trouble elsewhere.

Your place is not among them.

This last sentence surprises me, but again, I ignore the voice, screw my eyes shut, and try to form the first stanzas of the paternoster. But to no avail—vivid images of Percy and Arthur fighting the demon bull superimpose themselves over those of Jennifer bossing me around like I'm her own personal slave, then flash back to Owen and the giant bull before its flames take over the school.

"Are you getting answers to your questions?" Father Tristan asks behind me.

I stare up at the saint's statue; his face is taut with concentration as he spears the beast at his feet. I know his tale. The knight had been the only one brave enough to face the deadly dragon, saving entire villages and the king's own daughter.

My eyes travel down to the dragon at his feet writhing in pain, a look of sheer terror on its face. For once, I sympathize with it, which just goes to show how messed up my life has become.

"Not any answer I want," I finally say.

"Often it's not until much time has passed that we see the lesson we were to learn from our hardships," he says. The light of the candles reflects in his pale gaze. "You remind me of a friend I once had. He, too, had many questions. And those answers he did have left him dissatisfied."

"What happened to him?" I ask.

"He sought new ones."

"Did he like those better?"

"He died for them."

Well, that's just peachy. Is that what's going to happen to me too? But the thought of my potentially imminent death brings those of Agnès and my father to mind, and I shiver.

"Do not worry, child," Father Tristan says. "God is faithful, He will not let you be tried beyond your ability, but will provide a solution that you may be able to endure it." His voice lowers as if he's rewound his memory way back. "However scarred you may end up afterward."

Gloomy words from someone who professes to help people out. But then again, none of his sermons have been of the cheery sort. Perhaps he, too, is suffering from some chronic case of depression.

"Father, can I ask you a question?"

Father Tristan seems to shake himself out of his reverie and smiles. "What is it?"

"I've heard you speak of the Fey and their abilities," I say. "You speak of all that magic as being evil, and that it must be wiped away from the face of this earth, that we must send them all to Hell. And yet—"

"And yet I live here," he finishes for me, "in a world that only exists because of such magic, a practice clearly condemned by the Bible for leading down the path of evil. True. However, you need to understand that, sometimes, one needs to be with one's enemy to understand it and therefore be better able to defeat it. A worthy cause, don't you think? Damning the few to save the many."

His words echo those of Keva's, and I'm starting to wonder if they aren't right. Quiet as a haunting spirit, he moves away.

"You better get to class now," he says, "or you're going to get into trouble."

"Yes, Father," I say with a sigh.

I don't know what I was expecting, but somehow I feel a little relieved. I might not be literally sleeping with the devil and I don't ever want to, but I can withstand being near it. For now.

I know I've just told a priest I'm going back to school, but the last thing I want to do is go practice with a wooden knife while everyone else is training in EM.

Instead, I beeline to the back of the asylum, past a dark stairwell that buries deep into the ground, then stop when my feet reach the edges of the first row of fields.

My eyes scan the horizon, beyond the long hills where a long green line denotes the forest—the very forest that is supposedly the Fey's last standing line, where people are said to lose their minds or get swallowed up, not to be seen again for centuries.

I wonder what it would be like to come back here in a hundred years. Would the school still be here? Would I have to face the same problems, with bratty students and pitiless teachers? At least I'd be rid of my annoying family…

Drawn by the sweet scent of flowers, I continue on my way north. Soon, a single large rock rises up to meet me, the size of a small cottage.

Before it stands a beautiful woman, her long brown curls falling in a soft cloud over her lavender dress. As I hesitate to approach her, unsure whether she's a teacher or not, the woman turns around and smiles.

"Morgan," she says in a voice as sweet as the chirping of birds, "how very nice to meet you."

The hem of her dress starts to move on its own, and a very familiar bearded head pokes from around her ankles.

"Puck!" I say, surprised to see him so far from the school.

The woman laughs. "Yes, it was time for him to get some fresh air and a change of scenery. The poor little fellow's still afraid of closets."

And it's no wonder. The hobgoblin bounds over to me and nearly tackles me to the ground. I laugh—this is the warmest welcome I've ever experienced!

"I'm so glad he's made a friend," the woman says. Her eyes seem to be changing colors with every movement of her head.

Puck detaches himself from me and from my petting, and charges the stone with his tiny horns. He bounces off the rock and lands on his hairy bottom, dazed. The woman picks him up into her arms.

"How many times do I have to tell you that won't work on that stone?" the woman says kindly.

I notice then that the stone's blue-gray surface is covered in thousands of small runes.

"What do they say?" I ask.

The woman slowly passes her hand over the inscriptions without touching them.

"It's part of a ward," she says.

"A ward? Like a protection spell?" The runes look like they've just been carved, not a single patch of moss growing on the stone's smooth surface. "Is that why they say Fey people can't come here?"

"Unless they've been invited," she says.

My eyes widen at the thought that some old writing has that power. "So what Keva said was true," I murmur, remembering our sacred geometry class.

"I would hope you were at least taught the truth here," the woman says. "Otherwise, what would be the purpose of this place?"

My gaze drops to the bottom of the long runic text, near grass level, where a large symbol is carved—a five-pointed star inscribed within a circle. I take a few steps back.

"I used to think that was the sign of the devil," I say, forcing a laugh out, though the thought still makes me break out in a cold sweat.

"If that was the case, a lot of things around us would be considered evil," she says. "The inside of an apple, flowers, the passage of Venus around the Earth...No. That pentacle is a protection seal.

"Each point represents one of the four prime elements, with the fifth being the spirit. Then the circle that joins them all to preserve life."

"Preserve life?" I point to the large building in the distance. "You mean the school?"

"That's one way to look at it."

The woman starts walking back the way I came, and I follow her. She's still carrying Puck, who's now munching happily on a strand of her hair like a rabbit on a carrot, but she doesn't seem to notice or care.

"Can it do other things?" I ask. "That seal there?"

"Everything has more than one facet in life," the woman answers without stopping. "It all depends on how it's used."

Which means yes. I kick a pebble, and it bounces off the track a couple of feet away. I don't know who this woman is, but it's a good thing she's not a teacher. For one, I'd already have gotten detention otherwise, and two, her way of answering without answering would be problematic.

As we pass between the church and the asylum, we hear the bell ring the end of classes.

"I believe we're right on time for EM," the woman says, with a smile, a clear sign of dismissal.

"Damn this place to hell!"

I jump at the angry voice and find an old man ferreting around the flower bushes, his long beard caught in their spindly branches. I recognize him immediately as the crazy old man from the asylum.

I rush over to help the poor man. "How did you get out here?" I ask him, trying to untangle his beard from the bush.

"On my own two feet," he replies, his moss-green eyes flashing. "What a silly question!"

"I mean, how did you get out?"

The man looks even more outraged. "Through the door, of course!"

With her clear laugh, the woman approaches us. "It's too easy for you to get out, dear friend," she says in her singsong voice.

It seems her presence has a calming effect on the old man, for his features soften. In a few seconds, she has him freed and is holding his arm, probably to prevent him from escaping again.

Students are now streaming out of the school toward the practice field, all decked out in their training gear. And in their midst are two familiar faces.

"Morgan! Where have you been?"

Bri rushes toward me, Jack on her heels. Behind them is Lady Ysolt, her stony face menacing.

"I'm so going to get punished for this," I tell myself. "I just hope torture's a practice that's long been abandoned."

"Bah, nothing your death can't take care of, dear," the old man says, patting my shoulder as he and the lady leave.

"We've been worried about you," Bri says when she reaches me. She sounds more excited than worried, however. "What happened? We came to get you before lunch, but you were gone."

"Were you called into the principal's office?" Jack asks, looking nervously toward the odd pair who can still be seen walking to the asylum.

"No. I just woke up late." I shrug. "Then things just happened that kept me away."

"So why were you talking with Lady Vivian, then?" Bri asks, awed.

"And Myrdwinn, too?" Jack adds.

"Who and who?" I ask.

"The school's principal and the director," Bri says, a note of impatience tingeing her voice. "You were just talking to them. We saw you!"

"That's who those two were?" I shake my head. "But the man…"

"Myrdwinn," Jack says.

"Yes, he's gone a little senile," I say.

"Well, it's no wonder," Bri says, "considering how old he is. He was already here when my grandfather attended school."

"My granddad says that Myrdwinn was the school's president back when his grandfather was a kid," Jack says. "They even say he's the grandson of the original Myrdwinn, the enchanter who first taught knights EM."

I scoff. "That's not possible. That'd make him waaaaay over a hundred years old!"

"Which makes it perfectly reasonable for him to have dementia," Bri says.

I stare openmouthed at my two friends. Do they even hear themselves speaking?

Jack shakes his head at me. "I don't know how you do it," he says, "to be hanging out with KORT people and talking to the school's owners. You're either very lucky or in deep trouble."

Chapter 12

Once again, I'm relegated to a corner of the field to train on my own, but with a wooden sword this time. Curse my tendency to be easily swayed by the smallest kindness. I should've just skipped this part of the day too!

"At least give me something to practice on," I huff. I step sideways and bring the sword up, two-handed, in a mock parry. "Something I can hit to a pulp!"

"So much anger!"

I pivot and nearly thwack Arthur in the face. But the little turd actually ducks below the baton before tearing it out of my hands.

"Are you complaining because you can't do EM with the others?" he asks.

I brush my hair out of my face, noticing Daniel and his gofers staring at us.

"No," I say sourly.

Arthur raises his eyebrows, not buying it. "You should know hand combat. Many Fey use regular weapons, like we do. EM just allows us to level the playing field."

Not knowing what to do with my empty hands, I cross my arms and glare at him. "What is it you want? You're interrupting my class."

"Class is actually what I came to talk to you about," Arthur says.

I snort. "What is it, Mr. President? Did you come all the way over to a mere page to give detention?"

"Right on the dot! I see you're not as stupid as some say."

By "some," I assume he means Jennifer. I grind my teeth together, waiting.

"I hear that you missed all your classes today," he says, any trace of mockery gone, "but were not to be found in the infirmary. Is this correct?"

I nod, too annoyed to speak.

"Do you have a good excuse?"

Maybe that your girlfriend made me do cleanup duty last night, again, and when I was already dead tired and bleeding to death. I don't think my mental diatribe is reaching him, no matter how much I may glower at him, not that he'd believe me anyway.

"No," I finally say.

Arthur frowns, as if surprised at my response. "Very well," he says. "In that case, you are to clean the showers and restrooms in the mornings, for two weeks."

My mouth cranks open. "I have to what?"

"That means all eight sections of them, boys and girls, for each year," Arthur continues as if he hasn't heard me. "So I suggest you wake up a couple of hours early every day. Any questions?"

I'm positively fuming. "Yeah, did you have to come all the way here to tell me this, or did you only do it because you were dying to see my reaction?" I so do wish I'd smacked him in the head with my practice sword.

Arthur's hazel eyes bore into me. "Rules are rules," he says simply before stalking away.

"I really, really hate you," I say under my breath. I think I see his steps falter for a second, but I can't be sure.

"I did it! I did it!"

My class pauses to see Laura grow a wall of packed earth around her that's getting taller by the second. The girl's triumphant look morphs into one of panic as the wall grows higher than her shoulders.

"Control your gnome, Miss Adams!" yells Lady Ysolt.

"I can't!" Laura sobs.

"Tell it to stop!"

Laura shrieks as the wall of earth closes over her with a loud crash, rocks shooting out in every direction. Everyone screams and drops to the ground, everyone but me. Lady Ysolt flings her hands out, and a long green flash zooms out to divert the projectiles away from the class.

Time seems to slow down. I watch the stones curve in midair, then tear through the air toward me. Something sharp pierces my calf. I yell and keel over in pain, only to see a black shape slink away.

The jets of stones soar over me and land in the stands like artillery shots. Within seconds, everything's over. I look up from my bleeding leg to find the first three rows of benches demolished. I gulp. And to think that could have been me!

"Morgan, are you all right?"

Lady Ysolt races over to me and helps me up. She's so worried she's forgotten to call me by my last name like anybody who's not a knight ought to be called.

"I'm so sorry," she says. "I'd forgotten you were there."

Forgotten? I bark out a mirthless laugh. Of course she would. People only remember me when they have no other choice.

I pull away from her. "I'm fine," I snap. I wince when I try to put weight on my injured leg, but keep my mouth shut.

"Miss Kulkarni," Lady Ysolt calls out, "go take your roommate to the doctor's."

I mean to protest, but Keva leads me back inside the school, and I use this moment to escape from everyone, too tired to deal with people.

"You're shit out of luck, huh?" Keva says, leaning against a medicine cabinet as a nurse, an old man with a neatly trimmed beard and circular glasses, examines my wounds.

She chuckles. "I can't believe your own brother gave you toilet duty!"

The nurse's gentle fingers prod the ruptured skin until more blood drips down my leg.

I grimace. "If I could, I'd dunk him in it," I say to Keva.

"A feline," the man mutters in his graying whiskers. "How very odd."

"It saved my life, that cat," I say.

The doctor spreads a salve on my calf, some concoction of honey and other herbs, lavender perhaps and...

"Excuse me, sir," I say, "but is that comfrey?"

The man looks up from his bandaging, his eyes owlish behind his glasses. He looks more shocked than when he examined the deep lacerations left by the cat.

"Why yes," he says. "You've had this treatment before?"

"No," I say. "But we used it as a slug repellent back..." My vision blurs, and I sway on my stool.

He grabs my arm to steady me. I breathe in deeply and slowly until my sight goes back to normal.

"You need to get some food in you," the nurse says, "and some rest, or you're going to get really sick."

"No worries," I mumble, getting to my feet with Keva's help. "I never get sick."

"Eat something!" the man says again before the door closes on him.

Keva and I make our way down the hallway toward the dining hall. We pull the doors back, and a couple of students shove past us. I nearly fall down, but catch myself on the door's handle.

"You immature bastards!" Keva says. "If you think you can become knights with this kind of attitude, you're fooling yourselves."

I'm dead tired, famished, and filthy, but I'm quite sure that's not why people are avoiding me. No, I realize as people turn away from me, avoiding eye contact, they're staying clear of me for the simple reason that both Jennifer and Arthur have gotten on my back, and no one wants to feel their wrath by being associated with me. But at this point, I don't really care.

I settle down next to Keva and practically inhale my dinner. Food has never tasted so sweet, and, before long, my three plates are as clean as if they'd just come out of the dishwasher.

Keva stares at me in disgust—her standards for ladylike manners are obviously wasted on me. "Slow down, or you're going to choke yourself to death," she says. "My Good Samaritan moment's passed, I won't be taking you back to the infirmary."

I lean back in my seat, my bulging stomach threatening to pop my pleated skirt's top two buttons.

"There's no way they're from the same family," I hear some girls a couple of tables away whisper. "I mean, look at her."

"She's such a loser," another girl says with a snigger. "I mean, she was even held back three years!"

"Poor Arthur. It mustn't be easy to deal with a retard for a sister."

I steal a glance in Keva's direction, wondering how this is affecting her, but find her eating her chicken with all the airs of a grand lady; if it weren't for her foul mouth, she'd fool everyone into thinking she were royalty.

"What is it?" she asks.

"Considering your star-seeking status," I say with a yawn, "I'm wondering why you're sticking with me instead of keeping your distance like everyone else."

Keva lowers her fork and knife, then daintily wipes her mouth on her napkin. "First of all," she says, "I'm affronted you should think so low of me as to compare me to everyone else around here. Second, I do know you're dumb enough to have turned Jennifer into an enemy, though I'm sure if she knew you better, she wouldn't even bother. You've also managed to get disciplined more times in the few weeks you've been here than anyone else has in a semester.

"But one cannot get far in life if all one sees is just the surface of things."

She links her fingers together and rests her head on them. "In your short time here, you've managed to befriend a number of KORT members, a rare feat for a page. You're also on speaking terms with the dean and the school president, I've heard, and let's not forget you're Arthur's sister."

She raises her hand before I can interrupt her.

"I know he's sentenced you to disgusting menial labor for a couple of weeks, but we all know he's a stickler for the rules. And I also know that, before you showed up with Vivian, he was about to throw a search party for you."

She crosses her arms on the table and leans toward me. "Which shows he cares about you. So you see, you've still got your uses."

I shut my mouth with a resounding clap. Something's very wrong with her picture.

"You could have waited," Bri says, slamming her tray down on the table, startling me.

Keva shrugs. "You could have gotten here sooner."

Bri glares at her. "We would have if we didn't have somebody else's gear to clean."

"I was told to take care of this walking catastrophe, so I did."

I barely manage to keep myself from nodding off onto my plate as the argument continues throughout dinner. Finally, Bri jerks me awake to head back to the dorms. I drag my feet after them up the steep staircase to the top floor, where Jack leaves us to go to the boys' section.

"How are you going to wake up tomorrow?" Bri asks me. "We usually have the Lauds bells to help us, but they don't ring that early."

"Don't look at me," Keva says, pushing the solid door to our section open. "I'm so not waking up at three."

"I'll lend you my clock," Bri says. "It's the winding kind, so it works without a problem.

"You have one?" Keva says, alarmed.

Without bothering to answer, I head straight for the showers. If I go to my room now, I'm going to collapse fully clothed in bed and never wake up. And though Keva appears to be bearing with me thus far, I doubt she'd let me stink up the place without either pouring a pail of water on my face or throwing me out the window.

Before I manage to crawl into bed, two layers of skin dutifully scrubbed off, I make my nightly prayer.

Dear Lord, thank you for letting me survive yet another day. I apologize for all the bad things I've done and said, but really, if you were a little nicer to me and didn't give me quite so many things to test my temper, I would be much kinder. Amen.

Every day seems to bring me closer and closer to death. I go through my daily schedule in full walking-corpse mode: up at three, clean bathrooms, Mass at six, classes, then training, with a few hours reserved for meals and study. By the time the freshman boat breaks the lake's surface marking the beginning of the weekend, I barely notice that it's raining.

"Ask if I can come over this weekend," Keva whispers in my ear as I head to the car. "Just, uh…" She pauses, looking nervously at Dean. "Ask your parents instead of him. He doesn't seem too nice."

If I weren't so exhausted, I'd laugh—if only she knew how things truly stood. Instead, I slide inside Dean's car, where Arthur's already waiting, and we make the trip back to the house without a single word crossing our lips.

When we arrive home, Arthur pauses on the front porch.

"Listen," he starts, "about this week, I—"

I brush past him without waiting for the rest of his explanation, push inside, and head straight up to my room. I don't care what he has to say for himself. I don't care what anyone has to say to me. All I want is to be left alone to hibernate for the rest of the year.

My great master plan is defective, however, for I wake up a few hours later to a growling stomach. I stare up at the ceiling, making pictures of the tiny cracks and lines that spread out from the corners closest to the windows, wishing I'd been able to stay at my old school. At least there I had only one year left before I'd be free from this family.

My gaze slides down to the cross hanging over my door.

"I don't know what to do," I say to myself.

You could just continue with what you did last time, says my guardian angel, as if he's been dying for me to ask that question.

"And then what? They won't let me do any EM back at school, even if I did know how to handle elementals better than the rest of the class."

But that's because they don't think you can do it.

"Or they don't want me to," I mumble into my pillow.

I know I don't make any sense; they need as many knights as possible, and they'd never have sent me to Lake High if they didn't expect me to pull my own weight at some point. My eyes drop even lower, and I notice a note has been slipped under my door.

I roll out of bed and snatch it up; it's a message from Arthur.

Please come see me when you wake up. I'd like to have a word with you.
Arthur

"Don't think so, you moronic-two-faced-sucker!" I say.

I crumple the piece of paper and toss it in the wastebasket, then reach for my backpack. Smiling, I pull out the *Basic Dictionary of Runes*, glad that, even in my stupor, I haven't forgotten to bring this monster of a book with me. I'm still in my school uniform, but I don't care to change out of it and head downstairs, the old glove in my jacket pocket.

"Good afternoon, mistress," Ella says as I trot through her pristine kitchen.

I smile at her; Fey or not, the poor woman must not have an easy life, being in my mother's employ. I grab a couple of apples from the basket by the window and head out into the backyard.

The weather in Wisconsin's upper world is definitely not as peaceful as it is back in Lake High. The clouds rolling in from Lake Superior are the color of slate, promising rain by the foot.

"Better get to the shed before it starts pouring," I tell myself, accelerating the pace.

It doesn't take me nearly as much time to get through the broken window as last weekend, and I land in a respectable crouch without breaking anything. I take stock of the inside of the cabin. Nothing has changed since last I came here, which means nobody, not even a single spider, has gotten wind of my trespassing.

I sit on the spotless floor, close to the window, and take out my glove. Angling it to the gray light streaming through, I prod the ogham, its black surface silky smooth to the touch.

Wishing I knew how to differentiate gems, I riffle through the pages, looking for the rune that will match a black stone. Thankfully, there's only one in the whole book related to elementals, an onyx.

"Hagalaz," I whisper, reading the name off the page.

The stone seems to gleam, but the light disappears before I can ascertain whether it's actually responding to its name or just a trick of the light.

My heartbeat kicks up a notch. "Hagalaz," I say, louder.

The stone shimmers, and, for a split second, I can see a pale *H* form at its center, the horizontal bar droopy on one end.

"Saint George's balls, I did it!" I exclaim, holding the glove to my heart.

I don't think I've ever been this excited in my life, except perhaps the time I was allowed to hybridize my first iris.

I'm so eager to see what it can do that I nearly rip the glove to pieces when I put it on. I check the dictionary once more. The rune is a standard for ice. Does that mean I ought to practice outside? The pitter-patter announcing the beginning of rain makes the decision for me. I point my fist, stone first, to the empty wall opposite me.

"Hagalaz," I say.

I wait for a second, squinting. Was there a slight condensation of the air?

"Hagalaz," I say, louder.

The wall appears to pulsate with a dull yellow glow that intensifies until I see the outline of a door form. A few moments later, it opens, and in walks Arthur.

If I hadn't already been seated, I would have fallen down.

"Wh-What are you doing here?" I ask, quickly hiding my hand behind my back.

Arthur looks pissed, rainwater dripping off him onto the dusty floor. "What are *you* doing here?" he shoots back.

"Having a little fun," I say, not daring to look him in the eye.

In two steps he reaches me, kneels down, and grabs my hand.

"Ouch!" I try to pull away, but his grip's too strong. "You don't have to manhandle me!"

Arthur rips the glove off me, stares at the small ogham, and turns livid. "Were you practicing EM on your own?" he asks, his voice shaking.

"So what if I was?"

His fingers tighten around my wrist, and I wince.

"You're hurting me," I say.

"Do you even realize what could have happened?" Arthur yells, practically slapping me in the face with my glove. "Morgan, didn't you see what happened to your classmate?"

With a pang of guilt, I again remember Owen facing the fiery bull.

"Do you realize how dangerous it is for you to train like this, unsupervised? Not to mention this is the surface world, where any layperson can see you! I thought someone like you would've known better!"

I raise my chin. "I was in here, away from prying eyes. Nobody would've seen anything."

Arthur shakes me so hard my teeth rattle. "Not if you'd lost control," he yells. "Damn it, Morgan, somebody could have gotten hurt! You could have been killed!"

"Well I wasn't!" I retort. Not my best comeback, I admit, but I never expected this kind of outburst from Arthur, he who's always so controlled. "And yes, for your information, I do remember what happened to Owen. That's his name, in case you care to know. And that bull-salamander Fey didn't try to hurt me. He just wanted to go to the forest when they called him, and I happened to be in the way!"

Arthur's frown deepens. "What are you talking about?"

"The horn, Arthur. It heard the horn and tried to go to it. It wasn't planning on hurting anyone."

"What horn?"

A long pause settles between us, during which we stare at each other.

Finally, I ask, "You mean you didn't hear it?"

"Nobody heard anything," he says carefully.

I try to see whether he's making fun of me, but he's dead serious. Could I have heard wrong? Could I, in my shock and terror, have made it all up?

Arthur lets go of my arm and gets up. Rubbing my bruised wrist, I do the same.

"So what now?" I ask. "Are you going to punish me again?" I'm already feeling the loss of my one and only ogham, my dreams of telling everyone off gone up in smoke.

"No," he says. "I'm going to give you a private lesson."

"Concentrate," Arthur says, standing behind me. "You need to be able to feel the Fey through its iron casing when you call it out."

I try to feel whatever connection Arthur's talking about, imagining a link between my hand and the ogham. A prickly sensation, perhaps, or a thread attached from my finger to the gem.

"Hagalaz!" I say, pretending to want to push myself through my hand and the stone, and into the air in a shower of hail.

Nothing.

Disappointment, added to hours of practice without food, makes me sway on my feet.

Arthur sighs. "That's enough for today."

I lie down on the floor, my vision a blanket of fuzzy grays, and my ears ringing.

"Did you see anything?" I whisper, shivering with cold.

"No."

It's my turn to sigh. "Maybe...maybe I just can't do it."

"Then you wouldn't be able to go to Lake High," he says.

I rub at the spot on my left shoulder where an old ache has started to act up again.

"Maybe my father wasn't a knight after all," I say. "Maybe he was a layman and I inherited his lack of talent."

"Don't be ridiculous."

I close my eyes, trying not to show how disappointed I am. "You don't know anything about him," I say, hating how my voice quavers.

I feel something soft on my face and find Arthur dabbing my sweaty forehead with a handkerchief. "Better get going," he says, "it's nearly dinnertime."

When we get to the house, Irene jumps on us, all talons out. "What were you two up to?" she asks, deep suspicion seeping out of her in cold waves.

Arthur shrugs. "Just teaching her a few moves," he says. He makes for the staircase.

"What kind of moves?" Irene asks, sticking to him.

Ella slips a sandwich in my pocket before I follow them up. I hear a door close, then slam open.

"I asked you a question, buster!"

Irene's standing before Arthur's bedroom, her tiny hands resting in fists at her hips, over a wide metallic belt.

I remain on the landing, unsure what to do. The safest bet would be to head to my own bedroom, but I can't resist knowing what Arthur's going to say next. I'd always imagined him to be the golden child who couldn't do anything wrong, so seeing Irene get angry at him is surprising...and a little satisfying.

"I was trying to teach her to fight," Arthur says, popping back out of his room while buttoning up a shirt.

Irene's face goes white, then turns as red as a boiled lobster. Her voice drops a threatening two octaves. "You did what?"

My mouth hangs open, my mind unable to comprehend the one thing that goes against every physics rule—Arthur's lied? But why?

I make myself inconspicuous as Arthur pushes past her, then heads back down to the entry hall, Irene trotting after him.

"You heard me, Irene," I hear Arthur say as I tiptoe to the entrance.

"You thoughtless fool!" Irene yells. "You know better than to train *her*, especially out in the open, where anyone can see!"

These are words I've already heard, but with a completely different feel.

"Nothing happened," I say before Irene can hit him again. "And we were—"

"Was I speaking to you?" Irene snaps at me. She returns to Arthur. "And you, don't think because your father's away to deal with the hurricane that—"

"Am I or am I not the president of KORT?"

"I don't see how that's relevant!" Irene snaps.

"It's very relevant, Mother. It shows that people trust my judgment, not my money. Which is a lot more than I can say about you, especially after you hired that lawyer of yours."

There's a resounding slap, and I see the imprint of Irene's hand darkening his cheek. I gasp.

A car honks outside. "I've got to go," he says as if nothing's happened.

"Lucky for you that the girl's worthless," Irene tells him as he heads out the door, "but don't ever let me catch you doing that again."

Arthur waves at us, slams the door shut, and then it hits me; that little twerp's leaving me alone with our mother, who wants nothing more than to skin me alive!

"Where are you going?" I ask, following him outside before she can catch me.

Out on the gravel pathway that leads to the house's front gates is a fancy sports car, Percy at the wheel.

Arthur gets in the passenger's seat, while the latter waves at me with a big smile. Percy says something to Arthur, but Arthur just shakes his head, and the car leaves in a spray of gravel.

Oh no you're not!

I dash back inside, looking frantically about. Irene's nowhere to be seen, and I take my chances.

I grab her car keys and head outside. The car's waiting at the side of the house, a sleek, small thing as black as her temperament. Inside, I find her purse and a map of the region marked with small crosses. Evidently, she is planning on going somewhere.

"Sucks for you," I say, turning on the motor. "Guess you'll have to get a taxi."

It takes me a moment to adjust the seats, and then I move on to the next step, getting the car to move while hoping my little experience driving a boat on Lake Geneva will prove useful.

I shift the lever into the drive position, and the car moves forward. I press my foot down to stop, but hit the gas pedal instead and floor it. I nearly screech when the car bursts forward and comes two inches from taking down a creepy, modern-art statue. Panting, I finally manage to get the car to stop. I keep my hands on the wheel to keep them from shaking.

In the rearview mirror, I see Irene run out of the house, her skirt billowing after her. It's clear she doesn't approve of my little outing.

I don't wait for her to make it all the way to the car, and instead hit the accelerator again. I manage to destroy only a couple of rosebushes lining the road before I get the hang of it. Then I'm past the gates and on the main road.

With a loud cry of exultation, I tear along the streets, toward the lake. Thankfully, the rain's abated, and it doesn't take me long to spot Percy's vivid burnt-orange car swerve out of the traffic and get onto the freeway that leads to Oshkosh.

The only time I almost lose them is when I have to slam on my brakes to avoid running over an old lady crossing the street with her ugly dog. But the offensive canine and its mistress survive without a scratch, and I make my way onto the freeway without another hitch.

Arthur will soon find out he can't just keep me out of the fun.

Just so long as I don't get stopped by the cops...

CHAPTER 13

I nearly miss the exit, but manage to swerve through three lanes to make it without causing any accident. The sun is low on the horizon when I finally see Percy pull into a parking lot filled with trucks and motorbikes. I drive in after them, nearly toppling a whole row of those bikes like dominoes.

I park far away from everyone, fearful of causing some damage. Despite the lack of sign, I can clearly tell from the sounds spilling out that this is a bar.

I stay in the car for a while, contemplating what to do next. The boys are already inside. How they're managing not to get kicked out is a mystery. Surely they can't have come here to get drunk. Though this might be something up Percy's alley, I can't imagine Arthur breaking the law.

I decide to wait for a while longer. Perhaps they've come to pick someone up and are going to reappear soon.

Soon turns into minutes. When I see a group of three girls barely older than me exit, I decide to go in as well. I rummage through my mother's purse and find her makeup kit. With an unsteady hand, I manage to slap some on and look passable. Just so long as they don't ask me for my ID, I should be fine. As a precaution, I do leave my school jacket behind.

Doing my best to look tough, I stride up to the door, past a couple of burly men who eye me with caution and curiosity.

The inside of the bar is louder than I had expected. A lot of the conversations die down the minute I appear, but after a quick glance around, I find Arthur, Percy, and Lance seated at a booth around a really short man, intent on their conversation.

"Hey, sweetheart," a man calls out. He's wearing a black-and-white bandanna around his head, and his handlebar mustache is dusted with beer foam. "Didja get lost?"

"Nope," I say with a tight smile as I make my way toward the bar.

"Can I offer you somethin', miss?" a younger man asks, his tight muscles making his shirt bulge.

"Just some juice, for starters," I say, throwing the bartender a dazzling smile. "Long night ahead."

The man doesn't return my smile, and hands me a glass of cranberry juice.

"Haven't seen you around before," the man continues.

I turn around to look at what Arthur and his friends are doing. "Just passing through," I say without paying much attention.

The man inches closer until I can feel his breath on my arms. "Oh yeah? A travelin' girl, huh? I like the roads myself. Where you been?"

The little man with them is gulping down a pint of beer like he's been stranded on a desert island for too long. He doesn't seem too happy with his present company, though, no matter how inebriated he may be. Percy's talking to him, Arthur and Lance quietly brooding around them, but the man doesn't answer and instead reaches for another tankard.

A new group of people arrives, crowding in the bar next to me and forcing me closer to my neighbor. The guy seems to like the change, for he places his arm around my shoulders.

"Blake, can't you get that mutt of yours to stop barking all the time?" one of the men says, slouching against the bar. "It's been nearly a whole week I can't get my shut-eye."

"Trust me, Todd," another man responds, "if it weren't for Maddie, I'd have shot the darned thing already. It got so scared from all that strange wailing wind the other night, he peed all over the bed, and the wife won't believe it's him now."

The man behind me grunts as if sharing in his misery.

"Did ya hear about Hornby?" another cuts in. "Got his pants all in a twist over some joke some guys have done him."

"What joke?"

"Haven't ya heard?" the third man continues. "Said some kids took it in mind to play a trick on him and cut out some circles in his crops or some shit like that."

"Well at least we still got crops, eh?" the man with the pee-ing dog mutters. "Not like those poor folks down in Iowa and Nebraska."

All three of them take a long swig out of their beers.

"Just glad those locusts didn't get further north," the man named Mike finishes.

The guy next to me tightens his hold around my shoulders.

"You're a real hot piece of a woman," he says. I try not to frown at his breath reeking of alcohol. "Am sure glad you decided to stop by my neck of the woods, or we'd never have met. It's not every day we see someone as…fine as you."

On the other side of the bar, Arthur suddenly looks around, and his eyes meet mine across the crowd. Now that I've been spotted, I expect him to get up and march me back outside, but something the little man says makes him look away again. It's obvious now that they're trying to get the man drunk, but why I have no idea.

"So, sweet cheeks," the man whispers in my ear, "it's getting crowded in here. How 'bout we go someplace more private, huh? You and me?"

Without taking my eyes off what's happening in the booth, I raise my hand and push the guy's face away from me. "A minute," I say, getting up.

I weave my way around the crowd, narrowly missing a few perverts trying to feel their way up my skirt. I do so wish I were wearing heels for once, but I think my heavy boots are doing the trick, because people give up immediately.

"So he grabbed the b-bottle and s-s-s-smashed it on his own h-head, but it d-didn't b-break," I hear the short man hiccup. A wide grin stretches his flushed cheeks, and his ginger hair stands up in hirsute tufts. "Then he tried it again, and again, and again, and *still* it didn't break! He ended up p-p-passing out!"

The man roars in laughter, banging his tiny fists on the table. But none of the three boys joins in the fun.

"Tell me what happened to the people on the island, Nibs," Arthur says. Though his voice is low, I can hear him distinctly over the overwhelming drunken buzz that fills the bar.

The laughter dies abruptly. The little man doesn't look drunk anymore. Even his cheeks aren't flushed. "I wasn't there," he says, eyes shifting to the side.

Unfortunately for him, Lance is sitting next to him, blocking his exit.

"I didn't ask if you were there," says Arthur. "I asked what you knew about it."

The man's tongue darts out to lick his lips. Lance pulls a knife out of his boot, and the whole bar goes quiet. But the silent boy then pulls out an apple from his pocket and starts peeling it.

Though the rest of the patrons return to their drinks, the little man's more nervous than before.

"T-T-They're g-gone," he says. He drinks the remainder of his beer in one long swig, his Adam's apple bobbing up and down like a yo-yo.

"We know that already," Percy says. "What we want to know is how, who, and why."

The stranger sets his tankard down, wipes his chin with the back of his hand, and shakes his head.

A heavy hand grabs my waist, and the drunk man from before pulls me tight to his side. "Where're you goin', sweets?" Apparently he's managed to down a couple of shots of liquor before looking for me again.

His hand travels farther down my back, and I freeze. This has never happened to me before, thanks to my years at all-girls schools, and for an instant, my mind blanks.

"Get your hands off me," I whisper, my throat so tight I barely produce a sound.

The man tries to kiss me, but misses and goes for my neck instead. It's only been three weeks, but my recent training takes over, and I find myself kneeing the guy in the guts before cracking my elbow into his temple. The man drops to the floor, bringing a whole table with him in a resounding crash of breaking glass.

"He's getting away!"

I see a man, no taller than my hips, run out of the bar as fast as his little legs can carry him, a bright red hat anchored firmly on his head.

Lance rushes after the man, followed by Percy.

"You look great!" Percy yells at me, taking off after the other two.

Someone grabs my arm roughly, and I'm about to throw another punch, when I realize it's Arthur.

"I don't know what you think you're doing," he says, dragging me out of the bar under the intense scrutiny of the patrons, "but when this is over, we're going to have a talk."

I look back at the mess we leave behind. "Sorry about that!" I yell before the cold night air hits me like a punching bag.

"Go home," Arthur growls.

Percy and Lance are waiting for him in the car. To my surprise, I notice the little man's angry face staring at me from the back window.

"And put some clothes on!" Arthur yells, getting in the passenger seat right as Percy floors the pedal.

"Crap."

I run to Irene's car, fumble with the keys, manage to turn it on, then leave the parking lot without running over anyone—a real feat in and of itself.

Thankfully, there aren't many cars in this part of town, and none of them driving as crazily as Percy, so it's not too hard to pick out where the boys are going.

I follow them north, past the nuthouse where we go every Monday morning to catch the boat to school, down a series of empty fields, then finally stop in between a row of houses, close to a private wharf.

"Where are you going?" I ask, getting out of the car and running after the three boys, who are dragging the little man with them.

"Morgan, go back home," Arthur says.

I cross my arms, glad for my school jacket. "I don't think so. I want to know what you guys are doing to this poor man who obviously doesn't like water. Who is he, anyway?"

"He's just a clurichaun," Arthur says. "Nothing important. Now go away."

The little man glares at him.

"Obviously he's of some importance to you," I reply, "or you wouldn't have gone to such an extent to get your hands on him.

Which is quite rude, and against knight etiquette, I might add. By the way, what's a clurichaun?"

"A Fey critter that's known to bend an elbow,"[15] Percy says. He nudges the clurichaun. "Ain't that right?"

I must've looked as confused as I felt, for Lance adds, "He likes to drink."

"And that's against the rules then?" I ask, following them to a little boat moored by the water.

"Drinking's not against the rules," Arthur says, getting in the small vessel carefully. "But refusing to give us information in an important investigation is." He forces the little man after him. "At least on our end."

Percy and Lance hop in after them. I make to get in too, but Arthur stops me. "You're not coming. It's too dangerous!"

"If you're going," I say, "then I'm going too." I tap my foot on the wooden platform. "And if you don't let me on that boat now, I'll swim. You know I will."

"That ain't corral dust[16] she's sayin'," Percy says. "We all saw what she's capable of."

"I don't care whether she's lying or not," Arthur says through gritted teeth. "She's not coming."

"Fine." I take off my jacket, then proceed to undo my bootlaces.

"She could get hypothermia," Lance says.

I hear Arthur let out an exasperated snort, and I smile. Point for me!

"Don't hold him like that. You're hurting him." I try to pry Arthur's fingers off the clurichaun's neck, to little effect.

To be perfectly honest, this doesn't seem to bother the little man much other than he can't look around. Instead, he spends the whole ride staring at me, an indecipherable look on his face.

"So, what do clurichauns do," I ask, "besides getting drunk? Do you, uh, have a job?"

I hear Percy chortle.

"Nibs has been allowed to roam free on the surface world," Arthur says.

"So long as it's around this lake," Percy adds.

Nibs throws a series of curses at their faces. "This is our world," the clurichaun barks. "We lived in it long before you and the rest of your bare-assed people decided to join in."

"I think we'll agree to disagree on that one," Percy says, looking bored. He smiles at me. "There's always some debate goin' on 'bout what happened after Creation."

"Needless to say, Nibs has one job," Arthur says, shaking the little man, "and that's to be our informant. We pay him good money for it too. Isn't that right, Nibs?"

The clurichaun doesn't answer, but keeps his gaze uncannily fixed on me.

"Have we, uh…have we met before?" I ask. I rack my brains, but can't ever remember seeing a clurichaun.

"Your mother would know," he says with a smirk.

Irene? Why would she know, when I was raised my whole life on the other side of the globe from her? Unless this was something that happened when I was still a baby…

"So are you a, uh, earth elemental?" I ask. "Like a gnome? Or are you a dwarf? Do you always carry a lot of gold on you? Maybe in your hat?"

Nibs slaps my hand away when I try to reach for his baseball hat. He sneers. "I'm not a leprechaun, you dumb bitch."

I stare at him, openmouthed. Not the kind of answer I had expected; that'll teach me to try to play nice.

"We're here," Percy says as Lance directs the skiff to the shore.

The island is quiet, with not a single light to guide us but the ones of the city we've left behind and the quarter moon above us. Every single hair on the back of my neck stands up; this place is too quiet.

Nibs, still held around the collar by Arthur, leads our way to a forbidding, dark shape ahead of us. A deserted house.

"This it, then?" Percy asks, his voice sounding inordinately loud in the still air.

"Y-Yes, sir," says the clurichaun. "And another, f-further down."

"What are we doing here?" I ask them. There's something about the place that makes me want to turn around and swim back to the other shore.

"You're coming with us," Arthur tells Nibs, who's trying to pull away.

The clurichaun whimpers. We set out at a steady, but careful pace. Any minute now I expect to see something jump out of the shadows at us. Lance, beside me, has his knife out again, the blade gleaming in the dim moonlight. I wish I had a knife too, or a fork, or anything sharp.

Shaking, the clurichaun climbs up the steps to the porch, swallows audibly, then pushes the door open.

I hear a little *pop* behind me and nearly freak out, but a second later, the glow of a salamander encircles us, getting brighter and brighter until we can see inside the house like it's daylight.

"Wish you'd done that sooner," I tell Percy.

He grins at me. "Where would the fun be in that?"

"Be quiet, you two," Arthur growls.

The house looks like any other, rugs covering the parts of the floor where the scuffs and marks are heaviest, a set of worn-out but clean couches angled before a fireplace, books and magazines covering the coffee table.

It's not till we arrive in the kitchen that my heart does a somersault. On the table is a full meal, the chicken congealed in its dish, the soup moldy in the bowls. Whoever lived here never had a chance to touch their food. Either these people had to flee without getting a chance to pack anything, or they'd vanished in thin air. And despite how unlikely the latter may be, judging from the serene order reigning in the house, it looks the most plausible.

"I thought it was a couple of hikers that disappeared," I say.

"Yep," Percy says, opening cabinet doors, then shutting them closed again.

"So why are we here?"

"'Cause these here folks have gone too. We're just checkin' if the two are related somehow."

"Maybe they heard about the first disappearance, so they got scared and left," I venture.

"Perhaps. 'Cept we found one of the bodies this morn, and the other two are still missin'."

He doesn't expand further, and I'm suddenly too scared to ask.

"Looks like another kidnapping," Lance says, coming back from checking out the floor upstairs.

Arthur nods. "Fey or human, though, that's what we need to figure out now."

Next to the window, sitting beside a small water jug, rests a small rosebush. Its petals have withered and fallen around its now-black stem, and its leaves, curled up on themselves, look to be about to go the same route. Frowning, I reach out to the fragile plant. This is exactly the same kind of disease that had overtaken our arboretum back at Notre-Dame.

"Don't touch anything!" Arthur barks.

I pull my hand away as if I've been stung and look at him accusingly. As if I needed to be scared more than I already am.

"You don't know what could be poisonous or not," he says. He pushes Nibs in front of him. "Are you sure you don't know more than this?"

Head downcast, the clurichaun doesn't answer.

Arthur shakes him so hard his head bobs up and down and he loses his hat. "I know you were here," he says. "Kaede reported seeing you swim back the night these people disappeared, and we all know how much you hate water. So tell me. What. You. Saw!"

"N-N-Nothing..." Nibs squeaks out. "Much," he adds under his breath.

"Well, explain what you did see."

Looking defiant, the little man clamps his mouth shut. Arthur pulls out a dagger from inside his coat. He grabs the clurichaun's arm, pulls up his sleeve, and presses the tip of the blade to Nibs's bare skin. There's a sharp hiss and a slight smell of something burning, like feathers.

The little man growls, tries to pull away, in obvious pain. Sweat drops down his forehead like fat dollar coins.

Arthur cuts a small line down his forearm, and blood pools around the injury like a scarlet rictus.

"What are you doing?" I ask, jumping to stop Arthur. But Lance extends his arm to prevent me from getting any closer and shakes his head.

I watch, in horror, as Arthur draws his blade down the little man's arm.

"Either you tell me," he says, "or I shall remove your ogham."

Nibs swallows heavily. "Just...just one person," he finally says, his voice shaking more than ever. "Too dark to tell who. He's the one who took them."

"Where did he take them?"

"Nowhere," Nibs says.

Arthur presses his blade down even harder, and I notice a strange yellow object poking out slightly from the wound. Nibs cries out.

"Please, sir, I'm not telling lies! He left without taking anything with him."

"So you saw him leave then?"

Nibs nods eagerly.

"How?"

"B-By the waters."

"He had a boat?"

"N-No, someone came to fetch him." Nibs tries to pull away, but the more he does so, the more that yellow thing's coming out of his arm, and I soon realize it's his ogham.

"Who came to fetch him?" Arthur asks, relentless.

"Please, sir, you're hurting me..." the clurichaun whimpers.

"I asked who?" Arthur repeats, pulling his knife away without letting the little man go.

The clurichaun, seeing that the immediate threat of the blade is somewhat alleviated, thrashes about like a fish caught on a line. He bites Arthur on the arm, hard. Arthur lets out a slew of curses, brings down his other hand to hold Nibs down. Then, with a sickening *plop*, the ogham slides out of the little man's arm and bounces on the tile floor.

Nibs yells as if he's been stabbed to the heart, holding his arm close to his body. The whole house shakes beneath us as his yells turn into a high-pitched howl.

"Criminy!" Percy yells over the racket. "Get the thing to shut it!"

Arthur picks up the fallen ogham, pulls a small metal box out of his coat pocket, and slips the golden gem inside.

The moment he shuts the lid, Nibs drops to the floor like a dead spider.

"Did you just kill him?" I ask, stricken.

"No, he's just in shock," Arthur says, looking grim.

"Can't we..." I breathe in deeply to stop myself from crying. "Can't we just put it back in?"

Percy shakes his head. "It's a whole lot easier to let the cat outta the bag than get it back in."

Which I take to mean that once Fey lose their sources of power, it's nigh on impossible for us to get them to reconnect. Either that or we don't want them to.

"But he helped us," I whisper, still staring at the short man curled up on the floor.

"He lied to us," Arthur says, putting the little metallic bag back inside his pocket. "And people are dead."

"I thought Fey people couldn't lie!"

"They can twist the truth, which is just as bad."

Arthur heaves a sigh. "Come on, let's go check out the other place before we go home."

"What about Nibs?" I ask, indignant. How could they treat him like that, take what's most precious to him, then leave him like he's nothing more than a pile of dung?

"He's trapped," Arthur says without looking at the clurichaun. "He can't go anywhere while we have his ogham."

All three of them head back to the front door, arguing with each other about how well the Board's going to take the loss of one of their best informants.

I pretend to follow them, but hang back instead. I crouch over Nibs and pat his back. I pull my hand away quickly. His whole body's below freezing temperature, his skin showing a thin layer of frost.

"Nibs, are you all right?" I ask, my breath fogging in the air. "Do you need anything? Is there something I can do?"

But the little man either can't speak or doesn't want to.

My eyes water, and I sniffle. "I'm really sorry about what happened," I say. I take off my jacket and place it on his inert body. "I'm really sorry."

The dim glow of Percy's fire elemental dies out, leaving me in near-total darkness. Only the faint moonlight bleeding in through the kitchen door remains, delineating the black rosebush sitting like a vulture on the windowsill.

Feeling sick, I hurry outside, drop to my knees, then retch the little food I've ingested during the day. When the spasms subside, I take in deep lungfuls of the crispy night air, then pause.

I pass my hand over the grass, feeling its coarse brittleness under my gentle touch, and my stomach does another flip. Whatever disease has attacked the rose plant has also spread outside.

Walking with my nose close to the ground, I make my way farther and farther down the yard. Dried leaves crunch under my footsteps as I walk over the garden. The virus hasn't left an easy trail, jumping about from one point to another, often forcing me to backtrack and examine multiple trees and bushes before finding more evidence of its nefarious results.

Despite the obscurity, traces of the scourge lead me to a secluded area, surrounded by tall trees on one side and water on the other. Standing like guards before the shore are four large stones, like the warding stone I saw when I met Lady Vivian. Scanning my surroundings, I find a fifth boulder standing erect a few yards away, black and foreboding.

I stop at the edge of the clearing, remembering Jack's words, and shiver. Something here feels very wrong.

"Morgan! Morgan!"

The cry comes from behind me, back toward the house. The boys have finally noticed my subterfuge, and if I weren't totally creeped out by now, I'd be thrilled at the prospect of scaring Arthur. Instead, I start back up the way I came, running as fast as possible. I want to get off this island, and I want to get off *now*.

I trip and come crashing into Lance's extended arms.

"Whoa there," says Percy, "hold yer horses."

"Where the hell were you?" Arthur asks.

Lance helps me get my balance back before letting go of me.

"By the shore," I say.

"Where is it?" he asks, looking at my feet like they could be hiding something.

"Where is what?" I ask, not appreciating his sharp tone. Another foot closer and I'm going to kick him in the mouth, see if a few missing teeth aren't going to bring his ego down to mortal level.

"The clurichaun!" Arthur says, shaking my jacket in my face.

I raise my eyebrows. "Isn't he in the house?"

"Obviously not. We thought you took him!"

I shake my head. "He was cold, so I gave him my coat, but then I left him in the kitchen. You mean he's gone?"

Arthur looks at me with an air of disgust. Percy laughs next to me.

"You gave him your coat?" His laugh grows louder. "Mercy, but I've 'eard 'em all."

"What now?" I ask, tired of being treated like the village idiot.

"You do realize our uniform's got metal weaved in its threads?" Percy asks before exploding in laughter once more.

It dawns on me then that, while I wanted to help Nibs, I probably only increased his pain by putting my iron-meshed jacket on him; I might as well have finished him. A good thing he escaped instead, unless...

"You-You don't think that whatever's taken those people away got him too, do you?" I ask, my eyes darting about like a pinball.

"It's a possibility," Arthur says grimly.

"You know," I say in a failed attempt at sounding debonair, "I'm famished. Could we stop for some food on the way home?"

It's the cue for everyone to head back to the little boat, still waiting where we anchored it.

The ride back to the mainland seems longer somehow, and much more quiet, the lack of Nibs's presence weighing down on our shoulders like Christ's cross.

Chapter 14

"Give me the keys, Morgan," Arthur says with a resigned tone. "You stole Irene's car and don't even have a driver's license. This is not going to be pretty when we get back."

"I didn't steal it," I say, handing him the keys nonetheless. "I... borrowed it."

Arthur doesn't reply and gets in. I hurry into the passenger side, afraid he may leave me stranded as a form of punishment. I wouldn't be surprised if he made me walk thirty miles at night.

"Seat belt," he says, turning the engine on.

We arrive home past midnight. Casting furtive glances around in case Irene may be lurking about, waiting for me, I get back inside the house. But the place is deserted, except for Ella, who can be heard moving around in her kitchen downstairs.

I let out my breath, which I hadn't realized I'd been holding.

"Guess you're lucky," Arthur says, shutting the door. "Irene and Luther are out."

"I noticed, thanks." But I grin despite myself. "Are they often gone like this?"

Gingerly, Arthur shrugs out of his coat. "Mostly. They're in charge of the Americas, so it keeps them rather busy."

"What do you mean, in charge?" I ask, hoping Ella's got some sandwiches ready.

"The Fey don't remain in only one spot, Morgan, and a number of them live in the surface world. They need to be kept in line which means we have to constantly watch over what they do." He cocks his eyebrow. "Haven't you been paying attention in your lore class?"

I scowl at him.

"You should," Arthur says. "If you had, you would have learned that, back in antiquity, Fey people lived in broad daylight. Due to their powers, they were able to subjugate humans, and often used them as pawns in their power plays. And *that* is why we have to defend ourselves, unless we want to become slaves to them once again."

"Yes, yes, I know all about Carman and stuff," I say.

"It's not just her, Morgan," he says, looking tired. "They all did it. They all liked to play God."

He turns away from me and heads up the stairs, his arm held tight against his chest. I grab on to his shirt to hold him back.

"You're bleeding!" I cry.

He tries to shield his arm away from my prying eyes, but it's too late, I've seen the blood dripping freely down his hand, soaking up his shirtsleeve. How could I have not noticed it sooner?

"You're getting it all over the rug," I add before he can deny it.

"I'm fine," he says, "just a bite." He rushes up the stairs, and a moment later, I hear his bedroom door close.

Stomach grumbling, I hurry to the kitchen to pilfer some food. Ella, like a fairy godmother, has left two plates of cold pasta and chicken on the counter for us. I silently thank her, then rummage through the drawers and cupboards until I find the emergency kit.

Then, grabbing the two trays as well, I make my way to Arthur's room.

"Coming through," I say, managing to push his door open without spilling or dropping anything. "Aaaand you're half naked." I turn around and close my eyes. "So, so sorry. I...That is your flesh...wound...blood..." Saint George's balls, my brain's just been liquefied.

Arthur grabs the emergency kit from under my arm, and I dare to open my eyes again. He's thankfully managed to finish changing into his pajamas, but from the towel around his hand, I can tell the shower hasn't helped.

"You may need a couple of stitches," I say, trying to cover up my earlier embarrassment.

He rummages through the box and pulls out some disinfectant and bandages. When he removes the towel from his hand, I pull back in revulsion. His wound's turned a virulent red, and tiny bubbles of pus have already gathered around the edges of the bite.

"That's nasty," I say. "You sure that leprechaun didn't have rabies?"

"I'm sure," he says, his hands shaking while he unwraps the bandage.

"Here, let me help you." I grab the packet from him before he can drop it, and sit down on the bed next to him.

Gently, I take his hand in mine. His skin is cold and clammy to the touch, but the flush of fever is creeping into his cheeks. I prod his forearm, then his hand, testing the swelling.

"You, uh, you sure this guy didn't inject you with venom?" I ask.

"Maybe," he says, breathing heavily. He pulls away. "I'm OK, let me do it."

"Shut up," I say, trying to think.

I have no idea what to do against Fey poisoning. I would take him to a hospital if I didn't know they'd be as helpless as I. The only thing I've ever treated that was remotely similar was a viper bite when one of the girls got bitten during a hike in the Alps, and that was under the direction of Sister Marie-Bénédicte's careful instructions.

I swallow hard; I know I have a mixture of the antivenom in my mini-pharmacopoeia in the fridge downstairs…

Carefully, I help Arthur recline against the bed's headboard, noticing the dilation of his pupils. I bite my lip. "I'll be right back."

"I'm fine," he mumbles.

I run as fast as I can back to the kitchen, tripping over the last few steps nearly splitting my chin on the railing. It doesn't take me long to spot the small container, tucked on a back shelf. I grab it, and within a split second, I'm back upstairs.

"Time for some medicine," I say. "Give me your hand."

"I said I was fine," Arthur says.

"Please, you may play president all you want at school, but up here, I've got big sister prerogatives. Your hand."

Without another word, Arthur does as he's told. His hand has nearly doubled in size since I went down to get my unguent. I open the container and apply a generous layer of the paste onto the injury.

"What is that?" Arthur asks, crinkling up his nose in disgust.

"Herbs," I say, "mostly Calotropis and Gynura, with a mix of other stuff. It's an antivenom mixture. Just pray it works on Fey bites too."

Up close, I can see his hand's covered in tiny scars, pale against the honeyed color of his skin. I feel him staring at me as I take a clean compress, apply it to the bite, then wrap his hand with gauze. By the time I'm done, my heart is going at a thousand beats per minute.

"That should do it," I say, placing the last piece of tape to hold everything together. "But, uh, you should probably go see a doctor."

For some reason, I can't get myself to look into his eyes. I gather everything back into the box and get up in a hurry.

"Thank you," Arthur says.

"Sure," I say, still not looking at him. Before I leave his room, I pause. "Do you know where he might have gone?"

"You worried about Nibs?" Arthur asks.

"Y-Yeah."

Arthur throws me a look like I've just lost my mind. He raises the bandaged hand. "You've seen what he can do, and you're still worried about him?"

"It's not like you didn't deserve it," I mumble.

Arthur tries to straighten up and fails. "What?"

"Well, you were mean to him, and cut him up first." I point an accusing finger at him. "You can't blame him for defending himself, just like you can't blame a bee for stinging you when you've swatted at it."

"This is hardly a bee sting!" Arthur says, furious.

"Well, stealing his ogham is worse. You nearly killed him!" It's my turn to yell. "In fact, who says you didn't? None of us know where he disappeared to!"

"I can't believe this," Arthur says, outraged. "Haven't you seen enough? Your friend Owen's in the mental ward, along with a couple dozen more, I nearly lost my hand, and every day people disappear around the world because of them. And yet you pity him?"

"Exactly!" I know I've just treated his injury, but I'd throw my tray at his face if I weren't so famished. "What has he ever done that was really bad, apart from biting you tonight? You can't condemn a whole race, or people, or whatever you call them, because some individuals are rotten. Would you want to destroy all of humanity because a few happen to be scumbags?"

Arthur glares at me, fuming.

"I didn't think so," I finish.

I slam the door behind me before Arthur can say anything else, and storm off to my room.

I must be graced by my guardian angel, because the next day I don't see either Arthur or Irene, so I get to spend my Sunday in peace. I don't even see Arthur on Monday morning, when it's time to head back to school.

When Dean leaves me at the docking station, I go find Bri and Jack, already soaked through by the pouring rain.

"How was the weekend?" Jack asks me.

I shrug, thinking back on my private lesson with Arthur, the stolen car, the pervert at the bar, the creepy island, then the clurichaun's potential death. I don't even want to think about my spat with Arthur.

"Nothing special," I say. "I'm just glad it's over."

"Oh, I don't know," Keva says, joining us by the docking site. "I don't think my skin's getting enough vitamin D down there. It's giving me an awful tint."

"Not like you're going to get much of it in this weather," Bri points out.

"Freshmen, get ready!" comes Sir Boris's resounding voice as the longboat nears us in complete silence.

We've just sat down when Percy appears beside the teacher and talks to him in private. When he's done, Sir Boris looks straight at me, filling me with dread.

"Miss Pendragon and Miss Vaughan, come to the front."

Bri and I look at each other, but neither of us knows what's going on. If it had just been me, I'd have had a thousand possible explanations, but with my friend involved...I just don't have a clue.

"Yes, sir?" I ask when we get to the prow.

The bald man nods to Percy. "KORT business, hop out!"

Percy bows to us and helps us back to shore. "Ladies, if you please."

"What are you doing?" I whisper to him. "Why can't we go to class?"

"But you can," he says. "Just after a small detour, president's orders."

"A detour?" Bri asks. "Have we been summoned by KORT?"

Percy smiles at her, and, despite the lack of light, I can see her blush furiously. "To see a very special someone," he says.

My mouth runs dry. "If you mean Arthur," I say, "then it's really not worth it."

"Not Arthur," Percy says, grabbing a hold of both Bri and me. "Now 'old your breath!"

A brilliant green orb surrounds us, and then an invisible force projects us deep into the waters of Lake Winnebago at the speed of a bullet train, through to the other side above Lake High. I feel nauseous, and the moment we land, my legs buckle underneath me.

"It weren't so bad now, was it?" Percy asks, clapping my back.

"Let's not do this again," I say, feeling the ground beneath me roll up and down like the sea.

"Ah, you'll get used to it."

"Why are we here?" Bri's voice is cold.

I look up to find that we're standing in front of the asylum. Surely Arthur didn't want me locked up here, did he?

"We wanted to go see Owen," Percy says, all mirth gone from his eyes. "But we needed your approval first."

Bri lets out a long breath. "Why?"

"The lady here apparently needs some convincin'."

It's my turn to redden. Bri's staring at me, waiting for an explanation, but there's no way I'm going to tell her what I told Arthur on Saturday.

Bri finally relents. "Fine," she says. "Just...don't get him excited."

"We'll be careful," Percy says in a serious tone I've never heard him take before.

I try not to think of Bri's worried look as we trail Percy past the lobby, where the same man from my first visit still stands. Except this time, with Percy around, he doesn't make a fuss about there being more than the allowed two visitors.

"If you could divest yourselves of your trinkets," the man says in a bored tone.

"He means our Fey implements," Percy says. "Ya don't have to worry 'bout that yet."

He takes off his sword, belt, a dagger hidden in his boot, his vambraces, and finally a single emerald stud from his ear.

"Are you sure you got everything?" the man asks.

Percy nods with a smile, and the man leads us farther inside the complex, down the now-familiar dark corridors.

"Why are they making you take all of that off?" I whisper in Percy's ear.

"Nothin' Fey is allowed to come in," he says. "It's too dangerous."

We turn around a corner into the common room, where I immediately spot Myrdwinn sitting cross-legged on the floor, playing with what appears to be a set of runes.

The school director spots us as we make our way across to the other side.

"You're back in here, huh?" I ask him with a smile.

"Eeeh, I can get in and out when I want," the old man says, waving his hand dismissively. "I know all the ins and outs of this place."

He peers at me more intently; then his face lights up. "I know you!" he says delightedly. He runs over to me, his long beard trailing behind him. "Have you come for the pie? The taste *du jour*[17] is apple, my favorite!"

I blink. "Uh, no. We wouldn't want to deprive you. We came for a visit."

"A visit?" Myrdwinn claps his hands together. "How delightful. I've been longing for visitors."

"No, we didn't—"

But the old man doesn't let me finish and steers me instead toward the rest of the patients assembled there.

"I've been preparing a little something just for such an occasion," he confides. "You're going to love it!"

"I don't think—"

"It's music of the purest kind," Myrdwinn says, closing his eyes like he can hear it already. "It could make the angels weep."

He grabs a chair and stands up on it, then throws his hands up in the air to get everyone's attention. His lack of success doesn't seem to deter him, however, and he starts beating the measure with vigorous sweeps of his arms.

I don't know whether the patients are truly listening to him, or whether it's something else that's risen them out of their stupor, but some of them start to move back and forth, more and more violently, moaning and chanting incantations in a language I've never heard.

"Isn't this wonderful?" Myrdwinn cries from his perch, laughing like a maniac. "Cows would produce much better milk with this kind of music instead of listening to Mozart!"

17 Of the day.

A bald man stands up, screaming, tearing at his face like he wants to rip it off.

A couple of nurses rush in to quell the commotion.

"But we've just started!" Myrdwinn protests. "I was making art!"

"Shall we?" our guide asks, displeased at having been detained for so long.

He takes us down another hallway, and we end up in front a plain door with the number twenty-seven painted on it.

"Just a reminder to keep quiet," the man says. "You wouldn't want to disturb the other patients."

"Of course," Percy says.

We let Bri open the door to her brother's room and follow her inside.

The chamber is small, and dimly lit by a tiny candle in a corner. Sitting straight on the small bed is Owen, his gaze vacant.

Bri leans in to kiss him on the cheek. She murmurs something in his ear, brushes his greasy hair out of his face, then busies herself rearranging his pillow and covers. When she's satisfied he's as comfortable as he can possibly be, Bri moves away from Owen and looks at Percy and me expectantly.

"We've tried to make him eat," she says, her lower lip trembling, "but he won't take anything."

I can't bring myself to say anything; my throat's too constricted. To think that, just a few weeks ago, Owen was full of life and excitement. And now he's stuck in this depressing place, wasting away while his twin tries her best to get him well again.

I bite the inside of my cheek to stop myself from crying. I know very well why Arthur's sent me here now, the devious little bastard. He didn't like losing his argument, and now he's decided to torture me. And it's working.

"I need to get out," I say, bolting out of the room before I break down.

"Not the most pleasant place on Earth," Percy says when he catches up with me. "Never liked it much growin' up, and it hasn't changed since."

In the front hall, he proceeds to put his gear back on.

"You...you've been here before?" I ask. I can't imagine Percy ever being locked up here. He's got too much life and energy in him.

"Knew people who were," he says, buckling his sword belt back on. "Shall we?"

I look back. "What about Bri?"

"She's gonna stay a little longer."

Despite the building's thick walls, I hear the church bells calling us for morning Mass.

"Makes you wonder what they're thinkin' 'bout," he says as we cross the lawn toward the church.

"What do you mean?" All I can see is Owen's vacant stare, his body as lifeless as that of a puppet.

Percy sweeps his arm back to encompass the whole asylum behind us. "What is it that the Fey have shown 'em that they've ended up like this, haunted for the rest of their lives? It's like a spell that can't be lifted. Sometimes, I wonder if I were to get caught...maybe then I'd see what it's like, and if there's ever a respite in the constant hell they live in."

My footsteps falter, and I watch Percy's back as he strides toward his friends, his words trotting in my head. I don't know what's going on with Owen or anyone else in the asylum, and I wonder if their fates are worse than being killed like Agnès was. Or my father.

And for the first time since I've arrived, I wonder if that means Arthur is right and we can't survive unless we destroy all the Fey.

CHAPTER 15

"What was that all about?" Keva asks me as I join her and Jack in the Freshmen pews.

"I don't want to talk about it," I answer back, shifting uncomfortably on the bench.

"Come on, you can tell me," she says, wheedling.

But no matter how much she prods, pleads, or threatens me, I keep my mouth shut. Owen's plight is not mine to discuss.

"Fine, be that way," she retorts. "But instead, I want you to keep Puck away from our room, and especially away from my clothes, jewelry, and makeup. Besides, not seeing his ugly face first thing in the morning will be a great improvement for me."

"Sure," I say, distracted.

Across the rows, on the benches reserved for KORT, sits Arthur, a head taller than most, except for Lance and the cousins Gareth and Gauvain. He stares straight ahead, focused on Father Tristan and his preaching, the model student. Only once does he look in my direction, a quick flick of the eyes that tells me he knows he's won our argument and the little shite doesn't have the good grace to hide how much he relishes it.

I take a deep breath. I shouldn't let Arthur get to me like this, but no matter how hard I try, I can't help but foster thoughts of punching his smug face, a very unholy thought to entertain considering we're in church.

"And this I say to you," Father Tristan says, looking up from his pulpit, "be strong and courageous. Do not fear or be in dread of the devil's disciples, for it is the Lord your God who goes with you. He will not leave you or forsake you. May the Lord be with you."

"And also with you," we all say in unison.

"Bow your heads and pray for God's blessing," the priest continues, raising his hands over the assembly. "May the Almighty God bless you, by the Father, and the Son, and the Holy Spirit."

"Amen," I whisper, crossing myself before standing up.

"Go in peace."

It is the signal, and everyone does their best to hurry out while appearing not too eager to leave church. I, on the other hand, have no compunction about it, and manage to get outside before the rest of the crowd. A good dose of fresh air is all I need to stop my head from exploding.

Before I can get very far, however, I hear someone call me.

"Arthur, how delightful to see you," I say, not delighted at all.

A few feet behind him are Lance, Percy, and Jennifer. The latter throws me a furious look, and I give her a cheery wave in return.

"What is it?" I ask Arthur. "I don't want to be late for class."

"You won't be late for class, but you might miss breakfast."

"On your account? I don't think so."

I cut across the lawn to get away as quickly as possible without looking like I'm running away from him; which proves impossible.

"So?" Arthur asks, keeping pace with me.

"So what?"

"Did you see him?"

"Of course I did." I open the north door to the school building just wide enough for me to slip inside.

A moment later he's next to me again, and I wonder who he's gotten this annoyingly stubborn side from, because there's no way I exhibit the same genetic trait.

"What do you think now?"

"What do I think?" I ask, practically spitting in his face. "What do you think? This isn't a game, Arthur! Of course I feel horrible seeing what happened to Owen and to all the others, whether they're in there because of Fey encounters or something else. I wish I could do something about it. But that's what you wanted, right? So what? You want me to thank you for opening my eyes, is that it?"

I notice people staring at us, and I lower my voice. "But I'm not taking back what I said before. I still don't think it's fair to hunt every one of them down because it happens that some of them did...whatever it is they've done to us. That's not justice, Arthur. That's being a sociopath."

Arthur's brows lower. "You said you wanted to help them," he says, "but how can we help them if they remain under this spell put on their eyes by those creatures? And how can we protect the innocent from the Fey's devious and evil clutches? You don't know what they're capable of. Being sent to the asylum is the least of it! What about those who are kidnapped from their families, huh? What about those who are turned into monstrous hybrids so that no one, not even their own family, wants to come near them? What about those who, for the pleasure of some egotistical Fey, have been turned into trees or rocks? Have you asked them how *they* feel about the whole situation?"

Arthur takes another step toward me and jabs me with his finger. "I know it's not a game, Morgan. Lives are at stake, those of the laypeople, and ours! But what else can we do? We don't have their powers or abilities. Would you have us all turn ourselves over to be toyed with as they wish?" He jabs me again. "You say that some of them are innocent. And perhaps you're right. But have you ever stopped to consider that maybe, just maybe, they are laying low only because they're afraid that if they get caught abusing a human, we may punish them for their wrongdoing?"

I balk at the horrible image Arthur's painting. "I didn't know," I whisper.

"Of course you didn't know," he says, "which is why I sent you to see your friend. But instead, you thought to take offense." He moves away, eyeing me like it's the first time he's truly seen me. "I thought you had more sense than that, but I see they were right to put you with the freshmen."

And with those lovely parting words, he stalks off. And I get to feel very, very stupid. Especially when I realize a slew of people are still gawking at me, whispering behind their hands about what's just happened.

"Of course she wouldn't understand," Jennifer says with a smirk as she struts by me with her cohort of fans. "She's never had friends to call her own, or family who cared about her, so she wouldn't understand the pain of losing someone dear." She throws a long sideways glance in my direction. "But it doesn't mean that we have to cater to her emotional retardation."

Fists clenched, I stare at the flock of girls and boys as it cackles away around a corner.

"Just because I've lived most of my life apart from people doesn't mean I don't feel," I say under my breath.

"What have you done?"

A heavy arm lands around my shoulders, and I find myself looking up into Gauvain's dark face. He flashes me his lightning-white smile, but his good mood doesn't reach me.

"Getting Arthur angry, you mean?"

Gauvain nods energetically. "That's exactly what I mean, *chérie*.[18] I've never seen him lose his temper like that before."

Which makes my already low spirits drop a few more levels. This is just great. Not only have I made a scene, but on top of that, it's apparently a first with the head of KORT. Just what I needed, another reason to have people talk about me behind my back.

"How did you do it?" Gareth asks, towering on my other side.

I almost get a crick in the neck staring up at them, too confused to bother with an answer.

"You see, we've been trying for ages to get him to show a bite more emotion," Gareth says, his French accent thick. "But the most we ever got was cleaning duty."

"It's 'bit,' not 'bite,'" Gauvain says.

"It's the same thing, what does it matter?" Gauvain says before returning to me. "With you, he's not recognizable. He acts like..."

"A human being," they both say at the same time.

I shrug Gauvain's arm off. "I don't know what I've done, and I don't know why you'd want to get Arthur angry. It's really not very pleasant."

"You're our idol," Gauvain says to my back as I hurry to class.

"Our hero!" Gareth shouts.

"Our goddess!" Gauvain adds even louder.

I shut the door to the staircase behind me and welcome the blissful silence. Everyone is in the dining hall, I know, but I'd rather skip a meal than have to deal with more unwanted drama.

18 Darling.

Apart from a few stray comments and looks directed at me, the morning passes by without incident until we get to Sir Boris's class.

"Did you see the news board today?" Keva asks as she edges toward us while we're waiting for the teacher to arrive. "They finally named the three who are to be knighted."

"Yeah, we saw," Bri says, sounding tense. "Big deal."

"Her brother's gonna try for a position at KORT," Jack explains.

"Owen's out of the asylum?" Keva asks.

"Not Owen," I mutter, "Hadrian, her older brother."

"Oh." Keva seems to consider that for a moment, then says, "I hope he makes it. Then I'll be close to the sisters of *two* KORT members!"

"Miss Pendragon?" Sir Boris calls out the moment he walks in. "A moment, please."

I feel myself turn bright pink at being singled out. Everyone knows trouble's a-brewing when he focuses his attention on someone. I so wish the earth had opened up and swallowed me this morning. Not even Hell can be this tedious.

"Yes, sir?" I say.

He grabs a pile of papers, and I realize with dread that it's my series of late homework, already graded. He shuffles through them, as if he needs a reminder of the poor job I've done.

"You did quite well, considering you're new to this environment."

I look up from my boots in surprise. "Sir?"

"I wouldn't quite agree with you that goblins are such weak creatures," he says, handing me the whole stack. "You can't take Puck as a model of study. He's been domesticated for far too long. But otherwise, your work is thus far exemplary. Keep working like that, and you may move up through the ranks a lot quicker than you might expect."

I beam at him, thinking for the first time in my life how adorable and cuddly Sir Boris truly is. Refraining from hugging him, I get back to my seat.

"What did he want?" Bri asks.

"He's graded my homework," I say, staring at my papers like they're great works of wonder. "And he didn't fail me."

"Well, that's good then," she says, noting the red A marked on the top sheet. "Might shut Keva up for a while. I don't think she's ever gotten higher than a B plus."

We both grin at each other until Sir Boris calls us to attention and we are required to learn about the Alp-Luachra, a fairy that likes to burrow not in the ground or in trees, but inside people's bodies to eat them from the inside out. A most appetizing prospect right before lunchtime.

"I want everyone to write an essay on how to prevent getting infested with these Fey, and how they interact with their environment," Sir Boris says once the bells go off.

"A good thing he hasn't brought one of those gross creatures with him this time," Keva says on our way to the dining hall. "Can you imagine the ruckus this would have caused?" She shudders, holding on to her face without disturbing her impeccable makeup.

"You mean he brings Fey creatures in here?" I ask, trying to picture Sir Boris with a troll on a leash.

"Oh, sure he does," Jack says. "Which is really cool, because usually we only see them once they've lost their form and all that remains is their ogham."

"But he brings them *live*," Keva says.

"Do you remember the time Kaede's grandma came over for a visit during the first week?" Jack asks.

Bri lights up. "Yeah, she'd brought a kijimuna with her."

"A kiwi-what?" I ask.

"Kijimuna," Bri repeats. "They're these little fairies that live in the woods, usually found around Japan. Big heads, tiny bodies, and red hair everywhere. They were adorable!"

"They tied Sir Boris's mustache ends together," Keva says, "kicked him in the crotch, and jumped on the chandelier. They were caught only when the thing crashed down on K's grandma."

"Was she all right?"

"Oh yes," she says dismissively. "She had a bunch of protective charms on."

"Miss Pendragon?"

A young servant is standing before us, tall and spindly, his long hair pulled into a low ponytail. He hands me a letter before disappearing again in the mob of students.

"Uh-oh, someone's been summoned," Keva says with a smirk. "What did you do this time?"

"Nothing," I say, tearing the envelope open.

"It's from the medical wing," Bri says, reading from under my elbow.

Dear Miss Pendragon,

It has been brought to my attention that you may have the necessary qualities to be of help here at the infirmary.

Please see me at your earliest convenience after practice session.

Dr. Daphne Cockleburr

"Qualities?" Keva says, sounding skeptical. "You mean as a lab rat?"

"Still a better prospect than cleaning bathrooms," I quip.

Keva raises her hands. "Tough call."

Whack! I curl up in a ball, holding my head with both hands, trying not to cry like a baby in front of the fifteen-year-old boy. Today's class is sword training, which means I actually get to practice with the others for once—which made me very happy until I found out who I'd be partnering up with.

Daniel crows over me, triumphant. "You have to do my math homework now, Troll Feet," he says, pointing his wooden sword at me. "A bet's a bet, don't forget!"

I scowl up at him, but he seems unaffected as he swaggers about the training area, high-fiving Ross and Brockton.

"Up, Miss Pendragon," Sir Ywain, our weapons master, says. "In a battle, there is no time for dillydallying. Make sure your stance is proper so that your forte's always defending the line between you and the tip of your opponent's sword. And fix that grip of yours."

"As for you, Mr. von Blumenthal," he adds, wiping the smile off my partner's face, "you know very well our practice is scholar's privilege style, which means no attacks to the face."

Elias gets smacked farther down the field and lets out a loud yelp. The teacher runs off.

Muttering to myself, I get back to my feet and grab my practice sword.

"You done gloating?" I ask, angling the sword up, my right foot forward.

"I'm ready to teach you a lesson any time of day," Daniel answers, blowing on the strands of hair falling in his eyes.

Quick as a snake, he surges toward me, deflects my blow, feints, then hits me behind the legs. I drop to my knees as he comes back on my other side. He cracks his sword down on my arm and points it to my exposed neck. All in less than thirty seconds.

Panting, I hold my arm, still ringing from the blow like a tuning fork.

"Do you surrender?" Daniel asks.

"What do you think?" I say, using his sword to pull myself up and nearly bringing him down.

With a smirk, he stalks off to Ross and Brockton, who are still practicing a few paces away.

"That taught her good," Brockton says as he parries Ross's blow.

"I don't think anything can get into her thick skull," Daniel says. "My bet is, she's never gonna learn."

"At least you gave her a good spanking," Ross says. "She deserves it for giving our class a bad rep."

Pretending not to hear them, I gather up my gear and return it to the armory. I wouldn't be causing such trouble if people left me alone, people like Arthur and that stupid girlfriend of his. They should just get married so they can leave on their honeymoon and give me some peace.

By the time I make my way to the infirmary, my arm is still tingling. The medical wing is brightly lit with salamander lamps like in the dorms. From a back room come the moans of an injured person, and the distinct sounds of someone throwing up.

"Hello?" I call out. "Is anybody here?" I look down at the note again. "Mrs. Cockleburr?"

A stocky woman waddles up to me from a side door, a pencil stuck in her auburn hair to prevent it from getting in the way.

"What is it?" she says. "Another practice injury?"

"I got a note to come see you," I say. "About helping?"

"Are you Morgan?"

I nod, hoping nothing will entail cleaning.

"Oh good. I heard from Linette, that is Professor Pelletier, that you've got rather a deft hand with herbs, and just this morning I heard you had a healing gift."

I feel like I've just been thwacked again. "I beg your pardon?"

Dr. Cockleburr frowns at me. "You did treat a clurichaun wound overnight, didn't you?"

"I put a salve on one," I say, cautious. "It was meant for snake-bites, but—"

"How interesting," she says, taking notes on a small pad. "You prepared it yourself?"

I swallow with difficulty. "Y-Yes." I look about me, wondering if Arthur's in one of these sickbeds. He looked fine this morning, but things can go bad quickly—I'm one to know.

"Is something wrong?" I ask.

"Not at all, not at all," the doctor says, still writing. "And you have experience preparing other solutions?"

"Yes, but it was always under supervision."

"Perfect." Dr. Cockleburr closes her notebook and slips it back in her lab coat pocket. "So here's the deal. You are to spend your botanics classes with me instead, and I've already talked with Ysolt regarding trading half your EM time to help me out here with the patients and the preparation of remedies, since you already have some experience with it."

"But I can't skip EM!" I say. "I've got so much to catch up on, and I can't afford to—"

"Tut, tut," she says, batting her hand in the air like she's trying to get rid of a noisome fly. "Not everyone's meant to be a knight, you know. It doesn't make them any less worthy."

I gape at her as she hands me my new schedule.

"We'll be going over the basics of plant medicine first," she continues. "Then you'll help me with patients. You start tomorrow. Questions?"

"But I—"

"Excellent. See you tomorrow then."

She shuts the door in my face and I remain staring at it, open-mouthed. Finally, the meaning dawns on me and my cheeks stretch wide: Arthur's recognized my skills, and that's why he recommended me! That's right, I *am* brilliant!

Chapter 16

"Aren't you lucky?" Keva says, not at all sounding pleased. "Get to skip this grueling training to parade in front of hot knights."

"I won't be parading," I say.

"Please," she says, "everyone knows that the ones who usually end up in the infirmary are knights. And since you won't have just worked out, you won't be all sweaty and disgusting either."

"It's true," Bri says, "since they actually go all out in their fights. Maybe you'll get to see your brother, though he hardly ever gets injured."

"I really wouldn't want that," I say under my breath as the girls head over to EM class and I to the mending hall.

But what's waiting for me there is not at all the easy and carefree fate that Keva was bemoaning me, but grueling work that makes me break out in a sweat within minutes.

"Put that jar of honey on the corner shelf," Dr. Cockleburr tells me as I lug about a massive pot that's twice the size of my head, and weighs as much as a whale. "Come on, girl, don't take so long. You need to take these used bandages to the cleaners afterwards."

I wipe my dripping forehead on my sleeve before grabbing the large basket of bloodied gauze and wraps, the pungent smell of rotting flesh rising from its depths. I throw a longing glance toward her office, where I can see an herbal encyclopedia open at a page showing plants I've never seen before—guess working with plants will come later. Holding the basket as far away from me as possible, I make my exit.

"And tell them the water needs to be boiling," Dr. Cockleburr says before turning to a knight's bloodied foot. "Pike wound, you said Johnny?"

I hurry to the back of the building to turn in my grisly burden and the doctor's instructions.

"What do you mean boil it?" the woman asks, her cheeks rosy from the overwhelming heat in the room. "We can't boil it more than we already do."

"I'm just reporting what she said," I say, eager not to get in the middle of another argument. To my greatest relief, the woman snatches the fetid load from me and hands me a fresh, clean-smelling batch of bandages without another word.

"Maybe if we were allowed the use of salamanders like we used to, this wouldn't be an issue," I hear her mutter on my way out.

As I make my way around the building, I'm drawn to one of the bay windows where I can see the other students' training session. Flashes of colors burst over the field as different elementals are called upon, brightening up the darkening sky-lake. How much longer till I get to practice with them, or am I forever doomed to be no better than a cleaning girl?

With a sigh, I leave my vantage point and retrace my steps back to the infirmary. Before I even open the door, I can hear the loud roar of shouting voices. I push the door open to find half the senior year crammed into the room, going off about some accident.

I set my basket down on a chair, then squeeze past the crowd to the surgical quarters.

"And then the undine's ogham must've run out," a boy with spiky blond hair says.

The girl next to him adds, "Maybe he didn't recharge it properly."

"A knight of the round table wouldn't make such a basic mistake," another girl says. "Someone sabotaged him."

"And he wouldn't have noticed that, would he?" the blond guy snorts.

I find Dr. Cockleburr and a nurse attending a boy whose leg is open from the thigh all the way down to his ankle, part of his femur poking out of the deep wound.

I gag and turn away to avoid throwing up on the patient, but the doctor sees me and calls me over. "Morgan, where have you been? I need you to go see the boy in the consultation room. I think he's suffered a light concussion. Hurry!"

I stagger to the office, a small, windowless room with yellow walls. Sitting on the table, looking rather pale, is none other than Percy. He gives me a faint smile when he sees me walk in, but the effort proves too much, and he faints.

I hurry to catch him before he falls to the floor. The boy, though shorter than me, is much heavier than I had anticipated. I struggle to push him back onto the table, leaning against the wall for support, when someone comes over to help.

"Thanks," I say, my hands coming away slick and sticky. Light concussion, my ass.

"You're in charge of him?"

I whisk around to find Arthur standing behind me, and he's not happy to see I'm the one taking care of his friend.

"Why yes," I say, getting back to Percy. I need to find the source of his injury. "I work here, on your recommendation. Now help me take his coat off."

Arthur does as told, and we manage to take the heavy metallic garment off Percy's unconscious body, then roll him to his side, his blood-soaked shirt sticking to the table.

I grab the bottom of the shirt and rip it open, exposing a nasty gash down his chest. I let my breath out. The injury isn't as bad as it looks. Whatever sliced him open glanced off his ribs before it could pierce anything vital.

"He's going to need stitches," I say, grabbing the necessary tools from the cupboard, "but first, let's control the bleeding."

I press a fresh towel to the wound, hoping the blood loss will subside soon.

After what feels like an eternity, I raise the towel and find that my prayers have been answered. I disinfect the wound as carefully as possible, but even in his sleep, Percy winces.

"You've done this before?" Arthur asks, watching me from his corner.

"Once," I say, trying not to show my nervousness. "On a cat."

Arthur rushes over to me and grabs my hand before I can start on the suturing.

"Look, buddy," I say, holding his stare. "If you want to wait for someone with more experience to come stitch him up, let me know. But considering the mess that's out there, he may end up bleeding to death before that happens. So, what's it going to be?"

Arthur stares at me for another solid minute before finally letting me go.

"If it makes you feel any better, suturing a moving cat requires quite a bit of skill," I say, getting back to work. "At least Percy's unconscious."

My heart thrumming like the wings of a hummingbird, I thread the needle and hold it to the wound, align both sides of the injury to the best of my abilities, and make my first stitch. When the first knot is done, I cut the thread.

The wound seems so big and a piece of thread so little to hold all that flesh together, yet I carry on. I hold my breath, insert the needle perpendicular to the epidermis, push the needle through, then bring it back out the other side, tie, and cut. And repeat.

I can't keep from glancing up at my work to make sure everything's holding properly and that the needlework's not too shoddy, terrified of making a single mistake.

I barely notice when Arthur comes over to wipe the sweat off my brow with a small towel. "Do you need a break?" he asks.

I shake my head, intent upon my task. It's not until I've finished the thirty-second and final stitch, that I stretch up with a long sigh. My back cracks, and I feel the tendons in my neck pull.

"What happened?" I ask as I apply the antibacterial salve to the sutured wound with shaking hands.

"Training went awry," Arthur answers.

"No kidding," I say. "How?"

"We're not sure yet," he says after a slight pause. "Agravain, Percy, and Safir were practicing together. It appears Agravain's defenses went out at the last moment, just when Safir's attack was reaching him. Safir tried to pull back, but his sylph went haywire. Percy tried to cover Agravain and ended getting cut up, along with a couple of other students who were training next to them."

"Was there a problem with his gear?" I ask. Now that my task is done, I feel the urge to sit down before my legs give out.

Arthur hands me a stool and helps me down. "No. Agravain's in no shape to answer anything right now, but Safir says that they both checked and recharged their gear the night before, so his barriers shouldn't have failed like they did."

"What does it mean then?" I ask, recalling the earlier shouts and accusations. "Something's wrong with the ogham?"

"Perhaps," Arthur says evasively.

I close my eyes, feeling the adrenaline ebb away. It's so strange how things seem to be going wrong lately. Ever since I came here, in fact. I feel my innards shrink at the thought and sincerely hope no one else will make the connection.

But perhaps there's another explanation. After all, bad things have been happening all over the country of late that have nothing to do with me. Like the locusts that destroyed the crops in the Midwest, or the strange disease that killed all the livestock in Texas. And Luther thought it was the Fey who were behind the storms of hail and thunder that have been ravaging the East Coast…

Something nags at me, as if the answer's blatant and I keep missing it.

"How are you holding up?" Arthur asks, his voice low.

"I'm alive," I say, not opening my eyes. "And in one piece. Which is more than I can say for others."

My mind goes back to the screaming boy on the surgical table. Unless she's some kind of sorceress, there's no way Dr. Cockleburr can save his leg. I shiver, imagining the blow it'll be for him once he wakes up, no longer a knight.

The door to the room opens, and Dr. Cockleburr enters, followed by Jennifer who's looking dapper as usual. The girl's tense smile turns into a scowl the moment she sees me.

"What are you doing here?" she asks.

I keep my eyes on the doctor as she examines my work, my stomach knotted in tight coils. She lowers part of the bandage gently, prods the wound, then bends over it and sniffs.

"Very good," she finally says. "I didn't realize his injuries were so severe—fatigue, I suppose—but his pulse is steady, the wound clean. You handled it very well. You may clean yourself up as well and go. And you, young man, help me get him to a proper bed."

"Wait a minute," Jennifer says as I leave the room. "I'm not done talking with you."

"I don't have anything to say," I reply.

Jennifer follows me to the sink, where I wash the dried blood from my hands, letting the hot water take away some of the tension.

"I know what you're doing," she says malevolently. "You complained to Arthur that training was too hard for you, because you're new and unaccustomed to our way of life. But playing princesses doesn't suit you. It's like dressing a pig in human clothes. No matter what, the only thing you can do is roll in the mud."

I throw the soap back in the sink. "So what? The only one who's allowed to play princesses around here is you? Is this what this is all about? You afraid someone's going to steal your thunder?"

I stare Jennifer down—an easy feat considering I'm taller than her. If she wants to get into a fight, I'm all for it. Maybe then she'll shut her pretty mouth and leave me alone.

But Dr. Cockleburr walks in, carrying sheets dripping with blood.

"What are you two still doing here?" she asks, her brow furrowed. "Get out before I make you."

Still glaring at each other, Jennifer and I leave.

Outside the medical wing, the blonde girl turns on me once again. "Just know this. You may think you're being smart finding excuses not to practice because you lack the talent, but one day will come when you're faced with a Fey, with no chivalrous knight to rescue you. And on that day, as the Fey lays waste to you, you will remember my words."

"I'm too tired to deal with your temper tantrum right now," I say, turning on my heels.

But as I make my way to the dorms, I keep rehashing her dire warning. Jennifer may have said it out of spite, but the truth is that, no matter how much I'd like for her to follow the blonde airhead stereotype, she is right.

Dragging my feet, I engulf myself in the shadowy staircase.

"We need to talk."

I gasp and punch at the shadow beside me. Arthur ducks and sniggers.

"What was that supposed to be? Self-defense? You might try not to close your eyes then."

Ignoring him, I climb up the steps.

"Didn't you hear me?" he asks, hovering next to me. "We need to talk."

"I've got nothing to say to you."

"Fine, then you need to listen to me," he says, cutting my way off.

What is it with this boy and his constant nagging?

"What?" I ask when I can't get around him.

"I heard that last bit of your conversation," he says, having the decency to look embarrassed. "Where Jennifer explained your need for self-defense."

You mean her need to humiliate me? I silently say. I smile to him innocently. "Which means what?"

"That you need more practice."

I roll my eyes, and circle him to resume my way up to the dorms. "I haven't been cutting my training classes."

"That's not what I mean," Arthur says, keeping up with me. "I mean that you need EM practice."

I freeze on the steps. "I thought that I wasn't allowed to."

"That hasn't stopped you before," he says with a definite note of sarcasm. "I do recall you breaking into the shed in our yard."

"That was back home," I say, annoyed. "Here is here. Besides, I don't have access to any of the oghams."

"Which is why I'm giving you this."

He extends his hand toward me. Nestled at the center of his palm is a small, simple silvery band. I hesitate.

"What am I supposed to do with that?" I ask, my mouth dry.

"Wear it and use it for practice," Arthur says.

"But it's against the rules," I whisper. "You never go against the rules! What if you get caught?"

"The point of breaking rules," Arthur retorts, "is to do it intelligently so you don't get caught. I'm counting on you for that, which, I must admit, is quite a gambit."

I shake my head, still unwilling to take the ring. "What's the point? It's not like I can practice here, in front of everyone."

"What part of 'intelligently' did you not understand?" Arthur asks me.

I get flustered and shut my mouth before I can put my foot in it.

"The stone is small," Arthur says, "but that doesn't mean it's not powerful. So I don't want you to try to call it out on your own."

I frown at my brother, standing head-to-head with me despite my being a couple of steps higher. "I still don't get it."

He grins, slaps the ring in my hand, then rushes up to the second floor, where the knights' quarters are located. "See you later!"

Before I can unglue my jaw from the bottom step, he's gone. I stare down at the tiny jewel then, with growing excitement, I slip it on my ring finger.

"I don't know how to work with you yet," I whisper to it as if the Fey trapped inside can hear me, "but I thank you for your future protection."

"I want everyone to write an essay on the Aos Sí," says Sir Lincoln. "The main ranks of their society, how they lived before and after Milesians defeated them, where they fled, and their new habits and lifestyle."

I write the teacher's instructions in my notebook, wishing he'd call the Aos Sí a more regular name, like fairies or elves instead, but Sir Lincoln's always a stickler for precision.

"Do we have to go back all the way to the Tuatha Dé's fight against Carman, sir?" Keva asks.

"You can refer to it," Sir Lincoln answers, "but there's no need to go too much in detail. The essay doesn't need to be a hundred pages long. Fifty is good enough."

"But that's a whole history book's worth of writing!" I hear Dina exclaim.

"Your point being?" the teacher asks, his voice as cold as an Arctic wind. When Dina doesn't answer, he adds, "All this will be on your test before Samhain, so you better get this down, or I will flunk you."

Carman sure seems to creep up in conversations a lot these days. I almost expect her and her ten plagues to pop out on the front page of the news if this keeps up.

And then it hits me—the answer I've been looking for. I raise my hand.

"Yes, Miss Pendragon?" Sir Lincoln says.

"Sir, I've been thinking about what you said the other time," I say, ignoring the grunts of annoyance coming from Daniel, Ross, and Brockton, who are itching to get away.

"And what was that?" Sir Lincoln asks with a heavy sigh.

"About that Carman woman," I say. "Remember how you said that she was always accompanied by the ten plagues?"

"Well, that's what the poem says..." the teacher starts.

"So what if those plagues were appearing now?" I ask. "Like those described in the Bible, but they're because she's coming back? Is that possible?"

The teacher's face closes up. "Don't be preposterous," he says, curt. "She's been imprisoned for so long now, she might as well be dead."

"But she was only imprisoned, not killed!" I retort. "All these disasters that have been happening, the frogs in Louisiana, the pestilence in Texas, the gnats who killed those tourists in Death Valley, the hail and thunder on the East Coast, and even those strange boils that have spread on the politicians in Congress... surely that can't be all a coincidence?"

A silence greets my words, pregnant with fear and distrust. I pause as I recall what I saw on Island Park the night I followed Arthur, Nibs, and the others, and everything seems to click.

"That's what my parents were talking about," I say. "How all those bad things were centered around one point. It's all coming from Carman's prison, isn't it? And that prison's here, on that island!"

Someone gasps.

"That black sentinel the poem talks about," I continue without paying attention to the warning looks the teacher's giving me, or the growing fear on the students' faces around me, "it's that stone on Island Park! All along, her prison was right here, under our very noses!"

"They do say that she and her sons were sent over the Atlantic after the war," Keva says, a note of worry in her voice.

"Her sons, yes," Jack says, "but not her. Nowhere does it mention where the location of her prison is."

"But you're the one who said that was her stone!" I exclaim, shocked at this reversal.

"This is all stupid," Daniel retorts from his corner. "You're all going to go crazy scared just 'cause of what some stupid nobody who doesn't even know anything about our history is saying?"

"It's not stupid," I retort. "You're the stupid one if you refuse to see what's in front of your nose."

Daniel stands up so quickly his seat clatters to the floor. "I'll teach you who's stupid!" he yells.

I sneer at him. "Oh yeah, if you can't solve it with your intellect, there's always your fists, huh? Shows how often you get stumped mentally."

"Enough!" Sir Lincoln barks, his white hair fanning out around his purple face. "I don't see how this is related to the subject at hand."

"But I—"

"I'm speaking, Miss Pendragon!"

I look back down at my lap.

"Mr. von Blumenthal is right," he continues. "You should not speak thusly about things you know nothing of. Besides, I feel someone who's gotten a C on her last essay is hardly a reference on the matter." He flicks his hand. "Class dismissed."

I hear Daniel snort in derision before he races Ross and Brockton to the dining hall.

I curtsy to the teacher on my way out, but his ordinarily cheerful face is now wearing a sour look of displeasure.

"A word with you, Miss Pendragon," he says.

I try hard not to roll my eyes at him. "Yes, sir?"

"I'm going to ask that you keep your opinion to yourself from now on," the man says, his bushy brows unable to hide the gleam of disapproval in his eyes. "There's no need to cause a panic over nothing, however justified you feel you may be. Is that clear?"

"Yes, sir," I say, talking to the floor. I bow again, then hurry to join Bri and the others.

"Wonder what bit him," I say to them. "It's not like what I was saying was that crazy."

"Actually, it was," Keva says.

"You agreed to it too," I retort.

She shrugs. "Even crazies have a certain logic to them."

"Did you really get a C on that last essay?" Jack asks, as if my grade's more important than everything else. "Even after all I did to help you?"

"Hey, history's never been my forte," I say as we round the corner and the lunch crowd appears before us.

"If you don't improve by exam time, he'll definitely flunk you," Jack says, shaking his head.

"Look, I've already gone back three years. I doubt a quarter more's going to make much of a difference." Besides, I silently add, I'm still not sure I'll stay here past my eighteenth birthday.

I crane my neck over the sea of heads bobbing before the news board as students file their way into the dining hall. But all I can read is an announcement for a tournament during the Samhain festival, and that a spot at KORT will be filled with the new winner, in addition to the usual trials.

"What's Samhain?" I ask, trying not to think about Agravain's torn up leg—there's no doubt he's the one being replaced.

Keva laughs, and Bri shushes her.

"What?" my roommate asks. "I've got every right to laugh at her if I want to. It's not my fault she's an ignoramus."

"You could just tell her without making her feel bad about it," Bri says.

"It's a holiday to mark the beginning of winter, at the end of October," Jack says. He raises his voice to overcome the loud cacophony that reigns in the hall.

I thank the Fey girl who hands me my lunch plate, remembering Ella as I do so, and wondering if every servant in this society's Fey too.

"But it's better known around here as the Triduum of All Hallows," Jack continues, oblivious to my lack of attention. "You have All Hallows' Eve, All Saints' Day, and All Souls' Day. Samhain is an older lay term for it."

"And of course the professors have to make us work extra hard before the holidays," Bri adds.

"But that's next month!" I exclaim, horrified at all the work I still need to get done, and all the pages upon pages I need to memorize. Within seconds, I'm mentally drowning under a couple truckloads of books and papers.

"Yes, but think how glorious the celebrations are," Keva says, looking ecstatic. "Bonfires are lit everywhere, people are dressed all fine and pretty, there's a feast, dancing, rituals—"

"Rituals?" I ask. "We have to perform something?"

"Not you, silly," Keva says, clasping her hands before her in adoration. "KORT members. And some teachers. They've got to cleanse the land to help protect us."

"From what?"

Keva throws me her usual death stare. "From the Fey, stupid. What else would we need protection from?"

Jack nods. "Winter's the time when we see the most activity from the Fey world," he says, opening the door for us. "You've got to be especially careful of cross-quarter days, like Samhain."

A group of squires barrels through the dining hall doors, tossing each other an orb of water with the use of sylphs to keep it from splattering all over the place. I yelp as one of the guys' throws goes wide and the missile flies right past my nose to end its existence on the stone wall behind me.

Looking furious, Keva wipes the couple of drops that have besmirched her perfect makeup.

"You did that on purpose!" she yells, her dark cheeks getting even darker.

The boys laugh. "What are you gonna do about it, page?"

"I could go find an instructor or a knight," Keva says, cool and collected once more.

"Why not go straight to your mommy?" says one. "Maybe she'll care."

"Besides," the other says, "if the tall one had stayed still like she was supposed to, you would've been just fine."

"Ah, well, in that case, I could go straight to KORT," Keva says, "considering Morgan's brother is the president."

The laughter dies, and one of the boys leans toward Keva. Bri, Jack, and I tense up.

"You wouldn't want to do that," the squire says. "You see, if you did, everyone would know you're a squeak, and nobody likes those. Besides, we were doing her a service. I mean, look at her!"

The other boy shakes his head like something tragic has happened.

"She should thank us instead," the first boy continues. "She needs to realize she can't be compared to Jennifer."

They both laugh like it's the most ludicrous thing in the world and leave me seething in their wake. I wish people here left me alone like they did at Notre-Dame rather than be constantly belittled and insulted until I feel I'm no bigger than the size of a squashed pea.

"Don't worry," Bri says. "It'll pass, like everything always does."

I bite my tongue before I snap back; Bri's the last person who needs to get a snide remark from me.

As we're walking past the KORT section, another squire intercepts us.

"What is it *this* time?" Keva asks, exasperated. "Decided you wanted to get back at us?"

"Keva," Jack whispers to her, "this is a different person."

Keva looks the boy up and down. "You people all look the same," she says before walking away.

The guy doesn't let her get him sidetracked from his target, namely me.

"Morgan?" he asks, looking at me uncertainly.

I'm still mad, and I won't suffer another self-righteous dweeb. I stare at him, daring him to try anything with me. I twirl the ring on my finger; I may not be able to control elementals yet, but vengeance will be that much sweeter when I can.

"Uh, for you," the boy says, flushing to the roots of his copper hair.

He holds out a note to me, and I grab it, so surprised my anger gets flushed down the drain. If my instinct's correct, this could be…

"A love confession?" Bri says, voicing my own thoughts while the boy dashes away.

I turn the simple piece of folded paper in my hands, at once eager and intimidated. I've never had anyone confess to me before, and I'm not quite sure how to take it. Especially when I don't even know the guy's name.

"What are you waiting for?" Bri asks.

Her excitement finally overcomes my initial timidity, and I open the letter. Disappointment sinks its fist in my guts, though I'm too proud to show it. The crisp, tight handwriting is but a brief set of instructions given by none other than Arthur. So much for feminine intuition.

"Well, what does he say? Does he want to go out with you?"

"Of course not," I say, forcing myself to put the note safely away before I destroy it. "It's just a reminder from my brother."

Apparently my disappointment does not translate properly to Bri, for her eyes shine with greater excitement than ever. "Arthur? What does he want?"

I sigh. "Just reminding me to be a good girl and not get in trouble."

I grab my tray of food and go find Keva, sitting in a reclusive corner of the wide room—most certainly in an attempt not to get noticed by any more of Jennifer's fans. Bri sits down next to me.

"That's it?" she asks.

I smile at her and shrug. "What can I say? I'm the least reliable person in the family. I shouldn't taint his reputation."

Keva nearly chokes on her salad. "You can say that again!"

The moment I've returned my wooden stave to the armory, I remove myself from the rest of the class, eager to remain unnoticed. The last thing I need right now is to let either Jennifer or one of her groupies catch me during my little escapade, especially when it's tied to her fiancé.

Looking left and right for any sign of life, I make my way south, as per the instructions, past the dining hall, and down a set of stairs toward the sounds of clanging pots and pans, oven furnaces being fired up, and cooks yelling at each other.

I pause, glancing back down at Arthur's now-smudged directions. Am I really supposed to be down here, or did I miss a turn?

"What are you doing here, girl?" a plump woman asks me, her apron sprinkled with chicken feathers.

"I was, um, looking for—" Dang it, I really ought to practice my lying skills.

There's a loud crash by the kitchen door, and the woman forgets all about me to yell at some poor scullion who's dropped a large pot of beef stew on the floor.

I sigh in relief and hurry in the opposite direction until I'm sure I'm safe. My pace slows as I realize I'm in a completely deserted part of the basement, dust lying thick in the corners.

I crack open the first door I find. Torches set in sconces throw up enough light to show me rows upon rows of large wine and beer barrels lined up like a military regiment.

"Arthur?" I call out, stepping inside the cellar.

The door squeaks shut behind me as I venture farther into the chamber, until I'm sure either Arthur's not here or he's trying to scare me—in which case I'll have his hide tanned.

I trip and catch myself on a wine cask. Looking down, I notice a strange protuberance rising off the floor. As I bend closer, I find that roots have grown in between the flagstones, molding themselves to the floor.

"Stupid thing," I mutter, slapping the one that nearly had me losing my teeth on the flagstones.

The root rears up like a snake at my touch before pulling away as if stung. I let out a strangled cry, fall back, and knock my head on a barrel before I scramble to my feet and hurry back out the way I came.

I hear light footsteps run ahead of me. Then someone grabs my hand, pulls me inside another room and shuts the door.

"Let go of me," I say, pulling my hand out of the tight grasp.

There's a *pop*, and a small flame appears close to my face, singing my eyebrows, before it flies over to an old, musty torch.

"Oops, sorry about that."

"That was intentional," I say through clenched teeth.

Arthur's lips quirk at one side. "Nobody'll notice," he says. "Now let's get going."

"Get going where?" I ask, looking about us for more crazy roots.

The room is rectangular and filled mostly with disused furniture, broken jars, and baskets full of holes. A place where people are most likely not going to bother us.

"What spooked you?" Arthur asks, clearing some of the debris out.

"Have you been in the cellar?" I ask. "It's like there's an alien living in there!"

Arthur coughs back a laugh. "There are no aliens."

"Could've fooled me," I mutter.

"You've got your ring, I see," Arthur says, dusting his hands on the seat of his pants. "Excellent. Remember what I told you last time?"

My ears tingle with exhilaration. "You mean we're going to practice now?"

"Why else did you think I wanted to meet you down here?" he asks, pulling on the collar of his shirt, then rolling up his sleeves. "It's certainly not for your pleasant company."

I'm too happy to care about that last jab. Instead, I thrust my hand forward and concentrate on projecting the Fey outward before I realize I'm missing something.

"What's the matter?" Arthur asks, standing as far away from me as possible.

"I don't know the Fey's name," I say, "its rune."

"Perth," Arthur says, and I feel an answering prickling in my little finger.

I ogle at the jewel like it's just grown some teeth and bit me. "I think it felt you," I say, awed. "But I thought these things were only supposed to respond to the wearer?"

Arthur nods. "That was the first Fey I captured," he says. "And over the years, a link must have formed between us. It happens sometimes."

Wide-eyed, I scrutinize the tiny silvery circle. "How long have you had this?"

"Since I was five," Arthur says, motioning for me to get back to work.

EM practice, as it turns out, ends up in total failure once again. No matter how many times I try to project my thoughts into the ring and try to nudge the Fey inside it, it's pointless. The only thing I manage to do is give myself and Arthur a headache.

"Stop," he says, with a wide yawn. "That's enough for today."

"But I——"

A single look from Arthur tells me to drop it. I scratch at my shoulder, sorely disappointed. I had felt the Fey answer to Arthur's call, and he had been five feet away from me! Maybe it's not the oghams that are defective after all, I realize. Maybe it's just me.

"Does it always take this long for people to get it?" I ask, afraid to look at Arthur and read the truth in his eyes.

"Not usually," he answers. I can always count on him to tell me the truth, especially if it hurts. "But there have been cases before, where it's taken people a few months to finally show any ability for EM at all. Your..."

"Go on," I say when he doesn't finish his sentence. "You were going to say that there are cases when people were never able to do it, huh?"

Arthur lets a small smile slip. "Actually, I was going to say that it took this one guy over a year to be able to control his first Fey, and he ended up as KORT president. Turned out to be the best knight we'd seen in ages. Maybe you're just like him."

"Really?" I ask, daring to hope once again. Vengeance shall still be mine! Unless...I squint at him in distrust. "Are you pulling my leg?"

"Not at all," Arthur says, uncharacteristically nice to me. "You just need to work harder."

I stop just inches from him. "Who are you? What have you done to my brother?"

Arthur flicks my forehead with his finger. "Don't be a goose. I just mean you have to stop being so lazy. Now come on. It's late, and I'm beat." He extinguishes the torch. "Same time tomorrow!" he says, leaving me in near-total darkness and my forehead stinging.

Chapter 17

Bri was right after all. Over the rest of the week, the snide remarks and attempts on my life or honor subside. But it wouldn't have mattered, as I'm living in a constant semi-euphoria. Arthur's kept to his word and is still teaching me in the dusty storage room by the kitchens, despite the late hour and my lack of progress.

Right now, though, I want to smack his smug face with his stupid ring.

"How can you be so calm?" I ask him. I'm so frustrated with myself, I don't know how he can spend another second with me. Unless it's for the pleasure of seeing me fail.

"Would getting angry or annoyed get me any better results?" he retorts.

I snort. He's got a point. But it doesn't explain why he's still bothering wasting his time with me. He picks up a broken chair and smashes it on the ground.

"What are you doing?" I ask, scandalized. "We're already practicing against the rules. Why are you turning into a vandal as well?"

Arthur pulls off one of the chair's legs and slaps the wooden bar in his hand. "I've decided to try another approach."

"Which is?" I ask, taking an involuntary step backward.

An evil glint appears in his eyes. "I will attack you, and you'll have to fend off my blows."

"That's hardly fair," I say, taking another step back. "I've only got my bare hands."

"Who told you to use your bare hands?"

"You don't mean—"

"I do." Arthur readies his makeshift cudgel.

I raise my hands before me. "Wait, wait, wait. You do realize that I still can't do anything with this ring of yours, right?"

"Which is why I thought making you feel something more strongly could help you establish that link faster."

More like make me pee my pants. But maybe Arthur's right, and frankly, at this point, I'm desperate enough to try anything for a chance to get my ring to work.

"OK, I'm ready."

The words have barely left my mouth when he lunges forward, bringing the wooden staff down. I move out of the way a split second before it thwacks down onto an old school desk, splinters of wood flying about.

"You're not joking around, are you?" I ask, my mouth dry.

"If it's real, you'll act accordingly," Arthur says.

He twists toward me with a cross hit. This time I don't move fast enough, and the wooden leg catches me on the shoulder. I gasp and nearly collapse under the blow. Saint George's balls, this guy doesn't want to train me, he wants to kill me, slowly and painfully!

"Stop running away, and come at me with all you've got," he says, his voice low and steady.

I was wrong. Arthur's not being nice to me; he's a psychopath!

Without giving me time to recover, he comes at me again. I back away from him, but get caught between two tables. I topple over a couple of old rotting baskets, then throw myself away from the incoming strike. I hit the stone floor hard and roll away from Arthur's next blow, only to find myself stuck in a corner of the room, unable to escape my demented brother.

I see the wooden leg swing toward me. I close my eyes and hold my hands before me. *Please!*

I feel an answering tug in my ring finger. There's a whooshing sound, then the clattering of wood on stone. I open my eyes to find Arthur grinning down at me.

"What happened?" I ask.

"You did it," he says, offering to help me up.

"Haaaa!" I exclaim, pointing at him in victory. I grab his hand and flinch; my whole body's contused, my shoulder hurts like I've been quartered, and my head's so foggy I wonder if I might faint. But all of that's eclipsed by those three little words.

"What did I do?" I ask, blinking to try to clear my vision.

Arthur lets go of me with a hearty sigh. "You should really learn to stop closing your eyes. It's not going to help you in a fight."

The world slowly comes back into focus, an odd tingling sensation coursing from my hand and up my arm.

"Close your eyes," Arthur says.

"You just told me I had to keep them open."

"Just do it. It'll be easier for you to visualize."

Because I'm still stunned, I do as I'm told. Wrong move. I vacillate like a cabin boy on his first sea trip. I feel Arthur's strong hands grab me by the shoulders as I teeter, and he helps me settle back down.

"You OK?" he asks, his voice barely making it above the buzz in my ears.

I nod. "I-I think so."

"Maybe we've been training too hard," Arthur says, his voice soothing. "But, while you're at it, think back on what you were feeling when you let out the elemental."

"Hurt," I say, unconsciously shifting my shoulder. My mouth is cottony, making it hard to form the words. "Scared." I recall the moment I was on the ground, trapped, knowing that Arthur's next blow wouldn't miss. "I just wanted to make you disappear."

"Good," Arthur says. "Remember that feeling next time we practice. And as a reward for your success, I'll give you a days' rest."

For some inexplicable reason, the idea of not training with him tomorrow leaves me disappointed.

"And when you have this one under control, you can practice with others," Arthur says. "Just don't use Dagaz."

"Why not?" I ask, feeling myself slip into dreamland.

"Especially not when wearing metal," I hear him say as if from very far away. "It would be suicidal."

When I open my eyes again, Arthur's gone. I look about the room. If I thought it was messy before, it's nothing compared to what we've done to it during this practice session. Every single piece of furniture has been turned to shreds. And before me lies the chair leg Arthur had used as a weapon, neatly sliced in two.

My chest swells with pride—my work, and mine alone!

I can barely get my tired mind to shut up long enough to fall asleep. But it doesn't stop me from springing out of bed the next morning, still pumped full of adrenaline, a foolish grin slapped on my face.

"If you're that energetic," Keva tells me, applying her mascara, "tell your little furry friend there that next time he tries to sneak in on me while I'm changing, I'll have him neutered."

"No problem," I say, unable to get my cheeks to function properly again. Puck jumps into my arms, and I pet him hello.

"What is wrong with you?" Keva asks, arching her eyebrow at me in her mirror. She swivels around to face me. "You dreamed of a boy, didn't you?"

Still smiling, I shake my head, but Keva's already gone into la-la land.

"Can't be anyone from here," she says, "nobody's that stupid."

My smile falters. Keva slams her hand on her desk. "It's that Deacon guy, isn't it?" she asks, her eyes fiery with excitement. "I knew it! I told Bri there was something going on between the two of you, what with the way he looks at you…" She smiles impishly. "Like he wants to eat you."

I stare at her before bursting out laughing. "You mean Dean?" I ask, shaking so much Puck hops out of my arms. "Please, that's ridiculous. He's like a father to me, or a much older brother, that's all."

"Whatevs," Keva says. "I saw what I saw. You can be in denial if you want."

I wish I could tell her the truth, but I know that's impossible. Not only would I get Arthur and myself in trouble, but I might lose my ring, and there's no way I'd want to risk it. But despite that, for the first time in my life, I feel I truly belong somewhere, that I'm not a failure, and it feels really good.

"Where were you after practice yesterday?" Keva asks, applying lipstick. "We waited for you, but you never showed up."

"I had more work to do," I say, looking away. Keva is rather apt at knowing when I lie.

"Right."

The church bells ring, calling us to Mass, in time to prevent me from having to expand on the subject, and I rush outside.

"What happened to her?" I hear Bri ask my roommate as I skip on our way to church.

"Probably got a concussion at practice last night," Keva replies. "Would explain a lot."

Bri giggles. "She's gotten beaten up before. It's never affected her this way though."

"Well, why don't you ask her?" Keva retorts with a huff. "She's the one who's been coming back to the dorms super late every night."

I slow down to let my friends catch up and to avoid the odd glances from the rest of the school. The cool quiet of the church greets us as we head over to the pages' area. I glance over to the KORT benches but, apart from Jennifer, no one's arrived yet, not even my ever-punctual brother.

"What's going on?" I whisper in Keva's ear.

Noticing where I'm looking, she gives me her usual shrug. "If you're not going to answer my questions, I don't see why I should answer yours." She shakes her finger before I can protest. "No, no. That's the basis of relationships: give and take. Unless one happens to be a masochist, which is definitely not my case."

Father Tristan clears his throat, and we all turn our attention to his lithe figure, erect before the simple stone altar.

"In nomine Patris, et Filii, et Spiritus Sancti," he intones, his clear voice resonating around the domed ceiling.

"Amen," I say.

"The grace of our Lord Jesus Christ, and the love of God and the fellowship of the Holy Spirit be with you," Father Tristan continues, his hands and eyes raised to the ceiling as if he can see the Holy Spirit itself descending.

"And with you also," I drone.

The priest's clear eyes deign to lower themselves to our sinful forms. I do so wish he'd hurry, however blasphemous that might be. I just don't have it in me to be kneeling or sitting down for a whole hour, not today.

Besides, what is KORT doing? I've been here nearly a month, and I've never seen them miss a single Mass. They are the epitome of the good students, always following the rules and setting the right example. Except, perhaps, for the cousins and Percy.

"And so it is that summer is drawing to an end," Father Tristan says. "All Saints' Day—or, as many of you like to call it, Samhain—will soon be upon us. And if you are not ready, mentally and physically, the demons lurking in the shadows will pounce, eager for your demise. And they will show no mercy."

The doors open up, and in walk the eleven KORT members, Arthur at their head. They each kneel before the altar, cross themselves, then take up their habitual seats.

I throw surreptitious looks in their direction for the rest of the liturgy. They all look drawn, tense. Is it that my secret training sessions have been discovered?

I scrutinize Arthur more openly, but apart from a slight twitch in his jaw, he seems perfectly fine.

Once the service over, we stream out to get to the dining hall as quickly as possible. I scan the group of seniors ahead of us, searching for Arthur's broad back, but he and the rest of KORT have already disappeared.

It's not until we're at breakfast that Keva finds out what's going on.

"Apparently she didn't come back yesterday," she says, drenching her oatmeal in honey. "So something must have happened during her round."

"Who didn't come back?" I ask.

"Her squire is also missing," Keva continues, without bothering to look at me.

"Whose squire?" I ask.

"If you wanted to know, you should've been paying attention," she snaps.

"It's K," Bri says. "Knights go on rounds at the surface at least once a week to make sure everything's OK. Last night was her turn, but she hasn't come back."

"But I thought the Board was in charge of all surface affairs?" I ask.

Jack nods, his mouth stuffed. "Idz gof idz gloch dar schall."

"Bless you," Keva says.

"The area around Lake Winnebago's also under our supervision," Bri explains. "The Board's already stretched thin, so the lake is under KORT's jurisdiction too, even at the surface."

"Which would explain why Arthur and the others went on the island," I muse.

"They went where?" Keva asks, ears perked up.

"Never mind," I say and realize belatedly I've just made my second mistake of the day with her.

Glowering, Keva says, "Well that's all I heard. If you'll excuse me." She pushes her chair back and walks away imperiously.

"So what kind of trouble could she have gotten into?" I ask.

I remember the empty houses, the clurichaun's fear before he disappeared. Goose bumps rise along my arms.

"Who knows?" Jack says. "Could be anything. Fey, or even laypeople. Or it could be something stupid, like this one time, Gareth was found sleeping on duty. Only got caught because he didn't wake in time to go to church."

"It doesn't make sense," Bri says. "K's always been a stickler for the rules, more so than Arthur. She would never have fallen asleep while on duty."

"Maybe she was just delayed," I say. "And that's why her squire's not back yet either." I try hard not to think of this K suffering a fate like Owen's, or worse.

"I guess we'll find out later," Bri says, looking like her thoughts have followed along parallel paths to mine.

We're about to set our trays away, when the doors to the hall slam open and a girl stumbles in, her cheeks flushed from running.

"They've found Rei!" she yells, huffing loudly.

Everyone rushes out like the place is on fire. Bri, Jack, and I follow the crowd at an ever-increasing speed north through the school, past the church, and toward the large standing stone I'd once visited with Lady Vivian.

The stone is still there, towering over the growing throng of people, which is unusually quiet.

"What's going on?" Bri asks as we near the large group clustered at the base of the rock.

"Looks like they found something," I say, hopping up to get a better view, but all I can tell is that people are looking at something behind the warding stone.

"Let's get closer," Bri suggests.

To the annoyance of some onlookers, we push our way through. We're about to reach the front when a couple of salamanders send sparks flying in the air like some kind of signal.

"Why are the doctors taking so long?" I hear someone exclaim.

"Someone's hurt," Jack says.

"Thank you, Mr. Obvious," Bri says as she tries to peer from around a knight's beefy arms. She draws in a sharp breath. "It's Rei, K's squire."

"Excuse me," I say, forcing my way past the knight, and freeze.

Lying in a patch of dead grass is a young girl, her long black hair fanned out about her face. Kneeling next to her is Arthur, his hand resting on the pommel of his sword. He motions for Percy to come near him and starts talking to him very low.

"She's dead," Bri murmurs next to me.

I stare at the dead girl. Every single muscle in my body tenses. I let out a soft moan as I take in the dark lines marring her otherwise serene face, almond eyes closed to the outside world.

Memories of my last few days in Switzerland, memories I'd finally managed to suppress, come back to me full force.

"She's been poisoned," a girl says.

"How?" another asks.

The questions and theories are thrown out in a familiar pattern. At last, a couple of male nurses arrive, carrying a stretcher. They carefully lay the lifeless girl on it, then march back to the school.

I watch them pass by, unable to tear my gaze from all those black veins. Will this nightmare never stop?

"It's your fault!"

The people who'd started following the nurses back stop in their tracks and turn to face me.

"It's your fault this happened to her," says Jennifer, stalking toward me like a tigress toward its prey.

I feel myself grow cold. "No," I say.

She keeps advancing on me, her ice-blue eyes fixed on mine. "Wasn't this why you were kicked out of your previous school?"

My mouth goes dry. "No."

A disdainful look flashes on her perfect features. "There's no need to lie, Morgan. There's someone here who can tell us the truth. Isn't that right, Arthur?"

I look past her at Arthur, standing rigid as a Greek statue, his face as unreadable.

Jennifer looks over her shoulder at him. "I heard her classmate died in a similar way," she says, "and she was the primary suspect. Am I wrong?"

I clench my hands together to prevent them from shaking.

Don't listen to her, my guardian angel's voice breathes. *Don't cry before them, and stand strong.*

"Nothing was proven," Arthur growls, so low it might as well have never been said.

Jennifer turns back to me with a cruel smile. "Can anyone deny what I've said? And after her previous school, she's brought the killings to us. We've found Rei, Morgan, but where's Kaede?"

She's standing so close to me I can feel her breath on my face. Like a vulture, she circles me until she's standing behind me.

"Where were you last night?" she asks.

I flick my eyes toward Arthur, but he hasn't moved an inch, his lips sealed.

Clearly, he's not planning on saying a single thing in my defense. I take a deep breath, trying to deal with this betrayal. It's not the first time someone's stabbed me in the back. I should be immune to it by now. I look at the gray sky to keep the tears from pouring out.

"Well, if you're not going to answer," Jennifer continues, "perhaps I'll ask your roommate." She faces the crowd. "Is Morgan's roommate here?"

"She was with me," Arthur says.

Jennifer's triumphant look turns sour. "What for?"

"Do I really have to explain my every move to you?" Arthur quips, looking cold and distant.

Jennifer's composure slips. "No, I—"

Arthur strides after the nurses before she finishes, ignoring my grateful look.

"We're not done with this," Jennifer tells me through clenched teeth. "What I said was true, and nothing your brother says can undo that."

My stomach sinks as she walks away. She's cast her judgment, and now the eyes of hundreds of students pierce me like a thousand arrows pierced Saint Sebastian.

"You have no proof!" Bri exclaims though Jennifer's halfway to the school now. "If she had been guilty, they wouldn't have let her go."

"Maybe they couldn't find out how she did it," a guy ventures.

"Well, can you?" Bri retorts. "You know how she did it?"

"It could've been poison," someone interjects. "I hear she's good with those."

"Then the police would have found out it was," Bri says. "Or at least the Board. But no, they let her come here. And that's because they know she isn't the one behind it. Didn't you see the body? Who do you think would have the ability to do such a thing? You? No. A KORT member? I doubt it. But certainly not someone who doesn't even know how to do EM!"

I see a few people nod, whispering to each other. As they herd back inside, the noose around my neck uncoils a few notches.

"Thanks," I say to Bri when they're all gone.

"Don't mention it," she says. "I know you didn't do it. It was one of *them*. And believe me, when I find those Fey, I'm going to destroy them."

CHAPTER 18

The sweetness of September is swiftly replaced with the bitterness of October, bringing with it the first snowfall. Though the weather under the lake is milder, I can still feel a shift in the light, like all the colors have been muted.

What I wish would be muted instead are the rumors surrounding Rei's death and K's disappearance, but they're still going strong, spurred every so often by more supposed proof of my involvement.

"You shouldn't go in here," Bri says as Keva and I arrive before Sir Boris's classroom. "I mean, you should wait a bit."

"Wait for what?" I ask, pushing through anyway.

Taped to the blackboard are hundreds of newspaper cuttings and enlarged pictures of Agnès's dead body, and of me as I'm being taken to the police station. Jack's trying to tear everything down, though with difficulty. In their corner, Ross and Brockton snigger, and I feel Daniel's intense gaze follow my every movement.

Shock, then anger flare within me, warring with my desire to flee and never be seen again. But that's exactly what all these kids

248

want. I clench my jaw shut and head straight for my seat, to the disappointment of many.

Just pretend none of it's there, I tell myself in a now overly familiar self-hypnosis pattern. Pretend like everything's as it should be and nobody even knows you're here.

But it's hard to believe in my own words when the whole world is dead set against me.

"What is this?" asks Sir Boris when he sees the partially torn collage.

Jack hurries back to his seat.

"Who's the dolt who messed up my room?" he asks again, furious enough his Russian accent grows thicker.

Every student's eyes are kept studiously down as the teacher scans the rows, looking for the culprit. His gaze crosses mine and lingers there for a second before moving on.

"Very well. Mr. von Blumenthal, please clear this up. *Bistro!*"[19]

"But I didn't—" Daniel starts protesting.

"Whether you're the instigator is of no concern to me," Sir Boris says. "You seem like an enterprising young man. Surely you can get rid of this filth in under a minute. Now get a move on, boy. We haven't got all day."

Daniel glares at me as he gets up. I shrug, enjoying this tiny victory, for I know he's the one behind this.

But this instant of glory is quickly dispelled by the constant attacks I'm faced with whenever Sir Boris's back is turned. On my way to the blackboard, Dina trips me and I sprawl to the floor under the laughter of my classmates. Burning with humiliation, I quickly return to my seat.

"Morgan, watch out!" Bri shouts.

19 Quickly!

I duck instinctively as a pair of scissors zooms past me to embed itself, sharp end first, in my textbook.

"You did that on purpose!" I yell, looking at Daniel accusingly.

"I don't know what you're talking about," Daniel says with a sneer.

"Miss Pendragon!" Sir Boris exclaims. "What's the meaning of this?"

Glaring, I yank the pair of scissors out of my book before grabbing my backpack. I'm done with this place.

"Where are you going, Miss Pendragon?" Sir Boris asks, his face purpling with anger.

Angry tears stinging my eyes, I make my escape. I realize that I should be the bigger person, but it's awfully hard to turn the other cheek when all people want to do is squish me to a pulp.

Somehow, I end up by the kitchens. I veer left toward my secret practice room, eager to avoid attention. But once inside the storage room, I find it hard to get my composure back.

"I didn't do anything!" I yell, holding my hands before me as if I'm strangling someone.

My ring responds and a sheet of air blasts out, sundering the remains of an old desk in two. I stare at the result of my outburst, aghast.

"How is it even possible?" I wonder aloud, staring at my hand like it's a creature of its own.

But my fit of rage is far from over, and recalling what I've just had to deal with makes those roiling emotions bubble to the surface once more. All because of that stupid Jennifer and her big mouth!

Another blast of wind shoots out and pierces the wobbly cupboard in the back, drilling holes all over its dusty doors.

Panting, I look at my handiwork with smug satisfaction. If Arthur were here, he'd be amazed at my progress. Except he's not here, and, in fact, he's been very good at avoiding me these past few days.

And that, to my surprise, hurts more than anything else. After pretending to be on my side, to be helping me, the moment things got complicated, he's decided to shun my presence, both publicly and privately. It's like...I've been disowned!

"If you didn't want me as a sister," I shout, "you should've. Just. Left. Me. Alone!"

I punch my hand at every utterance, firing bursts of air with each stab, until not one piece of furniture in the room is left untouched. I keep on destroying everything around me, even as my head starts pounding and my shoulder aches so much I feel like I must have ripped my arm off.

Finally, when the Fey is no longer responding to my murderous desires, I stop.

"Serves you right," I mutter, seconds before I pass out.

"Drink this, dear."

I feel the cold touch of a cup being pressed to my lips and let cool water slip down my parched throat. I cough, and someone helps me sit up.

"How...?" I start.

"That was going to be my question to you."

I find myself staring into a pair of gray-brown eyes, and I give a jolt. "Lady Vivian!" I exclaim, fighting another bout of wooziness.

When I feel stable enough to open my eyes again, I wish that I was still unconscious—my secret training room is a wreck, and there's no doubt there's going to be hell to pay.

I give the principal a shaky smile. "Fancy meeting you here."

"Indeed." Lady Vivian gets up in one smooth motion, her ochre dress shimmering about her like liquid gold, then helps me up. "I see you've found a use for these old items."

Hands behind my back, I throw her another apologetic smile. "I, uh, they weren't as sturdy as I thought they'd be."

The torch on the wall gutters, throwing deep shadows on the principal's statuesque features.

"Well, what's done is done," the woman says with a sigh. She eyes me carefully, her eyebrows arched high. "I trust this shall not happen again?"

I gulp. "No, ma'am."

"Good. Now run along, or you're going to be late for your training session. I'll get someone in here to clean this up for you."

"Thank you, ma'am," I say, curtsying before dashing out of the room.

I thank my guardian angel for letting me off the hook on this one. With everything else going on, I certainly don't need to get on the principal's bad side as well. If only I knew what was causing those strange deaths, then I would get out of this bloody mess.

Could it be poison from one of those plants that only exist down here as I've seen in the Voynich manuscript[20] that Dr. Cockleburr's shown me? I mentally scratch that idea out—if it were, Dr. Cockleburr would know about it.

The only explanation I can think of is that it's Fey. But then, why would it have found itself in Switzerland first, then all the way here? The only thing the two places have in common is...me.

----••◄◖◗►••----

20 An encyclopedia of herbs and plants and their uses as medicine, but written in code. Only one example's ever been deciphered, and it resides with Dr. Cockleburr.

A light breeze drifts in from the arrowslit window and tousles my hair. I pause in my tracks, and shake my head at the ludicrous thought.

"We've been through this already!" a voice echoes down the hallway, startling me out of my own galling thoughts. "Why are we going over the same things over and over again? It's not going to tell us anything new!"

I flatten myself against the wall; eager to remain unnoticed.

"Yet every time a few details change."

My breath catches. That was definitely Arthur's voice; there's no doubt about it. I peek around the corner to find an empty hallway adorned by pennons[21] hanging down along the walls that I don't recognize—where have I ended up?

"Don't forget Rei's the one who told us of the Kruegers' disappearance," Arthur continues patiently. "And, as I found out just yesterday, the strange wind K and her were investigating turned out to be the wailings of a woman."

A collective gasp follows his words. Against my better judgment, I find myself tiptoeing toward the voices. I stop where the corridor turns. Along the outer corner, between two standing armors, is a set of ebony doors, into which a dragon-hunting scene has been carved. I jump back in fright when I see a dark shape zoom toward me, and realize that the reason I was able to hear this discussion is because Puck's been snooping around. Sneaky little bugger.

I draw closer to the narrow gap in the doorway left by Puck, without daring to peek in. There's no doubt this is one of those infamous KORT sessions, and they're discussing the murder. Which, I reason, completely justifies my eavesdropping.

"But if that's the case—" says Percy, sounding unusually tense.

---

21 Long flags, usually found on a lance.

"A banshee," says Gauvain.

"That's bad, real bad," Gareth adds. "They are omens of death."

"And we all saw what happened to Rei," another guy adds. "K's probably already dead too."

"I will not allow you to talk that way!" Arthur says, raising his voice. "Until there is definite proof she is gone from us, we will consider K alive and keep up with our searches. Banshee or no banshee."

"But that does complicate the equation," Lance says, with what appears to be a dash of excitement.

"Which is why every watch and search must now be done in pairs of knights," Arthur says, "and at least one of them must be a member of KORT."

Somebody bangs on the table. "That's not fair! We've already doubled our workload, and now you want us to go on duty three times a week? There's only eleven of us left, you know. Ten without K."

"I'm aware of that, Hector," Arthur says. "But that's part of the KORT package. If you don't like it, we can find a replacement for you as well."

There's a long pause, during which I can imagine Arthur's hazel eyes boring into whoever the unlucky bloke at the other end is.

"It's fine," the guy grumbles.

"Now that's settled," Arthur resumes, "we should find where this banshee's lair is, and fast. Samhain's almost upon us, which means its powers will triple. So if anyone wants to do extra rounds, on top of the ones already assigned, I need some volunteers."

Before the meeting ends and I get caught, I shrink away from the door.

"Well, you took your time, didn't you?"

I lower my eyes to the pristine floor as Dr. Cockleburr glares at me. There is nothing I can say that she'll find excusable, least of all if I've been doing things I shouldn't.

"Since you're over an hour late," she continues, "you'll stay here an hour later. I want the whole casualty room completely cleaned and disinfected, same with the ward. And that means bedding and drapes as well. And when you're done with that, I want you to take inventory of all the medicines and herbs we have in the pharmacy and note which need to be replaced or restocked."

"All of it today?" I ask, doing a quick mental calculation of the time it's going to take me to get it all done.

"No, by next year," she says, exuding sarcasm. "Of course today, now get a move on!"

It takes me three hours, fifty-six minutes, and twenty seconds to get the ward beds changed and the room scrubbed to Dr. Cockleburr's approval, and I haven't even started on the pharmacy. As I put the broom and bucket away, two squires bring in an injured knight, leaving a bloody trail behind them.

I groan as I pick up the bucket and mop once again.

"No time for that," Dr. Cockleburr tells me, pointing at the knight being lowered onto a table. "Help me with this one."

I recognize the girl, as her reckless behavior makes her prone to injury. I nod and rush to clean my hands and put on a clean apron. When I get back to the doctor's side, however, the knight, Marianne, looks at me with frightened eyes.

"M-Morgan?" she asks, blanching.

"You'll be all right," I say. I grab some gauze to soak up the blood, but the girl flinches away from me.

"N-No," Marianne says. "I don't want you near me."

"Don't be silly," the doctor says. "You're in need of surgery, and I can't do it on my own."

"No, not her!" the girl says, making the sign of the cross.

My hand falls back to my side, and I make to move away, but Dr. Cockleburr stays me.

"You're speaking nonsense," she says peremptorily to the knight. "You've told me before that you liked being treated by Morgan, that you felt you even healed faster."

"Witchcraft," Marianne mumbles, on the verge of fainting.

Dr. Cockleburr doesn't look happy, but ultimately, the patient has the last word, and she's forced to call Harry, a semiretired and nearly deaf nurse, to help her.

For a few minutes, I stand in the doorway, watching the pair operate on Marianne, before I finally get my limbs to work again and leave. But the more I pace down the hallways, the more my anger boils.

"I'm not going to stand by and let people insult me all the time," I tell myself. "Especially when the school isn't doing anything to help me."

I jab my finger at the school's standard hanging on the opposite wall, a shield before a wide oak tree, with a pentacle inscribed on it.

"How can you teach about defending the poor and the innocent when you don't even know how to do that for those within your own walls?" I accuse the flag. "But you've messed with the wrong girl. I'm going to show you how finding the truth is done!"

I humph, nodding vigorously at my brilliant statement. I'm going to show everyone that I'm not behind these murders. All I need is to find the real culprit.

Pacing, I rehash all that I know. Arthur and his minions had talked about some banned-she of sorts, whatever that is, and that it could be behind those deaths. And the way to find that creature is to track it by its howling cries.

Somehow, those words sound familiar. I frown, attempting to dig through layers upon layers of garbage in my memory, seeking a clue. I snap my head up.

"Aha!" I say, punching my fist into my hand. "The bar."

Adrenaline rushes through my veins as I recall the farmers venting about their dogs barking at the strange keening wind coming from over the lake. And the only place around there where one can live on the lake is Island Park, where the Kruegers disappeared.

None of us had seen anything back when we went to investigate with Nibs, but who's to say that outlawed woman wasn't hiding from us?

I toy with the idea of telling KORT about what I've pieced together, but soon give up on it. I could be completely wrong about this, and if that's the case, I don't want to have another strike against me.

Which leaves me with no choice but to find a way to get there on my own.

"Morgan!"

Something lands on my face, then falls on my plate and rolls away—a large piece of half-eaten carrot.

"What?" I ask, rubbing my forehead.

"We've been calling you forever," Jack says, looking concerned.

"What are you thinking about so intently?" Bri asks. "We know you didn't do it, you know," she adds more quietly.

And she should be discreet. Though all the tables around us have been cleared, it's hard to ignore the distrust and fear that crosses people's faces whenever I'm present.

"She's thinking about that man of hers," Keva says with a knowing smile. "I told you they were having an affair...You should pay up."

I frown at my roommate. "Will you drop that, please? First of all, there's no way there'd ever be anything between me and Dean. He's just our family lawyer doing what he's told."

"Uh-huh," Keva says with a roll of her eyes. "And everyone knows how top-paid lawyers are known for playing babysitters."

"Second," I continue, ignoring her, "I've got more important things to think about right now than guys."

"Like what?" Bri asks.

"Like it's-none-of-your-business," I reply.

All three of them stare at me with undisguised weariness, forcing me to concentrate on the bottom of my plate instead.

"I don't like this," Jack says in his soft voice. "She's up to something."

"Yeah," Bri says, "and that's bound to end up wrong."

"Of course," Keva adds. "Anything she does turns into a big mess."

I can feel their stares boring into me, eating away at my meager defenses. How can people ever keep secrets when they have friends so unabashedly curious?

"Fine," I say, "but you've got to promise not to tell anyone."

"Of course not," Keva and Bri say with heavy nods.

"I don't know..." Jack starts, but stops when the other two girls glare at him. "Yeah, OK."

I take a deep breath, suddenly regretting my decision to tell them what I've learned. "Well, I overheard something last night..." I stop and look around to make sure we're safe from prying ears. "I heard a KORT session."

"You mean you spied on them," Keva snorts.

"Call it whatever you want," I say. "They were discussing, you know, the deaths." All three of them lean forward in their chairs. "And they mentioned a banned-she something or other."

Jack chokes on the last of his food. "A banshee?" he repeats as Bri pounds his back.

I nod. "Apparently it's been roaming about on the surface near the lake, and that's what K and Rei were checking into the night they disappeared. Why? What is it?"

"Technically, they don't do much," Jack says. "But——"

"They usually only appear when someone's about to die," Bri finishes for him. "They're like carrion birds."

I try really hard not to picture Rei's body before me, but find it difficult and gulp the rest of my water down to hide my unease.

"So what's that got to do with you?" Bri asks.

"Well everything, of course!" I exclaim. "If I can find——"

"You mean 'they'?" Keva says pointedly.

"This banshee creature," I continue, "then my name will be cleared. I won't have to deal with all these stupid taunts, and I may even be able to go back to Switzerland, finish high school there, and be done with this wacko place."

"You want to leave us?" Bri asks, stricken.

I look away. "Well, I'd like to be independent as soon as possible," I say. "And if that means leaving..."

"You mean 'they,' don't you?" Keva asks again, her voice rising. "KORT members?"

"No, I mean I will look for it," I say, annoyed. "They've had their go at it, but they're obviously not getting anywhere."

"You can't be serious," Jack says. "You're not even a knight. What am I saying? You're not even a squire! What do you think you can do that they can't?"

And this is why I didn't want to tell them in the first place. I sigh in frustration.

"Seriously," Bri says, looking tense, "you know better than everyone else how much I'd like to see them all burn, but this is stupid. You're only going to get yourself killed—that's what banshees are known for, foretelling someone's death! Besides, you don't even know how to do any kind of EM. How are you going to get up there?"

I keep my eyes averted. There's no way I'm going to spill more than I already have, especially if they're not going to help me. I push my chair away.

"You're too young to understand," I say, tossing my napkin on the table. "I'm tired. I'm going to bed."

I have a feeling one of them is bound to break and tell someone about my plan. And that leaves me with but one solution: to go after the banshee tonight.

I watch Sir Ywain limp away before I take out the spare key and unlock the armory. If there's one good thing about all this stupid cleaning I've had to do, it's that I know where everything's kept.

I scan the shelves filled to bursting. What I need is a weapon.

"This'll do nicely," I say, coming upon a rack of swords.

I grab one whose hilt ends in a glimmering dark blue stone— not a gem I recognize, but the point is that the sword's made of iron.

I grab it, but its weight pulls me forward, and the tip clangs against the floor. I jerk around, ears open for any other sound. When no one comes over, I hurry to replace the sword back where it belongs and settle instead for a much smaller blade.

Knife tucked safely into my boot, I slink back outside, lock the door behind me, and head for the landing pad.

"I knew it," someone says behind me.

I jump to the side, ready to defend myself. Keva and I both stare at each other, and then I drop my hands back down, sheepish.

"If you think you're gonna get the banshee like that, God save us all," she says. "You might try not to close your eyes, for one."

"Yeah, yeah," I say, straightening my jacket. "How'd you know I'd be here?"

"I'm your roommate," Keva says. "Though frankly, you're so transparent anybody can read what you're going to do before you realize it yourself."

The wood creaks under us as we cross the wharf. When we reach the warding stone, I pause. Darkness has enveloped the fields ahead of us. I wish there were at least stars in this sky-lake, anything to dispel the sense of foreboding this lugubrious landscape is giving me.

"Changed your mind?" Keva asks, her voice ringing clear in the quiet of the night.

"Shh," I say, my heart beating faster. There's no turning back now, especially not with a witness.

Something glows in the darkness before us, winks out, then comes back, closer. Keva grabs the back of my jacket.

"Is that a Fey?" she whispers. "You step out of the school precinct, and you're toast."

My thought exactly. I wonder if I should get my knife out already, until I hear a soft meow.

"It's just a cat," I say, releasing the breath I'd been holding.

I shrug Keva off and head in the direction above which I believe Island Park lies. After a minute, Keva follows.

It's not until we're nearly to the forest and the school's no longer visible that I stop. I look up at the dark void that is Lake Winnebago.

"I really don't like this, Morgan," Keva says as the cat runs around my legs.

"I'll be fine," I say, more for my sake than hers.

I make a quick prayer to slow my heartbeat to a more acceptable speed, then point my hand down to the ground at my feet.

"Perth," I whisper.

A burst of green energy flashes out of my hand and pulverizes the ground, nearly taking out my foot at the same time.

"By Kali's mighty sword, you can use them!" Keva breathes.

"OK, let's try that again," I say shakily. "But without any maiming."

I'm about to call out the ogham's name again, when the cat hisses at me, then claws my legs to shreds.

"Get it off me!" I yell, trying to kick the animal away.

Keva comes to retrieve it, but not before it punctures more holes in me.

"Thanks," I say, wincing.

"Just…do your thing," Keva grunts, struggling to keep the cat away from her face.

I call out the ogham's name again, concentrating on what I want to see. The stream of air that comes out this time is wider, and I feel my feet lift off the ground.

"It's working!" I gasp when I've reached a couple of feet.

But I've cried victory too soon, as the green jet sputters, and I find myself toppling to the ground. I land on the packed earth, jarring my coccyx.

"Why don't you just give up?" Keva asks as the cat, who's gone completely bonkers, tries to claw her instead.

I remain flat on my back until I can catch my breath, then get ready for try number three.

This time, I manage to keep a constant flow as I rise into the air at ever-increasing speed. Before I know it, I break through some strange pressure and find myself drenched in freezing water.

Eyes closed and holding my breath, I keep the sylph's stream as steady as possible before I can drown myself.

I finally break the lake's surface to be greeted with a bitter wind. I try to stay afloat, fighting against my uniform and the dagger in my boot that keep dragging me down. I look about me, searching for my bearings.

I falter and take another big gulp of water. Coughing, I try to swim toward the city lights, if only to keep myself from getting hypothermia.

Then I hear it, carried on the air, the hair-raising sound of a woman's high-pitched cry. With a last burst of energy, I call on my ring's power. Half swimming, half flying, I travel over the lake until I land face-first on solid ground. With trembling hands, I pull myself away from the shore and the freezing waves lapping at my legs, then collapse under the shadow of a large rock. I roll onto my back, gasping as my bad arm gets caught under my soaked body, and stare at the night sky.

"Thank you, God," I whisper to the stars hanging high above me and realize, despite my fuzzy mind, that the ground underneath me is uncommonly warm for this time of year.

Chapter 19

Breath fogging in the air, I push myself to my knees, then forge ahead, toward the houses. The farther away from the lake I go, the warmer the ground beneath me gets, until my uniform's steaming about me as it dries out. Though it feels nice to regain feeling in my limbs, I know this is not a good sign.

"If it weren't for those idiots down there," I mumble, "I wouldn't have to go through this craziness."

I grip a tuft of grass, and it comes away in ashes.

"Please…"

A chill runs up my back. The voice is coming from just beyond the standing stone.

"No, please, I don't want to d—"

That strange moaning sound cuts the man's pleading short. My heart's thumping in my chest like it's trying to run away, as I should be doing. What was I thinking coming here all on my own just to prove a point?

"Stupid, stupid, stupid!" I tell myself before I bite down hard on my lip, realizing I've spoken out loud again.

Hands trembling, I reach for my knife and feel its reassuring presence in my boot. Ever so carefully, I slide it out of its sheath. I peer around the boulder for a split second before moving back out of sight, but it's no use. With this little light, I can barely make out anything but moving shadows.

"Sleep, sleep, little warrior," comes a high-pitched, sighing voice. "Sleep, and all your worries shall drift away like dust in the wind. Away, away they shall be carried, until you no longer feel anything, and the doors of the afterlife shall open to you."

Terrified, I cross myself multiple times at the horrible voice that manages to sound both sad yet eager. I'm about to cross myself for the eighth time when the ground starts shaking, small little tremors that quickly turn into bone-rattling quakes.

I steal another look around the stone. Across from me, another boulder is rising from the ground. I rub my eyes, but there's no denying it: that rock is definitely sprouting out of the earth like some magical tooth, nearly completing a semicircle of five standing stones.

A circle, I tell myself. A circle of stones, like in the poem. I knew I was right, but nobody ever listens to me. And now I'm going to die.

Keva was right. This is the stupidest thing I've ever come up with.

"Pretty, so pretty," the voice says. I see a shape wrapped in a dark cowl throw itself at the newly grown menhir[22] and rub itself over it like some gigantic cat. However, I know that it's no feline, but this banshee Arthur and the rest of KORT are so afraid of.

"Saint George's balls," I say under my breath, "what is going on here?"

22 Standing stone.

Every instinct I have tells me to get away before that creature sees me. But I find I cannot move an inch, not even to hide back behind my boulder.

Jennifer's dire words come back to haunt me—those predicting my death by a Fey with no one to protect me.

"Charlie, no!" A guy rushes over toward the creature. I hear the distinct hiss of a blade being drawn and feel myself let out a long breath—a knight's arrived, I'm safe!

"You'll pay for this!" the boy hisses.

The banshee rears up to her full height, which makes her about the size of an old woman.

But old woman or not, the creature is much faster than she appears. She pounces on the knight with a shriek, and he falls to the ground, motionless. The banshee kneels next to him, the low wail rising from its gray form. A slender, bony hand reaches out, claws clicking together as it grabs a long black knife.

"Stop!"

I find myself standing within the semicircle of stones, my own paltry knife held before me. It had seemed like such a wise choice at the time, but I think the sword may have been a better choice after all.

The creature freezes above the knight's body. Then two small dots of glowing yellow turn in my direction. I flinch backward.

A violent screech erupts, and I feel my skin try to crawl off my body. Before she can attack me, I rush the banshee. I must have surprised her, for I ram straight into her body, and we both roll onto the ground. Thrashing, the woman-beast screams in pain. I push myself up and rush over to the knight before the banshee recovers.

"Are you all right?" I ask, falling onto the soft earth next to him.

I try to feel for a pulse, but find that his body's slowly sinking into the earth, his right leg already halfway covered with the burnt soil.

I grab his shoulders as the ground tries to suck his body down like some hungry ogre.

"Over my dead body," I say, pulling with all my strength to get him out.

The boy shudders in my arms before going completely limp.

"Nonononono," I say, slapping his face while trying not to panic. "No time-out for you!"

The earth shifts around the knight's leg, and I hear the sickening sound of bones getting crushed. He screams, and I pull on his arms again until we lurch backward as his body tears away from the earth's rabid maw. With a horrified jolt, I realize half of his leg is missing.

"You're going to be OK," I tell him, trying to staunch the blood with my jacket.

If only I knew we were both going to make it alive off this cursed island.

"I'm going to take care of you," I say, looking around, wishing for help that's not going to come. "I'm going to call for an ambulance, maybe a heli—"

Something barrels into me, and I crash to the ground, hitting my head hard on one of the boulders. Air whooshes out of me, and I remain lying there, stunned. Training definitely did not prepare me for this crap!

I take a deep breath, then bite back a cry when a sharp pain answers me, searing through my sternum. I must have at least one rib broken, though judging from the lack of wheezing as I breathe, neither of my lungs got punctured.

Taking slow, shallow breaths, I carefully get back up on my feet. The dim world around me vacillates, and I lean against the stone for balance. Out of sheer will, I force myself to stay standing. Somewhere around is an angry Fey who wants to kill me, and I'll have a better chance to fight her off if I'm not lying on my back.

Something silvery on the ground catches my eyes—my knife! I hobble over to it and painfully lower myself to pick it up. Its handle is slick with what seems to be blood. I must have injured the banshee when we both fell together.

A tiny smile escapes me; at least I won't go down like a total loser.

A light rustling reaches me from behind. I turn around with a grunt. The monster lets out a shriek and rakes her taloned hands toward my face. I raise my arms protectively before me. The banshee's claws seem to hover over me for a moment, as if the air is resisting her. She lets out a terrifying wail, hunches down, and I feel a burning pain lance through me as her sharp fingers dig deep into my own mortal flesh. Tears burst into my eyes. I grit my teeth, try to push the creature away, take a step back, and bring down my hand still clenched around the knife.

The blade catches the monster in the face, and she yelps in pain before she attacks again. This time, I remember my training and slide my back foot around. The motion catches the creature by surprise, and she stumbles past me. I close in on her from behind, then plunge my knife into her body. I feel the banshee quiver like a fish caught on a hook. The Fey tries to reach back behind her, but I push its arm away as I twist the dagger in her back.

With a cry, she jumps away from me, nearly tearing the knife out of my hands. From beneath her deep cowl, the creature eyes me carefully. I don't know how much longer I can keep this up. I feel like I should have already turned to mush half a dozen blows ago.

"Well this is unexpected."

I whirl around at the sound of the voice just as something hits me in the temple, sending a dizzying number of stars into my vision before I crumple to the ground.

Chapter 24

"How much longer do we have to wait?"

The voice seems to come from very far, but I still recognize it. Arthur. I try to move, but my efforts are greeted with searing pain and a burning in my face and arms like I've been set on fire. Water. I try to pry my eyes open, but not a single muscle responds. I need water! My mouth is raw as if I've swallowed a beehive.

"I think she's trying to say something," someone says.

My lips open, and a tiny croak comes out. I breathe heavily, panic settling in. Why can't I move? What's happened to me? Visions of my night on the island facing the banshee flood back to me. What if I'm trapped, buried in the earth while I was trying to save that knight?

Morgan, listen to me.

I stop struggling the moment I hear my guardian angel.

Take deep, calm breaths, he continues, *and you'll get better. You just need to let the poison drain out of your system, and you'll be back to normal.*

I want to nod, say I understand, but have to contend with lying still. Soon, sleep's arms greet me, and I fall into a senseless slumber.

I'm running up a hill. A whirl of slate-gray clouds is growing larger in the sky, blotting out the sun, turning the day into night. I reach a circle of standing stones, but not a soul is to be found. My heart flutters, and bile rises to my throat—I'm too late! I look down at the foot of one of the stones and find a half-buried face. I gasp as I recognize Arthur's hazel eyes staring sightlessly at me. I fall down to my knees and start digging, but the earth keeps rolling and shaking beneath me. In the center of the circle, the ground opens up, seeking to draw me down into its depths. I try to scream, but my throat's closed up, and I don't make a sound.

"Lucan's awake."

The voice is soft and is coming from somewhere above me, pulling me away from my nightmare.

"How is he?" Arthur asks.

But that's not possible. Arthur's dead; I saw it. I try to shift, but my body won't move. My side aches. Then I remember the hooded figure, the knight with the missing leg, the fight, my broken rib, and then a heavy blow to the head.

"He's shaken," continues the first boy, and I now recognize him for being Lance. "Can't believe he won't be able to fight anymore. Says Charlie's dead, though we haven't found his remains."

"Does he remember what happened?"

"Barely. They found the banshee roaming about the island, but this one was vicious and attacked them."

"Which doesn't make sense," Arthur says. "Banshees usually like to stand back and watch people die rather than commit the killings themselves. And why would it have been there if the place was already deserted?"

"Lucan says he doesn't remember seeing Morgan when they got there," Lance says. "So we don't know if she's the one who saved him...or the one who drew them over there."

I keep my breathing as steady as possible and let the accusation roll over me.

"Any luck getting in touch with the Board?" Arthur asks.

"I'm afraid not."

Arthur sighs, then says, "They have their work cut out for them, I suppose. I hear they're now investigating that group of tourists whose bones were found picked clean by lice."

"Those in the Grand Canyon?"

"Yeah. I think we're going to have to solve the banshee problem on our own."

There's a pause.

"She still hasn't woken up?" Lance asks.

"How did you end up at the site so quickly?" Arthur asks back.

"Ran into her roommate, who told me what she was up to. When I got to the island—"

"Yes, yes, you found them both unconscious with Dean taking care of them," Arthur says, sounding irritated. "But it still doesn't explain how you ended up there alone, especially when you know that everyone must travel in pairs."

"Are you more upset that I got there alone or that I got to her first?"

My nose starts itching furiously, but I endeavor not to scratch it or scrunch up my face. If they know I'm listening, they'll stop talking, and I need to find out what's going on. It's obvious the two have already gone over this argument a number of times already.

"What about that lawyer of yours?"

"Dean?" Arthur asks. "He says that he went there on express order of the Board and found the two of them lying there. No sign of Charlie, the banshee, or anything, except for the knife."

"Lucan says it doesn't belong to either him or Charlie."

"She must've brought it," Arthur says. "Guess she's not that stupid after all."

"Unless it's their blood on it and not the banshee's."

This time I have to work much harder not to react and punch some sense into the boys. I concentrate instead on the fact that if it weren't for Dean, I may very well be dead by now. Note to self, I must thank the man for always saving me.

"We'll have to wait for the lab results for that," Arthur says. "But considering the injuries she's sustained, I doubt she and the banshee were in cahoots with each other."

"My thoughts exactly," Lance says. "Though…have you seen it?"

It? What are those two talking about now?

"I have," Arthur says, "and I think I may have an idea."

I feel the cool touch of callused fingers on my neck and tense up. The fingers go down to my collarbone, pulling my shirt with them.

I fling my eyes open and cover myself from the prying eyes, wincing in pain at the sudden movement.

"What do you think you're doing?" I ask.

My cheeks are burning, and I notice the same blush creep up Arthur's stunned face. We stare at each other as, for the first time since I've known him, he's at a loss for words. He recovers first and lowers his brow.

"If you were awake, you should have said so," he says accusingly.

"Do you try to get every unconscious girl naked?" I ask.

We both glare at each other under Lance's bemused look. Harry walks in on us, holding a bowl of water and a clean cloth draped over his arm.

"Back in the land of the living, I see," he says, a happy smile stretching his lined face.

"She's awake?" A head pokes around the doorjamb. "Morgan!" A sheepish Marianne shuffles in and grabs my hand. "I'm so glad you're OK! I thought for sure you'd be a goner and croak before I had a chance to apologize"—she throws a fearful look in Arthur's direction and leans closer to me—"for what I said to you the last time."

I shake my head. "It's all right. I understand."

Harry takes my pulse, checking it against his golden pocket watch.

"Still a little weak," he says, pushing me back down on my pillows. "Nothing a little rest and a good broth can't cure, though."

"How long have I been unconscious?" I ask. Marianne's recovery tells me I must have been out for more than a few days, at least.

"Over two weeks," Harry says.

I nearly jump out of my bed. "What?"

"Which is rather good, considering you should've been dead by now," the old man adds, looking at my pupils, then taking my temperature. "Your immune system's quite incredible, young girl, but let's not tax it more than it needs to be. You need to rest."

The old nurse turns to Arthur. "Which means she's not allowed to attend any meeting until Dr. Cockleburr's given her prior approval. Is that clear?"

With a stiff nod, Arthur exits, followed by Lance. Marianne gives me a quick hug that awakens the pain in my side.

"Get well ASAP," she says. "Samhain's almost here, and it would suck if you couldn't attend the feast!"

I'm left for the next few days to ponder my life at ease—though ease is not exactly what I feel. Every second of that dreadful moment on the island has been painfully carved into my memory, and I get to relive it with every waking moment. Then, three times a day, every day, Dr. Cockleburr comes to change my dressings, checking my wounds.

She's patient with me, and has given me my own room. Though I don't complain, I don't find that very comforting; there are only a few reasons I can think of why she wants to segregate me. Either I'm contagious, or I've become so disfigured she's afraid I'm going to scare her other patients to death. And when I feel the ridged scars marking my face, I'm afraid to see myself too.

At least she's allowed me to keep the Voynich manuscript by my bed so I can devour it whenever I want.

There are so many strange plants described in it, so many new species I haven't even heard of, that it gets my mind distracted from more pressing issues, like my recovery. Or the fact that we haven't caught the real killer yet.

"Are these only plants that exist down here?" I ask Dr. Cockleburr as she checks my vitals.

I shift around so she can place her stethoscope's cold bell on my back. I breathe in, hold, breathe out.

"Most of them, yes," she says before I repeat the exercise. "It used to be they could also be found above, but they've now gone extinct."

"Do a lot of extinct species live down here then?"

"I believe so," Dr. Cockleburr says, taking another blood sample from me. "But the land down here is much vaster than Lake Winnebago above, and much of it unexplored. At least by humans."

"So could there be dodoes still roaming about somewhere?"

The doctor's cheeks dimple for a very brief second. "It's possible."

"What about dinosaurs? Do you think they could be here too?"

"I don't know, Morgan," she says, losing her patience. "Why don't you try to get some sleep now, hmm?"

"Yes, ma'am," I say, chastised.

But sleep eludes me. That's all I seem to be doing these days—sleeping, eating, and catching up on even more homework that Bri and Keva bring me, the only two people who still visit me, not that anyone else has tried, not even Arthur.

Keva doesn't seem too pleased as she hands me Lady Ysolt's stack of papers.

"Can you please stop being so mopey and get the hell out of here so I don't have to carry your stuff all over school anymore?"

I grab the assignments from her along with Bri's carefully copied notes. Flipping through the notebooks, I can tell that I won't get bored stuck in the hospital bed here. There must be at least a hundred or so pages waiting to be memorized.

"Any clues on what's going to be on the test?" I ask.

Keva shrugs. "Beats me."

"You think you'll be well enough by then?" Bri asks.

"I don't know," I say. Our exams start in a couple of days, but Dr. Cockleburr's yet to give me her approval to get out of this bed. "I certainly hope so."

Keva lets out an undignified snort. "Please, just admit you're milking this as much as possible."

"Keva!" Bri exclaims, horrified. "How can you say that when she nearly died?"

"If she'd listened to me instead of going off on her own, she wouldn't be here now. Besides, look at her! There's not even a bruise left on her face—which is a good thing, mind. But it just proves that all she got were light scratches, nothing serious."

"They wouldn't be keeping her here if they thought she didn't need to stay."

I raise my hands to stop the argument. "Wait, wait, wait," I say, not sure I heard right. "My scars are gone? But that's no possible, I—could you hand me a mirror?"

With some reluctance, Keva hands me her pocket mirror. I can see her watching me curiously over it as I examine my pristine reflection, any mark of my fight gone.

"You don't mean to say," she starts, "you haven't looked at yourself since the day of the accident?"

"No," I say, tossing the mirror back to her. "I...was afraid of what I'd see." I pull the bandages still wrapped around my arms. The skin under them is smooth and flawless as a baby's butt.

"Exactly my point," Keva says.

"I don't..." I start, then shake my head. I know I've always been a fast healer, but this is pretty awesome.

I push my covers off and climb out of the high bed.

"What are you doing?" Bri asks, her small hands trying to keep me back. "You're not supposed to leave until they say so."

"You were pretending all along, weren't you?" Keva says.

I'm so giddy I could laugh my head off. "I thought for sure I was disfigured, and that's why they were keeping me here."

"Despite what it looks like, Morgan is vain after all," Keva says. "Brilliant. Now let's get out of here. I think I've seen enough of the hospital wing to last me a lifetime."

Chuckling, we leave the ward and head toward the exit.

"Morgan!"

Dr. Cockleburr's standing before the door, hands on her hips, looking dreadfully displeased.

"Who gave you leave to—"

"I feel perfectly fine," I say. "Good as new, in fact."

"We still have to do some tests," the doctor says, frowning. "We don't know if—"

"Like I said, I feel fine. Besides, I've been cooped up here long enough. I'll go crazy if I stay here a second longer." I sidestep her and wave her good-bye. "I promise I'll come back if I feel queasy at all!"

Rushing outside before she can protest further, I smash into someone else coming in, so hard I feel like I've just turned into a gong.

"I'm so very sorry," I say, rubbing my forehead.

"Am all right, no harm done."

"Bloody hell, Morgan, you've knocked Sir Percy down!" Keva exclaims, helping the knight up.

"Like I said, no harm, no foul." But Percy can't shake the fawning Keva away. "Glad to see you're doin' better, though," he says to me, then raises his eyebrows so high they get lost in his brown curls. "You need a hand gettin' back into your uniform?"

The blood drains from my face as I stare down at myself. I'm still wearing the hospital gown that I've been wearing all week long. Shame burns right through me; I've just walked in front of countless people with my bare ass peeking out!

"I'm perfectly all right," I say, bringing my gown tight around me.

I move closer to the wall in an attempt to keep my buttocks away from prying eyes. Percy laughs.

"I was just on my way out, actually," I say, looking to Bri and Keva for help, but they're both too awed by the knight to attempt to save my honor.

"Good thing I caught you then," Percy says, handing me a note.

"What is this?" I ask.

"Guess I'll be seein' ya soon," he says.

With a little bow, he touches his fingertips to his forelock, then leaves, making sure to give Keva a wide berth.

"What does it say?" Bri asks.

Anxious, I turn the letter around and open it as Percy's whistling dies away in the distance. I nearly rip the piece of paper in half as I pull it out, then read:

Ms. Morgan Pendragon's presence has been requested for a hearing at the next KORT meeting, to be held by week's end, at the ninth hour.

Staring at the fancy lettering, I hear both Bri and Keva groan.

"What?" I ask. "All they want is an account."

"You don't understand," Bri says. "A formal hearing with KORT is *never* a good thing."

"She's right," Keva says, backing away. "Means trouble for you, and I mean to stay well clear of it. See you around!"

Chapter 21

My summons to a hearing propagates through the school like wildfire. But this time, exam week and the upcoming Samhain festival are enough to dampen my own notoriety. I, on the other hand, plunge myself wholeheartedly into my studies. The fact that I've been ill turns out to be a great excuse to avoid both training sessions and my regular duties at the infirmary, and I use the extra time to hole myself up in the library.

Finally, the last day of exams arrives. Just in time, for I can feel my mind grinding to a halt as I stare at Sir Boris's questions. When the bell tolls, I let my pen drop on the table and stretch in my chair.

"What did you put down for the Fuath?" Jack asks as Nadia walks around to collect the tests.

"That they're linked to nymphs," I reply. "Aren't they?"

Bri clicks her tongue. "Only in so much as they both live in water," she says. "Fuath are Fomori, and by their very nature aren't the kind you want to come across."

Jack slaps his hand on his forehead. "They're the hairy ones, aren't they?" He grunts. "I knew it! I put down that they were scaly with pointy teeth that shot out when they sneezed."

Bri rolls her eyes at him as Keva comes over. "What are you wearing for tonight?" she asks, her eyes bright with excitement.

"Aren't we supposed to wear our formals?" Bri asks.

"Don't be such a nincompoop. Do you think people actually follow that rule?"

"I'm still wearing mine," Jack says. "We're going to be leaving the campus grounds, and our uniforms are safer than traditional clothing."

Keva snorts. "You think any Fey's going to attack when there's so many of us around? Please."

"What are you going to do?" Bri asks me.

I fling my backpack over my shoulder and head out. "Maybe I won't get to participate," I say

"Oh, right," Keva and Bri say simultaneously. "The summons."

"Do you need us to go with you?" Bri asks.

"Hey, don't include me in that," Keva says, "I've got higher priorities."

Bri throws her a warning look.

"No worries," I say. "I'm a big girl. I can get there myself."

"Very well said," Keva says, pulling on Bri's arm to get her going before she can word any objection. "We'll see you later."

"Right, later," I say.

"Don't take too long," Jack says, "or all the good food'll be gone."

With a sinking heart, I walk over to KORT's headquarters. I stare for a minute at the hunting scene carved into the black doors, sympathizing with the dragon surrounded by vicious hounds.

An appropriate depiction of my own life. I sigh. Arthur must really hate me.

I knock. The indistinct murmurs coming from behind the closed doors cease, then Gareth lets me in. He winks at me as I step inside.

The room is the most beautiful one I've seen in the whole school—tall arched windows let in light from the two angled walls, while colorful tapestries depicting knights on their various quests hang opposite them.

Along the wall closest to me are suspended twelve banners, each displaying different coats of arms. I immediately recognize the one at the forefront—two dragons standing back-to-back, the Pendragon sigil.

Taking up most of the room is a wide, ringlike table of dark wood, around which are enough straight-backed chairs to seat thirteen people, though only seven knights are now present.

Despite having met most of them, only the cousins smile at me, and Percy gives me a small nod. The others stare at me like I'm some cockroach that needs to be stomped on.

"Have a seat," Arthur says.

I go for the chair nearest me. The seat looks more like a throne, made out of a single piece of dark wood. I grab the back of the chair to pull it out, admiring the carving of an angel descending along the back, sword first, onto a horde of snarling demons depicted about the feet.

"Not there!"

I freeze at the shouted order and notice the shocked looks of the people around me.

"You told me to sit," I say, exasperated.

"Yes, but not there."

I raise my chin. Guess I'm not worthy of being at his hoity-toity table.

"I prefer to stand then," I say, staring straight ahead of me, above the heads of the seated knights. Maybe I should look bored, to show them I don't care.

"Miss Pendragon," Arthur says, "you are here now on trial for reckless behavior that not only nearly cost you your life, but those of others as well."

My jaw unhinges from its socket. "On trial, me?"

"As well as for theft," Arthur finishes without looking at me. "In the second case, we found a knife missing from our armory, which was presently found with you in the surface world."

"I object!" I say. "First of all, I did not steal that knife. I borrowed it. Second of all, who is to blame my reckless behavior, as you call it, but you people?

"You allow base accusations to be thrown at me that are false and unsubstantiated, turning my life into a living hell. Yet you take your sweet time with your so-called investigation of that squire's death and K's disappearance. How can you blame me for wanting to take things into my own hands and solve the case myself?"

"By risking other people's lives?"

"I got there after those two knights had already been attacked. You can't blame me for that."

Every knight there is poised at the edge of his seat, waiting with bated breath for the result of this exchange. Arthur pinches his lips together in displeasure.

"How did you find out about the banshee?" he asks.

I shrug. "Heard some people mention strange noises at night coming from around the island, and when I…overheard…people talk about a banshee roaming about…I put two and two together. It wasn't very difficult."

"Why didn't you report it to us?" Percy asks.

I let out a short, derisive laugh. "I was already being accused of murdering a person and kidnapping another. Who would have believed me?"

A silence settles over the assembly that seems to stretch on for hours. I shift my weight from one foot to the other, scared despite my bravado. Nobody's ever told me anything about these KORT meetings, least of all about trials. And here I am, facing both at once, and with no idea what type of punishment I'm facing. I pray it doesn't entail being quartered or beheaded.

"How did you manage to get to the surface?" a knight asks, a spindly boy with long black hair slicked back into a ponytail.

I cross my hands behind my back. "I, uh, I flew."

"You flew?"

I ignore the shocked looks crossing between the knights.

"You mean to say someone flew you there?" the boy asks.

"No. I mean I flew there."

"But that's not possible," another boy with spiky red hair says. "The only way to do that is with EM, and everybody knows you can't do it."

"Ah, but it appears that she can after all," Percy says with a tight smile. "And well, too, from the sound of it. A rare feat for a page, I may add."

Lance whispers into Arthur's ear.

"A moment, please," Arthur says, getting up, then heading for the back wall, where beautiful drapes of damask hang down in shimmery gold and burgundy, the colors of our school.

Arthur pulls one of the curtains aside to uncover a small passage into which he disappears. We all remain motionless, like the standing armors displayed outside, while we wait for him to come back.

When my legs are about to cramp up, the drapes open up again to let Arthur through. His face is pale, but otherwise betrays no emotion as he resumes his seat.

"The Board has spoken," he says, avoiding all eye contact with me. "Miss Pendragon is now forbidden from going anywhere without reporting to one of us directly. She is also not allowed to go anywhere beyond Lake High without supervision, which means the only way in and out for her is with the barges, like every other freshman here.

"In the matter of the theft, the Board agrees to drop all charges, as the knife was recovered intact. The case is now closed."

The moment the verdict is given, there's a flurry of activity as every knight rushes to join the feast outside. Each one passes by me without so much as a glance in my direction, not even Percy and the cousins, until only Arthur and I remain in the room.

He stops before me, opens his mouth to say something, but I throw him the dirtiest look I can muster, and he shuts it again.

I wish he knew how much I hate him right now, how much I wish I could shove his stupid rules down his throat and have him choke on them.

There's a slight clearing of the throat, and we both turn to find Jennifer. She gives Arthur a kind smile and reaches for his hand. I can tell she's enjoying this as much as a dog loves to roll in poo.

"Everyone's waiting," she says. "They can't start the festivities without you."

"I'll be right there," Arthur says.

"What about her?" she asks, threading her arm through his.

Arthur doesn't answer, but I know exactly what he's thinking: I can't go to the festival unless I'm accompanied, which means that I'd have to go with them, like an obedient lapdog. And there's no way I can watch Jennifer preen before me all night long.

Without a word, I flee.

I run past classrooms, down long hallways and dark staircases, not caring who sees me. Once outside, I keep running, across the now-empty courtyard, my feet pounding against the ground. I wish the Banshee had killed me. It would have saved me from this latest degradation.

And to think that I owe it all to Arthur and that stupid, evil witch Jennifer. I've never felt worse in my whole life, not even when I was at the police station back in Switzerland.

Burning tears stream down my cheeks. Out of all the people at school, it had to be Arthur. Why did he even bother teaching me how to fight and use oghams if I'm not supposed to use them? And now he's punishing me for it?

The party's lights rise in the meadow east of me and I veer in the opposite direction. The sound of distant shouts and singing carries over to me; everyone's having such a jolly good time while I have to watch my whole world crash and burn around me for the second time this year.

I wipe away at the tears angrily. I should not be crying, especially not because of Arthur. That boy doesn't deserve anything from me, except perhaps a solid kick in the crotch.

It's not until the forest's looming high over me that I pause. Panting, I stare back over my shoulder. Dusk has taken over the school, and the multiple bonfires are glowing like fireflies in the distant fields. I bet no one's noticed I'm gone, or even cares.

I really can't trust anyone; I see my error now, but the little girl who believed in fairy tales and happy endings has finally grown up.

I face the forest's foreboding recesses and, without a second glance backward, step inside them.

The darkness that lurks within the woods quickly closes around me until I can no longer tell which way I'm going. I dare not stop, afraid of becoming easy prey to some nocturnal beast should I stand still.

Breathing heavily, I force myself to go faster.

I try not to think about what I've heard of this forest, but the more I try to forget the stories, the quicker they come back to me. No one who's ever come here has come back out again, at least not intact, and I catch myself wondering if that is my fate too.

At least it's better than what I've left behind, I keep telling myself.

I trip on a root and sprawl down on the ground, dried leaves crackling under my weight. Something warm and bristly brushes against my legs and I yelp in horror.

I feel around the ground for a weapon and come up with a large stick. Eyes darting all around for the creature, I wield the branch before me, but the grunting seems to be running away and quickly dies down.

When it's quite clear I'm not under attack, I forge ahead deeper into the woods, too scared to stop again.

As my heartbeat finally slows down, I catch the faint echoes of a lively tune. Music! I'm saved!

Waving the bough before me protectively, I follow the merry sounds until I end up in a wide clearing. Standing in the middle of the glade is a solitary tree basking in a warm glow. It's not until I've taken a few more steps toward it that I realize the light is coming from the full moon shining above it, a silver disk larger than any I've ever seen in the upper world.

The music changes into a sweeter melody, full of tender promises, but I don't see anyone, nor do I see any of the Samhain bonfires that are supposed to blaze throughout the night.

A shiver runs up my spine and raises the hairs at the back of my neck. Could it be…Fey people?

"Stop right there!"

I jump at the voice, not sure whether I've heard right or if it's just the product of my imagination. I take another step.

"I said stop!"

I find the source of the voice, hiding in the oak tree's wide branches. A pair of eyes is shining straight at me like two glittering sapphires. I pull away from the massive trunk as a whole face emerges before me, followed by shoulders and a torso, until I find a little boy leaning toward me.

"Who are you?" I ask.

"Who are you?" the boy replies.

"I'm Morgan. Are you lost?"

"Are *you* lost?" he says petulantly.

I stare at the little boy hanging from his bough. He can't be more than five or six years old at most.

"Yes," I reply, giving up on the idea of teaching him manners. "No. I don't know. I just heard some music, and I wanted to check it out."

Cocking his head, the boy seems to think about it for a while.

"You'll have to get rid of your slave accessory if you want to enter," he says.

"My what?"

I look about myself in confusion. I don't have any chains on me that I can see. Then I catch the small glint of my ring, the one Arthur gave me, and I know that's what he meant.

I twirl the jewel around my finger, reluctant to part with it. It's the first present I've ever received, and one that's proven quite useful. But it also belonged to Arthur, and he turned out to be a big, fake, two-faced prick.

With a savage glee, I take the ring off and throw it to the ground.

"There," I say, "it's done."

The little boy smiles, revealing two rows of pointy white teeth.

"Excellent," he says. "Step inside, and welcome to our feast!"

I wait for him to open a door, eager to find out what the Fey land is all about. My foot's already tapping to the rhythm of the music. I stare at the trunk for a good minute before the little boy laughs.

"You must step through the circle at your feet, princess!" he says, disappearing once again into the oak tree's foliage.

"Princess my ass," I mutter, looking down.

It takes a moment for me to notice that the circle is, in fact, a small ring formed by a bunch of mushrooms.

"You've got to be kidding," I say, nonetheless stepping inside the band of fungi.

The world around me seems to flip upside down, and I close my eyes before I get sick. When I open them again, everything's changed.

CHAPTER 22

"Saint George's balls," I whisper, ready to freak out.

I stay rooted to my spot, my eyes roving about the festive crowd. There are so many Fey, all dancing to the cadence of the cheery music, their colorful dresses and long manes of hair and furs twirling about in a hypnotizing pattern under the twinkling lights of a thousand floating lanterns.

"Welcome to Avalon," the boy with the pointy teeth says, before disappearing up his tree again.

I pinch myself on the cheek hard enough to leave a mark, and my nerve endings' immediate response tells me this is definitely not a dream. Perhaps a hallucination then.

A purr the decibel of a lawn mower greets me, and I find a familiar black cat trying to imprint my boots.

"You again," I say, bending down to pet its luscious fur.

But the cat darts away into the crowd of dancers.

"Wait," I say, following after it. "You're going to get trampled!"

The cat disappears behind a tall woman's shimmering green dress, then dives between the furry legs of a satyr.[23]

"Come back here," I say, getting stepped on by a wide woman with a round, protuberant face that reminds me of a hippo. When the hippo-lady sees me, however, she hisses and veers away from me like I've got the plague.

A group of beautiful girls waltzes from across the glade toward me, their dresses so ethereal I feel they would disintegrate like clouds under my fingers.

"Oh, a new one!" one of them says, her limpid blue eyes twinkling.

"Can we play with her?" another asks, her cheeks as rosy as the ribbons tied in her golden hair.

They giggle, and I have a bad feeling it's not out of mirth, but something far darker. The first one draws closer.

"Of course we can," she says with a cold smile. "I'm sure she'd love to join us, wouldn't you?"

I don't move or say a word. I've learned not to trust pretty people, and these are definitely no exception.

"Oh, don't be afraid," a third girl with fiery red hair says, grabbing my hand so tightly my phalanges crunch. "Come play with us!"

She yanks on my hand so hard I tumble over and end up lying on the soft earth, gagging on some dirt.

"She's a wee little thing, isn't she?" the redheaded girl says with a gleeful laugh.

"Here, let me help you," says the one with the unsettling blue eyes.

Pulling on my hair, she forces me to stand up. I try to shove her away, but something cold and sharp jabs me near my jugular. I freeze.

---

23 A Fey who's half goat, half man.

"What do you want?" I whisper.

"Giving you a taste of what you do to us," the girl replies. "How do you like it?"

"Not that much," I say.

All around us, couples keep on dancing, oblivious to what's going on or pretending not to see us. I swallow hard, feeling the blade dig a little deeper into my throat.

"Let's not get hasty," I say. I try to move away, but the girl's grip is surprisingly strong. "Uh, parley?"

Another Fey girl approaches, sniffing me like a dog. "There's something different about this one, Blanchefleur," she says, scrunching her nose up.

"She's filthy, that's what," the one holding the blade says, her breath tickling my cheek. "Polluting Avalon."

The blade slashes down along my sternum and cuts my shirt open. I yelp, trying to hold the remains of my jacket together so as not to expose myself.

"Please let me go," I hear myself say. I know I've had a miserable excuse of a life so far, but I've suddenly grown extremely fond of it.

The girls giggle around me. "Hear how she pleads, Sister," says one.

"I think her cries will sound nicer to my ears," the one called Blanchefleur retorts, pointing the knife back toward me.

"I wouldn't do that if I were you."

Out of the corner of my eye, I see a tall figure emerge.

"Try me," the Fey girl says.

The knife is cold on my neck. Eyes closed, I wait for death to swoop down on me. A sharp pain vibrates in my shoulder, and I hear the girl yelp in surprise.

"I told you so," the man says.

When I open my eyes again, I find Blanchefleur getting painfully back up a yard or so away from me. I stare at the tall man—did he just save me?

He strides over to me, and the three Fey sisters bow low, displaying cleavages that would give every boy in my class a nosebleed.

I'm about to suffer from a nosebleed myself as I stare up at the man standing like a demigod before us. His black curls fall carelessly over his forehead and brush against the top of his shoulders that seem wide enough to carry four people. But what strikes me the most is the gold of his eyes, which are currently leveled at the three girls.

"You know better than to treat our guests this way," he says, his voice as smooth as hot chocolate on a winter night.

"But she's one of *them*," Blanchefleur says, full of indignation.

The tall Fey doesn't have to say anything; his presence alone exudes anger and repressed violence. I shiver, and not because I'm half naked. There's something terrible yet fascinating about him.

The girls prostrate themselves closer to the ground, waiting.

"What you have destroyed, you shall return tenfold," he says. "Is that clear?"

"Yes, my lord," the sisters say together.

The man turns to me, all smooth courteousness. The guy must be bipolar. There's no way he could switch moods so quickly.

"We meet again," he says. He makes a small bow. "Lugh, at your service."

I can't stop staring at him. "We…uh, we've met before?" I manage to squeak out.

The man tilts his head, and I feel myself go hot and cold as if my body's internal thermostat has gone haywire.

"You were somewhat out of sorts at the time," he says, "and I wasn't able to stay around." His gaze travels slowly down my body, and I hug myself tighter. "At least you're not drowning this time."

I gape at him—drowning? The only time that happened to me, Arthur saved me...Didn't he?

A thousand questions tumble over in my mind, so many my brain conks out and I'm left speechless. Just breathe, I remind myself. Breathe and accept the way things are, or go crazy.

"Is this Heaven?" I blurt out before feeling my cheeks light up like lanterns.

Lugh lets out a low chuckle. "I'm afraid not. The Gates of Heaven are closed to us...for now. But Avalon is a haven, a sanctuary against those of your kind, at least for the few of us remaining here. But never fear," he says. "Nothing more untoward shall happen to you here."

His hand warm on the small of my back, he steers me away from the revelers toward the edge of the clearing, where I can see tables with mounds of victuals stacked upon them.

"Blanchefleur," the man calls.

The Fey girl comes over to us, her brown curls bouncing lightly down her back with every step.

"Yes, my lord," she says, her voice lilting like the waters of a creek running over pebbles.

"Please take care of our guest."

"As you wish, my lord."

The man gives me a little push toward the Fey girl. "I will see you soon," he says before disappearing into the crowd once again.

Blanchefleur pulls me away none too gently, but I can't stop looking back for the stranger, hoping to catch another glimpse of him.

"Who was that?" I ask.

"That was Lugh," the Fey girl says, "prince of the Tuatha Dé."

My heart does a somersault. I've heard that name before, in Lore class. The Tuatha Dé had been a warlike group of Fey, ruling over their part of the world until they got defeated by the very ancestors of the current knights.

"I thought they were all dead," I say. I bite down on my lip—how brilliant of me to bring up this sour point with her, considering she's just tried to turn me into mincemeat moments ago.

Blanchefleur casts me a sidelong glance. "Defeated, yes," she says. "Dead, no. We were forced away from the upper lands to live the remainder of our days here, until Judgment Day."

She sits me down on a tree stump and pulls out a little jar from her pocket.

"What is it?" I ask as she opens it.

"An ointment, for your neck."

As she bends over my injury, I notice the nightshades adorning her hair, a flower known for being poisonous. I recoil.

"What, precisely, is in that ointment?" I ask.

The girl lifts her eyes to my face. "The list is long. Do you truly wish to hear it?"

I lick my parched lips. "I do wish to know if anything in there might be…injurious," I say carefully. "To humans, that is."

"Do not fear," Blanchefleur says, sounding disappointed. "Lugh wouldn't let anything bad happen to you now."

"How can I believe that?" I ask. "You tried to kill me earlier, if I recall correctly."

"And I would have if I could have," she answers.

As if *that's* supposed to make me feel better.

"And what about him, that Lugh?" I ask, still not letting her treat my wound. "What's he got to do with me?"

The Fey girl shrugs, her delicate shoulders poking out from her gold-and-blue dress. "How should I know?" she replies, holding me still. "Maybe he wants you as a concubine. It's been a while since he's bedded a human."

I sputter, and Blanchefleur uses that moment to apply her unguent. The moment the cream touches my skin, I feel a sweet, warm tingling spread down my body, and I let myself relax.

As the girl resumes her treatment, I scan the Fey crowd. Though they've been hunted and many of their kind enslaved, they don't seem to have a care in the world right now. Or maybe they're celebrating like there's no tomorrow because they feel their end is near, a little voice in me says.

In a way, that scares me even more. There's nothing more dangerous than one who feels cornered, and isn't that what we're doing to them? Reducing their territory and hunting them down until they have no choice but to counterattack or become extinct?

"There, that should do it."

I feel a strange assemblage of leaves and flowers wrapped around my neck like a collar. To my surprise, it doesn't hurt or itch, but rather feels warm to the touch, a warmth that spreads down to lodge in the pit of my stomach as if I've just had a full jar of wine. I hop back onto my feet.

"Thank you," I say.

"Don't mention it," she says with a grimace. "It only makes it worse."

Blanchefleur hands me a net of flowers and leaves, as well as a dazzling pair of shoes. "Please put this on," she says.

"What?"

Holding the net before me, I realize it's, in fact, a dress, as delicate as the one she's wearing. Definitely not something Sister Marie-Clémence would have approved, but better than the tattered remains of my uniform.

"Is there a more private place for me to change?" I ask.

Blanchefleur smirks, then leads me farther into the depth of the woods, where the music is but a faint trace in the air, like the sweet aftertaste of a cream puff. We stop by a large wooden throne lit up by a single flower-shaped lantern hanging over it. On its cushion sits the black cat, staring straight at me with its golden eyes.

"There you are," I say, grabbing the feline before it can escape again.

The cat gives a single meow of protest, but then settles comfortably in the crook of my arm.

"Hurry up," Blanchefleur says, taking the cat away from me and setting it back down. "The moon's nearly past its zenith."

"Which means what?" I ask, taking my muddy skirt off.

"That the festivities are almost over," the Fey says, looking longingly at the dancers.

"You can go ahead," I say. "I can get back there on my own when I'm ready."

With an elegant pout, she sits on the ground by the throne instead. "Don't tempt me," she says. "There are thousands of Fey out there that would pounce on the chance to kill you if they could." She lets out a sad sigh. "But if something were to happen to you now, Lugh would flay me."

I delicately pull the dress down over my shoulders, fearful of ripping it. The fabric is so light it barely feels like I'm wearing anything at all.

"I feel so very naked," I say as Blanchefleur combs my hair roughly before adjusting a diadem in it.

"You could remove it if you want," she says, all serious. "A lot of us like to go in our God-given attire without shame."

"I'll pass," I say.

A tiny creature buzzes over to land in her hair, a soft light emanating from its chest like that of a lightning bug. I nearly go cross-eyed as I watch the tiny, humanlike Fey reach up to Blanchefleur's ear.

"A pixie," I whisper, afraid to scare it away.

Without realizing it, I'm leaning forward, close enough that my nose nearly touches Blanchefleur's cheek.

"Careful, they bite."

I pull away quickly as the tiny creature flies away, like a giant bumblebee. Honestly, does everything pretty here hide fangs? My stomach responds by growling so loudly it scares the cat away.

"Let's get going, shall we?" Blanchefleur says, directing me back to the party. Noting my hesitance, she adds, "Don't worry. Didn't I say Lugh is watching over you?"

Yeah, I tell myself, and that's what troubles me.

Pixies whizzing in the air around us like tiny shooting stars, we make our way back to the clearing. This time, people are paying attention to me, willing, even, to invite me to dance with them.

As we pass by the buffet, I steal a couple of pears and a dozen tarts, then munch away happily as I take in the scene.

As the moon crests over the oak tree, the air thickens with the scent of roses and jasmine, and the music slows down to a spellbinding pace. My head starts to bob along with it, my food forgotten.

"Would you care to join me?"

The tall Fey prince, Lugh, is at my side, the cat in his arms. Both stare at me with pairs of identical amber eyes.

"To dance, you mean?" I ask.

Lugh gently lets cat down. "Keep an eye out for me, will you?" he says before the creature scurries away.

Then, with a smile, he offers me his hand and leads me within the circle of dancers.

Just think about where you step, I tell myself over and over again. Don't let your eyes roam anywhere lower than his philtrum,[24] and no higher than the tip of his nose.

"So do you remember me now?" he asks, his voice sending shivers down to the very marrow of my bones.

"Yes, charmed, charmed," I say, fixating now on his perfectly smooth chin.

Lugh gives a low chuckle and twirls me about. I trip, nearly losing my pretty new shoes, but he steadies me with his strong hands, and we continue as if nothing's happened.

"The first time we met," he says, drawing me closer.

I'm forced to look up or have my head crushed against his broad chest, and find myself caught in his steady gaze like a mouse by a snake, a very lovely snake at that; it's no wonder Eve faltered. I shake myself.

"Drowning, yes," I say. "It was quite…wet."

I blush all the way down to my toes.

"That's usually one of its outcomes," Lugh says.

"But I thought…" I stop myself from saying Arthur's name. I've been very good at not thinking about the git since I've gotten here, I'm not going to start now. "So you mean to say, you're the one who saved me?"

"In the flesh, if I may say so," Lugh says with a short laugh. "Why are you so shocked?"

I blink very fast, trying to recall that day, but the most I can pick out of my fatigued mind is the cold and darkness of the water before finding myself on the landing hill where Arthur and the others found me.

---

24 The dip above the upper lip.

"Why are you protecting me?" I ask. "What do you want from me?"

"Want?" the tall Fey asks. "Cannot the pleasure of your company be sufficient?"

Blanchefleur was right about the whole courtesan thing, I realize as my hands go clammy with apprehension.

"Maybe I saw something in you that was worth saving," he adds as he whisks me around the tree again.

"Oh, OK," I say. Maybe it's the dance and the lack of food, but I feel more and more light-headed and am having a hard time staying suspicious.

"You're putting the rest of the company to shame," Lugh says, squishing down any further thought of life preservation I was entertaining. "And the dress matches your violet eyes."

I giggle. At least this Prince Charming has a defect if he can't tell the color of my eyes from this close—or could fallen angels be color blind like dogs?

"There's really no need to flatter me," I say with a smile. "Besides, I already know how your people feel about me."

"And how is that?"

I lift my chin so the poultice around my jugular shows clearly.

"Ah, that," he says. "They just lost a sister a moon ago or so, and they're blaming your colleagues for it. Please forgive them. In their grief, they forgot their basic manners. Besides, you were wearing clothes that don't make people here feel at ease. But that's all well now, isn't it?"

One of the musicians, a young man with a long black-and-white Mohawk that reaches down to his rump, blows a lively trill with his flute, and the Fey orchestra picks up the tempo. We spin around the circle so fast I'm afraid I'm going to be flung out, but Lugh keeps me anchored, and I laugh with delight.

All my cares and worries seem to have disintegrated into thousands of particles. All that matters now is that I'm alive, amongst these beautiful if somewhat unusual people. And maybe it's because of this disparate group of Fey that my history doesn't matter—except for the minor detail of having trained with knights.

"So what happened?" Lugh asks as we pass a gnome skipping by, his bonnet askew.

"With what?" I ask.

"Well, it seems every time I see you, you're in trouble," he says. "What happened to you today that you made your way to our world?"

The words jar me back to reality in a most unpleasant way.

"Maybe," he says, drawing me close, "it means you should stay with us. It'll be easier for me to keep an eye on you then."

Though the tone is light, I sense that he's being serious. I tense up. Is this how people get caught in the Fey's meshes? By being promised a worry-free life, filled with light and sweets and dance and beauty? But that's what Father Tristan's warned us against. These are not angels, but devils, cast out of heaven like Lucifer. And everyone knows *he* was the hottest of the lot before he was sent to Hell.

Besides, I've seen what these pretty Fey people can do.

Lugh senses my inner conflict and pulls back, a look of sadness in his eyes.

"I heard you faced a banshee," he says. "If you stayed here, you could be safe. We could keep you away from the Sons of Darkness."

At his words, I stop dancing altogether as memories of the cadaverous creature bring shivers down my back.

"This is only an invitation," Lugh says quickly. "I would be sad to see you leave, but if that is your wish, there's nothing I can do about it. All you have to do is find a fairy circle, and you'll be back where you want."

I feel the knots in my shoulders untie. I'm free to do as I want, which is more than I can say about the way they're treating me back at school.

"So all I need is to step through that ring of mushrooms?" I ask.

Lugh chuckles. "Mushrooms, stones, trees, it doesn't matter which. Nature is nature, and a circle's a circle. All you need to do is visualize where you wish to go."

My eyes widen. "You mean to say those things are like portals?"

Lugh nods.

I whistle. "Fancy way of transportation. Wish the rest of the world knew how to use them."

With a tight smile, Lugh makes me spin around. I laugh.

"How could Father Tristan ever think you're demons?" I say. "That's so obviously not the case. You've fed me, clothed me, let me join in the fun, all with no strings—or chains—attached."

"And what makes you believe we're not demons?" he asks.

I open my mouth to answer, then pause. "Is this a trick question?"

"We're all from the same source," he says, lifting me up over a badger with a fancy yellow bow around its neck. "We're all... brothers and sisters, in a sense."

"So you mean to say that you're part of the Devil's cohort, trying to tempt humans into doing evil things and possessing our souls for... for your final battle against the Heavens?"

Lugh shrugs. "Would that be so far-fetched?"

I stop dead in my tracks, and a young Fey boy crashes into me. Lugh tries to get me going again, but I don't let myself be swayed.

"In that," he says at last, "we're more like you than you may think. Not everyone wants to use and abuse humans, just like not every human wants to enslave and destroy us. Our powers were God-given, there's no denying that, like everything else in this world. And with abuse, comes retribution. I can understand that. But we're not all bad, though God chose to turn His back on us, leaving us to our own devices in a hostile land. Isn't it natural for beings to fight for their survival?"

I gesture toward the clearing with a wide sweep of my hand. "This doesn't exactly strike me as survival," I say.

"Just because you've seen a small part of our world doesn't mean you know the whole picture," Lugh says. He takes a deep breath, then draws me in, so close I can feel the heat emanating from his body. "The question is, do you think we're bad?"

I lose myself in his intense gaze again, unable to look or move away. But I find I don't want to. His hand cups my cheek, then slowly follows the curve of my neck, traces my collarbone, and comes to rest on my left shoulder, over my old scar, leaving me feeling all warm and fuzzy inside. His face draws nearer to mine, his lips so close I can almost feel them. I close my eyes, tilt my head up—

Something slams into my back, and I fall forward, my lips meeting Lugh's. The world seems to stop as my heartbeat drowns out all other sound. I feel like I'm drowning again, but in a pleasant way this time.

"Get away from her!" someone says, jerking me backward.

CHAPTER 13

"Arthur, what are you doing here?" I whisper harshly.

Tightening his grip around my wrist, Arthur drags me after him.

Lugh cuts us off, frowning. "Where are you going?"

"Nowhere," I say, trying for the umpteenth time to free myself.

Arthur quickly scans the tense crowd. "I just wanted to ask her for a dance," he says through clenched teeth.

"That's no way to treat a lady," Lugh says. "I thought you people at least knew that much."

Arthur stiffens, releases me, then gives me a small bow. "Would the lady care to dance with me?" His voice is pleasant, but his eyes have a say-no-and-I'm-going-to-make-your-life-miserable quality to them.

With an inward sigh, I place my hand in his, give an apologetic glance toward Lugh, and let Arthur lead me away. The music resumes at a much slower pace, which gives him plenty of leeway to glare at me.

"What?" I ask, petulant.

Arthur keeps his mouth shut tight. Neither the beauty of the place nor the entrancing music seem to mollify him. He looks more like a panther, ready to spring the moment the cage door's open.

"Why did you run away again?" he finally asks, barely containing his anger.

"First of all, there is no *again*," I say. "Second of all, tell me which prisoner wouldn't want to be free?"

Arthur scowls. "You're not a prisoner."

"But having to tell everyone of my whereabouts is being free?" I retort.

"There's a good reason for that," he says. "You always get in trouble. Look where you've ended up now, right in the lion's den."

"The only one doing the biting here is you," I say, dipping into a low curtsy.

I hurry away, but Arthur keeps close to me. I stop at the buffet tables and grab a goblet of apple cider.

"Don't drink that!" he says. "It's what they want. It's how they're going to keep you here!"

Making sure he's watching, I slowly drink the savory liquid, enjoying every single gulp, and his look of horror even more.

"You little fool," he says, darting glances left and right. "As if coming here hadn't been hard enough."

I put the goblet back down, considering taking another cupful. The cider here is heady, and I can already feel its effects in the delicious warmth and fogginess pervading my body.

"You know," I say, pouring myself some more cider, "that is a good point. How did you get here? Especially with all your"—I point at his protective gear—"servant thingies."

Arthur puts my cup back on the table before I can take another swig.

"I told you not to drink that," he says.

I lick my lips, eyes focused on my drink. "You haven't answered me."

"I felt your ring," he says, checking our surroundings. "We need to get out of here, before the night's over."

I push Arthur's hand away and quaff the warm drink down, my free hand on his chest to prevent him from stealing it away from me again. When I'm done, I wipe my mouth with the back of my hand. Funny, I hadn't noticed before how vivid all the colors are, nor how everyone seems so soft and pleasant. Even Arthur.

I keep my hand on his chest, more to keep steady than to push him away. "You sh-should stop staring at me like that," I say. My mouth feels cottony, and I have a hard time forming words properly. "I'm not g-going anywhere with you till you tell me how you got h-here."

I'm not quite sure what Arthur's playing at, swaying back and forth before me like that, looking angry. He really should stop being so stuck-up.

"I had to let the sylph go," Arthur says.

I notice then the simple silver band on his pinkie, the one I'd had to leave behind to come here. But the ogham is gone. I feel a slight pang of sadness; that had been my Fey, the first one who'd responded to my call.

"It was that or let you be here alone without protection," he adds.

"Thief," I say, punching him in the shoulder before stumbling away.

Arthur catches up with me before I walk into a wide, spiky animal.

"I'm fine," I say, veering around the massive hedgehog-like creature. "Why does everyone feel like I need protection? You, and then Lugh, and then Dean, and then you. Is it cause you think

I'm gonna set the world on fire or something? I'm really not that bad, even if you think I've murdered all those people. I mean, I've even cleaned the toilets for two weeks without complaining. You should all take care of yourselves instead. You're the ones who are dropping like flies, not me."

Arthur slaps his hand over my mouth, then drives me back into a tree.

"Don't talk about that here," he says, hovering over me, his body tense.

My heart's going a gazillion beats a minute. I'm pinned against the tree like Christ to his cross, with no room to struggle.

"So maybe that one Fey was nice to you," he says, trying to reason with me. "But do you know them all here? What if one of them…" His nostrils flare with anger as he takes in the bandage around my neck. "Hell, Morgan, what if one of them had been the killer?"

I stop squirming.

"Oh, don't look at me like that," he says. "Of course I never believed you were behind those deaths. You're not talented enough. You saw the banshee, didn't you? You nearly died because of her! And now you come here, of all places? How could I not worry about you?"

He closes his eyes as if this long diatribe has wiped him out. I notice for the first time how pale he's gotten since our last training session together, ages ago, dark circles rimming his eyes.

"There, there," I say, patting him awkwardly. Nothing tonight, not even he, can make me feel bad anymore. "It's going to be OK."

The music stops abruptly, and people start screaming. Through the rapidly thinning crowd, I see the tables laden with food topple to the ground with a big crash, crystal plates and cups breaking into a scintillating rain. All that yummy food, wasted!

I want to rush over, but Arthur holds me back. Emerging from the forest's shadows is a large group of Fey, but these aren't the happy-go-lucky ones who have been partying in the clearing. These have a more feral look about them, like they're waiting for the smallest excuse to draw blood.

I involuntarily shrink away, my happy feeling gone. Their ranks part to let a large black horse through. The colt rears back, dripping wet, then lands amid the feast's wreckage.

The prince of the Tuatha Dé is suddenly there, a lone figure before so many hostile Fey. Yet his stance is easy and confident.

"That's quite an entrance there, Mordred," Lugh says.

A youth jumps off from the horse's back and hands the reins over to a woman whose curves would put Jennifer to shame. His jet-black hair is pulled back in a high ponytail, giving us ample view of his stern face and bare torso, which are both a strange shade of blue. He can't be older than either me or Arthur, yet he strides up to Lugh with all the confidence of a monarch.

"Who is that?" I ask Arthur. Apart from a troll, and perhaps an ogre, among the new faces, I've already exhausted my slim knowledge of Fey creatures.

"Don't know," Arthur whispers. "Just stay away from them, and try not to get noticed."

The youth continues to move along, past Lugh, inspecting the crowd, searching every creature's face like he's looking deep into their souls. And maybe he is, I realize with a shiver as he draws nearer.

"I don't recall you being invited to my get-together," Lugh said, putting himself between Mordred and us. "But of course, you're more than welcome to partake in the festivities, though you have made quite a mess of the victuals."

Mordred raises his hand. "Spare me," he says. "I don't have much more patience for you. I've come to collect my answer."

Hands deep in his pockets, Lugh shrugs. "I cannot speak for my people. Everyone's his own, and can do as he or she wishes." He flashes the intruder a bright smile. "Free will is, after all, the one gift the Lord Almighty was kind enough to bestow on us. You wouldn't want to take that away, would you?"

The blue-skinned guy gives him a cruel smile. "We got it because we fought for it."

A lumpy man the size of a dog approaches them. He bows to Mordred, the skin of his face flapping before him like it's been partially melted off his skull.

"A word, sire?" he asks in a raspy voice.

Mordred leans down to hear what the half-melted creature has to tell him. He stiffens, then straightens up.

"Seems like you have some interesting guests tonight," he says.

My throat dries up as his eyes first scour Arthur, then lower to me. Like a predator locked on to its prey, he makes his way over to us. As he comes closer, I see that the blue tint of his skin is the result of thousands upon thousands of thin lines tattooed on his body in tight coils and swirls that accentuate his sharp features.

He stops a few feet away from us. For a second, his golden eyes flecked with violet fix on me, and his eyebrows rise a fraction. Arthur comes to stand before me, drawing the man's scowl to him. Being the older sibling, I should technically be the one to protect him, but I'm forced to admit that I'm scared shitless.

"What is that one doing here?" the blue-skinned Fey growls.

I see his knuckles whiten as he clenches his fists, sending tiny sparks of blue-and-green lightning over his skin.

"Just a guest," Lugh says, striding over while maintaining a safe distance from Mordred. "Must've gotten lost. Tonight's his lucky night, though, as I'm in a very good mood and do not object to his presence."

A strained silence stretches between them while the three guys glare at each other, and I hope for the Fey's sake, and mine, that Lugh and Mordred don't make any sudden movements. Though he's taken off most of his weapons, I know Arthur still has a couple of hidden knives on him, and he's wound up as tight as a coil waiting to spring.

Maybe Mordred senses this, or maybe he decides he has better things to do, because he marches back to the edge of the trees, where his followers await.

"Time is running out, Prince," Mordred says, getting back up on his horse. "You better come up with an answer. Next time, I won't be so lenient."

He turns the colt around, and, as silent as the Angel of Death, he and his cohort are gone.

"Let's get a move on," Arthur urges me.

"But I—"

"Now."

We move through the dispersing throng, back toward the large oak tree at the center of the glade. Nobody seems to care about us anymore. But when we reach the tree, an unhappy surprise awaits us.

"The mushrooms have been trampled over," I say.

Arthur muffles a curse and looks about. But everyone else is too busy running away to help, and I don't see Lugh anymore either.

"Curse it," he says, "we need to find another fairy circle."

What was it that Lugh had told me? Something about circles being circles. And though some of the fungi are no more than unrecognizable lumps in the mud, the circle is still somewhat intact.

"Wait," I say before Arthur leaves. "Let's try it."

Arthur's about to protest, but I pull him inside the ring with me. Holding on to him tightly, I close my eyes and think back to the woods as they were before I came to Avalon.

It seems to take an inordinate amount of time for me to conjure the right image; I'd been so distracted by my own thoughts that I hadn't paid much attention to my surroundings at the time, just enough to realize that the place was dark, and cold, and not a little creepy.

I hear Arthur's slight intake of breath and open my eyes. Gone are the tiny lanterns glowing warmly in the air, and the scattering Fey. We're back in the woods by our school.

"I did it!" I shout, bursting with pride.

"Let's get out of here," Arthur says, dashing down the small hill. "It's nearly time for Lauds."

I glimpse the sky through the overarching branches and notice it's gone from deep black to a warm violet shaded with pinks and oranges. I can't believe it's near dawn. It feels like I've been gone for barely a few hours!

"Why aren't you coming?" Arthur asks, coming back for me.

I hesitate, still staying within my fairy circle. If I made it here, I'm sure I can make it back.

"Can you please stop making me worry?" he shouts. "Can you, for once in your life, think about someone other than you?"

"I didn't—"

Arthur cuts me off. "How do you think it felt to learn you were missing, not just from the infirmary, but the whole school, *again*? I kept on thinking I'd find your body lying somewhere, like we found Rei, or that you'd have disappeared like Kaede."

He stops suddenly and takes a deep, shuddering breath.

I'm too stunned to speak at first. I'd never have thought anyone cared about me that much, least of all him. I'm so used to being left to my own devices. This is completely uncharted territory for me.

"I'm sorry," I say at last. "I'll try to be, uh, better about it in the future."

Cheeks still flushed, Arthur nods. "You should also stop skipping classes," he adds.

"Don't push it."

Arthur flashes me a smile, then holds his hand out to me, just like he had when he invited me to dance. This time, I don't hesitate and take it. He closes his warm fingers around mine, and we race away.

The run back home is quiet, not that I can spare a single breath as I concentrate hard on keeping up with Arthur. I don't know where he gets all his energy from, but the bloke is bloody tireless!

When we reach the northern standing stone, Arthur finally slows down. Some of the night's great bonfires are still smoking in the distance as their embers burn down to ashes.

"Good," Arthur says, looking grim, "we haven't lost any time."

"Why?" I wheeze. "We've only been gone a night."

"Time over there can run differently," Arthur says. "Or so the tales say, and I'm inclined to believe them."

The desire to tease him rises in me despite my fatigue. "But what if we got here a year and a day later? Then these would be the fires from a year from when we left."

Arthur drops my hand, his lips thinning out in a scowl. "This is no laughing matter," he says. "You should pray this is not the case. A great deal can change in a year. Countries and civilizations have disappeared in less time than that, and, in case you haven't noticed, things were not peaceful when you decided to run away again."

"Some people just can't take a joke," I mutter, walking behind Arthur toward the church. We're too early, and the courtyard's empty, forcing us into an uncomfortable silence as we wait for the others to arrive.

I wonder if the whole school knows already of my punishment, then remember Jennifer's gloating face and know that's the case. I look back longingly at the line of trees along the horizon, where Avalon and Lugh await. Thinking about him reminds me of the kiss we shared, and I can't stop a blush from heating my face.

"You're thinking about him, aren't you?" Arthur asks in disgust. "You said you wouldn't go back there!"

"All I said was that I'd try to warn you before I leave next time," I reply, not liking his tone. "And why wouldn't I want to go back? They may not all like me over there, but I can't say it's much better here."

Arthur rolls his eyes. "How many times do I have to tell you, you're not a prisoner!"

I let out a very unladylike snort. "Puh-lease. Tell that to someone dumber than me."

"Look, this is all temporary," he says. "Maybe if you weren't foolish enough to wander beyond the school's protection all the time, this wouldn't have been necessary. As it is, we obviously can't trust you to not put your life and those of others in jeopardy, so until we've caught the one behind all these killings, you'll have to deal with it. You should be happy you didn't even get in trouble for doing EM."

"In public, you mean," I say. "Since you're the one who gave me that ring."

"True," Arthur agrees, to my greatest surprise. "No one was supposed to teach you how it works, least of all me."

"Why ever not?" I ask, too stunned to be mad anymore. "Isn't it the point for everyone here to learn how to use oghams, to become proper knights and protect Earth and all that?"

"Yes, but…" Arthur balks, at a loss for words. Guess not even he can come up with a good excuse, which is reason enough for me to grow deeply suspicious.

"Just why, exactly, would I be the only one not allowed to learn how to do EM?" I ask, seeing him grow more and more unsettled. "And why would I not have been sent here at fourteen, like everyone else? Or why not let me finish at a regular school instead?"

He's prevented from answering me by the appearance of the first early risers, who are none other than Gareth and Gauvain.

"Where were you yesterday, little mademoiselle?"[25] Gareth asks, giving me a lung-crushing hug.

"Don't tell me you were grounding her all night long," Gauvain tells Arthur.

"If you mean to say 'scolding,'" Arthur says, "then you're right. Somebody's got to do it, however annoying."

"Don't let him bully you," Gareth tells me.

"And if he does," Gauvain adds, "you let us know, and we'll pummel him." He stops at the church entrance to look me up and down appreciatively, until I turn crimson.

"It's no wonder he keeps you away from the rest of us," Gareth adds, his grin so wide his eyes are but half-moon slits.

"Enough, guys," Arthur growls, and the cousins burst out laughing.

"No, no, no need to get naked," Gauvain says, stopping Arthur from taking his jacket off.

"We'll be *chevalier-russe*,"[26] Gareth says, setting his own coat, which falls below my knees, around my shoulders.

"It's 'chivalrous,' you airhead," Gauvain says before adding to Arthur, "You'll need yours for the ceremony."

---

25 Missy.

26 Russian knight.

Before Gareth can start another fight, Lucan arrives, sitting uncomfortably in a wheelchair pushed by his squire. The cousins' faces fall at his sight, and I remember the night we faced the banshee. A good thing it was a knife she used and not poison, or Lucan and I would both be dead.

Knife. Poison. A thought strikes me, and I grab Arthur's arm before he can go to the section reserved for KORT members.

"Wait," I say.

"What is it now?" Arthur asks.

I ignore his sulky tone. "Those murders, I don't think it's the banshee."

Arthur straightens up, more alert. "Why not?" he asks cautiously.

"I just remembered," I say, "but when I was up on the island, it used some kind of flint knife to kill. There was no Fey magic involved, with poisoning or black veins or whatnot. And my lacerations—"

"Didn't show any sign of being contaminated the same way as Rei had been," he finishes for me.

We both stare at each other as the implications sink in. The church doors swing open to let in more students, breaking our moment of understanding. Arthur heads over to the cousins, who are arguing again, while I return to my bench.

When Bri, Keva, and Jack arrive, I greet them with a smile. Despite my new sentence, I don't feel quite so alone anymore.

CHAPTER 24

Bri and Jack's questions stumble over each other in a confused jumble of words the moment they see me, but Keva raises her hand, and they both shut up.

"What we first need to know," she says, "is where you got those clothes."

I blush, holding Gareth's jacket closer to me. I should've changed as soon as I got here. Keva narrows her eyes at me.

"So you were at the party," she says with an evil grin. "It's just that you weren't anywhere quite so…public."

"Ooooh," Bri says.

"That's so not how it was," I say.

Keva forces the blazer open to get an eyeful of the Fey dress. "Look at that," she says, loud enough to draw the attention of the squires seated before us. "Look at the finesse of the fabric, the delicacy of the design." She draws so close to me it almost feels like she's trying to smell my boobs.

"Back off," I say, batting her away.

Keva sits back with a deep, heartfelt sigh, tossing her braid over her shoulder. "You can tell the Pendragons are an old family, to be able to afford such a refined dress." She glances at me. "Whoever the fellow is, he's lucky. I've never seen you put so much effort into your looks before."

The entrance of a group of white-clad young men and women denotes the start of Mass, and I'm saved from having to explain my whereabouts. I know how they all stand on anything concerning the Fey here, and I doubt they'd approve of my little sojourn in Avalon.

Slowly, the procession makes its way down the nave, singing the Iesu Salvator Saeculi with voices so pure they could rival those of angels.

"Who are they?" I whisper in Jack's ear, pointing toward the formation as it marches past our pew.

"Fey," he answers in the same manner. "The history books say they've remained with us since Carman's defeat, but that they've vowed to never fight again, and to atone for their sins through constant prayer."

"Is that all they do?" I ask, unable to tear my eyes away from them as they fan out around the back of the altar.

Jack nods. "Yeah, they have their own room in the catacombs beneath the school, though they come out on special occasions like today, or to observe."

"Observe what?"

He shrugs. "Who knows? But that's what they call themselves: Watchers."

The whole school remains transfixed throughout the liturgy, which consists mainly of the choir singing hymn after hymn to the glory of God and of the knights who have fallen to protect us.

Kneeling before the altar, dressed in white-and-red robes, are three students, their heads bent down in prayer.

"What are they doing?" I ask Keva.

"They're about to be dubbed," she says, her face a mixture of admiration and envy.

"Dubbed what?"

"That means knighted," Jack whispers.

"Brothers and sisters," Father Tristan says, "before us today are three brave students who have proven themselves worthy of joining the ranks of knighthood, who are willing to put their lives down for the service of others and the protection of this land that was bequeathed to us by the Almighty.

"In King David's words, 'He whose walk is blameless and who does what is righteous, who speaks truth from his heart and has no slander on his tongue, who does his neighbor no wrong and casts no slur on his fellow man, who despises a vile man but honors those who fear the Lord, who keeps his oath even when it hurts, who lends his money without usury and does not accept a bribe against the innocent. He who does these things will never be shaken.' Are you ready to uphold these principles?"

"We are," the three kneeling answer in unison.

"Please present their arms," Father Tristan says.

Three knights move forward, each carrying a shield bearing the school's heraldic blazon, and lay them on the altar.

Father Tristan raises his hands over them. "Show us Thy mercy, O Lord."

"And grant us Thy salvation," the crowd says.

"Lord, hear our prayer."

"And give ear unto our cry."

"May the Lord be with you," Father Tristan says.

"And with your spirit," I mumble, my eyes roving to the unusual choir.

There's something odd about those Fey as they stand still as statues, their eyes fixed to the cupola above, oblivious to the ceremony unfolding before them.

Father Tristan finishes his blessing of the weapons and, looking regal, Arthur steps to the forefront. He stops before the three kneeling students.

On the other side of the transept, the whole of the knight corps is similarly decked out. The only one not wearing fancy armor is Jennifer, who manages to look politely bored in her deep blue gown that makes her hair look like a cascade of gold.

"Do you swear fealty to KORT and all that it upholds?" Arthur asks, his voice ringing clear.

"We here swear fealty and do homage to KORT," the three squires intone, "to ever be good knights and true, reverent and generous…"

I scoff at the thought of Jennifer having ever been able to utter such a vow. Bri digs her sharp elbow into my side, and I grow quiet.

"To shield the weak, be obedient to KORT's president, foremost in battle, courteous at all times, champion of the right and the good, and loyal to God Almighty. Thus we swear."

"Acknowledging your prowess on the training field," Arthur says, "and responding to the wishes of your sponsors, I am minded to make you knights. But know that to wear the arms of one is to hold a sacred trust, and that your obligations will follow you until your death."

From a pocket, Arthur pulls out a small escutcheon that shines dully before him, and hands it to the first kneeling boy.

"Wear this as a token of your fealty," he says.

With trembling fingers, the boy reaches out and takes the small token representing his new status. Arthur moves on to the next boy, then the girl after him, repeating the same speech each time.

Despite the novelty, this process is quite a drudge. I can even sympathize with Jennifer as my mouth extends in a wide yawn.

"Ouch," I huff when Bri elbows me again.

"A little respect, please," she says out of the corner of her mouth, her eyes trained on the altar and the four people before them.

I try not to nod off as Arthur steps back and the knights who'd brought in the swords and shields attach a pair of spurs to each of their protégés. When they're done, Arthur grabs the first sword, unsheathes it, and holds it before the first boy.

"Bear this sword with strength and honor," he says, "and may you never use it to hurt anyone for unjust reasons."

He slaps the knight on each shoulder, then the top of his frontal bone with the flat of the sword. "And may these blows be the only ones you'll ever bear. Rise, Sir Amir."

The newly minted knight gets up and, his curly head still bowed, receives the sword and the shield from Arthur.

Without a pause, Arthur moves on to the next boy, Bruno. When the girl, now Lady Claudine, receives her arms and weapon, I let out a groan of relief.

Thankfully for my now-bruised ribs, the chorus's angelic voices cover me and save me from another blow from Bri. The knights surround their newcomers with whistles and jeers. I watch them pass by, followed by Arthur and Jennifer. He looks tired and lost in his own thoughts, which seems to thoroughly annoy Jennifer, who keeps on whispering in his ear without arousing a reaction from him.

If she wasn't so disagreeable, I'd find the two of them quite stunning. But as things stand, they only make me gag.

"Let's get going," Bri says, "I'm starving."

Keva dusts her uniform. "No need to wait for me. I'm meeting my parents for breakfast. See you guys later. Or not."

Jack looks guilty. "My dad's here too," he says. "Sorry."

"What was that all about?" I ask as we trail far behind our classmates. "Why are their parents here?"

Bri doesn't look happy. "Parents are always invited to our tourneys," she explains. "They're about the only occasions when they're allowed back down here."

"Oh, that's nice," I say. I've yet to see my parents since I got attacked by the banshee, but I can't say I've missed them. "What about you?" I ask. "How come you're not meeting…"

Bri clenches her jaw so hard I can see the muscles work in her cheek. "They don't want to come near my brother," she says, then lets out a mirthless chuckle. "They fear being this close to him will taint them even more and destroy the little chance they think they have of making it on the Board."

"Well then," I say, forcing myself to be cheery, "guess we'll both be free of any parental supervision. What's fun to do at these things?"

Bri's brow unfurls ever so slightly. "The food's rather good I hear."

"Excellent," I say, the prospect of a meal reviving me. "Let's get going, shall we?"

Keeping an eye on my bread bowl of chicken and vegetables, and the other trained on the tournament taking place a hundred feet below, is no mean feat when you're climbing up the steps of an arena. By the time I reach Bri, I've spilled sauce all over Gauvain's jacket.

"What's so special about this tournament?" I ask, swallowing my brunch whole. "All they're doing is hitting each other with sticks. There's not even any EM being done."

"Wait until it's KORT's turn to go," Bri says, excited. "They actually have a full-on battle, with horses and lances and everything!"

"With old-school armor too?" I ask, imagining Arthur turned into a disgruntled robot.

"No," she says with a bright smile. "The armor's the only thing that's been changed over time. And a good thing too. A lot of people literally fried inside them when the weather was hot, and they weighed a ton."

She swallows the last bite of her corn dog. "The best part is that the top three winners of the regular knight games will be allowed to try out for a place at KORT."

"Really?" I ask, licking my fingers. "I thought there were only thirteen spots available, and all of them taken? Well, except for the two new vacancies."

"It's twelve seats, actually," Bri says. She boos the loss of a tall knight to a boy half his size. "The thirteenth's been vacant for as long as it's been created."

I think back to my one time inside the KORT room, and the ornate seat springs to mind, its dark wood carved with scenes of angelic battles. The one Arthur absolutely forbade me to sit in.

"It's meant only for the one who truly deserves it," Bri finishes.

I sniff the pungent smell of baked pies and caramel apples in the air. "So why doesn't the president sit in it?" I ask.

"It's too dangerous. If you're not worthy and sit in the Siege Perilous...you die."

I let out a loud laugh that makes people scowl at me.

"Seriously, though," I say to Bri, "nobody's sitting there because of some stupid urban legend?"

"It's not stupid; it's real," Bri says.

I let out a sigh. Sure, this whole place is out of the ordinary, and Avalon truly exists, but a magical chair that kills the poor bloke who happens to touch his arse to its seat...I shake my head. That's just too much.

"I'm going for some dessert," I say.

I get up, raising angry murmurs from the people behind me, and head back downstairs toward the sweets shops.

Despite the number of people seated in the stadium at the moment, the grounds around it are teeming with students and more family members than I'd ever have thought to see down here.

"Our kids are lucky to go to Lake High," I hear a woman tell an older couple. "They don't have to deal with the crazy weather above."

The old man nods. "Hear it's unseasonably cold up there," he says.

"Must be 'em," the old woman says, sucking around her missing teeth, and all three nod gravely.

I shake my head. If they hate the weather so much, why don't they move? Or better yet, couldn't they use EM to change it?

"I'll bet you two hundred my daughter beats your son," a red-faced man says to a stout woman.

Both are dressed in plain clothes, with not a single ogham in sight, which perplexes me even more. How could laypeople be allowed down here, especially after the rest of us have pledged a vow of secrecy?

Loud laughs erupt on the way to the forge, behind the dessert stands. Some of the people who'd been waiting in line before me stray off to the side to see what's going on, then desert the line entirely. It's not until I've secured a large piece of pecan pie that I decide to check out the commotion as well.

"What's going on?" I ask a woman whose husband is holding their son on his shoulders.

She shakes her head, as confused as I. With a shrug, I take another big chunk out of my dessert and force my way deeper into the laughing throng.

When I find the source of all the hilarity, however, my stomach contracts into a tight ball.

"They're coming!" Owen says, his face gaunt from weeks of starving himself. "They're going to kidnap us and feed us to the demons below!"

My whole lunch feels like it's coming back up my throat. How did he manage to escape the asylum?

I step forward into the circle of onlookers and try to appease him. But Owen, who barely reaches my shoulders, swings at me, and I'm forced to back out.

"I'm telling you they want you!" He laughs maniacally, making a toddler cry.

The tears draw his attention, and he points at her.

"Yes, the innocent too! They're going to bleed you to death, tear you apart, and feed your soul to Satan!" He pulls at his pale face, leaving deep gouges in his cheeks. "They're coming for the Teind!"

Spit froths at the corners of his mouth. The crowd has quieted now, and is watching him with fear and—the hairs at the back of my neck rise—with aggressiveness. Trouble's brewing, and the only person who has any chance of getting him back to the asylum's safety is his sister.

I dash back to the arena and take the steps four by four.

"Bri!" I call out.

The short girl whips her head around, her light brown hair tousled and her cheeks red with excitement.

"It's gonna be Hadrian's turn. Hurry up!" she exclaims, pointing at a couple of knights standing to one side of the fighting area.

I shake my head. "You gotta come," I yell over the loud cheering. "Trouble!"

Bri hesitates, and I feel guilty for bringing her the bad news. Finally, she reluctantly follows me.

We don't get there soon enough. Bri stops dead in her tracks when she spots her twin, her face drained of all color. Most of the crowd's left, and a few kids are now tormenting Owen. To my disgust, I see that one of them is Daniel.

"How do you like that, Feyblood?" the bully asks, kicking Owen in the ribs so hard the smaller boy's body is lifted in the air.

"Stop it!" I yell, pushing him away.

I interpose myself between the two boys before Daniel can kill Owen. I hear Bri's twin moan behind me, spitting up blood.

"Shame on you, abusing the weak like that," I say, hoping the nearby crowd will be enough to keep him away from me—I'm already familiar enough with his fists. "You'll never get to become a knight if you continue like this."

I shouldn't have said that. The boy's beady eyes lower with malicious fervor, and he smiles.

"But that's only towards other humans," he says. He points at Owen still on the ground behind me, mumbling about soul reaping and demons. "He, on the other hand, has clearly become Satan's puppet."

Bri runs over to get her twin back up. He must have recognized her, because he doesn't object to her help. I shift my stance to one of combat, lowering my knees and transferring my weight to the balls of my feet.

"That's a paltry excuse, even for you," I retort, keeping myself between him and Owen as he slowly circles us.

Like a pack of vultures, people come to surround us again, drawn by the prospect of more blood. Not one of them is willing to lift a finger to help us. I shake with fury at the thought of any of them ever pretending to stand by the noble code of conduct to which we're supposed to pledge ourselves. No matter where I go, hypocrisy is always prevalent.

"What's going on here?"

Still dressed in his full knight garb, Hadrian comes to stand before me, eyeing Daniel like one would a chicken about to be plucked.

"Are you the one who did this?" he asks. He sounds calm, but underneath it, I can sense a cold fury.

I smirk at Daniel. It's high time for him to get his ass kicked, and I'm pleased to be a witness.

"Name?" Hadrian asks, to my greatest surprise.

"Daniel," the boy spits.

"Year and order?"

"First, page."

Hadrian nods. "Noted. Be ready to hear back from KORT." And with that, he strides away, raising murmurs of disappointment in his wake.

I hurry over to Bri. "Let me help," I say.

I make to grab Owen's other arm. The boy's limping terribly, and his short gasps tell me he has some internal contusions. But the moment I touch him, the boy recoils from me as if I've just punched him.

"Morgan!" Bri says, stumbling to the side.

"I didn't——" I start, struck. "That wasn't——"

"It's OK," she says through gritted teeth. "I can take care of this." She pauses to whisper in Owen's ear and calm his whimpering.

Wringing my hands together, I watch them make their painful way back up the dirt path to the asylum, wishing I could be of some comfort to either of them, yet knowing my help is unwanted.

Still lost in thought, I head back toward the stadium's entrance, kicking up clouds of dust. I do so wish Hadrian had given Daniel at least one solid punch.

"There you are!" Percy says as he flings his arm over my shoulders with a laugh. "You ain't thinkin' 'bout scamperin' off, are ya? 'Cause the show's just about to start!"

Arm tight around my neck to keep me from running away, he drags me to a group of KORT members lounging about the south side of the arena, where most of the participants are waiting for their turn.

"Hey Arthur!" Percy yells, making my ears ring. "Look what I found!"

Standing a little apart from the others is my brother, tall and straight as a sapling, his light brown hair almost blond in the waning light. His full fighting suit makes him look even bigger than usual, gleaming where the metallic mesh cedes to layers of long, thin iron plates.

I grin, raising my hand to wave at him as he turns to look at us, then drop it just as quickly. Behind him are Irene and Luther, dressed in their usual gothic-warrior garb.

"You don't mind if we miss your performance, do you, Son?" Luther asks.

"We caught one of the main instigators," Irene says, itching with impatience. "He's in the catacombs right now, and we want to use the time to question him. Maybe today will be our lucky day and he'll spill the beans."

I clear my throat loudly as I approach them. "Hello, Mother," I say, not meeting her eyes. "Luther."

There's a moment of silence, during which I can hear the rest of the group wager who will get kicked out of KORT this year, and by whom.

"I heard you went after a banshee," Irene finally says.

I nod, watching the tiny flowers that adorn my new shoes, noting how they sparkle even in the dimmest of lights.

"You seem to be doing fine," she adds as an afterthought.

I can't help it; I look at her. Her eyes, heavily done with black, are cold, assessing, and I know that she wishes I were still in the hospital bed. I feel my heart give a painful throb, but keep my features as neutral as possible; no matter what, I cannot let her see me feel hurt.

"I still need to get ready," Arthur says.

"If you had a page, as is proper," Irene snaps at him, "it wouldn't take you this long to get ready." She gestures at the other knights around us, and I notice for the first time other boys and girls helping the KORT members put their armor on. Even the cousins have a pair of stout boys taking care of them.

With a huff, Irene struts away.

Luther pats Arthur's shoulder as he walks by. He doesn't say a word, but it's clear it's the pride of a father for his son. For one long second, my innards squirm with acrid jealousy of my brother.

I breathe in, let the air fill my lungs and purge me of the feeling, then exhale. I don't think I've ever felt such an intense emotion before, especially not one so dark, and it scares me.

"You OK?" Arthur asks me.

"I'm fine," I snap. I don't need anyone's pity, least of all his.

Not once did Irene come down to see me when I was nearly dying, but she has no problem coming to see her son parade around school like a lordling.

"Why isn't Dean here?" I ask. I'm sure that if he could, our family lawyer would be here with me, a silent but reassuring presence at my side, like he's always been.

"He can't," Arthur says, sliding his gauntlets into the belt holding his sword. "He hates water."

"Even with the boats?"

Arthur shrugs. "Never gets closer than twenty feet from the lake," he says, mocking. "If he can't get somewhere by foot or car, he takes a plane. Or the helicopter."

My eyes open wide, Dean—*my* Dean—is scared of something? And it's not even of bugs, or spiders, or Fey, but of water? Just the absurdity of the idea makes me want to giggle.

"Oh, Morgan," Gauvain calls out. His cousin's standing right next to him, talking animatedly to Lance and Jennifer, the latter of whom ignores me completely. "I wanted to ask you for something."

"What is it?" I ask, walking over to them.

"Oh no you ain't," Percy intervenes, pushing Gauvain out of his way to get to me faster. "I spotted the lady first!"

"You can spot this," Gauvain says, punching Percy in the midriff.

Thankfully for Percy, he's already wearing his armor, and the blow doesn't affect him. They both race over.

"I wanted to know——" Gauvain starts.

"If I could get your favor," Percy finishes, shoving his hand over Gauvain's mouth and poking him in the nose at the same time.

"You need a favor?" I ask, looking from one to the other. "From me? You do realize I'm the least helpful person on campus? Unless you need something from the infirmary."

Gauvain's brilliant-white smile flashes in his dark face. "No, a favor from a lady is a token of her...preference for a chevalier."[27]

"And comin' from you, pretty lady," Percy adds, "it'd be like our lucky star's shinin' down on us the whole time."

"So you want something from me?"

"Anything," Gauvain says, stomping on Percy's foot hard enough to make him lose his footing and hop a few feet away. "Like a kerchief, or a shawl."

"Or a ribbon," Arthur says, untying the one holding my hair back.

"Hey! Give that back," I say.

27 Knight.

328

Without paying me any attention, Arthur wraps the green-and-silver ribbon around his upper arm.

"The lady's s'posed to give it freely," Percy says, massaging his foot.

"It's mine," Arthur says. "Unless you want to challenge me for it?"

Percy grins. "Nah, we're fine. Right?" he asks, nudging Gauvain.

"Yes, very fine," the tall knight adds.

"That's what I thought," Arthur says, heading toward the back of the arena, where the racks of weapons have been brought out.

"Well, at least wish us *bonne chance*[28] then," Gauvain says.

"Good luck," I tell both boys before they leave to get their weapons as well.

My good mood flees the moment I notice Jennifer's livid face staring right at me. Gareth and Lance are gone from her side as well, leaving us completely alone.

"So you think you can display yourself around school like some floozy, do you?" she asks.

"I don't know what you're talking about," I say.

She pulls on Gauvain's jacket, letting it fall to the ground.

"You don't, do you?" she says. "What a beautiful dress, quite unlike any I've ever seen." She walks behind me, trailing her fingers up the back of my right arm, along my shoulders, then back down my left arm before facing me again

"Where did you get it?"

"I got it as a present," I say, holding myself back. This girl may not be a proper knight, but her earrings and ornate necklace are filled with oghams, which means I stand no chance against her.

28 Good luck.

Her fingers linger on my collarbone. "Such fine work, so thin and soft at the same time, yet I wonder"—she leans into me, slowly, like she's afraid to scare a bird away—"whether it's Fey."

A quiver of fear runs down my back. Jennifer feels it and, in one swift move, rips my dress apart.

I yelp in surprise and dive down to grab the discarded jacket to cover myself up.

"Traitress," she hisses. "So it was you all along, wasn't it, convening with them? The banshee event was a cover-up too!"

"Don't be ridiculous," I say.

"Get yourself and your filthy dress out of my sight," Jennifer spits, her face scarlet, "or I'll find a way to get rid of you, you little tramp!"

Feeling the sting of tears prick my eyes, I hurry away as a wave of cheers rises from the crowd in the arena at the appearance of KORT.

Chapter 25

The door slams behind me, cutting out all the outside noise. Why does the school have to be so centered on hierarchy? I'd love to give Jennifer a taste of her own medicine.

Looking down at the tattered remains of my dress, I heave a mighty sigh. That's twice now that I've received a present in my life, and twice it's been taken away from me.

The fresh evening air wafts in through the thin windows, brushes against my exposed skin. I rub my arms for warmth, and my hand grazes the old scar on my left shoulder—a raised cross that seems to have marked me for martyrdom from infancy.

My footsteps falter as I reach another of the slitted windows out of which I can hear the spectators' excited cheers. If a seat at KORT depends on skill and ability, there's also a factor of chance. Which means Arthur could technically be dethroned. I wonder how much Jennifer would enjoy having her fiancé ousted.

I force myself to turn away from the window and head deeper into the school. If it weren't for Jennifer, I would be out there like the others, cheering on the different knights. Like Percy, or Lance.

You're so overly dramatic, you know. You could go back out now. Bet that girl isn't even there anymore.

I glower, if you can glower at an inner voice. "Have you even seen my dress?" I mutter.

Nothing's preventing you from getting changed.

"Look, if I wanted to be rational right now, I'd be rational. Can't a girl be moody in peace?"

Come on, my guardian angel continues, *don't you want to see them fight? You could learn a thing or two...*

"Just leave me be!" I nearly shout, scaring a servant boy away. "I'm not going to go back out there tonight," I say, much lower. "And there's no need to wheedle me into doing it. I've made up my mind."

My guardian angel lets out a sigh of exasperation. Sometimes I'm amazed at my ability to keep myself company. Other times, like tonight, I wonder if it isn't a sign my mental health is deteriorating.

A low purr resonates around my ankles, and I find a pair of golden eyes staring up at me, as bright as the torches down the hallway.

"What are you doing here?" I ask, petting the black cat's furry head.

With a meow, the cat lets me pick it up.

"You look awfully familiar..." I pause. "You're not... You couldn't be..."

The few hours spent in Avalon, which now seem months away, come back to me.

"Are you Lugh's cat?" I ask. "Are you following me?"

I laugh at the craziness of this until the cat claws me. I drop the feline to the floor and clutch at my hand; four parallel scratches are now etched into the back of it, deep enough to show blood.

"You stupid thing!" I hiss as it licks its paw disdainfully. "I don't care where you're from or who you belong to. Just...stay away from me!"

The cat looks decidedly unconcerned. Before I walk away, however, it tenses and sniffs the air. Then, staying low to the floor, it slinks away through a door to the inner courtyard.

"Good riddance!" I yell after it, closing the door on the cat so it can't get back out again.

But I remember the hundreds of rare and precious plants kept by Professor Pelletier, some of which are poisonous. If the darn creature's dumb enough, it might get killed, or, worse, it might pee on all the plants and kill them instead!

I crack the door open again and call out.

"Here, kitty, kitty," I say, making kissing noises.

But the dark garden remains quiet, except for the soft cooing of a couple of doves in the fruit trees that border the building, and the occasional wisp of music carried by the light wind from the festivities. For a split second, my hand clenches around the door handle. The tournament must be nearly over now, and I'm stuck here, still in my torn-up dress, looking for some dim-witted animal.

With a heartfelt grumble, I let go of the door to comb through the small pathways, peering into the bushes and around plants and trees in search of the annoying cat.

"She's always watching, always, and there's nothing I can do about it!"

My hand freezes on a low-sweeping branch—sounds like someone's having a lovers' spat. I hear a soft voice reply, too low for me to make out the words.

"No, I can't stop her!"

The barely contained anger ends with a heart-wrenching cry. I jerk back in surprise, letting go of the branch, which snaps back into my face. I clasp my hand over my stinging mouth, and right on time, for the darned cat chooses that moment to brush past me, toward the angry couple, and nearly makes me scream.

"I don't know how much longer I can keep doing this," the man says. "It's tearing me apart from the inside, and every day she grows stronger…"

"Cat, come back here," I whisper harshly. "Cat!"

I stop at the edge of the pool of light thrown by a round lantern hanging from the branches of the massive apple tree. Within the amber glow is a woman sitting on a stone bench, a man lying down with his head in her lap. Definitely not a fighting couple. I remain transfixed as the woman makes soothing noises, brushing the man's light brown hair back from his troubled face. From the long tresses and her midnight blue gown, I know it must be Vivian.

I take a few steps back, afraid of getting caught like some grubby old voyeur, then hurry away as quickly as possible, giving up on my hunt. I nearly make it to the building when I catch a furry backside a couple of bushes down.

Very slowly, I tiptoe up to the creature, then pounce on it.

"Got ya!" I say as my hands grab the furry beast.

Except it's fatter than I recall, and a lot heavier. I turn toward the light to get a better look.

"Puck!" I exclaim, so shocked I almost drop him.

The little creature burps in my face, letting me know he's recently had a mixture of sweet milk and blue cheese.

"Lovely," I say, wrinkling my nose as I gently set him back down on his bum.

Puck jumps back up on his tiny hooves and runs around me in close circles that prevent me from going anywhere.

I chuckle. "Stop it, Puck. I need to get out of here, and I'd rather not trip on my way."

But the little hobgoblin won't quit his antics until I stop moving entirely. I cross my arms and tap my foot.

"What is it?" I ask.

Puck stops his insane twirling and hops up to grab my hand. To my surprise, he leads me back toward the apple tree, but before we reach the bench on which Vivian and that man are, he veers left.

I soon find myself faced with a wall of tangled roots, the kissing hedge, but Puck doesn't stop there and instead bounds between two wide shoots. After a moment's hesitation, I follow him. I've always avoided this section of the garden before, and I catch myself growing embarrassed at the thought of getting caught here.

As I make my way through the maze of gigantic roots, I feel the ground shake underneath me and have to hold myself to stop from falling. To my utter surprise, I realize that the roots are shifting beneath me to make a very treacherous-looking set of stairs that lead below ground.

"I don't think this is such a good idea," I tell Puck in a loud whisper.

Yet I keep going down, one step at a time, farther and farther into the ground, until my feet reach a patch of soft earth. I stop before a wide archway gaping at me like a toothless mouth. The air here is much cooler, making me shiver.

Before I can backtrack, Puck rams into the back of my legs, forcing me forward.

The moment I step through the threshold, my skin tingles as if I've just walked through a giant spider web.

"Where are we?" I whisper, terrified to make another movement.

When my eyes adjust to the dimness, I realize that I'm inside a small, barren room.

"I don't know why you wanted me to come here," I tell Puck, feeling brave again now that I find we are alone down here. "There's no milk, no cheese or cookies, nothing."

A slight rustle reaches me, like drapes made out of beads being pushed back, and a small glow appears in the back of the chamber.

"What the—"

I cross the alcove toward the light and find it's coming from a small round bowl of black polished stone.

I reach for it, feeling the runes carved in its rim with my fingertips. The glow emanating from it makes the stone seem translucent. I clutch the bowl to my chest, and the roots that had been hiding it from sight fall back in their original place.

"You shouldn't do that!"

I stop breathing, heart hammering, my hands holding the vessel closer to me. I slowly turn around, but I'm well and truly alone in this tiny room.

"Don't tell me what to do," Jennifer's voice answers, muffled.

I instinctively recoil from them before I realize there's a small door hidden behind the curtain of roots dangling along the curved wall of the chamber.

I press my ear to the door. What is Jennifer doing down here, and who with, when she should be at the party with Arthur?

Every still-functioning cell in my brain is firing signals that tell me this is none of my business, but the dumber part of me, the one that always wants to know what's going on, tells me I need to find out what other evil plan the Queen of Hell has hatched.

The small door swings back at my touch without a sound. I let my eyes adjust to the sudden flickering light of torches before I edge forward into what I find is the vast cellar.

"You see how she is, simpering in front of everyone else like she owns the place," Jennifer continues, talking to some unknown guy. There's no doubt in my mind who she's talking about, however.

The door closes behind me, blending in so perfectly with the rest of the wall, I can't see it anymore. I have a second of panic before I realize that nobody's seen me come in, and I'm perfectly out of sight.

My dress rustles about my ankles as I step around the ceiling-high rows of barrels to get a better look.

"Anyway, we shouldn't be meeting here anymore," Jennifer says. "It's too dangerous. We could get caught."

"It's safer," the boy answers. "You saw Rei. You don't want that to happen to you as well, do you?"

Jennifer snickers. "Please, with her here, I say it's probably safer out there. And don't tell me you actually like her."

"I never said anything," the guy says back. His voice sounds familiar, though I can't quite place it.

I crane my neck around another barrel of alcohol, but the next row is empty as well.

"You know, there's something awfully strange about her," Jennifer says.

"What do you mean?" the boy asks.

"Well, for one, why make her come here now? I mean, they've kept her away all those years, why bother bringing her here at all? I'm telling you, there's something wrong with this picture."

I hold my breath as the two of them speak. Despite my abhorrence for her, I have to concede that Jennifer's got a good point, one I've asked myself a gazillion times.

"Perhaps it's because her abilities were latent," the boy says, calm.

"Please, she didn't even know how to do any kind of EM when she got here," Jennifer says.

I lean against the wall of casks, doing my best not to make a sound.

"But she comes from a long line of strong blood," the boy continues. "It would have been stranger if she hadn't been able to use elementals. Besides, you saw how much she's improved in so short a time—she was able to get herself to the surface without anyone's help."

"Stop defending her!" Jennifer says, her tone as sharp as a samurai sword. "About that, you never told me how you ended up being the first one to save her."

For the first time since I've been eavesdropping, the guy lets out a sigh. Frankly, I'm surprised he hasn't been annoyed with Jennifer sooner.

"I couldn't very well explain why I was outside the school walls, could I?" he asks. "It was either that or have us exposed, and I would never let that happen. Besides, it was my duty as a knight, and would you like me as much if I turned away from my vows?"

With a jolt, I finally realize who's been talking to Jennifer all this time. I stoop down so my eyes can peer through the holes left between the stacked barrels and hold back a gasp.

A few feet from me are Jennifer and Lance, standing so close to each other that if one sneezed, the other would be sure to be covered in spittle. My hand clenches convulsively around the stone bowl as I watch them embrace. I guess Lance is no robot after all. Then the second shoe drops. That little tramp! How dare she fool around with another boy, however pretty he may be, while she's engaged to Arthur?

Something grasps my hand, and in the next second, I feel tiny, sharp teeth sink into the meat of my thumb. I scream and fling the bowl aside, sending Puck flying into a cask. He hits it so hard one of his horns sinks into the wood and gets stuck.

"Who's there?" Lance calls out.

There are some hurried footsteps, but I'm too concerned with the blood flowing freely down my hand to pay much notice. I wince as I prod the wound; this is definitely going to need some stitches. I just hope I'm not going to catch leptospirosis[29] or some weird Fey disease.

"You!"

The cry of outrage gets me to look up as Jennifer advances toward me like a banshee.

"How dare you spy on us!" she yells. Her blond hair is unusually disheveled, and her alabaster skin shows red spots of anger; even in enraged she manages to look pretty.

"I was here first," I say. "What were you doing here? Oh wait, never mind, I already know."

I look pointedly over her shoulder at Lance, who's turned a few shades paler, but doesn't look away. Jennifer slaps me, her blow stinging my cheek with such force that it echoes in the cellar.

"Jennifer, you should calm down," Lance says, finally approaching us.

"Don't tell me what to do!" she yells. "I'm sick and tired of everyone dictating my every move, my every word! I won't have any of it from you too!"

Puck manages to extricate himself from the cask, his horn coming out of the wood with a pop. The wine pours out of the new hole like a fountain, flooding us. Jennifer squeaks as a burgundy wave hits her dress, splattering her and Lance together. Using the diversion, I run away as fast as possible.

---

29 Disease found in domestic animals transmittable to humans, usually in the form of jaundice and fever.

CHAPTER 26

The morning bells draw me away from my dream—a boggy mess where I'm caught fighting Jennifer, who turns out to be a monstrous Fey in disguise, while trying not to fall in the ever-widening hole that's opened at our feet.

I make a final punch, my fist getting caught in my covers, and end up falling face-first out of bed.

"Better hurry," Keva says, already decked out in her pristine uniform. "This is the last day of fun before we have to go back to the everyday drudgery of school."

I grunt, sitting up like a mummy.

"At least my parents aren't here today," she says, "so I'll be able to actually enjoy myself."

I rub at my eyes before the pain in my sore hand reminds me of the previous day's events, and how much I hate parties.

I take my time to extricate myself from the bedding and put on my last clean uniform. Then we go find Bri and Jack who are waiting for in the hallway.

340

"What's the matter with you guys?" Keva asks as we drag our feet towards the staircase like we're going to a funeral instead of a fair.

Daniel barrels through us, knocking Bri down. Jack and I both catch her before she can plummet down to the bottom of the stairs.

"Watch it!" Jack yells.

"Sorry," Daniel sneers. "Didn't see Crazy here."

"She's not crazy!" Jack retorts, shaking with rage. "So shut it."

"Well, her twin's in the loony bin," Daniel says, "and you know blood doesn't lie."

With a chuckle, he rushes down to the ground floor, Ross and Brockton laughing at his heels.

"I swear," Jack mutters, "if he says anything more to you about...I'll—"

"Get pummeled into mincemeat," Keva finishes for him. "Not a very wise choice, I'd think."

"Let's just get going," Bri says, sounding tired.

Subdued, we make our way to church while everyone around us is laughing and making plans for the last day of the festival which is to consist of games and contests.

"I don't know how to break this to you," Keva says in a listless tone, "but you guys are really no fun right now. So once Mass is over, I'm gonna explore the fair on my own. Deal? Great then."

I ignore her. Keva will never change and will always place her own interests first.

"How is your brother?" I ask Bri when we get inside the church.

She kneels on the prie-dieu, her head in her hands.

"He's not doing too well," she says, her thin voice barely carrying over the muted din of the growing crowd. "He seems... more agitated."

"How so?" Jack asks. "Is he getting bored?"

Bri shakes her head. "I don't know. He doesn't make sense. He keeps talking about a reaping or a tithe…It's just horrible to see him so scared and not be able to do anything about it."

She lets out a muffled sob. Feeling awkward, I pat her back lightly.

"He's safe, though," Jack says, looking as much at a loss as I am. "People are taking care of him while he…recovers."

Bri lets out a small chuckle that shakes her frail shoulders. "Safe?" she asks, sounding near hysteria.

I look around, noting the curious stares thrown at us. Keva, on the other hand, is doing her best to ignore us.

"Safe?" Bri repeats a little louder. This time, there are more than just a few casual glances in our direction. "Do you know how easy it is for them to get out of there? Just to get to visit someone, you have to jump through twenty thousand hoops, but can they even keep an eye on their patients? *No!*"

"Shh," Jack says, his face and neck red.

"What if he gets out again?" Bri continues.

"I wish we could help, truly," I whisper soothingly, "but what can we do for him?"

Bri turns her fevered eyes toward me. "We can get rid of all those filthy Feys," she hisses.

I'm too disturbed to pay much attention to Mass, and barely manage to mouth the appropriate responses. Instead, my thoughts keep whirling between Bri's fervent hate for the Fey, yesterday's strange events with Puck, and Jennifer's cheating. I scratch my itchy hand, which still bears the mark of Puck's teeth.

Everything's so crazy now, I'm afraid of going even more insane if I stay here.

At that thought, the image of Lugh's golden eyes swims back before me like in a dream, bringing with it the recollection of that terribly embarrassing moment when we kissed. It's strange how soft lips are, like trying to kiss a marshmallow, except with teeth.

When Lauds is finally over, I rush toward the exit, in desperate need of calm and quiet.

"Morgan?"

I turn around at the sound of Father Tristan's soft voice.

"Yes, Father?"

"May I have a word with you?"

Sighing inwardly, I follow him to the back of the church. When we've reached the apse, he turns to face me, his unblinking gaze making me squirm.

"I've noticed you haven't been to confession yet," he says.

I eye him with circumspection; is he angry or just stating a fact?

"I, uh, didn't really think it was obligatory."

"It's not," Father Tristan says. "But I thought you may need it."

"Why?" I ask. "You think I'm always up to no good?"

A tiny smile appears on the priest's wan face. "I didn't say that. However, it's always best to make sure you are cleaned of all sins before you go out into the world. You never know when Azrael may erase your name. And when that happens, wouldn't you want to present yourself with the scales as much in your favor as possible?"

I shiver at his mention of the angel of death. What is he trying to convey to me? That I'm going to die soon? Is this a threat?

I swallow convulsively before I manage to answer. "Do you tell this to everyone here?"

"No," he says after a pause. "Yet most people go to confession at least once a week, and they don't get in trouble as often as you do."

A cold fear washes through me. Does he know of my time in Avalon?

"I don't have anything to say," I mumble, "except, perhaps, that I don't get along with everyone at school, and I often wish I could strangle them. I do believe that is my worst sin, Father."

Father Tristan doesn't respond right away, keeping me rooted to my spot while he examines me. I try really hard to keep my expression as blank as possible, willing him to believe me.

The church doors slam open before he can further question me, however, and we turn at the sound of someone running toward us.

"Morgan!" Bri calls out on the brink of panic. "I need your help!" She skids to a stop and grasps my hands and squeezes them so hard I'm afraid my wound's going to open again.

"What's the matter?" I ask. "What happened?"

"It's my brother," she says, on the verge of tears. "He's gone!"

"Where?" I ask, trying not to freak out as well.

"If I knew that, I wouldn't have come here!" Bri yells.

"All right, all right," I say. "Let's think about this for a minute. When did they notice he was missing?"

"I'm not sure," Bri says, sniffling. "Around the time when the bells for Lauds rang, I think."

"OK, so he can't have been gone for more than an hour," I say. "He can't be very far. He's probably just roaming about the school. Have you asked anyone if they've seen him?"

Wringing her hands, Bri shakes her head. "I just came straight here. I was hoping that you...I..."

"Take a deep breath," I say. "Nothing's going to happen to him. Let's just go around and ask people if they've seen him. And we can ask Jack and Keva to help too, and the prof—"

Without letting me finish, Bri dashes away. With a quick curtsy to the priest, I follow suit.

Outside, the sky-lake is dark, pressing down on us like a water balloon about to pop. Everyone's at the fairgrounds already, leaving the school mostly deserted, and Bri was so fast I can't tell where she's gone to.

I hesitate. If past behavior can be relied upon, it would seem Owen may like the crowds. So I set off at a light canter toward the music and laughter.

"Morgan!" Percy calls out, an air rifle slung over his shoulder. He waves me over to the shooting stand where Gareth's watching his cousin take all of the targets down with a sour look.

"Look who's come to join us, guys," Percy says, nearly poking Gareth's eye out with his rifle.

"Where were you last night?" Gareth asks me. "You disappeared without a mace!"

We all stare at him, and Gauvain pauses in his shooting. "You mean 'trace,' idiot. What would she need a weapon for?"

"Because it's been getting dangerous outside," Gareth retorts, crossing his beefy arms over his wide torso.

"So what's the hitch in ya giddy-up?"[30] Percy asks me in his southern twang.

"My friend Owen's gone missing," I say. "You guys wouldn't happen to have seen him?"

30 What's the matter?

I look hopefully at the three boys, but they stare back at me with such blank looks I might as well have been asking them to paint the Sistine Chapel over.

"What's he look like?" Percy asks.

"He's about five-five," I say, "dark hair, dark eyes…"

"That's about any freshman boy out there," Gauvain says, passing his rifle back to the amazed man in charge of the stall.

"Well, he's crazy," I say, grasping for words. "You know, the one who got into an accident with a salamander at the beginning of term?"

The three boys nod heartily, and hope surges within me. If KORT starts looking for Owen, then he'll be found in no time!

But Gareth adds, "I remember the bull. It was quite wild. But…I don't remember your friend."

Percy and Gauvain nod again, and I feel myself wilt.

"OK then," I say, starting off again. "Just…keep your eyes open for me, all right?"

"Will do!" Percy says, waving his weapon high in the air and smacking Gauvain with the butt of it. "And come hang out with us when you've found 'im!"

I make my way around the crowded field, occasionally stopping by booths or vending stalls to ask more people for Owen's whereabouts, but all I get are shrugs and shakes of the head.

When I've gone around the grounds a couple of times, I spot Jack skulking next to the mirror house, eating fries halfheartedly. When he sees me, his face brightens up.

"Have you seen Bri?" he asks me.

"We're looking for Owen," I say, stealing some of his fries.

"You mean he's escaped again?"

I nod, devouring the rest of his snack. "I've asked everyone here, and no one's seen a trace of him."

"You don't think that he's back at the asylum, do you?"

"I don't know…" I say. "I guess I could go check it out."

"I'll go with you," Jack says. "If he's not there, then I can help you guys look for him too."

We both set off back toward the school, only to be stopped by Arthur, who's sitting at a table with Lance and other KORT members.

"Where were you yesterday?" Arthur asks me. "I didn't see you at the tournament. You know you're not supposed to leave without—"

"I was *in* the school," I say.

My eyes move over to Lance, sitting on the bench next to him. Unashamed, he looks back at me with his light gray eyes.

"So what are you up to now?" Arthur asks, breaking my string of silent curses at his fake friend.

I glare at my brother, annoyed at all these questions. Does he really think he can have me leashed like some dog?

"Nothing," I shoot back. "Come on, Jack."

Jack limps after me, though somewhat unwillingly.

"What?" I ask when he's stopped for the fifth time in his tracks.

"Well, I don't understand…" The shy boy looks away as if I'm going to bite his head off at the smallest word.

"Go on," I say, trying to calm myself down.

"Why do you hate him so much? It's really not very smart to get him mad at you. You're only going to dig yourself a deeper hole."

"Let's just go see if they've found Owen," I say. "Then we can worry about more trivial things."

We're almost all the way back to the school when a large gust of wind catches me in the middle of my back and propels me off my feet. I land on the hard earth, biting my lip.

"Are you OK?" Jack asks to the sound of distant laughter.

I let him help me back to my feet as a large group of people stomp over our way.

"Nice one, Daniel," Ross says, high-fiving him.

"Now, now," Jennifer says, pulling away from the middle of the pack with a mock frown. "We shouldn't play games like these with special-needs people."

She walks over to me, her miniskirt swishing around her wide hips. I should've known she would find the first opportunity to get even with me. But if she wants me to divulge her secret, she's picked the perfect spot.

Jennifer stops before me. Her frown deepens as she's forced to look up. With visible effort, she relaxes her jaw and smiles.

"You've cut yourself!" she says, sounding to untrained ears genuinely concerned. "Here."

She takes out a yellow tissue from her pocket and dabs my lip with it. I try to pull away from her, but her other hand shoots out and grips my arm like a vise.

She leans into me. "You better keep your mouth shut, or you're going to regret it," she whispers, pressing the kerchief hard into my mouth so that my teeth dig deeper into the cut.

I wince and try to get away, but Jennifer doesn't let me go. A growl starts out low in my throat, and I lash out, punching her as hard as I can.

Jennifer falls unceremoniously to the ground to the collective gasp of her fan group.

"What did you do that for?" a squire girl asks, rushing over to help Jennifer.

"You better stay away from me," I say to the blonde girl as she gets back up, holding her eye. "Stop messing with me, or else you're really going to regret it."

"She was just trying to help you!" the squire says, outraged.

"Didn't I tell you that she's become more violent?" Daniel says. "She should be locked up like the wacko that she is." He smirks at me. "Your status as Arthur's sister isn't going to protect you forever, you know."

His words are accompanied by murmurs of assent. I hold my tongue—a little late, but nothing I can add will make things better now.

Without another look at them, I continue on my way to the asylum.

"Hey, wait up!" Jack calls out.

I slow down enough for him to catch up. He steals a few side glances at me, looking worried.

"Did you have to go that far?" he asks.

"What?" I ask, unable to contain my anger any longer. "You think like them too? That I'm some monster waiting to jump anyone who's unfortunate enough to get in my way?"

Jack cowers away at my tone, and his reaction only riles me up more.

"Are you scared of me, Jack?" I practically yell. "You think I might kill you too? Well if that's the case, what are you still doing hanging around me for? Go away!"

Eyes wide, Jack darts away like a scared rabbit. The moment he's gone, my anger disappears, and I'm left feeling like a deflated tire. I want to call him back and apologize, but it's too late for that now.

I realize my hand is hurting and slowly unclench it—blood has seeped through the bandage and, pushing it back, I notice the stitches have burst out. I sigh. Time for me to make a quick stop at the infirmary.

"What did you do to yourself?" Dr. Cockleburr asks me, dabbing my mouth with as much delicacy as a rhinoceros pawing the ground.

"God nogged o'er 'y zome gids," I say, my newly bandaged hand limp on my lap.

Dr. Cockleburr humphs. "I don't know what I'm going to do with you," she mumbles. "A shame, for someone training to become a nurse to be caught in fights all the time."

I grin and immediately regret it as I feel my wound stretch.

"You better take care of yourself, girl," the portly woman tells me as I make my way out.

"Yes, ma'am," I say, eager to get away and resume my search for Owen.

I make a sharp turn into the hall that leads to the exit, when my ears prick. I hurry over to one of the windows and listen carefully. Above the distant sounds of laughter and music is the muted sound of a horn. It dies out, then, seconds later, picks up again.

And this time, the call is answered by a keening wail a few feet away from me that raises every hair on my body.

CHAPTER 27

"Owen!"

I run after the stumbling boy, jump over a fallen potted plant, slam into a door, and propel myself into the staircase where I've seen him disappear.

"Owen, where are you going?"

The sound of bare feet slapping against the stone floor comes back down to me, and I climb up the stairs in pursuit. I now really regret having sent Jack away; if this keeps up, I'm going to be running up and down all over the school, and I'll be dead before lunchtime.

"Owen, come back here," I call out.

His head pops up over the balustrade, the torches behind him throwing his face in deep shadow.

"They're coming," he says, drool coming down his chin before landing a few steps above me. He laughs. "They're coming for me!"

I try not to break eye contact with him while I close the distance between us. "Who's coming for you, Owen?" I ask, keeping my voice calm.

"*Them*," he answers. "You've heard the call too, haven't you?"

I'm but a few steps away from him now, so close I can see his dilated pupils, the balding spots at his temples where he's torn out his hair, and the barely scabbing wounds he inflicted upon himself yesterday.

Slowly, I reach out to him. My fingers brush his sleeves, then the cold flesh of his wrist. He giggles and flees.

"Owen!" I call out, running after him.

I land on the second floor. Both hallways on either side of me are empty, the sun peacefully slanting down through the open windows.

"Saint George's balls, Owen, where did you go now?"

I try a classroom door, but find it bolted. With mounting worry, I try each door, finding most of the rooms either locked or empty. As I round the corner, however, I see the boy at the other end of the hallway stiffen. A second later, the distant sound of a horn reaches me.

I expect Owen to scream again, but he turns around and marches back toward me, his features rigid.

"So you decided to come with me?" I say with a false cheeriness. "Are you hungry? I can go get you some sweets if you want."

But Owen doesn't seem to hear a word I say. He walks by without so much as a look at me, his mouth resolutely shut.

"Owen?" I ask, pulling on the back of his dirty jacket.

Owen doesn't slow down and keeps on marching, pulling me behind him. I tug harder, but the thinning cloth of his coat rips in my hands, and I stagger backward.

Without a trace of hesitation, he goes for the KORT room's large black door and opens it wide.

"What are you doing?" I ask, rushing after him. "We can't go in there."

I squeeze past him and move about the empty room. "There's nobody here, see?" I say, gesturing around me. "Just some old table and chairs…"

Owen stands still as a rock, his eyes glazed over. I use that moment to sneak a peek behind the long drapes where I saw Arthur disappear during my hearing. All I find, however, is a tall mirror at the end of a dark alcove that takes up half the back wall.

I poke my head back out the drapes. "Nope, nobody here eith—Owen, *no!*"

The boy's moved the Siege Perilous back. I dash toward him, my feet getting caught in the drapes. I fall, scraping my hands and knees, struggle to get back up, then run toward him.

I'm still feet away from Owen when he sits on the polished black wood of the chair. I gasp, expecting the ceiling to come crashing down on us.

For a moment, nothing happens, and I let my breath out—those legends were wrong after all.

"Owen?"

I take a tentative step toward him and freeze as his head snaps back, his wide-open eyes two pools of black as if his pupils have bled into the rest of his eyeballs. Which I know is not physically possible.

Facing me, the angel carved on the back of the chair seems to move. My eyes widen as I realize it's crying, tears of black trailing down its perfectly symmetrical face. The demon it's about to skewer with his sword opens its mouth, and more of the black goo pours out of it, climbing up the ebony chair.

Before I know it, the strange liquid's enveloped Owen's hands and feet, spreading up and over his limbs. A guttural cry's wrenched from his thin throat, like his innards are being torn to shreds. He starts struggling against his bindings, his movements getting more jerky and feeble.

"H-Help," he gasps before screaming again.

His eyes, clear for the first time since the accident that sent him to the asylum, are staring straight at me.

"Please," he whispers, his body shaken by spasms.

I lurch forward, grab him under the shoulders, and pull.

"Come on," I say, gritting my teeth and trying not to touch the foul substance still creeping up his body.

Another shudder runs through him as the black liquid reaches his navel, and he lets out a shriek that nearly bursts my eardrums. I pull even harder, sweat dripping down my face and back.

"Try to push yourself!" I yell.

Owen stops screaming so suddenly I let him slip from my grasp before I realize what I'm doing and tighten my hold on him again. His breath comes out in short gasps, like he's drowning.

I don't care anymore if the black stuff gets on me or not. I need to get him out of there! I grab for his arms, my hands plunging into the dark slime, and find myself grasping the chair instead. I move my hands around, but can't feel his limbs.

"Owen, where's your hand?" I ask, my throat clenching with fear.

But the boy's too far gone from the pain, and he doesn't respond.

"*Owen,*" I say, getting more and more frantic, "lift your god-damned hand so I can get you out of there!"

The black liquid reaches his sternum. Owen's shoulders convulse.

"No!" I scream, tearing at the slime as fast as I can, trying to get it off him. "Nonononono!"

My hands are a blur, but the more I fling the goo off from Owen, the faster it seems to be climbing up his body. Soon it reaches his chin. His head falls against the back of the seat, his mouth open.

"Please don't, please don't, please don't…" I cry, tears pouring down my face to lose themselves in the black mixture.

The liquid pours inside his mouth, cutting off his last gurgling cry. Within seconds it closes over his nose, reaches over his scalp. The last thing I see are his eyes, staring into mine, before the darkness envelops them and he's gone.

I sink to my knees before the now-empty seat. Owen. Gone! What am I going to tell Bri?

I don't know how long I remain prostrated before the Siege Perilous. I don't even notice when the blackness that's stolen Owen away disappears again, leaving the seat as pristine as it was before.

All I can think of as I clench and unclench my hands is how cruel God is to make me witness my friend's death, but also be the one to have to bear Bri the news.

In a spurt of rage, I push the seat violently away from me. It topples backward and falls with a loud thud, making the floor shake.

Then, out of the sudden, deep quiet that's descended upon me, comes another long, terrifying scream.

I smack my head up into the side of the table as I look about for another victim, when I realize the screams are coming from outside.

I rush to the window. Long shadows are now enveloping the courtyard below me, distorting everything in sight. I can see the asylum north of where I stand. On the other side, going west, is the road we take to and from the landing pad, where the boats are waiting the coming of the weekend to send us back to the surface.

Frowning, I squint at the three long shapes on the hill, their graceful keels curving up into three stylized dragon heads. I blink a few times, then squint again as a dull flash of blue reaches me once more. My breath catches in my throat; running between those boats while waving a knife is a girl, and just a few steps behind her, taking its time, is a blurred-out shape.

My heart quickens, and I run out of the room, bumping into a white-clad man standing in the doorway. I bounce off the wall before tearing down the hallway toward the stairs that lead to the exit.

"Help!" I cry out, sprinting so fast a stitch develops in my side.

From the ground level, I can barely make out the boats. Another sharp scream rings out in the air, then is just as abruptly cut off.

"Leave her alone!" I yell as my feet pound down the wharf.

I reach the first of the boats, but find its surroundings empty. Without waiting to catch my breath, I race to the next one. Lying on the blackened grass behind it is Jennifer, a dark shape bent over her.

My blood runs cold, and I throw myself forward. My fingers graze only air as the shape moves away from me, revealing the rest of Jennifer's body. I land on my knees on the burnt-out grass next to her.

I gather Jennifer's limp body in my arms and look up, but the dark figure's gone.

With trembling hands, I shake her by the shoulders.

"Wake up," I say, unable to contain a sob. "Wake up. It's gone. The thing's gone!"

But Jennifer's limpid blue eyes don't open to glower at me like they usually do.

"Come on," I say, shaking her more forcefully. "This isn't a joke, Jennifer!"

Someone pushes me aside and grabs her hand. "What did you do to her?"

My mouth opens and closes without uttering a sound as I watch Lance take Jennifer's pulse, his movements frantic. Someone else arrives, the same squire who'd come to Jennifer's aid after I punched her.

"It's her!" she says, pointing her finger at me as more people appear. "She's the one who did this. I saw her!"

"What?" I mumble.

"You didn't have enough beating her senseless," Daniel says, scowling at me, "you also had to try to kill her!"

"I didn't—"

"You said you would make her pay," the girl says, bursting into tears, "and now you have!"

"You're a witch, admit it!" a boy spits at me.

"You're trying to kill everyone around you!" someone exclaims.

"She's probably got Fey blood in her," Daniel says. "Always said she was a troll."

"Or maybe she's a demon escaped from hell," the squire retorts.

Helpless, I watch as Lance picks Jennifer up in his arms like she weighs no more than a bag of feathers, and hurries away.

At the end of the pier, he runs into Arthur.

"She's still alive," I hear Lance say before he continues on down the hill toward the school.

With that one word, it's like the whole world's been lifted from my shoulders. I sink farther into the ground, unable to move another muscle. I don't even react when a pair of shiny black boots enter my vision.

"Come with me," I hear Arthur say above me.

I don't even care that two knights have to drag me with them like some convict. All I know is that I've at least saved one person, and it's all that matters.

CHAPTER 28

I'm half dragged, half carried back to school. My ears are buzzing, and my head feels like it's about to burst like a champagne cork. It's not until we've reached the second floor and I see the large KORT room door wide open that I balk.

"Come on," a knight says, shoving me inside.

I trip on my own feet, but manage to stay upright with the help of Percy, who's holding my other arm.

"Y'all right there, Morgan?" he asks. "Come on over 'ere, and 'ave a seat."

I slump onto the cool stone bench, my eyes riveted to the Siege Perilous. Though the inky liquid that poured over Owen is now gone, sucked back into the chair, I can still see the boy as he was, just moments ago, his gaunt face distorted with pain.

Hunched over, I let out a whimper. I can hear people trying to push their way in to get a better view of me, but Gauvain and Gareth shove them back out.

"Enough!" Arthur yells. "I want everyone who's not a KORT member or an eyewitness to leave this room immediately."

With mumbled words of protest, students file back out, leaving a small group behind.

"Murderess!" Jennifer's friend hisses at me on her way to the other side of the room, followed by the rest of their pack.

I watch them fight over who gets to sit farthest from me.

Someone knocks at the door, and a second later, a freckled face appears.

"What is it?" Percy asks.

"I c-came as a w-witness," Jack says, in obvious awe.

"Take a seat with the others," Percy says, motioning toward the bench.

I try to give Jack a small smile, but he studiously avoids my eyes. To my surprise, he doesn't stop next to me, but goes to join the others, and I know that he's going to talk against me. A feeling of betrayal washes over me, but then I shake it away. I can't blame Jack; my situation isn't very pretty right now.

"You're finally learning, Smith," Daniel says. "Thought you'd been taken in by her, like the others. But the witch hasn't won you over yet, huh?"

There's a collective sniggering that gets cut short when Gareth walks over to take a seat. The giant guy pulls his chair out and sits down heavily in it. Daniel lets out a loud cry.

"Oh, excuse," Gareth says. "I didn't realize."

And, very slowly, he lifts his seat to let Daniel pull his foot out from under it.

In another time, another place, I'd have been delighted at the sight. But right now, I can't bring myself to care.

A moment later, the door opens again to let in a pale Lance. He marches straight to his seat besides Arthur's.

"How is she?" Arthur asks him.

"We're not sure," Lance says with visible difficulty. "Dr. Cockleburr says that she's showing the same signs of poisoning as Rei, but, from her first observations, it appears something may have stopped its progress. It does look like she was in a fight, however, as she's bruised around the eye."

"Is she conscious?"

Lance shakes his head.

"It's her fault!" Jennifer's friend yells out, standing up and pointing her finger at me. "It's because I stopped her that Jennifer's alive! I—"

"Silence!" Arthur says. "Sit back down. You will be given the opportunity to speak later."

Arthur turns back to Lance. "You were the first knight on the scene," he says. "What did you see?"

"I'd heard of a commotion at the landing docks, so I hurried up the hill. When I got to the boats, I saw that girl push Morgan away and Jennifer already unconscious. I checked her vitals, then picked her up to take her to the mending wing."

Arthur nods. "Did you note anything strange?"

"I saw a dagger lying on the ground, but I was too concerned about getting Jennifer help to pay attention to much else."

"All right," Arthur says, taking notes. He then looks at the back of the room, where the witnesses are huddling together. "You." He points to Jennifer's friend. "Stand up, and give us your name."

"Sophie Williams, sir," the girl says.

"Status?"

"I'm Jennifer's squire, sir."

Gareth stands back up, holding up an old, but well-cared-for Bible.

"Place your hand on the Bible and swear to speak the truth and nothing but the truth," he says, "and may God be your witness."

Sophie places her trembling hand on the Bible and whispers, "I swear."

Gareth sits back down, causing Daniel to scramble to get his feet away as fast as possible.

"So what did you see happen, Miss Williams?" Arthur asks, pen at the ready.

"I went looking for Jennifer, sir," Sophie says. "She'd gone to the infirmary after being punched in the face by *her*."

"Morgan had punched Jennifer?" Arthur asks, sounding mildly surprised. He clears his throat. "Please explain."

"Well, we were walking together to get to the fairgrounds," Sophie says, "having fun, when we came across that murderess. She'd slipped, and Jennifer went to help her. But instead of getting thanked, she got punched in the face!"

I let out an involuntary cry of protest—how dare she lie so blatantly, and after swearing to God on top of it! I'm halfway up when a small sign from Percy makes me sit back down.

"But when Jennifer didn't come back, I decided to go check on her. That's when I saw her, sir."

"Saw who?" Arthur asks, his voice level.

"That murderess." Sophie spits out.

"You can call her Morgan," Percy says, in his usual bored drawling. "Or Miss Pendragon. Your choice."

"Please continue," Arthur says.

The girl glares at me. "She was running up to the boats, and I heard Jennifer scream. So I ran up there too, but when I got there, she was already down, and that murd…Morgan was trying to kill her."

"How exactly was Morgan killing Jennifer?" Arthur asks.

I'm amazed at his composure while I'm being accused of yet another murder. I stare, wide-eyed, at his strong features as he looks back and forth between Sophie and his growing stack of notes.

"She was slapping her, sir."

Arthur looks up at Sophie, his eyebrows cocked. "Slapping her?"

"On the face!" she says to add weight to her account.

"Very well," Arthur says. "Did you hear anything at all, from her or around you?"

Sophie looks stumped for a second. "Not really, sir."

"What do you mean, not really?"

"Well…" Sophie bites her lower lip, throws an accusing look in my direction as if this question is my fault, then adds, "She, that is Morgan, was talking to herself."

"And what was she saying?"

Sophie shrugs. "I'm not sure. I-I was too busy trying to save Jennifer. And then Sir Lance arrived."

"Thank you," Arthur says, "you may sit down."

"But I know she was trying to kill her!" Sophie adds. "She'd threatened her. And look at her hands—they're black, black with the poison she used on Jennifer and the others!"

We all look down at my hands, and she's right; my palms are blackened, though I know it's not because of Jennifer. Hiding my hands deep in my pockets, I momentarily squeeze my eyes shut as visions of Owen's terrified face come back to me.

"Yes, thank you," Arthur says while Gareth forces Sophie back down on the bench with one large hand on her shoulder. "Next."

Daniel gets up then. He gives me a tiny smile of derision, then states his name. "Daniel von Blumenthal, sir."

Staring down at my lap, I slouch back against the cold wall. I know exactly what he's going to say, or the rest of their group—it's Switzerland all over again. In their eyes, I'm a psychotic killer who itched to give Jennifer her due. Well, they might not be entirely wrong on that point, but I never actually wanted her dead. Maybe permanently disfigured or incapacitated…

I choke back a gasp. Maybe it is my fault she's now dying in a bed somewhere in the infirmary, I realize. Have I not wished, multiple times, for her to pay for all she's put me through? Though I'm not the one who's hurt her, except for the black eye, maybe my wishing it so is what caused it.

"Morgan?"

I jerk my head up and blink at the faces staring at me expectantly. I realize that everyone's already spoken, Jack included, and that it's now my turn to give an account.

"Yes?" I ask, standing up so quickly it makes me dizzy.

Gareth comes to stand beside me, offering me the Bible.

"Place your hand on the Bible and swear to speak the truth and nothing but the truth," he says, "and may God be your witness."

I place my hand on the crackled cover. "I swear," I say.

"Please state your name and status," Arthur says.

I cast him a mocking look—as if nobody in here knows me. "Morgan Pendragon. Page."

"Please state the events leading to the recovery of Jennifer's unconscious body by Sir Lance."

"First of all," I say, "I would like to make some clarifications."

Arthur's pen stops over his papers. "Very well," he says with a sigh.

"When I saw Jennifer this morning, I was looking for my friend's brother. Jack can attest to that."

Jack flinches at the mention of his name, but I ignore him.

"However I didn't fall down on my own, as was stated," I continue. "I was attacked."

"Attacked?" Arthur asks the top of his nose scrunching in concern.

"Yes. By them," I say, making a sweeping gesture toward the group sitting on the other side of the long bench.

"How so?"

"It was an elemental attack," I say. "A sylph."

"You're quite sure about that?"

I nod.

"And you saw them do it?"

I hesitate. "Not exactly," I admit. "But it wasn't the first time I've been subjected to bullying from Daniel, so I assumed—"

"Let it be noted that the accusation of an attack is an assumption by the accused," Arthur says, making further notes.

I clench my fists, but keep on with my story—now's not the time to go berserk. "While falling down, I split my lip open, and under the pretense of helping me, Jennifer threatened me."

This time, Arthur can't help but look at me.

Sophie springs up from her seat. "Lies!" she yells. "We didn't hear her say anything!"

Gareth, who's back in his original place, has to force her to sit down again.

"What did she threaten you with?" Arthur asks me.

I glance quickly in Lance's direction, but his face remains blank. "I-I'd seen her do something the night before, and she didn't want me to tell anyone about it."

"What was it?" Arthur asks.

Conflicted, I stare at my brother. I feel like I should tell him the truth, tell him that his darling fiancée is cheating on him with one of his best friends. But then I imagine how much this will hurt him, and I just can't bring myself to do it, especially not in front of everyone else.

"I can't tell you," I finally say.

"That's because she's lying!" Sophie yells again before Gareth shuts her up.

"If it's anything illegal," Arthur says, his voice cold, "then you must bring this up."

"It wasn't anything...illegal," I say. "But it wasn't something she wanted others to know either."

For a while, the only thing that can be heard is the sound of the wind sighing outside the windows, and the distant screams of children playing. I shift my weight from one foot to the other, hoping Arthur won't force me to reveal the secret.

"Continue," he says, resuming his writing.

"I went to the infirmary myself," I say. "For my lip and my hand."

"Yes, Dr. Cockleburr did mention it," Arthur says. "So when did you see Jennifer next?"

"I'm not exactly sure how long it was," I say, finding it more and more difficult to speak. "But I heard her scream, and when I went to look, I saw someone was chasing her up by the boats. I couldn't tell who, I was too far, but I saw her try to defend herself against it with a knife. So I ran over to help."

"How long did it take you to get there?"

"I don't know. A couple of minutes? When I got to the boats, she was already on the ground, and this...shadow thingy was over her. When it heard me, it ran away."

"Did you get to see who it was?" Arthur asks.

I shake my head. "Like I said, it was a black shape, somewhat blurred...I couldn't make out anything from it except that it was bigger than me."

"It?" Arthur asks, sitting straighter in his seat. "You don't think it was human?"

I hesitate. "No."

The room erupts in cries of protest.

"This is stupid," Daniel says, louder than everyone else. "It's obvious she's lying. Fey can't penetrate through the school's barriers!"

Arthur raises his hands, and the assembly quietens. "Let the accused finish her story," he says. "Why didn't you think it was human?"

"Well, I tried to tackle it," I say, "and it moved really fast out of my way. Too fast to be human. Even then, I should have touched it, but my fingers didn't feel anything, just…cold."

More angry murmurs break out around the room.

"I grabbed Jennifer to shield her," I say, "but when I looked up, it was gone. I didn't even hear it leave. And Jennifer…I tried to wake her up, but when she didn't, I panicked. And that's when that girl, Sophie, pushed me away."

"Now let me ask you this," Percy asks me. "Where exactly were you when you saw Jennifer and this 'ere, uh, black shadow critter?"

I feel the blood drain from my face. "Here," I say.

"'ere as in school?" Percy says. "Or…?"

"In this room," I whisper.

The scratching from Arthur's pen stops. "Why were you in the KORT room?" he asks me.

"I'd followed my friend's brother in," I say, choking on the words. "He'd escaped from the asylum, and when I saw him after leaving the infirmary, I followed him here."

"He came 'ere?" Percy asks.

I nod. "I saw Jennifer through that window."

Percy gets up to stand where I'm pointing. "You do have a better view of the dockin' area from 'ere," he says.

"So what happened to the boy," Arthur asks, "your friend's brother?"

I burst into tears. "He-He sat d-down where h-he shouldn't h-have," I hiccup, "and I couldn't s-save him!"

"What do you…The Siege Perilous?"

"But that's not possible," one of the knights says. "Everyone knows that—"

"He's gone!" I yell, hysteric. "It ate him! It took him. It—"

Percy's holding me in his arms, making soft, soothing noises. I cry into his shoulder, soaking his clothes, but he doesn't let go of me.

"You should've come straight to me," Arthur says, pacing the KORT room, empty now but for him, Percy, the two cousins, and myself.

I'm sitting on the stone bench, eyes lowered to my clenched hands.

"Then Jennifer would be dead," I say, trying to ignore my pounding headache and my left shoulder throbbing in tempo with it.

"So you think you saved her?" Gauvain asks me.

I shrug. "Whatever that...thing was doing to Jennifer, I interrupted it, and she's still alive, isn't she?"

"We don't know how quickly the poison works," Arthur says.

"Well, it ain't that slow," Percy says. "If it only took Morgan a couple a minutes to get up there, then that critter didna have much time with 'er. But you 'eard what Lance said, She did 'ave some of them veins turned black."

"What I find troubling," Gareth says, "is that the *créature* was on school property at all."

"Yes," Arthur says. "Either Morgan's wrong about what she saw——"

"I know what I saw," I say.

"But you'd just seen your friend die," Gauvain says. "We can understand if it made your brain confused."

"I was not confused," I say, much louder than I intended. "I know what I saw. I didn't make it up. How could I?"

"But if that's the truth…" Gareth says. He stops, looking somber.

"Then the barriers are compromised," Arthur finishes. He passes his hand over his face, looking exhausted.

Percy pushes himself away from the wall. "I'll go check it out," he says. "Will be back directly."

He raises his hand to his forehead and nods at me as he strides past.

"Anything we may help for?" Gareth asks.

Gauvain tosses a pebble in Gareth's direction. "With, idiot. You should study your prepositions more."

"Just check on our supplies," Arthur says before a fight breaks out between the two. "And post on the news board that there's a curfew as of today. No one, except for knights on duty, is allowed outside the school. Anyone who's found to break the rule will be expelled."

"Eye to eye, *Capitaine*," Gareth says, snapping his heels together in salute.

I hear the cousins' bickering voices die down as they disappear down the hallway. I envy their ability to be so carefree, like nothing in the world can get them down, no matter how horrible or threatening.

"You," Arthur says with an accusing tone.

I lift my eyes up to him shaking his finger at me.

"You," he repeats.

"I did not leave the school grounds," I say, defying him to find something to criticize about me.

Nostrils flaring, he watches me carefully, then says, "No. You didn't. And that's an issue."

"What do you mean, an issue?" I ask. "I did everything you told me to. I even went out of my way to help that…your girl-friend. What more do you want from me?"

"For you to stay out of trouble," he says. "But apparently that is too much to ask of you. So from now on, you are consigned to our home."

The words take a while to sink in. Then I jump up to my feet. "What did you say?" I ask, shaking with rage.

"You heard me," Arthur says, turning away. "You can't be trusted. And if that's the only way I can keep you out of funny business, then so be it."

"By locking me up?" I laugh when he doesn't answer. "Really? That's the best you can do?"

"Damn it, Morgan!" Arthur yells, spinning around so we're standing nose to nose. "How else am I supposed to keep you safe? No matter what I say or do, you always manage to slip through the cracks and invite trouble. Do you think I want the next body we find to be yours?"

I push him away. "Why do you keep on wanting to protect me all the time?" I ask, shoving him again. "I never asked for any of this! I never asked to be in this godforsaken place! I never asked to become a knight!"

I'm crying freely now, but I can't stop myself. I'm tired, tired of seeing people die in front of me, tired of not knowing anything about everything.

"That's twice now that you're trying me for killing someone," I say, punching Arthur in the chest over and over again until my knuckles are scraped raw. "Why didn't you guys just leave me to rot in a cell in Switzerland when you had a chance? Things would have been a lot easier, and you wouldn't have had to deal with me!"

Arthur grabs both my fists and holds them down behind me, locking me in place so I can't fight anymore. Gasping, I glare at him instead.

"You will do as I say," he says, his hazel eyes so dark they almost look black. "And that's final."

CHAPTER 29

Whistling a funeral march, Percy follows me down the corridors as I look for Bri—the last thing Arthur's allowing me to do before I head back to the surface and get locked up for who knows how long. The high-pitched version of Chopin's classic grates on my nerves as I try to find the best way to tell her that her brother's dead.

"Hey, ain't that the girl you're lookin' for?" Percy asks, pointing with his chin.

Looking down from a fifth-floor window, I see the small figure of a girl running toward the meadow, her short dark hair in disarray. My heart sinks at the sight—that's definitely Bri, and she's still looking for Owen.

I whirl around and rush back downstairs under the confused looks of students coming back from their day of fun.

"Bri!" I call out when Percy and I pass the wharf on our way west. "Bri, wait up!"

"There!" Percy says.

We run past the last boat and into the fields surrounding the school. We run until we reach the western warding stone, out of breath.

"Where is she?" I ask Percy, panting.

The shorter boy looks about. "Not sure," he says. "But that girl's mighty quick!"

A cackle makes the hairs at the back of my neck stand up. Hand on his sword, Percy crouches into a fighting position, but a haggard face pokes around the monolith, a beatific smile peeking from under his beard.

"It's Myrdwinn," I say, stopping Percy from skewing the crazy old man.

"Yeah, I noticed," Percy replies. "You spotted anyone round 'ere?" he asks the old man.

Myrdwinn laughs, pulling on his extended earlobe. "Just a lil' mite running like she got her ass on fire," he says.

"Where?" I ask. "Which direction?"

"Just down the next hill," Myrdwinn says, shuffling over.

With a loud sniff, he grabs my hands and turns them over to show their blackened palms. He sniggers.

"Thought you were the *chosen* one, eh?" He laughs, drool dripping into his beard. "Well, you're marked now. There's no more escape!"

I pull my hands away. What does that degenerate old man mean? That I'm going to die next, like Owen?

"Come on," Percy says, chivying me away. "Let's get yer friend back and give 'er the news."

Casting a backward glance at Myrdwinn, I run into the muddy fields, struggling to crest the hill without slipping. But over here, we can see someone's small footsteps have preceded ours.

"Bri!" I yell again, stumbling in the mulch. "Wait up!"

Bri finally hears me, for I soon see her plod back to us.

"Did you find him?" she asks, her uniform soiled from slipping in the mud herself.

Now that I've found her, I can't bear to tell her the truth. I watch a flock of crows take flight from the distant treetops. For a moment, I wish I were one of them, free to roam about the earth with no worries beyond finding food and shelter.

"Well, where is he?" Bri asks.

"We did. Find him, that is," I say. This is so not a great start. "But…he's gone."

"Gone?" Bri repeats. "You mean he escaped again?"

I shake my head. Why is she making this harder on me? "I mean he's *gone* gone," I say, "as in…" I clear my throat and kick a tuft of dirt aside.

"I don't understand," Bri says, looking back and forth between Percy and me. "Did he leave school? Did my parents come pick him up?"

"No," I say.

"He sat in the Siege Perilous," Percy says, coming to my rescue.

With a sharp intake of breath, Bri sinks to the ground.

"No," she whispers, as if denying it is going to make everything OK again. "No, it's not possible. You must be wrong."

"I saw it myself," I say, trying real hard to keep my eyes dry. "He'd gone crazy!" I want to kick myself at the use of the word, but keep going, "I saw him when I came out from the doctor's, and I kept calling and calling him, but it was like he couldn't hear me. So I followed him, and we ended up in the KORT room.

"At first, I thought he'd just gotten confused. That maybe he was looking for someone, you know? And I…I looked away for a split second. And when I looked back, he'd sat down on that cursed chair. I tried, I really did, but there was nothing I could do!"

Bri remains motionless for so long I wonder if she's fainted with her eyes open. Finally, I hear her tiny voice.

"You're sure about this?" she asks.

"Quite sure."

Despite the open air, I feel like I'm suffocating. Yet I can't even imagine what Bri must be feeling like now, when her own twin is gone and there's no more hope of him ever coming back to her.

I put my hand on her shoulder. "Is there anything I can do for y—"

Bri slaps my hand away. "Don't," she says. "I don't need your pity. I just...I just want to be alone for now."

"OK. OK, I can do that. But...are you sure you don't want someone with you? I could go find Hadrian if you want."

"I said *leave!*" she shouts.

I shrink back, then turn away and head for the docking area. There's nothing more left for me to do here before my exile, nobody else my presence can bring bad luck to.

Silent as a shadow, Percy trails after me. I repress a shiver. If I do bring disaster everywhere I go, maybe it's not such a good idea for Percy to come along. But I hold my tongue, knowing that no matter what I say now, nobody's going to listen to me.

Back on the surface, the world is as dreary as I feel. Winter hasn't officially started, yet the lake's surface is already patched over with ice, forcing Percy to use a salamander to break through.

To my surprise, Dean is waiting for us at his usual spot, his tall, lanky frame dark against the night sky.

"How did you know we were coming?" I ask, my teeth chattering.

373

"Arthur sent your parents a message," Percy says as Dean hands me a warm coat.

"So quickly? How?"

"It's called scrying," Percy says. "Just need a flat reflective surface, and ya can use it to see what's happenin' elsewhere. Ya can also communicate that way. Real prattical when we can't use regular tech, like down there."

We head for the car, which has been left running on the side of the old cemetery. Inside, Percy sinks deep into the leather seat.

"You're coming too?" I ask, pushing him farther into the car so I can climb in.

"Sure thang," he says, eyes closed. "Gotta make sure the miss is safe and all."

I feel my blood boil and dig my fingers into the seat. "This is ridiculous," I say. "I don't need someone to watch over me twenty-four seven. It's not like I'm going to do anything."

My protest goes unheard, however, as I soon notice Percy's deep and steady breathing. I let out a grunt, and the rest of the drive back to Fond du Lac is done in absolute silence, except for the occasional muttering from Percy in his sleep.

When the car pulls into our driveway, the door to the mansion opens to let Irene out.

"Thanks for coming along," she tells Percy, looking tense. "And you can tell my son we'll be coming in later."

Percy gives her a sharp nod, but before heading off again, he pulls me aside.

"Arthur had a message for ya," he says low in my ear. "Don't trust anyone."

"Yeah, great, thanks," I say with a derisive snort for this sudden brotherly concern.

Percy shakes my elbow. "He means it, Morgan. Ya can't follow no one till he comes back 'ere for ya. Ya hear?"

"I hear," I say.

With a small bow, Percy leaves me behind with my mother and Dean. Irene ushers us inside before closing the door and setting the lock.

"Luther's asked to see you," Irene tells the tall lawyer. "He's in the office, going over the maps."

Apprehensive, I watch Dean disappear into the depths of the house—there goes my last line of defense against my mother.

A strained smile on my face, I make a small curtsy. "Good evening, Irene," I say, inching toward the stairs. "Lovely weather, isn't it? Well, I'm knackered, so I think I'm going to go to—"

"I'm so glad you're safe!"

The declaration is so unlike her that I wonder if perhaps I've misheard. She must've said she was mad I was safe. Yeah, that would be more in character. But the worried look on her face seems to contradict my reaction.

"Uh, me too?" I say, ill at ease. Surely something nasty must've happened since yesterday, like a massive blow to the head. Either that or it's some kind of devious ploy to get me off guard.

Irene grabs both my hands in hers. "We were so worried," she says. "We heard everything that…What's wrong with your hands?"

I wipe my hands on my skirt self-consciously, though I know the strange stains won't come off.

"It's from when my friend sat on the Siege Perilous," I say. "All this black stuff came out…It must've somehow stained me while I was trying to take it off him."

Irene pounces on me at those words, pulling my collar down to uncover my neck and shoulders.

"What are you doing?" I ask, backing away.

Sighing with obvious relief, she lets me go. "Nothing's changed."

"What is that supposed to mean?" I ask. "Were you afraid I'd turned into some kind of alien?"

Her sudden cold look disconcerts me, though I should've expected it. I knew it had been a trick, as if God would actually give her a soul overnight!

"You look tired," she says, strutting away. "You should go to your room. I'll have Ella bring you dinner."

I take her suggestion for what it is—an order. Once in my room, however, I can't keep still. I find myself pacing about, tossing one wild idea after another as I try to decipher her cryptic words.

There's a small knock at the door, and Ella walks in, carrying a tray laden with warm food and dessert.

"Thank you," I say, not feeling hungry at all, which is a definite sign that something's bothering me.

The tiny woman's form starts to take that translucent sheen she takes when she's about to disappear.

"Wait," I say. "Can I ask you something?"

She turns to me, her clear eyes blank.

"What's going on?" I ask. "What is it that they're not telling me?"

I wonder for a brief moment if I haven't just made a mistake confiding in her, but I quickly brush the thought aside—who else is better informed of the goings on of a family than a quiet, unobtrusive servant? I take a long drag of my tea to hide my nervousness.

"You should be careful, mistress," Ella says timidly. "They're going after you."

I nearly choke on my drink. "What? Who's going after me? Students? Are they mad?"

Ella draws back from me, looking like she wants to turn into a dust mite.

"I won't hurt you," I say, forcing myself not to scream. "Just tell me who's going after me, and why. Is it my parents? Fey people? Jennifer?"

But Ella's lips remain resolutely shut, and she disappears from view, evading any further questioning.

"Ella!" I call out after her, but I'm now well and truly alone, and I know that, even if I spent the whole night looking, I won't be able to find her if she chooses not to be seen.

Frustrated, I slam my cup back down on the table, sloshing tea on my hand. Who says stuff like that and then doesn't provide an explanation?

I resume my frantic pacing, stopping occasionally to chomp down on a piece of lettuce.

You could just look for the answer yourself.

I pause at the unbidden words. Where would I look for something like that when I can't even leave this madhouse?

Who said you had to leave this place?

Once again, my guardian angel is the voice of reason. With my parents as Board members, surely I can figure something out. I crack my door open and peer outside. The lamplit hallway is deserted, much to my relief. I tiptoe down the carpeted corridor, halting for the briefest moment before Arthur's empty bedroom, then creep down the stairs.

"The incidents seem to be concentrated mainly around Georgia, Colorado, and Ontario..." I hear Luther say from his office.

Holding my breath, I inch toward the door. My parents must have forgotten I'm here to be talking so loud.

I put my eye to the keyhole, through which I can barely make out a part of the wall-length mirror. In it, three reflections can be seen, crouched over a table.

"But if you look carefully," Luther says, sweeping his hand over a map, "they seem to be converging."

"To Avalon," Irene says in one breath. "You know what that means."

"Honey, you can't assume they're behind all of this," Luther says in a tone that suggests they've had this discussion many times before. "We can't afford to start a war we're not ready to fight."

"Are you saying you don't believe they can do it?" Irene retorts.

"We need solid proof," Luther says. "If we attack them directly, on their own territory nonetheless, it could spell trouble for all of us."

"Maybe if we got our prisoner talking," Irene says, getting more agitated, "we would get our proof." She bounces away from the table, too flustered to remain in one spot.

"I should never have listened to Myrdwinn," she says, even louder than before. "If we'd gotten rid of her when we had a chance, we wouldn't be in this predicament!"

"He had his reasons," Luther says.

"Which he never explained to us," Irene retorts, "and that is deeply suspicious. He *is* losing his head, after all. This was all a mistake. I knew from the moment I laid eyes on her! And look at all the crap we have to deal with now!"

Goose bumps ripple down my arms as I realize she's talking about me. The hallway seems to tilt dangerously for a moment. I must have made a noise, for I see Irene twirl toward me.

I barely have the time to fling myself away from the office before the door opens and Irene's small figure is outlined in the doorframe.

"What are you doing here?" she asks, catching me at the bottom of the stairs.

This time, there is no disguised warmth in her voice, but an unsettling wariness and, I realize for the first time in my life, hatred. I can't make myself answer.

"You should be in bed," she says, grabbing my arm so tightly it hurts.

She frog-marches me back to my room, her grip extraordinarily strong for a midget of a woman. She shoves me inside, and I slam into the bed.

"I will not tolerate any eavesdropping in my own house," she says. "You are to stay here until further notice. For your own good, of course."

She shuts the door firmly behind her, and the distinct sound of a key turning in the lock reaches me. Locked up by my own mother, a mother who wishes I were dead instead.

Bruised up, I curl up on my bed, comforting myself that tomorrow I'll find a way to get out of this jail and never come back.

CHAPTER 30

I hate being locked up. I hate it, hate it, *hate it*. I accentuate that last thought with a kick to the door and am rewarded with a sharp pain in the toe. Hobbling, I make my way back to the bed and sink into it.

You're always complaining, my guardian angel retorts. *At least you're in a nice warm place, getting fed as much as you want.*

"Stuff it," I mutter into my pillow. "Like you're having such a hard time. Besides, you're the reason I'm in this mess."

Don't blame me for your situation. I merely make suggestions. It's up to you to follow them or not.

"And I did, and now I regret it," I say, flopping over onto my other side. Never has a soft bed been this uncomfortable.

Finally, as I've found myself doing for the past week I've been stuck in here, I walk up to my desk and press the set of runes carved into the wall above it. A second later, Ella appears.

"Yes, mistress?"

"Sit down, Ella," I say, pulling the chair out for her.

The tiny elf looks at me warily, then shakes her head. I sigh and drop into the seat instead, holding my head in my hands.

"Can you tell me…" I start. What is it I want to know? Where Arthur is, for one. I thought that we'd finally come to see eye to eye after Avalon. But he's cast me aside like a broken doll and hasn't even bothered to come see me. Secondly, I'd like to know how close those dunces are to catching the murderer. And thirdly, if I'm ever going to get out of here again.

"Have you seen Arthur?" I ask before she can dematerialize. "Is the school in lockdown? Has something else happened?"

With every question, Ella grows paler.

"There's nothing you can tell me?" I exclaim, frustrated. "No news, no nothing?"

Ella keeps staring at me with her big brown eyes flecked with gold.

"Have you been told not to say anything to me?" I finally ask, exasperated. "Am I truly a prisoner here that I can't even be told the smallest thing?"

I spring off my chair and start pacing, wearing the rug thin. Why did she ever bother to give me a warning if now she won't even say a thing?

I come to a stop before the trembling Fey. "I don't suppose that, even if I promise not to say a word, you'll tell me?" I ask.

Ella keeps her mouth resolutely shut. I sigh and rub my forehead.

"OK. Then how about giving Arthur a message?" I ask. "Would that be possible?"

Biting on her lower lip, Ella looks down. I'm afraid she's going to refuse again, when she gives me a small but decisive nod.

"You can do that?" I ask, suddenly doubtful. "I mean, you can leave this place?"

Ella swallows audibly. "Sir Percy is outside the gates."

"How come he can't even bother to come see me then?" I mutter to myself as I sit down to write. The note, addressed to Arthur, is short and sweet:

> Get me out of here, or I swear I'll leave this
> hellhole in twenty-four hours and skin you alive.
>
> Your sister,
> Morgan

I hand Ella the note, but, as she takes the slip of paper in her trembling hands, I pause.

"Just, could you come see me after?" I ask. "I'd like to know what Percy said. And, thank you."

With a small curtsy, Ella disappears, and I'm left alone to sink further into insanity in the meantime.

A few moments later, there's a small knock, and I look at the door. "Ella, is that you? Are you already back?"

But the small tap comes back again, from the window. Outside, a pair of golden eyes is staring straight at me.

"You again!" I exclaim, crossing my room to open the window.

In walks a black cat. I'm not sure if it's Lugh's cat or not, but he's been visiting me every day since I've been held captive here. He shakes the snow off his fur, then proceeds to clean himself. I close the window again, noting the dark clouds hovering over Lake Winnebago.

The cat meows, then rubs himself on my arm, purring loudly. With a sigh, I pat his tiny head.

"You wouldn't happen to know what everyone else is doing, would you?" I ask him. "Like why I haven't seen anyone around here?"

The cat just stares at me, as if I'm already supposed to know the answer.

"Yeah, didn't think you did," I say, looking away.

The cat drops down to the carpet, then follows on my heels as I resume my nervous walk around the room. How long should I expect to wait to hear from Arthur? An hour? A day? Two? No—I said twenty-four hours, and I meant it.

"Ouch!"

I glare down at the cat, who's just scratched my ankles. He looks up at me, all big-eyed innocence.

"What is it?" I growl.

I roll my eyes as he meows sweetly, begging for food. I go over to the desk and press the runes set in the wall again.

This time, it takes longer for Ella to appear, and when she does, I let out a strangled cry.

"What happened to you?" I ask, running to the small Fey who's sporting bruises all over her face and exposed arms.

"Did you fall down the stairs?" I ask, though I know that's impossible.

I swallow hard. "It's not Percy, is it? Did you give him my message?"

She nods once, then keeps her eyes on the floor. She stiffens, and I realize she's seen the cat. I try to smile.

"Please don't let them know," I whisper. "He's the only friend I've got. Actually, I was wondering if you could give him some food?"

Her next words surprise me. "You should leave here," she whispers.

"What?"

"You can't trust him."

"I can't trust who?"

But she's gone mute again. I grab her by the arms, and she winces.

"Please, Ella," I say, relaxing my hold on her, "I don't understand. Who can't I trust?"

She gasps, her mouth opens to say something, then her body turns to mist, and I'm left holding nothing but air. I stand frozen for a moment, mulling over her last warning, until I hear the cat meow again.

I try to call her back, but this time, Ella doesn't reappear. Something splatters against the window, and I whirl around, only to realize that the snow's turned to hail. Something else hits my window, leaving a long gray-green mark. Puzzled, I draw closer to the glass pane—and have to hold back a shout of surprise.

The whole snowy landscape has turned to gray as thousands upon thousands of insects swarm about, blotting out the waning sun.

"Flies," I breathe. My hands go clammy as my prior worries come back full force. "A plague. It can't be anything else." Which means that Carman's getting closer to freedom.

My gaze drops down to the overcast garden below, and I start at the sight of a hunched figure detaching itself from the barren trees. My blood runs cold as I remember another stooped shape on the island by the standing stones. I blink, and it's gone. I shake my head. It must be stress that's making me see things.

The cat hops onto the windowsill and paws the glass pane.

"You want to go back out?" I ask him with a shake of the head. "You're insane…"

He meows at me. I pat his small head, but he circles around on himself, and meows again.

I can't stop myself, I laugh. "I'm not following you in that."

I stop as an idea springs to mind. My father's killers are out there somewhere, doing their best to free Carman. I have no doubt about it. But I'm the only one who believes that and, therefore, the only one who can do something about it. Which means I've got to get out of here. Now.

"Actually, that's a great plan, Skipper," I tell the cat, who doesn't seem to like his new name. "Maybe, if you're who I think you are, you could take me to Lugh. What do you say to that?"

The cat yawns as I throw my bedcovers to the ground, rip my bedding off, then tie the sheets together. When I'm done, I fasten the end of my makeshift rope to the radiator, then stare at the ground below.

"Saint George's balls," I gasp, "this is way more terrifying than I thought."

Before I can chicken out, I slam the window open, letting a swarm of flies in. Shielding my eyes, I throw the other end of the rope over the windowsill, then follow after. I see the cat hop onto the edge of the window, watching me in return as I hover over the emptiness beneath me.

I have to force my quickly numbing fingers loose to lower myself as thousands of flies swarm around my face, forcing me to shut my eyes.

I take another careful step back and reach lower on the cloth ladder. My foot slips and I squeal as I swing against the wall. My fingers slide down on the soft sheets. I scrabble to get another purchase, but my shoes keep slipping on the ice and snow. My hands are cramping, definitely not a good sign. Movies are all lies; ropes made out of bedsheets are definitely not the way to go.

I grind my teeth together as I try to get another good grip, but the wind slams me into the house, and I let go completely.

Time seems to stop. I feel my body fall backward, light pooling from my bedroom overhead, the cat long gone.

Dean's head pops out of the window, surrounded by a now-easing cloud of flies. He lunges down, grabs my coat, and I jerk to a stop.

For a moment, we both keep still, as if frozen. Then slowly, inch by careful inch, Dean pulls me back up through the window. We both fall onto the floor, breathing hard.

When I feel like my heart's not going to burst through my chest anymore, I look up to find Dean eyeing me furiously. I look away, shame burning my cheeks.

"Yeah, not my best moment," I say. My voice drops. "Thank you."

Lying on the floor in a pile of broken dishes is my dinner—mashed potatoes splattered on the carpet and up on the wall, peas and carrots scattered under my bed. And, a few feet away, the remains of a bowl of milk, the cat sleeping beside it, his chest rising and falling in quick breaths.

Definitely can't count on you, can I? I think, prodding him with my foot.

Still glaring at me, Dean motions for me to follow him.

For the first time in over a week, I get to leave my bedroom, my failed escape notwithstanding. When we reach the kitchen, Dean heads straight for the stove and starts bustling around with pots and pans.

I plop down onto a stool and watch him prepare some hot chocolate.

"Where have you been?" I ask, despite knowing he won't answer. "My parents are always out, Arthur hasn't shown his face, and none of my friends have bothered to call on me. It's just been me and Ella all this time, and she's not much of a talker."

I look about the kitchen in search of the Fey, knowing this is her territory.

"Where is she, by the way?" I ask. "I called her earlier, but…"

Dean turns around and sets a cup of hot cocoa before me. I put my freezing fingers around it and smile up at his dark, brooding face.

"Thanks."

I lift the cup to my lips, blow on it to cool it down, then remember the cat upstairs and set the cup back down.

"I'll be right back," I say, getting up. "I left my furry friend in my room, and I know he's been hungry."

But Dean motions for me to get back to my hot cocoa and goes up to fetch the cat instead. I smile as I watch his broad back disappear down the corridor—if he weren't a layperson, he'd be a heck of a great knight. Definitely loads better than Arthur.

With a snort, I look up at the stove, still picturing Dean making me hot chocolate, when I notice a large gap in the wall above. I cross the kitchen and hesitantly reach up to touch the large hole left in the stones—a hole that should be filled with Ella's ogham.

Her last words come back to me: *You should leave here.*

Before I know it, I'm in the entrance hall, grabbing a jacket. I take one last look at the stairs up which Dean's gone.

"Sorry," I whisper to him, knowing he's probably going to get in trouble because of me.

I fling the door open and rush across the snow, all the way down to the gates, where Percy's bright orange car is parked.

I knock on Percy's window, jerking him awake. He stares at me, bleary-eyed, before he unlocks the passenger door and I climb in.

"Drive," I say. "Hurry!"

"Why? Where to?" he asks while doing as I ask.

"The lake. And step on it!"

The drive is tense as the car eats up the miles, occasionally skipping on patches of ice. Thankfully, at this time and in these weather conditions, most people are home.

The tires screech as Percy breaks before engaging the car into the small path toward the cemetery. Through the leafless trees, I can see a few of the mental institute's lights twinkle across the fields.

The moment the car stops I jump out of the car. I hear Percy slam the door shut as I rush away. The snow crunches under our feet as we march through the weeds toward the water. Twice I trip as my foot gets tangled up in roots, and twice Percy catches me.

"Now will ya tell me what all the fuss is about?" he asks as we reach the shore, crossing his arms. "Ya ain't gonna make it down there without me, ya know?"

"Touché," I say, my breath fogging in the air.

We both look at the ice-covered lake reflecting the city lights in the distance.

"Yeah, I'm terrible at coming up with good plans," I admit, "but I need to go back there."

"To school?" Percy asks, sounding shocked. "But Arthur forbid it?"

"I need to speak to him, it's urgent," I reply, hoping he can't tell that I'm lying.

"I s'pose," Percy says, digging his hands in his pockets. "Definitely would change from babysittin'."

"So are you going to help me or not?" I ask him.

Percy lets out a theatrical sigh. "I s'pose I'll have to," he says. "Ya're crazy enough to dive in there on yer own if I don't."

Disguising my cry of victory into a cough, I grab his hand, and we both step onto the frozen water together. Half walking, half sliding, we make our way farther onto Lake Winnebago, until the sheet of ice beneath us threatens to break.

"Well, here goes," Percy says.

A green bubble rises around us in a protective cocoon. Then Percy aims his hand down, and a jet of bright red bursts forth. A split second later, and I squeal as we drop into the pitch-black waters.

I expect to see the top of the school within minutes, but something happens in the water, and we get jostled around.

"Hold on tight!" Percy shouts in my ear.

We wheel about, then torpedo our way deeper into the lake until I'm not sure which way is up or down anymore. I squeeze my arms around Percy's neck so hard I'm sure I must be choking him. Just as I'm about to get sick, we break through the lower barrier of the lake and pitch through the air toward the ground at bullet speed.

I scream as the dark ground below comes rushing toward us. At the very last moment, Percy changes our course, and I let go. I roll for about ten thousand miles in the tall grass, then finally come to a stop, bruised and with about five dozen bumps forming on my cranium.

"What was that all about?" I ask, picking myself up.

I wipe off the slick water dripping down into my eyes and sticking my hair to my face. "What happened that we're all wet? This didn't happen the last time."

"Blood," Percy says.

My hand stills on its way to squeezing the thick water out of my hair. "What did you just say?"

"Looks like we swam through blood," he repeats, spitting on the ground.

"I knew it," I say, too grossed out to dare move again.

"What didja know?"

"It's the plagues." I lick my lips and regret it immediately. "That's…seven now, I think. Maybe eight."

"Whattaya talkin' 'bout?"

There's a small pop and fizzling, and two small orbs of fire appear between us, hovering in the air at eye level.

"You're as foul as I feel," I say, watching the blood pooling in the grass at his feet.

"Cold shower?" he asks me with a crooked smile.

Before I can reply, he sprays me with the coldest water I've ever felt, but I bare myself to it gratefully.

"That should do it, eh?" Percy says with a large grin. "You now look brand-spankin' new!"

He turns about, orienting himself. "School's that way," he says. "Let's pony up!"[31]

I hesitate. We've landed in an area close to the forest, and I feel it beckoning me to come forth.

"Whatcha doin'?" Percy asks when he realizes I'm not following him. "Afraid Arthur's gonna clean your plow?[32] Dunna worry 'bout it, I'll talk to 'im and save yer pretty backside from a whippin'. Not that you haven't deserved it, mind."

He motions for me to follow, when a girl runs straight into him, and they both topple to the ground together. Quick as a cheetah, the girl comes back up into a low crouch, her face reflecting the gold of Percy's roving lights.

"What are ya doin' here?" Percy asks, getting up a second later. "Ya shouldna be outside school boundaries. It ain't safe."

The girl's scowl turns into a smile of derision that doesn't reach her piercing blue eyes. "Oh, schoolkids, just my luck."

"Blanchefleur?" I ask.

The girl tenses, then turns toward me. "Lady Morgan," she whispers.

A low cackle reaches us through the tall grass, one that fills me with fear.

"Down!" I scream as a black shape jumps into the air toward Percy and the Fey girl.

31 Let's get going.

32 Going to beat you up.

Percy reacts on instinct and dives to the side, but Blanchefleur pivots slightly on one foot, and the creature lands inches from her, long claws digging into the soft soil.

"It's her," I say, my throat dry. "The banshee."

.

Chapter 31

A good thing I haven't had anything to drink all day, or I would pee myself. The black cowl turns toward me, and a too-familiar wailing emerges from its recesses.

"Morgan, watch out!" Percy yells as the vicious creature bounds toward me.

I throw myself to the side, feeling the banshee's tattered robes brush against my legs as she hurtles past. I reach to my belt for a knife, then realize that, once again, I'm weaponless. I watch as the banshee's dark form collects herself, my limbs shaking so much I can't get back to my feet.

Before she can attack again, however, Blanchefleur launches herself at the creature, the glow of her long, crystalline blade flooding the area in a silvery light. The banshee throws her arms out in defense and lets out a loud cry as the edge of the sword digs deep into her forearm. Claws out, the banshee lashes out and wrenches the blade out of Blanchefleur's hands.

I watch the sword twirl in the air, then land, hilt first, in the tall grasses, where its light slowly goes out.

I hear Blanchefleur gasp as one of the banshee's blows lands and she falls.

Using the sound as guidance, I rush forward to stop the banshee from killing the young Fey. The creature shoves me out of the way, and I fall to the ground, jarring my arms and knees.

Percy's own orbs of fire flicker in and out of existence as he dodges and attacks the creature consecutively.

"Get back to school, Morgan," Percy says as he pulls out a pair of twin daggers.

His weapons gleam red as he hurls himself toward the banshee. Holding one blade at an angle before him, he thrusts with the other, hitting her in the shoulder. But the dark Fey spins away, then pounces on him, her claws raking the air before his face.

Desperate to save him, I crawl about the ground. My fingers close against something long and cold to the touch— Blanchefleur's sword. I raise the weapon before me, and it flares out in a brilliant white light, blinding me momentarily.

"What're ya doin'?" Percy yells at me as he slowly forces the banshee back.

I crack my eyes open and see the dark creature evade another knife sweep, then run straight at me. I yelp and duck under the long, bloody talons.

I feel my blade connect, and tighten my grip around the handle for fear of losing the weapon. With a snarl, the banshee rounds on me again.

I raise the sword back up in time to counter the creature, and stumble backward under the force of the blow.

"Morgan!" Percy shouts.

I make the mistake of looking at him. There's a heavy pain in my shoulder. My feet lose their grip on the ground. I see the blade's light pierce through the banshee's hood to reflect in a pair of dull white eyes, then we're both propelled away from each other, and I ram into the solid earth, the air leaving my lungs all at once.

I hear padded footsteps then a grunting form appears above me. For a second, it looks like my life is over. The banshee leans toward me, blasting me with the putrid stench of rotting fish.

"Master will be pleased with me," she croaks.

Master? I shake my head to get the ringing out of my ears, but only manage to make myself dizzier.

I watch the banshee reach for me, when a large ball of green explodes against her, throwing the creature into the air. I hear a muffled cracking of bones as she lands in the dried grass.

"I told ya to go back!" Percy yells.

"Couldn't...leave you...alone," I gasp.

He pulls me to my feet. "You OK?" he asks, making one of the red orbs fly toward my face so he can examine me.

"I think so," I say with a shaky breath. "Thanks."

"Don't mention it," Percy says.

A screech rends the air, and Percy drops down to a low crouch just as a large black shape barrels into him. He lands, sprawling in the tall grass, rolls onto his back, then flips himself upright again.

"Percy!" I shriek.

I try to go to him, but falter as the world around me tips. I blink in the darkness. I think I see the banshee's misshapen form scurry toward me. I raise my hands up, but the sword's gone. I look about my feet, searching for the weapon.

Someone pushes me roughly to the side.

"Dagaz," Percy mutters as the banshee reaches him.

There's a loud bang, and the sky is streaked with the white flash of lightning, followed by an agonizing shriek.

"Stupid human," Blanchefleur says, pulling me away from the growing smell of burning flesh.

Mouth agape, I watch the scene unfold before me, Percy and the banshee wrapped in incandescent fire before the light goes out. I remember Arthur's warning, how Dagaz's use is like committing suicide.

There's a rustling of clothes and metal, the sound of a body falling to the ground, then nothing.

"Percy?" I call out, my voice cracking.

I crawl toward the spot where I last saw him. Blanchefleur rushes around me, her sword once again in her hands.

"Is he..." I can't bring myself to say it.

Blanchefleur pokes a body with her feet until it rolls away. "Stupid human," she repeats. "Of course lightning would be drawn to him, what with all that metal he's carrying."

My breath rushes out of me, and my throat constricts. "Percy?"

"He's still breathing," Blanchefleur says, scornful, "though gravely injured." She gets up in one graceful move and scans the area. I hear her swear.

"What is it?" I ask, taking Percy's pulse, then feeling his burning face.

"We lost her," she says.

"The banshee? Why was she after you?"

"I was after her," Blanchefleur snarls. "She killed my sister; she has to pay for it."

Coming to stand beside us, she holds her sword up so its light can shine onto Percy's injured body.

His clothes have partly burnt away, showing pale skin beneath.

I draw in a sharp breath—covering most of his torso is a bright red Lichtenburg figure. The lightning-shaped burn goes from his shoulder all the way down his back, branching out over and over again like a leafless tree. My heart skips a beat as I realize that Percy really could have died, and all because of me.

"I need to go get help," I say.

"You're not going to find any," Blanchefleur says. She sheathes her sword, throwing us back into the decreasing darkness.

"The school can't be far. There are healers there who ca—"

"It's too late for that now," Blanchefleur says.

"I don't understand."

The Fey's blue eyes look straight into mine, reflecting the pale dawn. "It means your school's probably already under attack by now."

As if to corroborate her words, I hear the faint but distinctive sound of the tocsin[33] ringing in the distance. I rock onto my feet.

"What?"

"Fomori invasion," she says, pointing up.

I look at the sky-lake. Streaks of light pink are bleeding into the midnight blue and, with them, strange dark clouds, the first I've ever seen down here. As I peer more intently at the odd-moving patterns, I realize that those aren't clouds, but four-limbed creatures descending from the lake, crawling along the barrier that separates the lower world from the surface.

"But I thought Fey weren't allowed to step into our school unless invited or…"

"Or enslaved?" Blanchefleur finishes for me. She shrugs. "The barrier's been breached. And on that note, I've got to go."

With dread, I realize that all those black spots are converging toward the school.

I look back down at Percy. His ordinarily smiling features are now distorted with pain, though he barely lets out a sound. Remorse gnaws at my insides; I can't leave him like this.

"Wait!" I call after her before she disappears. "We can't let him die!"

Blanchefleur grimaces at Percy.

33 Alarm bell.

"Please!" I beg her. "He saved our lives."

After another moment's hesitation, she lets out a deep sigh. "Help me take off his armor," she says, "and I'll take care of him."

"You will?" I ask.

"I wouldn't say so if it weren't true," she retorts, flashing me a look of contempt.

Right, the whole Fey-can't-lie thing. I grab both her hands in mine. "Thank you so much! I owe you one."

Blanchefleur pulls away, wincing. "Just get it clear in your little head. I'm not doing this for you. As you said, I owe him a favor, and so I shall repay it before it's too late."

"Right, right," I say as I hurry to take Percy's armor off—not an easy task considering all the knots and how some of the metallic plates have melded together.

"Are you sure you want to go there?" Blanchefleur asks as I pull the vambraces off Percy. "It might not be wise, especially for you, since the reaping's nearly done."

"What's that supposed to mean?" I ask, taking Percy's steel-toed boots off. "Do his pants have to go too?"

Blanchefleur leans over me, then points at his torso. "Just that, and it should be fine," she says.

I place Percy's shirt on top of the growing pile of iron items. "There, all done," I say, dusting myself off. "Don't forget your promise."

"A word given cannot be taken," Blanchefleur says, carefully kneeling down next to Percy's unconscious body.

I watch her closely as she places his head onto her lap.

"Are you all right?" I ask, noticing for the first time the gashes in her shoulder.

"You better hurry if you hope to still find your school in one piece," she tells me without looking up.

I don't have to be told twice. My feet pound the ground as I run full speed across the fields, following the trail of Fomori crawling on the sky-dome above me.

"Dear God," I pray under my breath, "please let them be OK!"

Fighting a stitch in my side, I reach the large standing stone that's a mile west of the landing area. As I near it, I realize the boulder's cracked in two, as if it's been struck by a giant hammer. I crest the hill, arriving by the first longboat, and suck in my breath. From here, the breach in the barrier is obvious; it's like an angel's punched a hole through the sky, and now hundreds of creatures are dropping through it to land on the school below.

Using the boats for cover, I hurry toward the front of the wharf, coughing on the smoke billowing up from the burning keels. Beyond the flames awaits a nightmarish vision of chaos.

I see Laura and Diana run up the hill toward me, pursued by a Fomori—the Fey's even uglier in reality than in the book illustrations, and, for once, I wish I'd been wrong and that they were extinct.

Before I realize what I'm doing, I'm sprinting down to their aid. The creature's long limbs quickly catch up to the two terrified girls. It smiles at them, showing two rows of jagged teeth in its brown-green face, its eyes glowing with a white-blue, feverish light.

I slide down the remaining few feet and tackle the Fomori to the ground.

"Run!" I yell to my classmates.

I don't have time to watch them escape as the creature bounds my way. Its webbed hands whip down toward me, thin spikes out.

Rolling away, I see its sharp claws dig into the earth where I'd been standing.

I use that moment to kick the Fomori in the face, hearing its jaw crunch under my boot heel. Without waiting for it to retaliate, I scramble away and into the thick of the battle.

I skid to a stop before a group of knights fighting off a couple more Fomori, their sweaty faces lighting up with the various elementals they're calling.

I dive behind a tree. What am I doing here? I don't know how to fight, I don't have a single EM to control, and I still have no weapon.

"I should've borrowed Blanchefleur's sword," I mutter as an explosion shakes the ground, so loud it momentarily overcomes the sound of the tocsin. My ears ringing, I see more and more Fomori arrive—too many for us to fight, too many for us to survive.

"Please, dear God, have mercy on us," I pray out loud.

One of the Fomori falls down on the gravel path between me and the school, writhing beneath an iron net. But the other Fey march past him, oblivious to their comrade's pain.

"Don't try to capture them!" a knight yells. His dark hair looks familiar. He whirls around to stab a Fomori in the guts, and I recognize Hadrian, Bri's older brother. He pulls out his sword, wet with dark blood, and helps a girl up. "Remember to aim for their vitals!"

"Get everyone inside the school!" someone shouts nearby, bringing me back to my senses. "They haven't gotten through the main defenses yet!"

"Gather all those who can't fight inside!" I hear Hadrian shout again.

I'm about to dart inside myself when I notice a squire cowering beneath a bench, his eyes wide with terror. Just two feet from him are a couple Fomori, their slitted noses smelling the air like hunting dogs on a scent. The hairs on my arms bristle as the creatures' big heads snap toward the boy, drool falling from their spiky teeth and onto their slick, murky brown bodies.

The boy screams as one of the monsters reaches down and grabs him by the hair, its maw gaping wide open, ready to chew his head off. I grab the first thing I can find, a large rock, and hurl myself at the creature. The stone connects with its temple, and its webbed fingers let go.

"Inside!" I yell to the kid as both Fomori turn on me.

The first one swipes at me, and my jacket rips in two. I topple backward onto the ground, hitting my elbow on the bench. Breath cut short, I remain still for a moment, and blink up at the hideous creature.

The Fomori sneers at me, if such a thing is possible from a creature that has no lips. Then something crashes into it with the force of a bull, sending it flying into the bench. Before the second creature knows what's happening, there's a bright flash, and its head rolls off.

"Morgan, *ma chère*,[34] what you doing here?" Gareth asks me, helping me up with his gauntleted hand. "Thought you were upstairs, safe and bound."

"No, they didn't tie me up," I say as we dodge under shots of fire that have sizzled astray. "Which is how I've found myself here."

"What about Percy?" he asks. "Weren't he keeping his eyes over you?"

He holds out a beefy arm to keep me back and swings his broadsword up, cleaving a Fomori in half before it can finish a knight who's fallen down.

34 My dear.

"He's injured and can't come," I say, helping him lift the unconscious girl he's just saved.

"Like most of us here, *hein?*"[35] he says.

I sweep my eyes around the gory scene, afraid to look too closely at the bodies scattered about, afraid I may recognize anyone. Afraid one of them may be a friend... or Arthur.

"What do they want from us?" I catch myself asking. "Why are they fighting us like this?"

Gareth shrugs. "Why does any war start?" He waves at me. "Well, better get you inside before I find my poet cousin and see what trouble he's plugged into."

"Great idea," I say.

We reach the main building, crack the western door open, and push the fallen knight's body inside.

"Tell them to get the lady to scry for the Board's help," he tells me, wiping blood and sweat from his eyes.

"Who?" I ask as I try not to succumb under the knight's weight.

"Vivian," he replies. "If she hasn't done already."

"Help, right," I say. "I'll go look for her."

"*Brave petite,*"[36] Gareth says with a sparkling smile before he charges into the fray once again.

"May God protect you," I whisper, "and the rest of the knights."

A soft moan brings me back to the injured girl, and I shut the door behind me. If I thought the outside was chaotic, the inside halls of the school are completely topsy-turvy.

"Can anybody help here?" I call out, grabbing the knight under the arms to get her to the infirmary. But without Gareth's help, it's impossible to lift her. "Anybody?"

---

35 Eh?

36 Brave little one.

A strained-looking, but otherwise impeccably dressed Keva appears at the end of the hallway.

"Morgan? What are you doing here?"

"Nice to see you too," I say, gritting my teeth as I pull on the body with all my strength to move it a couple of inches. I look over my shoulder. "A little help?"

"Right," Keva says, running away.

Great, just great. I try to pull the girl a little farther up the flagstones, but her armor catches on something, and I find myself sprawled on the cold floor.

"Now's not the time to be sleeping, you know."

My eyes roll back to find two pairs of boots a handspan away from my forehead.

"What do you expect from the likes of her?"

To my surprise, the voice belongs to none other than Daniel. The boy bends down and lifts the girl up by the shoulders, motioning for me to grab the feet. Between the two of us, we manage to get the squire to the infirmary, where the nurses and Dr. Cockleburr are running about like chickens whose heads have been cut off.

"Morgan, perfect timing!" the doctor says when she sees me. "Go grab some clean water and soap and come help me."

"Right away," I say.

I dash for the dispensary, stopping only long enough to wash my hands. I try not to think about all these students lying on tables and beds, groaning and sighing in pain. Only one of the beds in the ward is quiet—Jennifer, despite the insanity going on around her, hasn't moved a micro-inch.

I find Dr. Cockleburr in the intensive care unit already performing surgery.

"Is that Sir Boris?" I ask, unable to tear my eyes away from the deep slashes running down his torso.

"It is. Now get to cleaning."

Sloshing water over the side of the basin in my hurry, I nearly drop the soap on a couple of occasions, then finally manage to mop up the already suppurating wound.

"How did he—"

"Was the first to respond to the attack," the doctor says, tying up the last knot around Sir Boris's quadriceps. "Fought a dozen Fomori on his own. Maybe if the old fool realized how much age and paunch he's gained since last he was in a full-blown attack, he wouldn't be in this mess."

"Aren't you afraid?" I ask as I watch her sure hands fly over Sir Boris's injuries.

"There's no time for that," she says. "You can't let those feelings get in the way, or people die." She casts me a glance. "But then again, I'm not on the front lines, am I?"

She moves over the now cleaned wound. I hand her retractors then hold up a candle so she can see if anything's been torn inside as well.

"And maybe if Lady Vivian had paid attention," I hear her mutter, "we wouldn't be under attack at all."

The name jars my memory, and I nearly drop the light.

"What are you doing, girl?" Dr. Cockleburr snaps. "If you keep this up, this poor man's going to bleed to death. And I'm not letting anybody die in my clinic today. You got that?"

"Y-Yes," I stammer, handing her a new needle and thread.

I watch her sew up Sir Boris, wishing her to go faster—the sooner I can get out of here, the sooner I can give Vivian Gareth's message and my own warning about Carman.

The moment Dr. Cockleburr drops the scissors back onto the table, I thrust the bandages into her arms and rush out of the room.

"Where are you going, Morgan?" she asks, her eyes nearly popping out of her head.

"I have an urgent message," I say, slipping on the floor slick with blood.

I don't bother to clean myself up as I run back outside the infirmary. I plaster myself to the wall to let a couple of squires carry in another injured knight. If this keeps up, there won't be anybody left to defend our school.

I slap myself to get the awful thought out of my head. There's no point in going over what-if scenarios. Nothing good ever happens if you give up without trying.

I push myself away from the wall and run down the hallway, searching every face I pass for Vivian's familiar features.

"Have you seen the principal?" I ask Elias who's running around holding weapons.

The boy shakes his head.

"Gianakos, what are you doing?" an older man yells in a stentorian voice, his arms bulging under the weight of massive hammers. "We need to get as many tools and weapons out before they get to the forge!"

"Try the KORT room, she may be communicating with the Board," Elias says before hurrying after the burly man.

Without waiting a second longer, I dash up the stairs, taking them three at a time, reach the second floor, then propel myself down the hallway toward the KORT room. I come crashing through the open door, stopped only when I slam into the large table.

"Lady Vivian?" I call out, rubbing my sore thighs. "Lady Vivian, I've got a message for you!"

Nobody answers. The drapes behind Arthur's usual seat are standing wide apart, letting the first full rays of the sun reach inside the small recess and reflect back on the tall mirror suspended inside.

"Saint George's balls!" I cry out, hitting my fist on the table. "Why is no one ever present when I actually need them?"

Muttering to myself, I cross the room back toward the door, when a large explosion rocks the whole building. I have to hold onto a chair to stop myself from falling. The vibrations seem to last forever, reverberating down to the marrow of my bones. They must have gotten to the forge, I realize.

There's a slight scuttling sound, as of a child running, and a small, bearded head appears at the door, crowned with two tiny horns.

"Puck! Just the one I wanted to see!" I try to stand up a little straighter. "Where is your mistress?"

The hobgoblin cocks his head questioningly. I want to growl in frustration, but, afraid to scare the creature away, I force myself to take on a soft tone.

"Vivian, Puck. Have you seen her? Do you know where she is?"

The hobgoblin's face lights up, and he darts away.

"Hey, wait for me!"

I have to force myself to unclench my fingers from around the chair to run after Puck before he disappears again.

Puck takes me down the western staircase, which happens to be the one most packed with people, the battle raging just beyond its walls. I try not to look out the tall windows; I have yet to see or hear of Arthur, and it scares me to think that, like Sir Boris, he may be lying somewhere, shredded to pieces.

But no matter how well I try to keep a low profile, being one of the tallest people around still makes me stand out.

"Morgan!"

"Not now, Keva," I say, looking for Puck.

"But the doctor is looking for you!" she says, pushing her way through the throng toward me.

"Tell her I'll be there as soon as I can!"

I round a corner and find the hobgoblin hopping down the corridor, his tiny hooves clicking on the stones. He pushes the door to the arboretum, looks back to make sure I'm still there, then scampers outside.

To my surprise, however, it is not Vivian I find in the courtyard, but a tall man dressed in white, his blond hair falling around his shoulders like a halo.

"Who are you?" I ask. "Where's Lady Vivian?"

The man drops his gaze from the sky to my face, and I have a momentary start when I notice his eyes are so pale they look almost white. A blind person?

"You should not have come here," he says, his voice soft. "You're putting everyone here in danger."

I flare up. "I'm not the one who started this whole invasion thingy," I say, lifting my chin in defiance, even if he can't see me.

The man's lips quirk up. "I suppose you may be right about that."

I narrow my eyes at him. "Wait, haven't I seen you somewhere before?"

The man stares at me with his blank eyes, motionless.

"You were there," I breathe, bringing a hand to my mouth in shock. "The day Owen died, you were there, I saw you!"

The man nods. "My role is to observe and pay homage to the Almighty."

"A Watcher?" I swallow back the tears that threaten to pour forth, then rub my blackened hands on my skirt. Take a deep breath, I remind myself, and think about the most pressing thing right now.

"Do you know where Puck went to then?" I ask.

The man raises a long-fingered hand and points to the back of the apple tree.

"Choose your path wisely, daughter of the Gibborim," the man says, casting his eyes upward once more, "for the stones are being raised, and the gates shall soon be opened."

"Will do," I mumble, backing away. The guy is obviously bat-shit crazy to think of himself as a Watcher when he's blind.

When I'm certain the man's no longer paying attention to me, I turn around and hurry to the make-out hedge, where the wall of tree roots and branches rises up to meet me.

"Puck?" I call out, ducking under a low-lying bough.

The tree seems to recognize me, and a narrow passage opens up in the hedge of roots, leading into the ground. After a moment's hesitation, I follow the twisted steps down until I reach the small chamber. The niche in which I'd found the strange bowl is now empty, and I feel a strange sense of loss at its disappearance.

"What are you doing?"

I flinch at the harsh tone before I realize it's coming from beyond the door to the cellar, still ajar. Maybe Puck's gotten caught causing some mischief or other.

I tiptoe to the door and peer through. All I can see is the first line of wine and beer casks that crosses the chamber.

"You shouldn't even be down here!" the man continues, still angry.

I let out the breath I'd been holding. Whatever Puck's doing, it doesn't sound like he's with Vivian right now—which means I'm back to square one.

"I wouldn't if I didn't have to," another man answers derisively, his voice strangely familiar. "But circumstances, you know..."

I don't know what pushes me to do it, but instead of going back up into the courtyard, I creep into the cellar.

"You're not going to succeed," the first man says. "You don't even have all the ingredients." A low laugh erupts.

I pause and peep between two casks. Ahead of me are two figures, the closest one with his back to me. The air between them seems to spark.

I squint at the man facing me, and my jaw drops open when I recognize him as Vivian's lover.

I see him tense up, and, for a moment, I wonder if he's heard me. But the man continues, "You should get out while you still can. The Board's on its way, and your troops are already retreating. There's nothing more you can accomplish here."

"You're wrong on that point, Myrdwinn," the stranger says.

Myrdwinn? As in the school's director? Impossible, this man's young. Maybe it's Myrdwinn Junior…

The stranger lifts his hand, and a black wave envelops the other man until he's gone from sight. When the clouds of darkness finally dissipate, Vivian's man is lying on the floor, immobile.

A tiny, furry hand grasps mine, and I almost squeal in terror. Heart racing, I realize it's only Puck. He's pulling me away from the scene, looking agitated. I start to follow him, but cannot stop myself from looking back at the two men.

I jerk back when I see a dark eye peering at me through the hole between the vats. I trip and hit my head on a draining valve.

With a muffled gasp, I sink to the floor as more and more of the man's face comes into view, a face that's been familiar to me all my life.

"There you are, Morgan," Dean says. "I've been looking all over for you!"

Chapter 32

"Come, Morgan. It's time."

"Y-You can speak," I whisper, too terrified to move, let alone run away.

"Of course I can speak," Dean says. "It's fascinating how much people will say in your presence when they think you're mute. As if not speaking means your mind's defective."

My brain balks at what his presence here means. "But you hate water," I say.

A chuckle shakes Dean's shoulders. "A great way to easily keep my cover all these years, don't you think? Now come on, let's get out of here."

Ignoring his order, I stare up at Dean's long face. Our family lawyer, my own knight in shining armor, has been a fake all along?

I swallow with difficulty, my throat dry and raw as sandpaper. "And you can manipulate elements."

"Please," Dean says sarcastically, striding around the barrels of wine until he's feet away from me. "Have you ever seen me wear one of your paltry devices?"

My eyes widen. "F-Fey?" I whisper, almost too scared to let the word out.

"Bingo. I always told Irene you could be quite bright when you chose to. Well, 'told' isn't the exact word, but you know what I mean."

"You can't be," I say, the shock still impeding my neurons. "Fey can't withstand the touch of iron…You couldn't have been able to live with us, drive…take a plane."

"It's called a seal, Morgan," Dean says. "I thought you knew all about those."

"But you saved me," I say, louder, still trying to make sense in a world that's disintegrating before my very eyes.

All those memories of my time growing up in Europe, being shuffled from one boarding school to the next. But Dean had always been there to pick up the broken pieces and set them right again, to tell me that everything was going to be all right, that I had nothing to worry about.

"You even got me out of jail!"

Dean's eyebrows rise high over his dark eyes. "Of course I did," he says. "How else would I bring you here? Now enough with all the questions, and get up."

A terrifying thought strikes me like a well-sharpened ax. I bite hard on my lip to stop it from trembling.

"The murders…was that you?"

"Not directly, no," Dean says with an exasperated sigh. "Now get the hell up and follow me."

"No." I sink farther into the wine barrel behind me, as if it's going to swallow me up.

His hand strikes out, tiny dark bolts of lightning firing out. I scream and raise my arms over my face. Pain shoots down from my shoulder to the tip of my fingers, and I hear Dean curse. Breathing hard, I slowly lower my arms to palpate my body, looking for any hole or missing limb. Instead, I find Dean leaning heavily against the wooden casks behind him.

"You will come with me," he says, wiping blood from the corner of his mouth. "Whether you like it or not."

"Or else?"

"There is no else," Dean says, grabbing me by the arm and forcing me to my feet.

"Let. Me. Go," I say, struggling against his hold.

My shoulder, still aching from my fight with the banshee, hurts like I've been stabbed with a red-hot poker. A spasm sends goose bumps down my arm, and, to my surprise, I see Dean wince.

"I said to come along nicely," he mutters.

Without letting me go, he raises his other fist and clocks me in the face. My vision goes momentarily dark. I feel Dean catch me before I collapse on the floor, then fling me over his shoulders like a sack of potatoes.

I try to move, resist some more, but my whole body feels like someone's pulled my plug. As if through foggy lenses, I see Puck scutter away behind Myrdwinn Junior's prone body, and I remember I have yet to give Vivian the message. Then Dean makes a sharp turn, and I lose them both from sight.

My body swings back and forth with every step Dean takes, sending sparks of pain down my left arm. I hear Dean's labored breathing as we make our way slowly up the stairs. The noises of battle greet us before we even reach the ground floor. My heart lurches inside my rib cage—what is going to happen to all these people?

"Morgan?"

I blink and look sideways at the indistinct shapes moving toward us from a side hallway. Though I can't distinguish anyone's face, Bri's voice is unmistakable.

"Who are you, and what are you doing to Morgan?" Bri asks.

I want to tell her to stay away, warn her to take cover, but only manage a half-choked gasp.

I feel more than see Dean strike Bri down, the hairs on my body rising from the blast's aftermath. I want to punch his back, scream Bri's name, but the air feels like it's gotten as thick as cream, and my movements get sluggish.

The cool air whips around me the moment Dean pushes the outside door, carrying with it the acrid smell of smoke coming from the burning forge and wharf. Without hesitation, he marches forward into the fray. Even in the midst of battle, the sounds of steel hitting sharpened bones, and of rattling explosions, seem dim.

I hear someone call my name, someone who sounds strangely like Arthur. I strain to lift my head. I think I see a gleam, hear the distinct though oddly distant sound of someone battering furiously at something, but then my head falls back against Dean's dorsum, and I pass out.

I wake up the moment I'm dropped into snow's freezing embrace. I roll over and heave, my whole body shaking with the effort. Once I think I'm safe from fainting again, I sit up to see where we are.

I know we've reached the surface—the snow, bright sunlight, and the distant rumbling of cars make it obvious—but it's not until I see Dean sitting against a tall stone that I realize where exactly.

"Island Park," I croak. I blink as the sun's reflection makes my eyes water. "Why are we here?"

But Dean won't answer. He doesn't move from his sitting position, and, upon closer inspection, I note the sweat beading on his pale features. His eyes are closed and his breathing labored. Could he be ill?

My first instinct is to go to him, like he's always come to me in times of trouble. Then I recall the nightmare that's still unfolding down below, and I decide against it.

Slowly, I get to my feet, my knees creaking, then take a long step away from the cairn and toward the shore, leaving deep imprints in the thick blanket of white. No boats can come here in this season, but perhaps the ice is strong enough that I can walk on the lake back to the city's safety.

"I wouldn't do that if I were you."

The low voice sends shivers down my spine. I look over my shoulder; Dean's eyes are open. He jerks his chin toward me, and I feel something brush against my legs before I hear the chilling laugh.

"Massster," the banshee hisses, prostrating herself at his feet.

I nearly fall back down into the snow.

"Master?" I repeat. Dean is that creature's master?

Using the standing stone behind him for support, Dean slowly gets up. It all starts to make sense now—that night I ended up fighting the banshee on this island, the reason he'd been the one to save me...

"You were here that night, weren't you?" I ask, anger boiling in the pit of my stomach.

"Now you realize," Dean says, avoiding my eyes.

I reel back. This isn't possible. Dean—*my* Dean—in league with the banshee who's been killing all these people? But pieces of the puzzle finally come together—how Ella tried to warn me, and then disappeared in the process...

"Ella," I say, recalling the hunched-over shape in the yard. "You killed her too, didn't you?"

"A necessary sacrifice for the freedom of a great one," he says.

"You mean a degenerate man killer," I say and have the pleasure of seeing anger flare on his otherwise expressionless face.

"You killed my father," I murmur, feeling my eyes go wet.

Impassive, Dean looks at me for a long moment. He sways as he pushes himself away from the stone, toward me. The banshee rushes to his aid, but Dean shoves her away.

"You're the one who got those Fomori in?" I ask, hating how my voice trembles.

"I needed a diversion," Dean says. "And with the Board safely away, the plan seems to have worked, don't you think?"

"A diversion?" I repeat. "To get all those people killed?"

Dean shrugs. "Nothing more than what they're doing to us," he says. "At least their deaths are quick. Much better than spending eons as a slave until your powers are so depleted you cease to exist."

"And me? You tried to poison me!" I exclaim. "That's why that cat was asleep when you brought me back inside, wasn't it?"

The spilled bowl of milk, the insistence I drink that stupid hot cocoa of his...For some reason, this hurts me even more.

"Why me?" I whisper.

"You're the missing ingredient," Dean says simply. His dark eyes come to rest on my face, then slide down to my left shoulder.

He stumbles toward me, and I back away. "Stay away from me," I say, looking between him and the dark cowl that covers the banshee's deathlike look, "you and your gofer."

"Trust me," Dean says, "if there was a way around this, I would have found it."

"Around what?" I ask, confused by his tone. Could he actually be sad about this? A spark of hope flickers in my chest; if Dean doesn't truly want to hurt me, maybe I still have a chance to get away. I take another step back, feeling the ground slope gently down. "Why did you bring me here?"

"To fulfill your destiny," Dean says.

And with a sudden burst of speed, he jumps to my side and grabs my arm, his thin fingers digging into my flesh. He jerks me after him.

"You're hurting me," I say, feeling woozy once more.

"It'll be over soon," Dean says through gritted teeth.

The banshee hovers around us, one moment pacing ahead of us, the next pushing me in the back to make me move faster.

"Are you going to kill me?" I ask.

Dean has us hurry toward the circle of stones until we're standing in its center beside a small, oblong knoll that wasn't here the last time I was on this cursed island.

"I have ffffinished the circle," the banshee rasps.

I see that, where there had been seven stones before, there are now eleven of them forming a circle around us like a rough draft of Stonehenge. Dean lets go of my arm and strides to a wide gap in the circle.

"I see," he says, his crisp voice reaching me over the whistling wind. The banshee's gray form moves about Dean like a will-o'-the-wisp, excited.

"I did everything Massster asssked," she says.

"Yes," Dean says, reaching behind him, "but you missed a spot."

I see something glint in his hands before it gets buried in the banshee's tattered robe. A keening wail arises from the Fey. Her clawed hands reach out for Dean as she sinks slowly into the cover of snow in a gray heap.

"You've served me well," Dean says before pulling his hand away.

If I had any food left in my stomach, I'd be throwing up right now. I know how horrible the banshee is, how she's attacked me and those knights, how she's left Percy on the brink of death.

Yet…a small part of me can't help but feel pity for the creature and the way she was used. Had it not been for Dean, would she still have committed all those atrocities?

Small tremors that rapidly increase in intensity shake the ground. As the wail turns into a howl of pain, I realize that the banshee's struggling to dig out of a growing hole in the ground, her claws raking through the snow uselessly.

"Massster!" she pleads.

A poem comes back to me from the depths of my memory, one Jack recited in the library before an ancient stele.

Four men to raise the stones their blood did shed…

A frisson runs down my neck—all those people reported disappeared, four in all.

Four Fey their essence over the cairn did spread…

And now this banshee, a Fey, is being fed to the earth to complete the circle—the circle that's supposed to be a prison—thereby reversing the process…

My mind loses track of my surroundings, and, next thing I know, I'm lying in the snow next to the churning earth, pulling on the banshee's bony arms. There's a strange resistance, as if the ground's sucking away at the banshee's body, inexorably dragging her farther and farther down.

Dean's hand grabs the back of my jacket and tries to haul me away.

"Stop it!" I yell, anger flaring through me.

Again, I feel that numbing pain shoot down my left arm from my shoulder. Dean lets me go with a curse.

"Come on," I say, gritting my teeth as I pull harder at the creature's arms.

With a sickening crunch, the banshee's suddenly released, and we both tumble backward. The earthquake continues for a while longer, then slowly fades away.

Shaking my head, I look about for the creature. I find the banshee stretched out in her tattered cloak a foot away from me.

"Are you all right?" I ask, half crawling, half walking over to her.

The creature whimpers as I try to feel for a pulse, then snaps at me. I jerk my hand away, but not fast enough, as she claws down my side, tearing my jacket from collar to sleeve, nearly ripping my arm off in the process. The banshee then quickly pushes herself toward the lake, leaving a dark path of blood in the snow behind. Then, with a final gasp, she rolls over onto the frozen water, shatters the ice with one long talon, and sinks into the dark waters.

"You fool," Dean says, panting.

He's holding his right side like something's bothering him, and for the first time in my life, I hope he's in intense pain.

"What, did I foil your plans?" I ask, a self-satisfied smirk on my face.

"Not exactly," he says, grabbing me by the wrist and forcing me back to the center of the stone circle. "Though it does change some of the variables."

As we reach the knoll again, Dean pulls his knife back out and slashes my exposed arm. I scream as pain explodes down my body, sending stars into my vision. Sweating profusely, he tugs on my arm so the blood falls freely onto the small mound, turning the snow scarlet.

"No!" I yell frantically. "Let me go! What are you doing?"

"Undoing something that should never have been allowed," Dean mutters.

Once again, the ground shakes, and Dean releases me. I scramble backward, away from the earth, which, I know, is going to try to swallow me whole. But the ground doesn't attempt to suck me in, and I watch, mesmerized, as a large rectangular stone engraved with runes slowly emerges from its depths. Then stops.

Dean folds over, as if the strings that have been holding him up have abruptly been snipped.

A semi-hysterical laugh bubbles out of my mouth, harsh in the suddenly quiet air. Wrong move—Dean's head snaps up, and he glowers at me. He staggers back up, and I cower away, expecting him to come straight for me and finish the kill.

We both spot the knife at the same time, its dark blade gleaming dully in the sunlight. For a moment, we stare at each other, then pounce for the weapon at the same time.

My hands close on the wooden handle first. Too easy. I turn around as Dean's fist flies toward me, and I duck, then spin away. Too easy. He turns around and throws himself straight at me, and the knife gets ripped out of my hands.

Dean stops, staggers, rights himself until I can see the wooden handle protruding from his side, marring his usually pristine suit. He gasps, then smiles at me.

Sitting in the snow, panting, I watch him stumble over to the empty spot in the circle—the spot where the last remaining stone needs to be raised to free Carman.

"No!" I cry out.

I try to get up, but all my strength went into that final attack, and I can't do anything but watch as he falls to his knees, then sits back.

"You did it on purpose," I whisper. "You made me kill you…"

Dean turns his face to me, slowly, as if even that small movement is painful.

"Dry your tears, Morgan," he says, almost tenderly.

And to my surprise, I find that I am crying, the salt of my tears stinging the myriad scratches on my face.

"It's going to be all right," he says. "It'll be over soon."

"W-Why?" I hiccup.

Dean winces, takes a rattling breath, then hunches over. "Why not?" he replies, his words slow. "Look at the world around you, everyone always fighting over the most trivial of things, destroying everything without sparing a thought to anyone else but themselves. Soon enough, everything will be in ruins anyway. I'm just...helping the process along...while...while liberating my p—people. A noble p-pursuit in-deed."

A low laugh escapes him that ends up in a racking cough.

Already low vibrations are coursing through the island as the ground soaks up his blood. My mind's going at the speed of light now, trying to find a way to stop him. Dean's head twitches back, muscles straining in his neck. And the answer comes to me.

"Hold on," I say, crawling toward him.

Time seems to slow down. Every movement I make takes a century as Dean sinks deeper into the soil.

"Don't die," I say, teeth chattering as the snow soaks through my clothes. My left arm, free from the protection of my jacket, is completely numb. I fling it forward, blood pouring from the wound in a shower of scarlet drops.

In the distance, I hear something shatter, then the voice of Arthur crying my name out. But I stay focused on Dean as I drag myself toward him, intent on saving him before he disappears entirely. Just a few more yards, and I'll reach him.

"Let...it...be," he says, giving another shudder.

"I can't," I say. "I can't let you die."

Dean's usual derogatory smile lifts his lips for a split second before another grimace erases it. Just a few more feet, and I'll be able to grab his hand.

"Morgan!"

A sparkling shape appears behind Dean, long and forbidding. I raise a hand in panic.

"Arthur, don't!" I yell.

But it's too late, and I watch the long sword slash down, cutting Dean down across his back. For a brief instant, Dean seems to be unaffected by the blow. Then he falls forward, disappearing in the thick layer of snow, and doesn't get back up.

"Nooooo!" I yell, beating the ground with my frozen fists.

"Morgan!" Arthur says, jumping over Dean's body to rush to my side. He seems relieved, and smiles. "Are you all right?"

He tries to help me up, but I push him away.

"You killed him! You killed him!" I say, beating feebly at his chain mail.

I barely register the fear etched in Arthur's proud features, or the dried blood caking the side of his face. All I know is that he's killed the one and only person who's ever been there for me. I feel like my head's about to explode.

"It's all right," he says, holding my injured arm up in his warm hands. "I'm here now. I'm going to take care of you."

"You murderer," I say, sobbing.

Arthur blanches. He turns my arm over to expose the long gash extending the length of my humerus, then rips a part of his shirt off and proceeds to bandage my cut.

He's tying off the knot when the ground beneath us heaves and rolls, like a buried giant's just rolled over in its sleep.

"What's going on?" Arthur asks, crouching low to keep his balance.

"It's happening," I say, shaking.

A gale whips up around the cairn, lifting the snow from the ground in a small tornado. Above us, large clouds are gathering, blotting out the sun and giving everything an eerie glow in the growing darkness. I turn to look at Arthur, but I can't see anything before me. My heartbeat accelerates—the ninth plague!

"Arthur?" I call out, my words snatched away by the intensifying wind.

Another gust lashes at me, then I feel myself lift off the ground and get flung away. Just as I'm afraid I'm going to find myself in the middle of the lake, I crash into one of the tall stones, bounce off it, and land in the mud.

Mud? Head pounding, I manage to push myself halfway up. With growing horror, I see that the ground around the central altar has vanished, turned into a gaping abyss from which blazing heat emanates.

"Arthur?" I call out, terrified he may have fallen into the dark hole. "Arthur?"

I look about me frantically, shielding my eyes from the debris flying around. Then, just as suddenly as it started, the wind dies down. A lightning bolt streaks through the sky, followed by another and another. A loud gurgling rises from the crater, and the earth seems to belch out a miasma of dark, foul liquid before it heaves again and closes up.

Trembling from head to toe, I watch the scorching mass of darkness move over the ground, burning everything it touches.

Then, with a strange sucking sound, the mass rises over the ground and slowly solidifies until, to my astonishment, there stands a young woman, her long jet-black hair framing her chiseled face. It takes a moment for her pitch-black eyes to focus, then she extends her pale hands before her, fingers splayed, turns them around, then touches her face, as if she herself can't believe she's real either.

"Saint George's balls," I mutter, unable to look away from the beautiful creature.

And I know, without a trace of doubt, that it's Carman.

Her hearing must be as sharp as a dog's, for she drops her hands immediately to her sides and looks over to me.

"I have you to thank, don't I?" she asks, her voice a soft breeze on a hot summer day.

She advances toward me, her dark dress made out of thousands of crow feathers fluttering about her.

Rooted to my spot, my head still spinning, I let her reach me without uttering a sound or moving a single muscle. Up close, she's even more stunning, her cheeks dimpling as she makes a half smile.

"Pretty little thing, aren't you?" she says.

She reaches for my chin, and, the moment her fingers graze my skin, I feel like I've just been pricked by thousands of needles. I want to pull away from her touch, but her fingers dig deeper into my face until I feel she's going to shear my jaw off.

She brings her other hand softly down my cheek, leaving behind a long, burning trail. The sickly sweet smell of early putrefaction emanates from her, cloying the air like a nauseating perfume. I want to scream, but though I open my mouth, no sound comes out.

Her hand travels slowly down my jaw, then closes around my neck, crushing my thyroid. I feel my eyes bulge out as I try to gasp for air.

"Dain should have killed you like he was supposed to," Carman says with a soft smile.

Dain? Does she mean Dean?

She inches her head forward, then murmurs in my ear, "You shall pay for my son's death."

Dean's her son?

Black dots swim in my vision. They grow larger with every passing second as pain shoots down from my shoulder. Then, before I pass out, Carman pulls away suddenly. The air whistles as Arthur's sword swings down between us. I cough, gasping for breath.

"You all right?" Arthur asks without looking at me.

"I-I think so," I rasp. "Still alive."

"Then get away from here," he says, his sword held protectively before him.

"Where?"

But before he can answer me, Carman strikes. She's so fast, all I can see is a dark blur. Arthur parries left, then right. He steps back until he's standing against one of the megaliths. He slashes up, then drops down as the stone behind him shatters in a loud explosion, but a large chunk of rock hurls into him, knocking him over.

"Arthur!" I yell, my voice breaking.

Spasms rack my body, and I curl up on myself, biting down on my lip so as not to scream, until I taste blood. My left arm is pulsing to the rhythm of my heart, and I wish the banshee had ripped it off me—maybe then it wouldn't hurt so much.

I feel someone lift me into a sitting position, and find myself staring into a pair of limpid gray eyes.

"How bad is it?" Lance asks, lifting my hair to examine my face, then raising my bandaged arm for inspection.

The piece of cloth Arthur had wrapped around it is soaked through, but I shake my head. There's no time to worry about me; Arthur needs help. With a nod, Lance gently reclines me against a stone. Then, in one smooth movement, he pulls his sword and dagger out and hurries over to join the raging battle.

Watching Arthur and Lance fight is like watching a coordinated dance. When one parries, the other attacks; when one moves forward, the other sweeps around, their movements quick and sure, marked by the clanging of the swords. Then, as if by some unknown agreement, Lance and Arthur jump in opposite directions, a silvery net stretched between them. The next moment, the long mesh is entwined around Carman, the iron glowing red as it burns into the primeval witch.

A high-pitched laugh erupts from the Fey woman as the net melts to her feet before it gets swallowed by the mud.

"Fools," she says, her voice echoing all around us. "You think to use these paltry tricks against me? *Me?*"

She roars the last word, and a strong blast of wind batters against the two boys. Lance manages to resist it, but the gale sends Arthur reeling backward.

Red and black sparks arc through the air from Carman's extended hands and spear Arthur on the spot. A cry escapes his lips as the force of the discharge hits him. His body lifts up then falls back down with a dull thud.

I want to run to his aid, but my body no longer responds to my will, and I watch him stumble up, helpless, as he and Lance throw themselves completely into the fight. I bite my lip as Carman dodges another attack, a constant smile on her relaxed features like she's playing with two eager puppies. At this rate, they're both going to be dead.

Something hits my arm, and I wince. I turn my head around with some difficulty, only to find Puck's furry little body getting ready to run into me again. But his movements are impeded by the large object he's dragging behind him.

The stone bowl. An instant longing for the carved object flares up inside me, immediately quelled. Dizzy, I close my eyes, too tired to guess what game the hobgoblin's trying to play with me now. But Puck pries my fingers open and slips the bowl into my bloody hand.

The stone is warm to the touch, and, in my fogged-up mind, I have the sensation that it is responding to my heartbeats. I crack my eyes open again to find Puck huffing and puffing while pointing at the inside of the vessel. To my surprise, the bowl is filling up with a clear liquid. I watch Puck make suction noises as if he's drinking from a cow's teat. *Drink?*

I stare at the now-full container. I take a shuddering breath, then try to lift the bowl. At first, my arm won't budge and remains inert. On the other side of the stone circle, another explosion makes the island shake. Some of the liquid splashes over the sides and onto my injured arm, but the bowl quickly refills until it's full to the brim once more.

Again, I try to lift the object, gritting my teeth against the pain that makes every muscle and tendon feel like it's going to snap. Then the bowl's smooth surface touches my lips, and the warm liquid trickles down my parched throat. It tastes of honey and fruit, and leaves a pleasant tingling sensation behind. Somehow, my mind seems to clear up, and my skin begins to glow. I give a start when I notice a soft golden light envelop my left arm, travel up past my elbow and reach my shoulder.

It seems to stop at my old scar, where the glow intensifies, making the cross stand out red against my pale skin. Slowly at first, then more quickly, the lines of my scar extend, switch directions, making sharp angles, and I stare, mesmerized, as a five-pointed star inscribed within a circle appears—a pentacle!

For a moment, the symbol brightens, forcing me to close my eyes. When I open them again, the glow is gone, and so is my scar, leaving a perfectly smooth patch of skin behind.

"What in the world…" I whisper, touching my shoulder gingerly before I realize that nothing aches anymore.

The improvised bandage around my arm falls apart under my touch, revealing a long, pale line that runs from my elbow to my wrist, the only remaining trace of the wound Dean had given me.

"Healed," I murmur, turning my arm over, back and forth. "I must be dreaming…"

A strange prickling makes the hairs at the back of my neck rise, and I snap my head up. Without a second thought, I sprint toward Lance, who's trying to fend the witch off Arthur's still body. Before them, Carman raises her chin, arms spread open at her sides, and I know that this is the end.

I dive as an explosion rends the air. I land on the two boys, bringing Lance down as well. I grit my teeth as an inexorable pressure threatens to crush us, bearing down on us with all the weight of a family of ogres.

The power then lifts away, and I look over to Carman. The witch is glaring at me like I'm the vilest of creatures, as if I were the walking corpse and not her.

The mud at her feet turns black, smoke rising from it in long tendrils, then rolls toward us like a large, dark wave. On instinct, I raise my arms before me in defense, and, to my surprise, the lavalike flow deviates from its path and pulverizes another of the large stones instead.

Carman snarls, no longer the beautiful angel, but a vicious demon instead. I brace myself for another attack, when an enormous, black horse gallops toward us.

"Enough," a familiar voice calls out. "The others are coming. We have no time."

A lithe young man jumps off the horse, and I recognize him as the Fey who interrupted Lugh's party. Mordred doesn't spare us a single look as he kneels before Carman.

"Please, my lady," he says, eyes downcast, "our numbers have greatly diminished, and I fear we will not be of much service to you any more today."

Carman hesitates. Then her frown smoothes out, any trace of her demon self vanished.

"Where to?" she asks.

"I will lead, my lady," Mordred says, rising to help her up onto the Fey horse.

In a couple of bounds, the creature and its evil rider reach the lake, then plunge into its deep waters. Mordred follows after them, pauses on the shore to look at me, and our gazes lock together.

Arthur's moan draws my attention away for a second, and, when I look back, the Fey's gone.

"Morgan, I need your help," Lance says, his voice tense. "Now!"

I kneel beside Arthur. His armor's shred to pieces, his torso a big open wound. I grab his hand; his skin is cold and clammy to the touch.

"His pulse is weak," I say mechanically.

A crazy thought enters my mind. Carman's release has brought on the tenth plague—the killing of every firstborn. But Arthur can't die of that, can he? He's the second born, the second! I should be the one to die…

I tear the remainders of my jacket off and use them to try to stanch Arthur's blood flow, pressing down into his wound.

Arthur lets out another groan, but his eyes remain closed.

"How long till they get here?" I ask.

"I don't know," Lance says. "It could be now, or it could be an hour from now."

"We can't wait that long!" I don't add that Arthur could very well die any minute now, but we both know it.

I try not to panic as blood bubbles to Arthur's lips. At least one of his lungs must have been pierced. I blink away the tears flooding my eyes. Arthur takes another gurgling breath, chokes on more blood, then stops moving.

"No!" I scream, punching his chest above his heart. "No, you can't die on me, you hear me? You. Can't. Die!" I punctuate every word with another punch, but it's useless. Arthur remains unmoving.

I let out a long, guttural cry, tears flowing freely down my face. I hold my brother in my arms, rocking back and forth.

"No," I sob, bending over his light brown hair stained black from all the blood.

This is all my fault! If it weren't for me, he'd still be alive, attending school with all his friends, then hanging out with Irene and Luther on weekends.

"I'm so sorry," I whisper, kissing his forehead, slick with tears. "So sorry." I lift my head up to the heavens above. "Please, God, please don't let him die like this...Please!"

Lance's hand seizes my shoulder and squeezes. "Morgan," he says.

I turn a tearstained face to him, but he's not looking at me. I hear a gasp, and drop my gaze down to Arthur's face. His mouth is open, and he's breathing through it in small, shallow gulps. Under my fingers, his skin is knitting itself together.

"What have you done?" Lance asks with awe.

"I'm not doing anything," I say, staring in shock at the now blemish-free skin. "I don't even—"

Arthur's eyes flutter open, and his hazel eyes meet mine. A small smile spreads on his flushed face. He reaches up and winds his fingers in my hair, then pulls me closer to him, so close his breath tickles my neck.

A sudden warmth spreads down my face, and I find I can't pull away from him. My lips open in protest, but no words come out—too much trauma in one day has turned my brain to mush.

"Nice to see you, Morgan," he whispers, and an answering smile spreads across my face.

I'm about to hug him when someone yanks me back by the hair.

"Get your filthy hands off him!"

CHAPTER 33

Dazed, I look up to find Irene standing above me, her face purple with anger.

"Mother," I say as more people file in behind her, dressed in fighting garb.

"Do *not* call me that," she says, seething. "And you," she adds, pointing at Arthur who's getting up, "get some clothes on. You look indecent."

"That wasn't my first worry while fighting off Carman," Arthur says, unperturbed.

At the mention of the Fey, Irene turns pale. "That can't be," she says curtly. "The prison…"

Yet the ruined stones, the debris littering the muddy ground, and the scorch marks about the place are a dead giveaway.

"How…" she starts, then looks at her son. "Why did you end up here, when your own school was under attack?"

"Saw your lovely lawyer carry Morgan off," Arthur says in his usual nonchalant way while buttoning up the coat Lance has handed him. "So I decided I'd follow. We ended up here."

"And you?" Irene asks, turning to Lance.

"Followed Arthur," the usually quiet boy replies, "and this little fellow."

Puck, still holding on to the bowl, hobbles over to me, and I gather him into my arms, where he curls up into a small, shivering ball. I find myself glad that he managed to stay out of harm's way.

"What is that filthy beast doing here?" Irene asks, pointing at the hobgoblin.

"That is Puck," I say, tightening my arms around the small creature, "and he saved my life." How, that's still a mystery to me, but considering I'm still breathing, I figure I've got plenty of time to worry about that later.

"It's the Sangraal," someone whispers reverently.

"The Sangraal?" a woman repeats. "But it's been lost for ages!"

I look down at the vessel still clutched in Puck's small hands, its rim covered in small runes—this is the holy cup that's supposed to have magical powers? I remember my glowing skin, my injury healing, and my scar disappearing. Huh, that would explain things.

Before I can wonder at the meaning of its reemergence and its role in my speedy recovery, Irene shoves me back and grips my left shoulder.

"Gone," she says. She pulls away, a look of mixed terror and rage on her features. "Guards, tie her up."

Confused looks are exchanged by her men in an exact mirror of my own.

"Did you not hear me?" Irene sputters. "Tie her up! And use your iron netting to do it. She's dangerous."

I want to laugh at the absurdity of the situation, say that Carman's already gone, escaped under the lake somewhere. But the men come forward carefully, as if approaching a wild boar.

One of them pulls out a long lace of metal that glimmers in the hazy light.

"You can't be serious," I say. Why would they want to tie me up, and with iron bindings to boot?

"Don't you dare lay your hands on her," Arthur says, standing before me.

"Step away from her, Arthur," Irene says, her composure back. "You wouldn't want anyone questioning your position now, would you?"

Arthur doesn't move, and I draw closer to him, taking comfort in his presence. But that's the wrong thing to do, as Irene goes around her son and grabs me by the hair once more, pulling me away.

"Stay away from my son, you monster!" she hisses.

Puck whimpers against my chest. I try to smile, chuckle, but I can't help tears from pricking my eyes.

"Monster?" I ask, looking at the people around me.

But nobody's meeting my eyes. Not even Arthur, who's looking straight ahead as if I'm not here.

My smile wobbles. "This is a joke, right? Ha ha. Now drop the act. It isn't funny."

With a grunt of disgust, Irene turns away from me, and the two guards grab me roughly by the arms. I resist, clutching on to Puck.

"This is ridiculous," I say, my voice rising three octaves with my growing fear. "I didn't do anything wrong! Arthur, tell them!"

But Arthur remains mute. I swallow my anger and sense of betrayal back down. I shouldn't have expected more from him, but, after all we've just gone through, I had hoped.

"Take your hands off me," I say, breathing in to keep myself cool and collected. "I'll follow you."

There's a moment of hesitation. Then the two guards take their metal wiring away, though they remain at my sides—as if I were stupid enough to run away now.

Two boats are waiting for us by the shore, the Pendragon coat of arms painted on the front of their black hulls. I climb into the first boat, the two men close to me. When everyone's aboard, the boats push themselves away from the snowy bank in complete silence before the familiar green glow comes up in a bubble around us and the crafts dive into the freezing waters of Lake Winnebago.

The sight that greets us upon our arrival is one of destruction and desolation. People have streamed out of the school and are busy collecting the dead or helping the few injured soldiers who haven't gotten to the clinic yet.

The long barges land north of the wharf, which is now but a pile of smoldering embers. A fleeting thought of Laura and Diana crosses my mind, and I wonder whether they are safe.

"Take her to the KORT room," Irene says, "while I gather the Board to decide her fate."

I step out of the boat with as much dignity as I can, which isn't an easy task when two tall, burly men are holding on to you like a criminal.

"Just a moment," Lance says, stepping uncharacteristically to the forefront.

Glaring, Irene tries to go around him, but Lance is much taller and stronger than she is and keeps cutting her off.

"Get out of my way, boy," she says, exasperated. "I could have you in chains for this."

Lance's knuckles whiten on the grip of his sword, but he doesn't move. "I can't let you take her right now. I need her."

"Whatever for?" Irene asks.

"I need to take her to the infirmary," he says, his voice level.

My mouth drops open, and I nearly drop Puck, who uses that opportunity to jump out of my arms and scramble away. I hadn't pinned Lance for a caring guy, especially with regard to me, but this is proving me wrong. I throw a challenging look in Arthur's direction; this is how a true chivalrous person ought to be. But Arthur's pointedly avoiding my eyes.

"She's fine," Irene says, her voice cold.

Someone whispers in her ear, and she casts a look at Lance and Arthur, both covered in blood and soot, and she finally relents.

As we pass by the asylum, which is now but a mass of rubble, I see some of the nurses try to calm down a group of their patients as they stare and scream at the remains of what once had been their home. In the midst of them, I catch the eye of a single man, his pale skin lighter than his white hair. A heartbeat later, he turns away from me as the stench of burning flesh reaches me, making me gag.

"The Fomori," one of my two guards says as we walk by a large bonfire. "Gotta make sure they're completely destroyed."

Shuddering, I accelerate my pace until we reach the great northern door and step inside the building.

The moment we walk into the medical wing, Dr. Cockleburr assails me.

"Where have you been, missy?" she calls out from her corner, where she's placing a brace on a boy. "Do you even realize how much work there is to do around here? But you decide to skip out on me and—"

She stops when she realizes the two men next to me aren't there just for decorative purposes. She frowns and pulls the bandage tight, making the boy wince.

"What's going on?" she asks, hurrying over, wiping her hands on her stained apron. "Morgan, who are these people?"

"Board members, I assume," I say, trying to ignore everyone's stares.

"What happened to you out there?" she asks, tut-tutting. "You're going to have to get changed before you resume your work here."

"That's not going to be possible," the taller of the guards says.

"Are you injured?" Dr. Cockleburr retorts.

"No, ma'am," says the guard.

"Then what are you doing in my clinic?" she asks, her thick eyebrows drawing down. "I'm already overcrowded as it is. Get out."

"We can't, ma'am," the other guard says. "We have to keep this one under control. She may be dangerous."

Just focus on the light fixtures, I tell myself as the too-familiar feelings of shame and humiliation burn my cheeks red.

"Morgan, dangerous?" Dr. Cockleburr asks in surprise. "That's preposterous. She's one of the better healers around here, a true natural!"

"And that's why we're here," Lance says. "Is Jennifer still…"

The doctor motions with her head to the ward, and I find myself shuffled forward. Dumbfounded, I follow Lance's broad back to Jennifer's bed. One thing's for sure, though, it's not because of me that he's worried, after all.

Jennifer hasn't changed since last I saw her. If it weren't for the tiny network of black veins that now reach her neck and the bottom of her face, she'd look like she was resting. But, from experience, I know what those black veins mean, and Jennifer shouldn't even be alive anymore.

"Go ahead," Lance says, pushing me gently toward the front of the bed.

"What is it you want me to do?" I ask. "Fluff her pillow?"

"Heal her."

I snort. "Right. Let me pull out my magic wand and get right on that, sir."

Lance doesn't laugh. Neither do Arthur nor my guards. They all watch me like they really are expecting me to perform a miracle for them.

"This is stupid," I say, crossing my arms. "I'm not a magician. I can't do what you're asking me to do. Don't you think I'd have healed her by now if I could?"

"You saved him," Lance says, pointing at Arthur, who's staring at me so intently I'm the one who looks away first. "I saw it with my own eyes. His ribs mended. His skin grew back together. He'd stopped breathing, and now look at him!"

"All hail to the new Saint Lazarus," I mutter under my breath.

"It's true," Arthur says. He touches his chest where the lacerations had been. "I felt your touch, right here."

I roll my eyes. These people are impossible. And yet...yet I can't deny that something miraculous happened on that island.

"But that was all God," I whisper. "I prayed to Him, and He answered me..." I raise my bare arm and turn it over, exposing the long, pale scar that newly adorns it. My hands are still stained black, but all my other scratches and bruises are gone, and I hadn't prayed to God then.

No, I healed because Puck made me drink out of that cup, which these people say is the Sangraal. Then could it be that I truly did heal Arthur? My eyes widen in consternation.

"No way," I exclaim, despite myself.

"Could you...could you at least try?" Lance asks, a note of pleading in his voice.

I start at his question, having momentarily forgotten his and the other men's presence. I sigh.

"OK," I say. I raise my finger before he can thank me. "But… don't expect anything to come of it."

I turn back to Jennifer, observing her still body. What did I do to Arthur to mend him? Hold him in my arms, cry, and kiss his forehead. I shudder at the thought of having to kiss Jennifer.

Settling for something less drastic, I sit on her bed and lift her head to let it rest on my lap. I lay my hand on hers and lean over her until my long hair hides the four men from my sight.

Closing my eyes, I start to pray.

Our Father which art in heaven, hallowed be thy name. Let thy kingdom come, thy will be fulfilled, as well on earth as it is in Heaven.

A light tingle spreads from my head, down my shoulders and arms, and all the way to the tips of my fingers.

Give us this day our daily bread. And forgive us our debts, as we forgive our debtors.

My hand feels warm on Jennifer's. My initial reflex is to pull away, but I force myself to stand still.

And lead us not into temptation, but deliver us from evil. For thine is the kingdom, and the power, and the glory. Forever and ever. Amen.

"Look," I hear someone whisper.

But I dare not open my eyes for fear of breaking my concentration, and start the Paternoster over. The words tumble out of my mouth, too low for anyone else to hear, more and more rapidly, in an endless litany.

My mind is empty of everything but the prayer and Jennifer lying in my lap. Nothing else matters. Nothing but the desperate hope that perhaps she will be saved after all, and the fear that I may fail.

I feel movement, hear a gasp.

"By all that's holy," someone exclaims, "she's done it!"

Someone leans onto the bed, and I sway backward, breaking my contact with Jennifer.

"Jennifer," Lance says.

As if in a dream, I see the boy grab the blonde girl's hand and press it to his lips as her eyes open. Her pale face has a translucent quality to it, but gone are the lines of black that had striated her body just moments before.

A sudden wave of fatigue washes through me, leaving me with the feeling of a shipwrecked sailor who's just spent days swimming for survival.

A pair of hands grabs me by the shoulders before I fall over on the bedspread. I want to push them away; a nap is just the thing I want right now. All I need is an hour, or a century.

"This is proof that she's like them," Irene says, her sharp tone cutting through my tired thoughts.

"This is proof that she's saved not only me, but Jennifer as well," Arthur says right next to me.

"Don't play with words," Irene retorts. "Only the Fey can do that, and that means only one thing: she needs to be locked up."

That last statement has the effect of twenty gallons of ice water being poured over me, and I bolt upright.

Irene notices my reaction and smirks. "Don't tell me you hadn't figured it out by now."

CHAPTER 34

"You can't do that. She hasn't done anything wrong," Arthur says, staring Irene down.

"I'm afraid you have no authority on the subject," Irene says, motioning for the guards to grab hold of me.

I'm so weak that they have to carry me between them. My feet drag on the stone floor as they head for the exit. I don't even have the energy to protest.

"Where to?" they ask.

"The only place around here that'll hold those of her ilk are the catacombs," Irene replies.

"You can't be serious," Arthur says. He hurries over to Irene's side.

"I am," Irene replies with a vicious smile. "Well, at least until we figure out where her ogham is."

Ogham. A hysterical laugh shakes my shoulders at the concept of having one of those stuck in me somewhere. Don't they remember how long it took me to get one of the elementals to work? And now they expect me to have my own source of power?

The laughter dies when I see nobody's finding any of this funny. "Oh, come on," I say. "Obviously I'm not the one who healed them. Well, I did, but I didn't." I lick my dry lips, then clear my throat. "What I'm trying to say is that it's because I drank from that bowl, the Sangraal, nothing more."

I feel my guards tighten their hold on me, and one of them crosses himself.

"I grew up in a Catholic school," I whisper to him. "Don't you think I'd have...melted by now if I were a devil? Or at least been struck by God?"

But it's useless. Whatever I say, these people are not going to believe me. I should be used to this behavior by now, but my naive faith in humanity always bounces back to bite me in the ass.

Eyes half closed, Irene observes me like I'm some lab monkey. "That's exactly my point. And the proof is that your seal's gone."

"My seal?" I blow on a loose strand of hair that's fallen over my eyes. Why does that ring a bell? I reach up to my shoulder where my scar used to be, where I saw it transform into a pentacle after drinking from the Sangraal—the same symbol I've seen on the tall monoliths protecting our school. Was that what Dean was talking about?

"What's been keeping your abilities at bay," Irene adds. She stalks up to me, her short skirts swaying back and forth around her narrow hips. She circles me like a vulture, then stops so close to me she's forced to look up to stare into my eyes. "It's what allowed you to pass for human all these years," she hisses.

"I'm sorry," I retort, "but I always thought that, out of the two of us, you were the monster."

She cuffs me, the sound of the slap echoing in the now-still room. But I don't try to make myself small this time. I won't let this woman keep treating me like I'm unfit to even be the dirt on which she walks.

"Oh, that struck a nerve, did it?" I continue.

A muscle twitches at her temple, and she raises her hand for another strike.

"That is *enough*!"

Lady Vivian strides over to us, her face flushed with anger. I brace myself for another reprimand, but the head of the school turns on Irene instead.

"What is the meaning of this, Irene?" she asks.

For the first time in my life, I see my mother quail. Luther arrives, looking concerned.

"I'm sure there's an explanation," he says, looking back and forth between his wife and me. "Honey?"

Irene jerks away from his touch. "She's gotten her powers back. She's become a liability."

Vivian casts her brown eyes down to my bare shoulder. She looks as beautiful as ever, not a single strand of hair out of place, or a speck of dust on her velvety dress; it's as if the battle that's just happened never reached her. Yet she seems paler, tiny lines crinkling around her eyes, over her sunken cheeks.

"So I see," she says. "But I wouldn't necessarily say she's dangerous, would you?"

"That's exactly what I'm saying," Irene spits out.

Vivian's face turns stony. The atmosphere in the ward becomes tense, electrified, like on a stormy day.

"I don't think it's the power one has that makes one dangerous," she says, her voice calm, yet carrying a dangerous edge to it, "but rather how it's used."

Irene looks away, obviously uncomfortable with the topic.

Vivian straightens up. "Let her go," she says to the two men still holding me. When the guards don't move fast enough for her taste, she adds, "Don't forget who her father was."

Irene blanches.

"You know who my father was?" I ask, my knees going weak.

"Of course," Vivian says. "Everyone here does. He was a great knight, the best of his generation."

"That doesn't make up for her mother," Irene cuts in.

"Not her adoptive one, that's for sure," Vivian retorts. "Which is why I hereby dissolve your guardianship of the Gorlois heir. All her inheritance must be relinquished, or at least what's left of it."

Irene squares her shoulders. "And to whom should I transfer the custodianship?" she asks.

"Well, to me, child," Vivian says with a bright smile. "I'll give you a week to get everything settled."

Irene barks out a laugh. "To you? I'm not a fool, old woman. I know how far your authority goes, and in this matter, I stand firm. She's a Halfling. She can't go around free."

Vivian's violet eyes flash. "We shall see about that," she says before striding away, her long dress flouncing behind her.

The moment Vivian's gone, Irene rounds on me. "Don't think you're going to get out of this so easily," she says. "Everyone around here now knows the truth about you, that you're just some half-Fey bastard." She snaps her fingers into Arthur's face. "And *you* better stay away from her."

His face pales, but Arthur remains mute.

"I don't understand," I say as Luther pulls Irene away for a private talk. How could Irene not be my own mother? Granted, she's never shown much love for me, but I'd always thought...

My whole life now seems like one big fat lie.

"I don't understand," I repeat.

"Gorlois was once engaged to Irene," Arthur says, "before he disappeared."

Frowning, I lift my eyes to his concerned face. "What are you talking about?"

"When Sir Tristan, who'd gone to his search, failed to come back within the year..." He shrugs. "She married my father two years after Gorlois left."

My breath catches in my throat. I watch Irene shake her head at her husband. "But-But...that means..."

"When Sir Tristan came back," Arthur continues, "Gorlois was already dead. But he'd left something behind. A little baby girl...you."

I jerk back at his words, unable to process the data. There is one thing that seems clear to me, however.

"You knew," I breathe. "You knew all along."

Arthur's lips thin out, but he finally nods.

Rage wells up inside me, unchecked. I jump to my feet, but the guards hold me back. "You traitor!"

"Please, hear me out," Arthur says.

"So you can spew more lies?"

He winces, but keeps on going. "You don't understand," he says. "There was a reason this was kept from you—"

"What? You were afraid that the freak would go vicious if she found out the truth?"

"Don't say that," Arthur whispers.

"Afraid the rest of them will learn you and your family have been hosting a demon in your house? Afraid the school will stop seeing you as a perfect person?"

Grabbing me by the shoulders, Arthur shakes me. "Don't be a fool. What they think is no concern of mine. What you think about yourself, however, is."

"Please, don't pretend like you care now," I say. I should've trusted my instincts from the start—though fairies may exist, and knights in shining armor are still around, there is no such thing as a Prince Charming. "And stop ordering me around like you own me," I add as my guards pull me away at a sign from Irene. "You're not even my brother!"

Shackled and closely guarded, I follow Irene and Luther back outside under the curious stares of hundreds of students. We march toward the back of the church, where small stairs lead us belowground. Luther pushes a small door open, and I'm dragged into a damp hallway, past dark, empty rooms, and down more steps.

Finally, we stop before a bolted iron door. Luther inserts a key, turns it, then pulls the screeching door open.

Without a pause, my guards shove me in. Unable to catch myself, I land with a heavy thud and smack my head on the grimy floor.

Rolling over onto my back, I see Irene smile, the light of one of the guard's torches distending her features.

"Welcome to your new home."

STRANGE PRANK GOES AWRY - THE AUTHORITIES ARE STUMPED

In an odd turn of events, the elaborate hoax, which started a few months ago and involved the replacement of the native cairn on Island Park with monoliths worthy of Stonehenge, has turned sour.

The police, after getting reports of explosions originating from the island, found upon arrival that the circle of standing stones had been destroyed. When called upon to comment, the chief of police refused to say a word, claiming the investigation was still under way. An eyewitness, who wishes to remain anonymous, stated that the place reeked of sulfur and that blood had been found on the premises.

Some locals are accusing Natives American tribes of being behind the vandalism.

"You saw how they was protestin' when the stones were found first," Mr. Ethan Pearson, owner of a small bar just north of Oshkosh, stated. "They just can't take a joke. Those kids, or whoever they were, didn't hurt no one, and look what they did, blowin' the whole place up like it's Armageddon!"

Whether these accusations prove to be true, or the act of destruction was performed by aliens, as another group claims, nobody knows. The authorities were still trying to work out how anyone could have brought in those gigantic stones without being noticed in the first place.

But that is not the end of the story. Scientists have been called in to analyze a plant that was discovered growing out of one of the stones. According to a member of the staff, it may be a genus of completely unknown origins. Most baffling of all is that the plant is inextricably attached to its rock and is resisting any attempt at being cut out, no matter the tool used.

Perhaps those who state this is all a trick played on us by aliens aren't too far from the truth after all.

About the Author

Alessa Ellefson is a bit of a globe-trotter--born in Texas, she was raised first in Spain, then Belgium, before landing in the US of A to study... math (the one subject she'd vowed never to take again after graduating from high school). In terms of writing, she's tried her hand at a number of different genres, including screenwriting and poems.

Blood of the Fey is her first published novel (her previous stories are tucked safely away for fear of adding more horrors to this lovely world). It is also the first in the *Morgana Trilogy*, though many more tales are jousting in her head for the next spot at the end of her pen.

More information on what goes on inside Alessa's devious mind can be found at www.alessaellefson.com

95658009R00248

Made in the USA
Lexington, KY
10 August 2018